D0340194

Mary's Land

Mary's Land

Lucia St. Clair Robson

BALLANTINE BOOKS

NEW YORK

Maps by Mapping Specialists, Inc.

Library of Congress Cataloging-in-Publication Data
Robson, Lucia St. Clair.
Mary's land / Lucia St. Clair Robson.—1st ed.
p.   cm.
ISBN 0-345-37196-8
1. Maryland—History—Colonial period, ca. 1600–1775—Fiction.
I. Title.
PS3568.03185M37   1995
813'.54—dc20   95-1735
CIP

Text design by Ann Gold

Manufactured in the United States of America

First Edition: September 1995

10 9 8 7 6 5 4 3 2 1

For Karen Ann Lichtenstein,
dear friend and member emeritus
of the rascal rout of rogues,
rufflers, and writers.

Acknowledgments

Thanks to Dr. Lois Green Carr, historian and author, for her insights on the Brent family. I'm also grateful to her for correcting some of my more egregious errors of fact. Those that remain are my fault entirely.

Rebecca Seib-Tout, Executive Director of the Piscataway-Conoy Confederation, shared information on the Piscataway people that I couldn't have found elsewhere.

Roxane Ackerman, keeper of Native American history and lore in Gayhead, Massachusetts, was of great help. The collection in the Gayhead library included glossaries of the Algonquian language that were invaluable.

Reverend Eleanor McLaughlin suggested sources of historical information on the worship of the Virgin Mary. Father Hallock Martin set me straight on the intricacies of ecclesiastical vestments.

Pete Wigginton of the State Department of Environment answered questions about sources of drinking water for the early Maryland settlers.

Nick Carter of the Maryland Department of Natural Resources loaned me reference material on the flora and fauna of the Chesapeake Bay area.

My longtime friend, Tom Gauger, and my brother, Buddy Robson, both technoadepts, helped me make the transition from my çoal-powered computer to the mystifying universe of megabytes.

Eric Smith goaded me into writing about Maryland, more of a charge than I imagined it would be. Thanks a whole lot, Eric.

And thanks to the Ginnys. Ginny Stang trusted me with her books on Maryland history. Ginny Stibolt, as always, answered my incessant questions about botany. She and her husband Ken also made it possible for me to become better acquainted with wild turkeys than I ever thought I would be.

Sam Droege can answer any question about birds, and answered mine.

As always, I'm in literary debt to the staff of the Anne Arundel County Public Library system and to librarians and archivists throughout Maryland.

I'm particularly grateful to the historians, archeologists, reenactors, and staffs at St. Mary's City and at Plimouth Plantation, Plymouth, Massachusetts, for making this story come alive.

The folks at the Gloucester City Records Office, Gloucester, England, have kept tabs on generations of inhabitants of their part of the country, the Brents among them. Because of them the information was there when I needed it.

Thanks to my agent, Ginger Barber, for her patience and advice.

And finally, Pamela Strickler, my editor of fifteen years, hauled me through the maze of Maryland history by the scruff of my neck. And a long haul it was. Thank you, Pam.

Life goes on like a carrier's cart over ruts and stones.
—Old English saying

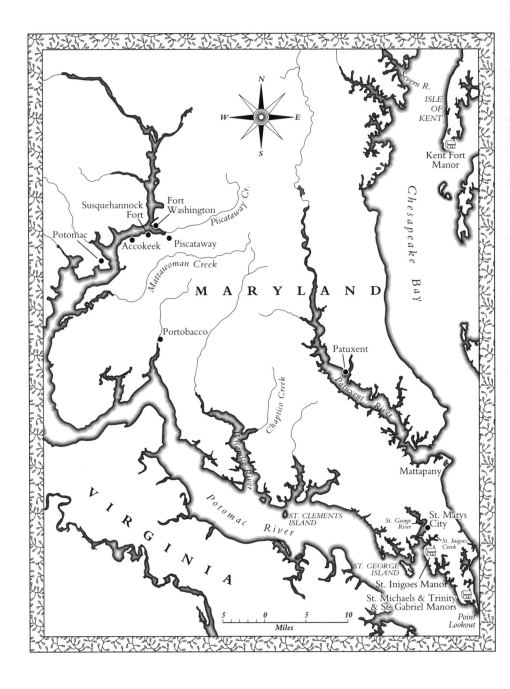

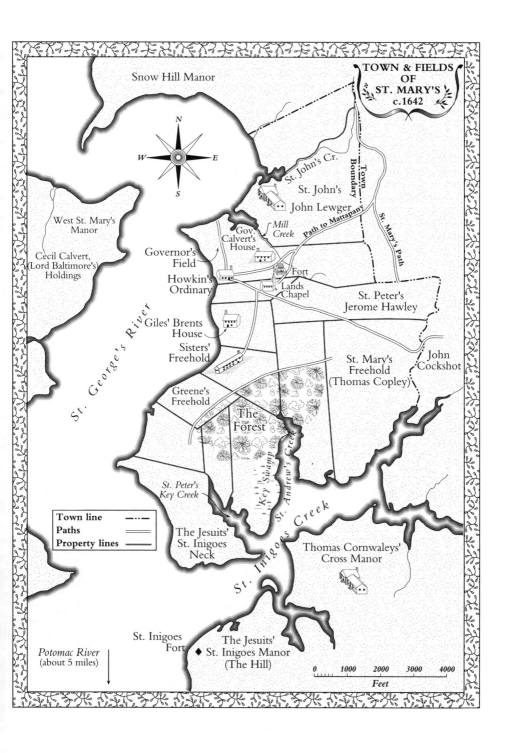

Mary's Land

Chapter 1

By 1638 the world had long since gone from flat to round, but people still disappeared off the edge of it at Bristol. Ships converged from the earth's oceans and anchored in the two rivers that embraced the city. Green ginger and raw brown sugar from Jamaica, wine from Crete, cloth and glass from Venice, hawks from Algiers and bracelets of Barbary gold flowed into Bristol's port, then trickled outward into the city itself.

Seven centuries of smoke had blackened the plaster and exposed timbers of the steep-roofed buildings. In the ancient ward, the gabled upper stories, patched and propped, jettied out over the streets until they almost met. Four and five stories high, they formed deep canyons that sunlight only penetrated through a haze of sulfurous coal fumes. Bristol's commerce churned along at the bottom.

Anicah Sparrow elbowed Squib's bony ribs and pointed her chin at the bawd mincing across the sewer. The padded frames of the woman's old-fashioned farthingale skirt were so wide she could have set out a meal on them. The hem swept through mud and filth for yards around her.

"Be she the whore from the house on Grope-cunt Lane?" Squib squinted up at the bulk and gaudy grandeur of her.

"Aye," Anicah said. "And me ticket to the theater."

Anicah knew her. She ran a flogging school where she used the whip's tang to whet the dulled appetites of old men. Anicah recognized most of the more successful denizens of Bristol's stews. She had had her hands in their pockets at one time or another in the last few years. She had never found in them more than enough to buy a scant meal at the cookhouse—oat frummity, dark bread, a lump of cheese and a noggin of small beer.

Anicah was bigger than Squib, but small for thirteen. She was slender and agile and fast on her feet, useful qualities in her profession. The greasy smoke from Bristol's chimneys had deepened the honey-brown of her skin to the color of polished walnut.

The continual rain of soot had blackened the tatters of her tow-linen shirt and knee breeches. Under the shirt, her shoulders protruded like the knobs on newel posts. A knit cap pulled down to her dark eyebrows hid her hair and ears. Her eyes were the hue and sheen of very dark amber, set in hunger-bruised hollows. Her wide-eyed gaze gave her the look of a startled fawn, with a glint of feral cunning.

In the August heat the flogging school mistress wore her travel cloak open and thrown over her shoulders. Her breasts lolled over the rim of her tightly cinched bodice. Under their smear of rouge the nipples were the color and texture of old sharkskin. She used a switch to clear a path through the merchants and beggars, mongers, thieves, skulking dogs, seamen common and exotic, and country yeomen staggering under their loads of produce.

In the distance a trumpet announced the play. The bawd hurried her pace, and Anicah and Squib walked faster to stay behind her. They darted through the press and dodged the immense dray horses pulling sledges of coal and hogsheads of wine and tobacco. As she walked Anicah assessed the farthingale's generous overhang.

"Mayhap we c'd both fit, Squib."

Squib grimaced and pinched his nose shut at the idea of venturing under the bawd's skirts. He was no kin to Anicah, but the closest to family she had. He was small, with an explosion of red hair and a scattering of freckles. Anicah had named him after the small firecrackers, because like them, he sparked, bounced, made a lot of noise and vanished.

"I'm to the baiting," he said. "Pritchard's entered a brace of Devon mastiffs. 'Twill be rum sport."

Anicah was tempted. Blood would flow at the baiting. Firecrackers would liven the bulls before they were slaughtered, their flesh sweetened by the mastiffs' teeth. There would be baying dogs and shouting bull paunchers. Food vendors and ballad mongers would cry their wares and the usual drunken brawls would erupt.

But today's play was one of the Avon scribbler's bawdier offerings. Its like wasn't often staged in Bristol, even though the Puritans held less sway here in the west country than in the rest of England. Anicah had sneaked into the theater only once before. She couldn't pass up this chance.

"I'm fer the droll," she said. "Meet me at the High Cross at cockshut."

She and Squib hooked their little fingers and tugged, increasing the tension until Squib had to let go. It was a ritual that brought them luck.

"Beware the hawks," Anicah said.

Squib grinned, as though hawks, bailiffs, were his friends. As though if the catchpoles found even a stolen farthing on him he wouldn't be tied to the tail of a cart and whipped through the town. As though if he were caught with more than two shillings worth of goods he wouldn't be hanged.

"Afore ye brush off, amuse the old whore fer me." Anicah could see the theater's gate ahead. The time had come to board this bark before she sailed over the horizon.

Squib scooped up a double handful of dust and trotted ahead while Anicah closed the distance between herself and the farthingale. She hitched her breeches under the raveled length of ship's line that served as a belt. She winked at Squib, and he pitched the dust into the face of a solicitor just passing in front of the bawd.

"Damn me!" The man stopped so abruptly his broad-brimmed hat fell off. The bawd's skirts hit him first, then carried by her momentum, she thumped into him herself.

The lawyer looked as though he'd walked into a swarm of

bees. Anicah laughed as he tried to clutch his satchel to his chest, wipe the dust from his eyes, catch his hat before the plume hit the sewer, fend off the bawd, and protect his purse all at the same time. Anicah poised for the plunge.

"This could be worse than hanging," Anicah grumbled. She lifted the stained hems of the heavy silk skirt and satin petticoats and slid into the fetid twilight beneath them.

The bawd didn't endanger her health by bathing, and she wore nothing to cover her privities. Light from under the swaying hem revealed that above her gartered red hose her lumpy thighs rose like peeled tree trunks into the canopy of the wire frame. Disease and hard use had thinned her muff. The wisps of hair looked like a bird's nest that had barely survived a hurricane. A cloth bag dangled from a cord around her waist.

Anicah could mark her progress only by noting when the cobbles gave way to the theater's stone steps. She took her thin-bladed shiv from her belt and cut the cord holding the purse. Through the cloth she could feel a few farthings and a thimble. The old whore operated on credit or kept most of her money somewhere else, though a place safer than this Anicah couldn't imagine. She stuffed the purse down the front of her shirt.

She thought her crouched legs would give out before she felt the rough wood of the theater's floor under her bare feet. When Anicah judged she had traveled a safe distance from the ticket taker, she bent over and let the bawd flounce away, dragging the skirts over her back.

Anicah stood up and took a deep breath. She flexed her cramped legs and mingled with the throng. She didn't see anyone foolish enough to dangle his drawstring purse from his belt. A few still hung them under their clothes with slits in their breeches or skirts for access. Most wore them fashionably sewn as pockets into the slit. It was a new style that required a different technique for stealing things out of them.

As she looked around she poked a finger through one of the holes in her knit cap and scratched. She pulled a lock back through the hole and wrapped it twice around her finger. It was growing out. She had sold her dark mane to a wig maker a few months ago and she didn't miss it. It had provided too fine a pasturage for her six-legged livestock.

Anicah viewed a crowd as a poet his ink and blank paper, a stone worker a quarry, an actor his script. The beauty and charm of her art lay in improvisation. Success depended on choosing the right victim. She preferred merchants to the fops of the upper ranks. Merchants carried coin. Gallants lived on credit.

She chose a hulk of a man swathed in acres of green holland, as though a bed curtain had fallen over a wine butt. Grime marked the opening of his pocket, but finding it by feel under the skirt of his satin doublet and among the folds of his knee-length breeches would be difficult. She brushed against him as though pressed there by the crowd and slipped her hand into the slit. She closed her stiffened, forked fingers on the snuff box sitting atop his sack of coins and drew it out.

She wanted to make another dive for the purse, but he moved away. She dropped the box down the front of her shirt and joined the mob sitting on the ground closest to the stage.

This was an old theater, unroofed, with scarred wooden floors and rickety boxes. Tiers of galleries rimmed the circular brick wall surrounding the stage. Well-fed west-country squires and merchants and their wives and maids leaned out over the low walls and called to friends. The grooms and apprentices in the upper tiers were even noisier, but none made more commotion than the gallants. Many of them sat on the stage so they could have an unobstructed view.

They combed their shoulder-length locks and retied the ribbons in them. They spat over the side and smoked and diced and sang to entertain themselves. Anicah could tell that most of them were drunk. If they didn't like the performance, so much the better. Riots were good for business.

Around her the groundlings roiled in their usual ferment. They had decided that the entertainment should have started. Anicah joined them in hooting and yelling.

"Please, gentle people." The theater manager cowered in the center of the stage, as far as he could get from the flying garbage. "The fairy queen is shaving, but our humble offering will commence anon."

"Which end would her majesty be shaving?" Anicah shouted.

Once the play started Anicah leaned forward to hear the dialogue over the hisses and catcalls and the gallants' lewd exchanges with the wenches selling oranges. In spite of the flying fruit and the groundlings' loud farts by way of criticism, Shakespeare drew her in with his magic. When Snug, Bottom, Flute, Snout and Starveling bumbled onto the stage, she roared a welcome along with the others. She forgot she wasn't part of the play and she leaped up to answer an actor's line or shout objections.

William Shakespeare had died more than twenty years before, but Anicah understood every sly aside. Like her, he spoke flash, the argot of vagabonds, petty criminals, Gypsies and prostitutes. But she could appreciate his eloquence too. The actors' labored delivery and crude improvisations could not clip the wings of his graceful, lascivious wit.

She left the theater happy but not much wealthier than when she went in. Her stomach rumbled and she started off at a fast walk toward Broad Street and the High Cross at the center of Bristol. The streets were more crowded than usual, as people sat outside to escape the ovens August had made of their houses. As she passed the shops, vendors called out "What lack ye, lad? What lack ye?"

She broke into a trot when she heard shouts in the distance.

"Away to the wicked cross with ye, papists!"

She rounded a corner to see a gang of boys pelting a small group of people with sewer filth. They must have been recusants, Roman Catholics who refused to renounce their outlawed religion.

"Malignants! Jesuited papishers!" someone cried. "Foul anti-Christs!"

The two men in the group, their short capes flapping, darted into a narrow alley. A pair of cloaked and masked women and a few maidservants followed them. They ran up the precipitous stone steps to the inn called the Cocklorel and slammed the door behind them.

Anicah selected a turd and hurled it. It hit the wall and stuck. "Spawn of the devil," she shouted. She held no particular animosity toward them, she just enjoyed hectoring as a sport.

She noticed, however, that when the urchins grew bored and left, more servants arrived with trunks and satchels. These particular papists, country gentry by the look of them, were about to take a trip, probably a sea voyage, since the Cocklorel catered to that trade. Anicah stared at the inn and wondered how she could lighten their load.

Chapter 2

T he Cocklorel's small second-story chamber had no windows. In the oppressive heat a heavy blue pall of tobacco smoke hung over the long table and the ponderous, high-backed chairs. The wail of a fiddle and the oaths and laughter of the inn's less genteel customers drifted up through the floorboards.

Margaret Brent's gray eyes reflected no particular emotion, but her skull throbbed with the pain that had been her companion all day.

"Captain Fleete," she said. "I am unacquainted with the fees expected in the city. Canst thou tell me how much garnish is required to bribe yon minstrel to cease?"

Henry Fleete halted the fistful of mutton en route to his mouth. "Fiddlers are not like other extortioners, Mistress Margaret. The more you give them, the longer they hang about."

"Damn me, but they have become a public nuisance." Margaret's brother Giles tamped tobacco into his pipe. He lit it with the slow match, a saltpeter-soaked cord smoldering in its iron holder.

As with most men and some women too, years of gripping a pipe's stem had worn semicircular grooves into two of Giles Brent's lower and upper left teeth. He didn't have to open his mouth to slide the pipe between them. Next to him, his brother Fulke sat encircled by a wreath of his own smoke.

The fumes made Margaret's throat ache and stung her eyes, but she knew no purpose would be served by asking them to stop.

They would stare at her as though she had requested them to cease breathing. She agreed with the late King James who wrote that tobacco was "loathesome to the eye, hateful to the nose, harmful to the brain, and dangerous to the lungs." And she intended to better her fortunes by trafficking in it.

She supposed she should have stayed in the garret room with her sister Mary and the inn's generous complement of fleas, but she was too restive for that. She certainly couldn't take her unquiet thoughts for a walk through the streets. Her brows twitched at the memory of being pelted with filth little more than an hour ago.

In any case, she was eager to hear about the wild country that waited for her far beyond the horizon, and Henry Fleete was the man to tell her. He had lived in Virginia and traded among the Indians for almost twenty years. His dealings in the fur traffic had brought him back to England for several months, but he would return to Lord Baltimore's new colony on the same ship that would carry the Brents there.

Margaret Brent possessed the same long, narrow face her brothers Giles and Fulke did, but her features were too large for it. From between heavy brows her nose rose to a bony knob, then dropped again. She had a wide mouth, as sensuous as Giles's, but not as noticeable between the overhang of her nose and her jutting chin. Silver strands threaded her faded brown hair at the temples. She wore her hair in the current style, with curled locks hanging loose in front of her ears and the rest pinned up on the back of her head.

She was tall with broad shoulders, a long back and wide hips. "Hamper-arsed" was what the village folk whispered, and "mackerel-backed." They thought she couldn't hear them, but Margaret didn't miss much.

Her dress was subdued for a woman of her station, and a wide collar covered the square-cut scoop of her gown's neck. But she wore her brown silk overskirt fashionably separated in front and pinned up to hang in big loose folds over her blue lawn petticoats. Her skirted bodice was tightly cinched under her stomacher, a U-shaped panel that extended below her waist.

Salty moisture itched under the stiffened buckram of the stomacher. Margaret tried to move her legs, cramped from riding sidesaddle since before sunup, but Giles's mastiff and whippet occupied the space under the table. Margaret's chair was too heavy to move so she kicked the mastiff with the toe of her pump. The rushes spread on the floor rustled as he stirred. He grunted and farted contentedly, but he didn't budge.

Margaret had been taught that dignity was worth the price of any discomfort. She traced her lineage through her mother to John of Gaunt and Thomas Woodstock, sons of King Edward III. Women descended from nobility did not fidget. She shifted ever so slightly in her clothes anyway to ease the torment under her stomacher. She had pitched convention to the winds already. A little squirming would hardly matter. Besides, Captain Fleete was much more interested in the saddle of mutton and the local sherry than in her.

Margaret was used to being ignored. She was thirty-seven years old, and men as a species had not paid attention to her even when she was young. The only exceptions had been the Jesuits who had educated her in France, and the few failed gentlemen lured by the dowry her grandmother had settled on her. But Margaret had other plans for the money than handing it over to some belching, dottering, out-at-elbows country squire with bad breath and worse manners. She had invested it in the woollen trade and had done well. The profits, on deposit in London, were financing her share in this mad venture.

The thought of just how mad the venture was struck her now. She twined her trembling hands in the folds of her petticoats and half opened her mouth to announce that she and her sister would take horse for home at first light. She and Mary could occupy their days with prayers in the room set aside for them in the family's manor house.

But the house had passed into her eldest brother's irascible possession. And Margaret imagined herself and Mary growing smaller each year, more stooped and shadowy. Eventually the huge family portraits lining the gallery would have more sub-stance than they.

Even worse, she and Mary would have to continue attending the heretics' church services or pay fines and risk imprisonment. They would have to endure the hatred of those around them. She thought again of the screaming urchins and the excrement that stained her cloak.

Lord Baltimore, however, was a Roman Catholic. In the new protectorate he called Terra Maria, Mary's Land, Margaret and her kin could practice their religion openly for the first time. Bal-timore said he had named his colony after King Charles's wife, Henrietta Maria, but Margaret wasn't fooled. She thought about the wonder of a vast expanse of country named for the Holy Mother. She sat back in her chair and said nothing.

Fleete, with an impish twinkle in his bleary blue eyes, leaned toward Giles. "D'ye know the difference between orthodoxy and heterodoxy, Squire Brent?"

Giles sucked on his pipe and tensed. Religion was what most people debated these days, and rancorously too. "Nay," he said cautiously.

"The first is a man who has a doxy of his own. The second makes use of another man's doxy."

After an instant's pause Margaret began to shake. Laughter rumbled up from deep inside until she had to hold her stomacher to keep from breaking the laces that tied it in place. This was the first time she'd laughed since she started the journey from north-ern Gloucestershire six days ago. It felt good.

Fleete relaxed, though he had hardly been tense to begin with. He had heard the rumors that Margaret Brent and her sister had been indoctrinated by the hated Jesuits into an implacable piety.

He gave Margaret a sham of a rueful grin. "I beg you to par-don my bear-garden discourse, Mistress Margaret."

"Thou art a wag, Captain Fleete."

At thirty, Henry Fleete's pockmarked face sported a nose mis-shapen by brawling. His pale hair was thin and so was his small spiked, reddish beard. He had on breeches of brown fustian and a leather doublet laced up to cover the clumsy patches in his linen shirt. For all that, he possessed an outlandish flair.

Instead of ostrich plumes, his hat was adorned with broad, coppery feathers, iridescent in the candlelight. He said he had plucked them from a turkey. He also said that turkeys lived in the forests of America in such great numbers people could not hear each other shout for the noise of their garbling. He had told so many stories equally preposterous that Margaret suspected he lied for the sport of it.

"Might I examine thy blower, Captain?"

"Certes." Fleete handed the pipe across the table to her.

Along its three-foot stem stretched the carved image of a catamount half hidden in vines. The panther stared out at her as though a living spirit dwelled behind its yellow painted eyes. She wondered what hand had graved its lines into the wood.

"Wast thou really captured by the salvages and didst thou reside five years amongst them?" She gave the pipe back to him.

"Aye, Mistress Margaret. They took such a fondness to my person they insisted I share their hospitality."

"Canst thou say something in their tongue?"

Fleete spoke in a low, lilting cadence that made Margaret's scalp stir. It evoked a place and a people so far away and strange she could not begin to imagine them.

"What didst thou say?"

"I said that I am better proficient in the Indian language than mine own."

"Captain Fleete is much esteemed by the salvages." Giles emptied the last of the sherry and stamped his boot to call the serving wench on the ground floor.

At thirty-four, Giles was not a young man. His thin blond hair fell in loose curls about his shoulders. The ends of his moustache turned up in a perpetual smile and a stiletto-shaped beard clung to his undershot chin. The lids of his blue eyes drooped, giving him a sleepy, dissipated look. His quilted yellow satin doublet had broad shoulder welts that made his torso and waist look even thinner than they were.

Giles was his father's fifth son and had no prospect of inheriting either of the family's two manors or even living there. As a Roman Catholic he was barred from holding office, attending the university, joining the army or navy, or pursuing most professions. He was too proud to woo some rich merchant's daughter for her portion and a place in her father's business. For people of the Brents' class, a gentleman was not a gentleman unless he owned land and had tenants to call him "Squire."

Fulke was the second son, and his plight was even crueler than Giles's. Perhaps so narrowly missing wealth and station by the order of his birth gave Fulke his morose and resentful air. At forty-three he seemed a wan and shabby version of his younger brother.

The serving maid carried in a bottle of wine and a beef pie the size of a keg lid. Giles caught her by the arm and pulled her close so he could whisper in her ear.

"Fer shame, squire." She giggled. As she turned to go Giles slapped her on the bottom.

Henry Fleete sucked the marrow from the mutton bone, then waved it like a baton as he talked. "Maryland is without question the most pleasant and healthful place. And the Potomac the greatest river in the world." He poked his knife into the pasty's crust to let out the steam.

"The air is temperate in summer and mild in winter." Fleete didn't let talking interfere with eating. "Its verdant shores and forelands intertwine like lovers' limbs with the great Bay of Chesapeake and its mighty tributaries and meandering creeks. The deer are as numerous as cuckolds in London. You shall like it, I assure you, Mistress Margaret."

"I'm sure I shall." Margaret knew that Fleete, a Protestant and hardly a man of quality, had received a patent of two thousand acres, built a manor house, had bound servants and seated tenants in Mary's Land. He had reason to be effusive.

"The women who go there as servants have the best of it,

even the wild Irish," Fleete said through a mouthful of pie and gravy. "The wenches have hardly set foot on shore when they are courted so diligently that the virginity that has plagued them soon troubles them no more."

Margaret's cheeks and nose grew apple-red, and even heedless Henry Fleete knew he had misspoken. He belched and concentrated on the pasty.

He looked relieved when two boys, filthy as chimney sweeps, appeared in the doorway. Margaret could almost see the vermin stirring in their hair and clothes. She drew her skirts closer about her.

"Here's a brace of knaves," Fleete called out jovially.

"Lord bless ye, kind masters and mistress." The tallest stepped boldly into the room with his small, redheaded companion close on his heels. The redhead coughed pitifully into his shirtsleeve. "Please forgive me brother," the tall one said. "He's sickly." He spoke with the broad west-country burr that Margaret and her brothers' accents only hinted at.

"Damn me!" Giles waved his handkerchief at them. "We'll suffer no mumpers here."

"Spare us a penny and we shall give lung to a ditty whilst we caper like so many barb'ry apes on a leash." With her most beguiling smile Anicah jigged a few agile steps.

"You shall dance when I thrash you for your impudence."

"Ye must be a soldier, so fine and all." Anicah was not intimidated. "A military cove will damn us first, then tip us a sixpence, whilst an autem cackler calls down God's blessing and parts not from a thin farthing."

Margaret gave Giles a quizzical look. He had spent enough time in the stews to learn the language.

"Autem cackler is the canting term for a nonconformist," he grumbled.

"Art thou opposed to the Puritans, lads?" With her cool iron-gray eyes, Margaret surveyed Anicah and Squib.

"We do hate them, mistress," Anicah said. "For they are enemies to mirth, and they do not plant anything better than what they would root out."

Margaret arched her brows, surprised at the mother wit.

"Have a care, Mistress Margaret," Fleete warned. "Now they accost us at table. Soon we shall waken with them standing, hands outstretched, at the foot of the bed."

"I misdoubt we shall encounter them where we are going," Margaret said.

"Such urchins are like the cats that roam the gables and dung heaps." Giles wrinkled his long nose. "They quarrel and pilfer and stink." He regarded Anicah and Squib as though they were the anatomized remains of an executed criminal on exhibit. "They're as bad as Gypsies." He pointed his knife at Anicah. "The bigger one even looks like a Gypsy."

"What's needed is a piper who can entice their hordes into the holds of our ships for transport to America," Fleete said. "Their labor is sorely needed there, but the wretches would rather starve here than find ample store in the new country."

"We come from honest weaver folk, me brother and me." Anicah stared, wide-eyed and earnest, into Giles's face.

Margaret was amused. Like the cats to which Giles had compared the urchin, he knew whom he could most easily cadge.

"The pressmen took our father," Anicah said, "and sent him to fight in the low countries. He left us with no more than what a dog might drag off the malt heap. His ship was surprised by Algerine pirates who docked his yard." She made a slicing motion to illustrate circumcision. "Then they cut off his daddles for refusing to renounce Christ."

"Daddles?" Despite herself Margaret was intrigued.

"Hands, kind mistress." Anicah held out her grimy pair, palms down. Squib continued to cough delicately, as though reluctant to disturb gentlefolk with his tragic sufferings.

"Pirates and circumcision and amputation," Giles said jovially, "a common ruffler's lie, but told with flair."

"I expect gibberish of this wretch, Giles," Margaret said. "But speak you the king's English."

"Rufflers are beggars who claim to be seamen maimed in their country's service." Giles fumbled in the folds of his breeches. "Here's a farthing then for your ailing brother."

"Beggin' yer pardon, sire." Anicah looked him in the eye and spoke almost chidingly. "I'd not sell me brother fer a farthing, ailing or sound."

The men laughed, but the child's dignity stirred something in Margaret. She had seen England's poor thronging the roads. Families dispossessed by the enclosures of common fields trudged with their worldly belongings on their backs. Crippled soldiers, orphaned children and out-of-work weavers begged by the waysides. The entire country seemed to be on the move, impelled by crop failures or the king's ever-increasing levies, or by the annual waves of pestilence that beat at the doors of highborn and low and left death and madness in their wake.

Margaret knew she would meet other beggars before she left England's shores, but she felt compelled to give alms to these two. It would be her gift to a wounded and divided land she might never see again. There was no use asking Giles or Fulke to give more money. They rarely carried coins.

"Go upstairs," she said. "Knock on the second door. Tell my sister I said to give you sixpence and God's blessing."

"The Lord's blessing on you, mistress." Anicah and Squib bowed low as they backed from the room.

"You've granted a pair of rogues and dissemblers and belike bung-nippers entrance to your chamber, Mistress Margaret," Fleete said.

"Scapegraces perhaps," Margaret said.

"Rogues." Fleete speared the last of the beef in the bottom of the bowl. "Rogues and thieves."

Chapter 3

When Anicah reached the dark, narrow back stairway she whispered in Squib's ear. "Whilst I wheedle her for chink," she said, "foist whate'er y'can."

"Y'didn't flash the maunds."

"Nay." Anicah held up her palms and she and Squib squinted at the ugly sores, one in the center of each hand.

Anicah had made them from unslaked lime and soap and rust. Beggars usually bound the mixture with rags and waited until the lime created ugly wounds, but Anicah had learned to sculpt them to look almost as realistic when viewed in dim light.

"The papishers set store by 'em," Anicah said, "but the old huddle looked wise to the rig."

"Aye. She had peepers like boiled gizzards."

A single lantern filled the narrow, low hallway with the stench of burning whale oil. When Anicah reached the head of the stairs, she stood a moment to calm her pounding heart. Since her stay in Bridewell prison, she had rarely been between walls or under a roof. The massive beams and closed doors threw a tenuous fear over her, as though she had walked into a spider's web in the dark.

She knocked on the second door.

"Bess?" a voice called from the other side.

"Nay, mistress. I come with a charge."

The door creaked open and Anicah and Squib slipped inside.

Mary Brent closed it behind them. In a hushed whistling of silk, she sat on the edge of the bed. Anicah was shocked to see her fingering a circlet of beads, a popish bit of witchery.

A white linen bertha covered the chest that the plunge of her neckline would have exposed. Pale brown curls framed her narrow face. The rest of her hair was pulled back into a knot. She looked old to Anicah, at least thirty. She was tall and angular, with translucent skin stretched across her high-set cheekbones. She had a small mouth and large eyes of Coventry blue.

Her eyes made Anicah as uneasy as her sister's had. Mistress Margaret's eyes seemed to read Anicah's thoughts the way a parson drew sense from the tiny black loops and lines in a Bible. But under the tranquil blue surface of Mary's eyes lurked something that was, if not mad, at least peculiar.

A few candles lit the edges of the portmanteaus and trunks stacked between the sagging bedstead and the lowest point of the sloping ceiling. Squib inched toward a chest whose open lid revealed a tumble of lace and linens.

"Art thou a child of Egypt?" From her seat on the bed Mary Brent's gaze was almost level with Anicah's. "Thou hast an Egyptian's swarthy complexion and an exile's eyes."

"Nay, mistress. Me father was a Spaniard, with belike a nipperkin of Moor. He raised us in the true religion." Anicah's voice trembled. "Till he 'n' our mother was backed by pestilence."

"Backed?"

"Kilt, mistress." Anicah coaxed a tear into trickling down her cheek.

"So you are orphans, poor dears. Will you be sailing with us to the land of the Perizzites?"

"Nay, beggin' yer pardon. Only your gentle sister asked us. . . ."

" 'Get thee out of thy country and from thy kindred,' " Mary said suddenly.

Startled, Anicah almost turned to leave, thinking she was being dismissed.

" 'And from thy father's house unto a land that I will shew

thee.' " The passion in Mary's soft voice and the wild innocence in her eyes set the hair to stirring at the nape of Anicah's neck. " 'From the wilderness unto the great sea toward the going down of the sun shall be thy coast.' "

Anicah glanced at Squib, but he seemed unaffected by Mary's outburst. He stared artlessly about him while a train of lace-edged linen disappeared under the hem of his wool jerkin.

"If you are of the true faith," Mary said, "then you must come with us to the coast where the sun goeth down."

"Beggin' your par—" Anicah began again.

" 'And I will appoint a place for my people Israel and will plant it,' " Mary said. " 'That they may dwell in a place of their own, and move no more, neither shall wicked people trouble them as before time.' "

"An't please you, mistress," Anicah put in desperately when Mary paused to draw breath. "We have a charge from your sister."

"Margaret?"

"Aye." Anicah was anxious to escape before gizzard-eyes came upstairs. She glanced at the clothing lying across a trunk. "Mistress Margaret asked me to fetch the black wool gorget to protect her from the night humors. And a silk handkerchief. She charged me to tell you we might have half a bull for our trouble."

Squib gave a small gasp. It was a bold request.

Mary laid the shawl and handkerchief over Anicah's out-stretched arm. "Half a bull?"

"Half a crown, mistress." Anicah held her palm out as though to receive the gratuity, but also to reveal the sore.

"What is this?"

"I know not, mistress." She offered her other hand. "They appear on me daddles from time to time. Mayhap y'could spare a sixpence for the healing of 'em . . ."

"Blessed Mother of God." Mary crossed herself and fell to her knees.

She took both Anicah's hands in her own long thin ones. Her spidery touch made Anicah long to jerk away from her and flee this dim, close cell. She thought she would suffocate with the odor of lavender like sweet decay and the rue and wormwood scattered to repel fleas.

"The holy Virgin Mother hath sent us a sign. She hath blessed our going out of Egypt." Tears streamed down Mary's face and dripped from her sharp jaw until Anicah worried that they would dissolve the stigmata. "Forgive me, most Blessed Mother, for doubting your holy design."

Anicah withdrew her hands and maneuvered Mary to her feet and back onto the bed. "We must take yer sister her things, mistress." She was so nervous she was willing to forego the half crown. She herded Squib in front of her and had her fingers on the latch when Mary called to her.

"A token for thee and thy brother, messengers from the land of Egypt. Where we are going we shall have little need of it." She held out her hand and Anicah, at arm's length, took the coin gingerly. Mary Brent seemed not to notice that Squib had gained considerably in girth since coming into the room. "You are the dark children of this dark city," Mary said softly. "But you bear a light within which even you cannot see. God's blessing on you." She made the forbidden sign of the cross.

"And on you, mistress." Anicah lifted the latch and slipped out behind Squib.

She hurriedly crossed herself in the opposite direction to undo whatever sorcery the papist's gesture might have called up. Then she and Squib pelted down the winding stairs and through a hall reeking of urine. They cut through the clouds of steam and smoke and oaths in the kitchen and ran out into the rear courtyard. Anicah led Squib past the stable and into the alley behind it.

They darted down a dozen black, aimless passages and up and down the steep stone steps that climbed the hills from one level of Bristol to another. Only when they arrived at the street lined with chandlers' shops and seamen's taverns and brothels did they slow down. The smell of tar and pitch, spices and old fish thickened the air here. A dank fog poked stealthy fingers among the buildings. The rectangles of light from the open alehouse doors seemed to glow through gauze.

The woman sat smoking a pipe in a dark doorway. "Thrupence for a dog's portion, lads," she called out. "A sniff o' me cunt and a lick."

"I'd charge ye naught to kiss me arse," Anicah said cheerfully.

They followed the ancient city wall, with houses clinging like barnacles to both sides. Then they turned a corner and the world opened up before them. In the middle of the street, just beyond the stone quay, hundreds of masts tilted every which way. The River Frome's tide was at its ebb, and the ships lay beached on their hulls in the offal washed into it by the last rain or tossed there by the Tom-turd men. A full moon illuminated men-o'-war, privateers, East Indiamen, merchant vessels and those for the coasting trade, which usually meant smuggling.

By the time the church bells rang nine of the clock the rest of Bristol would be quiet. Here the clatter and bustle went on most of the night. The comings and goings of ships danced to the restless rhythm of the winds and tides, to the waxing and waning of the moon, not to the predictable rising and setting of the sun nor the convenience of men.

Anicah and Squib trotted to the half-built hull of an Irish coaster and slipped inside the ribs. Squib leaned over and rested his hands on his knees while he caught his breath.

"The papist tabby be daft."

"All papishers be daft." Anicah remembered the stories of Catholics sacrificing Protestant children in their idolatrous rituals and serving them up with wine in a eucharistic stew. "They be full of dodgery and paternosters."

"What'd she give ye, Ani?"

"She tipped us a bull." Anicah held up the crown.

Squib squealed with joy.

"I'll break it with ye tomorrow." She slipped it into the bawd's purse. "The secret is to get among quality and make of yerself such a vexation they pay to be rid o' ye."

She helped him decant the loot from under his jerkin. Besides the silk handkerchief and wool shawl Mary Brent had given Anicah, Squib had stolen linens and scarves, a pair of velvety lambskin gloves, a silver buckle and watch and a feather fan, broken and bedraggled from being stuffed into the jerkin.

"Prime swag," she said. "Sweet's your hand, Squib."

Squib beamed.

"We'll visit the fence first light."

"I can go wi' ye?" Squib held a linen sheet while Anicah laid the goods in the center and tied the corners to form a bag.

"Aye."

"We be snacks then?"

"Aye, snacks. Partners." Anicah slung the bundle over her shoulder. "Meet me at the mouth of the fence's lane at the eighth bell."

"We'll buy rum rigging, suits of holland."

"And eat till we don't know whether to shit or spew." She grinned at him.

Squib waved as he headed off toward his lodging on a bulk, the overhang of a shop window. "God keep ye, Ani."

"And you." She went off singing into the clutter of the quay, completely fog-wrapped now. She was giddy with plans for her wealth, but she was as cautious as always. She threaded a confusing meander among the thousands of noisome hogsheads of salted herring and cod.

As menacing as the docks and their swaggering seamen and keel bullies might seem, Anicah felt relatively safe here. Escape and concealment were easy among the stacks of lumber, cargo and sledges. Gangs of drunken young swells armed with swords and bludgeons harried other parts of the city for the lark of it, but they rarely dared to come here.

Anicah ghosted through a deserted area of the wharf. She looked around before ducking into an overturned hogshead half hidden behind a broken and discarded sledge tilted on its side. Anicah never slept in a place with only one exit, but the barrel was missing its bottom. Pushing her bundle ahead of her she crawled in and settled herself cross-legged with it between her knees.

She emptied the contents of the snuff box she had lifted from the merchant at the theater. Sneezing, she pulled a grimy, folded piece of paper from her hat and put it inside. Her mother had told her it was her father's will. It was the only relic of the father she'd never known. She couldn't read it and didn't know anyone who could. She put the box into the cloth bag that hung around her waist inside her breeches.

She pulled out the wool shawl and plumped the bundle into a pillow. She lay on her side with her head on it and drew the shawl over her. Even in August the air here was chill at night.

As she lay curled on her side she held onto the crown inside the old whore's purse around her neck. She traced the coin's sharp, round rim with her thumb and fell asleep thinking of the shoes and wool stockings she could buy from the undertaker this winter.

She awoke when a hand grabbed her ankle. She kicked out with her other foot, felt it connect solidly and heard the gratifying sound of a man's grunt. The hand released her and she scrambled on her hands and knees out the bottom end of the hogshead and into a fishing net.

Chapter 4

Anicah thrashed in the net, struggling to break free from the hands that pulled it tighter around her.

"Stand back." The voice sounded loud yet far away, as though it had traveled through a pipe to reach her. She lashed out and her fist hit bone, her knuckles wedging neatly into an eye socket.

"God's nigs, he pegged me peeper," a voice said.

A blow across her shoulders knocked her to her knees. Bolts of pain shot to the tips of her fingers. The cudgel hit her next in the stomach, and she gagged. She curled over and tried to raise her arms to protect her head, but they were too intertwined in the net.

"Undamaged, ye jingle brains." The second voice sounded near her ear.

An arm encircled Anicah's head. Ignoring the tarred net in her mouth, she sank her teeth into the man's sleeve and the flesh inside it.

"Damn me!" With his other hand the man cuffed her ear, setting her head to ringing.

She felt the crease and pull of a rope around the net and her chest. More coils fell around her and tightened until she was gasping for air. Someone balanced a lantern on the hogshead. Anicah struggled onto her knees and scowled up at the three men standing over her.

They didn't look like catchpoles, sheriff's deputies. Under their cloaks they were stylishly dressed in loose satin breeches with lace ruffles at the knees and knitted silk stockings. The clothes ill-suited them.

The three hauled Anicah, still struggling, to her feet. Two of them held her, while the third loosed the rope and unwound the net. He pulled her hands behind her and snapped fetters onto her wrists. He retied the rope, leaving an end in front to lead her.

"What's this, then?" He grabbed the cord around her neck and yanked, breaking it. He opened the purse's drawstring and shook the contents into his palm. "The bungnipper's got a crown." He held the coin up.

" 'Tis mine. A kind mistress tipped me it."

"Where be this mistress?"

Anicah glared at him.

"Foisting more'n a shilling will see you twist."

She spat at him.

"We bagged a bravo, lads." His laugh sounded more like a bark. "Mayhap he'll not plead." He stooped to look directly into her face. His breath made her nose twitch. "And if ye plead not, ye'll don the iron doublet."

He seemed pleased with the prospect of Anicah being pressed to death. "I once had the privilege of escortin' a woman to the press yard and puttin' the halter on her chest. Ye c'd hear her bones crack as they added the weight. She bore two hundred and fifty pounds fer but a pissin'-while before she begged to go back to court and plead."

"Ye may kiss me breech." Anicah regarded him disdainfully.

"Come along, then." The leader used the rope to haul Anicah to her feet. He started off and Anicah followed a few paces. Then she dug her heels in and swiveled at the hips. She yanked the line from his hands and ran a few clumsy steps.

"Settle 'im."

The cudgel hit her and she thought her head was exploding, her brains shattering. The glinting shards pierced her eyes and flew outward.

"The jakes is in the corner. Neither piss nor shit elsewhere." The man unlocked the fetters from Anicah's wrists. He put his foot to the back of her breeches and shoved her into the dank room. She recognized it as one of the storage vaults honeycombing the ground under Bristol.

Anicah's ribs and back ached from the cudgel blows, and her thoughts revolved in a slow, disorienting spin. The taste of bile made her stomach recoil. She rubbed the knob on the back of her head to ease the throbbing.

The wind from the heavy door slamming behind her set the dense fog of tobacco smoke to swirling in lazy eddies in the light from a single candle. It had burned almost to a stub, and its flame guttered in the breeze, then gathered itself to flare again. It seemed to float in the darkness.

The pain behind her eyes was so intense she had to squint into the candle's pale aura. It stood next to several beer bottles on a rickety table. The three men seated there glared at Anicah as though she were responsible for the wind. Then they went back to studying their cards and puffing on their pipes.

Anicah could make out the shades of people sitting hunched against the walls and the glow of embers in their pipes. When the room and its occupants began to tilt and wobble, she pressed her bruised shoulders against the stone wall and slid down until she was crouching on the floor. She shut her eyes, trying to regain her balance.

"Spirits caught ye, did they, ye pitiful rattlebrain?" The woman's voice came from behind a pipe's red glow in the shadows at the far side of the room. "Yer whore of a mother must be happily rid of ye."

"A turd in yer teeth, ye buttock-whore." A sudden rage shook out pain and self-pity. Anicah launched herself at the voice. She bumped the table as she charged past. It tipped, scattering cards and bottles. The candle rolled onto the floor and went out, leaving the room dark as pitch.

" 'Od's nigs. Damn ye altogether." The card players scrambled to rescue the bottles before the last of the beer gurgled out.

Anicah groped along the wall, found a neck and got her hands around it. She ducked her head and squeezed as her victim thrashed and clawed and gurgled.

Someone lit the candle and strong hands grabbed Anicah's hair and the back of her breeches. The boy she was strangling pried her fingers from his neck and began coughing and gasping. She glimpsed his crimson face before she was flung against the wall.

"Ferocious little ram cat." The woman who'd started the trouble had moved to sit at the table.

"I'll drub you, you draggle-tail. . . ." Anicah tried to rise, but a hand pushed her down.

She stared up into a face as ugly as a mummer's mask. Smallpox scars cratered his cheeks. One eye was yellow as a cat's, the other the color of dark lager. They glared at her from under the tangled brush of an eyebrow that met at the bridge of his nose.

He stood there long enough to be sure Anicah wouldn't move, then settled himself onto the stool and picked up his cards. His breeches hung loose on his splayed legs, and his knobby knees poked through large holes in his brown fustian hose. The rest of his clothes were black as soot. A greasy leather cap perched on his head.

Once Anicah's eyes adjusted to the gloom she could see that most of the room's occupants were men or boys, but a woman lay on a thin pallet nearby and cried softly. The desperation in her sobs made Anicah want to cry herself.

"Cease yer flinging of snot about," she said.

The crying stopped abruptly.

"She bears a fardel of troubles." The boy sitting next to her was the one she had tried to throttle.

He leaned against the wall with his long legs pulled up against his chest. Even sitting he towered over Anicah. He had a straight sturdy nose and generous mouth. A shock of black hair half covered his eyes. He had the unwhiskered jaw of a boy, but a fine set of cheekbones were beginning to show through the soft flesh of childhood. He wore a plain wool jerkin, reddish-brown homespuns and the clumsy, mud-caked shoes of a farmer.

He gazed at her with his mouth half open and a lost and bewildered look in his dark blue eyes.

"Stop staring like a cat turned out of a basket," she snapped.

He handed her a brown bottle. Anicah glanced at him over the top of it. The country boob was too simple to take offense.

"My name's Martin Kirk," he said.

Anicah took a drink and kept the bottle. She leaned her head back and let the beer work its wiles. She intended her silence to discourage his chatter.

"Spirits got you, did they?" He was obstinately friendly.

"They never." But the thought of being caught by spirits almost panicked her.

She knew boys who had vanished. One day they were pilfering and roistering, drumming on the shop stalls with their cudgels, and the next day they were gone. Rumor said they were sold to ships' masters and sent across the ocean to be worked to death or eaten by cannibals and wild beasts.

Spirits. Folk whispered it, as though the men who stole people were supernatural, invisible. Like the Reaper himself the spirits took both male and female, but unlike Death, they preferred healthy youngsters to the old and infirm.

"I'm not supposed to be here." Martin interrupted her thoughts again. "They've made a mistake."

"Stuff it, ye walloping great looby." She hit his arm as hard as she could and bruised her knuckles on him.

"Aren't we in a pet." The woman at the table cackled as she dealt the cards. "Ye'd rather dance the gallows jig, would ye, than serve seven years in the plantations? A puny dung-heap rat like yerself will expire in America ere the ship weighs anchor for the return."

Anicah ignored her. Now that she could see her, she recognized Joan Parke. She knew from experience that quarreling with Joan required more energy and space than she had at her disposal right then. Joan had been in Bridewell prison when Anicah's aunt was sent there for rioting and took Anicah with her.

Anicah rubbed the knot on her head and considered the jilt called fate, who smiled most fondly at those she was about to betray.

Chapter 5

Margaret and Mary Brent stood on the stone quay waiting to climb down into the battered wherry. The Brents' maids and servants had already crowded into the second boat. The watermen lounged on their oars and made no move to help their passengers embark.

This was not the first time Margaret had been smuggled out of England. As Catholics she and Mary could not receive a religious education in their own country. They had sailed to the continent twenty-five years ago to study with the Jesuits in Liège. The smells and sound of Bristol's waterfront carried Margaret back to that time. She had felt afraid then, lost and abandoned. She felt the same way now.

The predawn darkness, the hood of Margaret's cloak and her travel mask narrowed the world to a shadowy tunnel. In the distance she heard the creaks and groans of ships riding at anchor. From the darkness came the steady beat of a drum guiding a lighter toward shore. A dense fog amplified the hollow thumps and gave them a ghostly resonance. Margaret thought, with grim satisfaction, that each drumbeat was causing an echoing throb in Giles's head, aching from his excesses. For the past week he had behaved as though he would never see a dram or a doxy again.

Mary's lips moved silently. Margaret knew that under her cape she was engaged in the illegal activity of reciting her rosary, a miniature one made to hide in the palm of her hand. But the rosary wasn't the only illegal item with them. At Margaret's feet sat a small chest. The missals and crucifix, the chalice, paten and altar cloths inside it would get her and Mary imprisoned or at least fined heavily if discovered by the authorities. In either case the ship would sail without them.

A Jesuit priest and physician traveling with the Brents started down the steep steps in the side of the quay. He held his hand out for Margaret who searched with her toe for a secure footing on the slimy, tilting stones.

"Hurry it along," one of the watermen grumbled.

A sallow band of light at the horizon silhouetted the masts. The wherry had to be away from the wharf before the sun rose. The king's officers were not likely to challenge the boat and its cargo once it moved among the anchored ships and the schools of smacks and tenders that serviced them.

The Brents and the Jesuit, Father Poulton, were leaving England's shores without taking the required oath denying papal authority. It was a serious offense. The watermen, however, were used to dealing in illicit goods, and the papists' money was as good as any.

The wherry glided so smoothly and silently away from the quay, it seemed suspended between the black river and the gray tent of fog. The oarlocks creaked rhythmically as the boat nosed through the plumes of mist rising off the surface. Against the lightening sky the lines of the ships' rigging formed an entanglement so vast the vessels themselves seemed imprisoned in it.

Raked bowsprits pierced the fog, as though clearing the way for the broad bows that appeared, then vanished into the mist. Tiers of guns formed a menacing bristle at the bulwarks and gun ports. The hulls dwarfed the wherry as it glided among them.

"Damn me!" Giles stared upward.

Margaret followed his gaze to see that they were moving under the privy hole in the overhanging prow of an East Indiaman. The square rim framed a sailor's naked buttocks thirty feet overhead. Margaret leaned over to avoid the fall of excrement. She suspected that the watermen had rowed them here to express their view of the Roman Catholic religion.

A warm wind, made capricious by the river's curves and high banks, ruffled the surface. It filled the sails of the smaller boats and sent them bucketing along.

"Such a sweet zephyr." Father Poulton smiled from the bow. "I predict we shall catch a fair wind and arrive before Michaelmas."

Giles leaned forward and lowered his voice. "You know, Margaret, that we shall have to stay out of sight until we're under way."

"We understand," Margaret said.

"Mary." Giles looked sternly at her.

"Yes, Giles."

"We'll be among heretics on this voyage. We are not to say our beads or hold mass where we can be seen. Those are Lord Baltimore's orders."

"Of course, Giles," Mary said.

Of course. Giles looked dubious.

He knew that if Mary hadn't come with them she likely would have ended up a prisoner or suffered a martyr's death. No matter how often the ecclesiastical courts warned her family, she politely declined to attend services in the local Anglican church. She had already cost the Brents a fortune in fines.

The wherry bumped into an ancient, high-rumped Dutch flute, broad of beam and round of stern. With a squeal the prow plowed a furrow through the barnacles and beards of algae. Lighters loaded almost to capsizing swarmed around the ship. A bleating ewe swung wildly in a sling overhead.

The ship's bulk looked to have settled into an abrupt bulge at the waterline, like a man whose love of pasties and puddings had caused his flesh to form a roll above his breeches. It carried, fore and aft, galleried superstructures from which the decorative paint had long since flaked off. The narrow aftercastle towered three levels above the stern transom. The ship looked as ungainly as a gourd and likely to roll over in the slightest breeze.

"How shall we board?" Margaret asked.

Giles nodded up at the ewe, her legs splayed over the net's rim. A sailor leaned out with a hook to snag the sling and pull it toward the rail.

In the darkness Anicah sensed the clutter on the deck around her. Someone grabbed her arm and heaved her forward through the tangle of cordage. She barked her bare shin on a stack of barrel staves before hands shoved her roughly through a square opening, black as a well. The big country boy, Martin Kirk, followed her. He stepped on her fingers.

" 'Od's ballocks." Anicah lost her footing. She expected to plummet to her death, but the soggy planking came up abruptly, bruising her tailbone. The air was hot and rank.

When she tried to stand she hit her head on the ceiling. Someone lit a whale-oil lantern and hung it on a hook, but it gave off more smell than light. It did illuminate a heap of mildewed sacks of ticking. The sodden straw stuffing formed a huge lump in the bottom of each, but Anicah grabbed one and sat on it.

This was the 'tweendecks, the area between the main deck and the hold of the ship. As far as Anicah could see the compartment was packed with bodies lying two or three to a pallet. From the blackness beyond the lantern light she could hear coughing and rustling and grumbling about being woken up.

A seaman caught Anicah's wrist and replaced the fetters that had chained her to the gunwale on the trip here. He locked the other iron ring around Martin Kirk's wrist.

"There's been a mistake," Martin protested. "I'm not a criminal. My parents signed a contract with your ship's master to deliver me to a planter in Maryland."

"There are them as change their minds and try to escape." The seaman rapped him hard on the head with his truncheon.

As Martin fell Anicah hauled with both hands on the chain so he landed next to her on the pallet. Being shackled with him was a piece of good luck. His weight and size would help her maintain proprietorship of the bed.

Anicah had learned that the tall, surly individual in the greasy leather hat was called Harry. She wasn't surprised when he stepped off the ladder and began kicking the occupants off of the nearest pallet.

One of them scrambled to defend his estate. Harry was pounding his head against the boards when two seamen separated them by thumping them with their clubs. Cursing, the loser dragged his things farther back into the depths of the 'tweendecks. Those nearest Harry edged away.

Anicah could see that he had claimed the spot by the hatch. He was the last man to enter and the seaman chained him to the ladder. Anicah pulled her dazed companion to his knees and dragged their pallet next to his.

"Ye made a prime job of it, squire," she said.

It was a bold move, taking up some of the space he·had fought for. He glanced at her, then leaned his head against the ladder and closed his eyes.

A rustle of canvas coverlets and a fresh murmur of complaints rippled along the ranks of occupants as Anicah's companions tried to claim pallets and space to lay them out. Then Joan Parke arrived.

"A cluster of poxes on ye," she screamed up at the sailors. "Ye prefer to usher at the back door, d'ye?"

"We've no use for a three-penny upright whore infest'd wi' a clap," one of them shouted down at her.

"Filthy buggers," she muttered. "I wot I am not man enough for 'em."

"Would none o' them tip ye threepence fer a flourish, Joan?" Harry didn't bother opening his eyes.

'D'ye care to dance a blanket jig, Harry?" She dropped her small satchel at his feet.

"I'll find ye."

"Move forward with the rest of the wenches, ye burnt-arse whore." The seaman prodded her with his truncheon, then took the lantern and ran up the ladder. As soon as his bare soles cleared the opening a heavy wooden grate slammed over it.

"Bite me arse," Joan called after him.

Anicah could trace Joan's progress into the darkness, damning everyone to the devil and raising protests when she stepped on people.

Anicah had noticed that the women weren't shackled, and she considered announcing that she wasn't a boy. But at least here she might feel the occasional brush of a breeze to ease the stifling heat. And though the smell of ordure, vomit, sweat, tar, and whale oil was strong here, it would be worse there.

Martin Kirk began to sob softly next to her. Anicah leaned her back against the hull. She stared up at the heavy beams and the planking of the deck above. She imagined it sagging, collapsing. She could hear the lap of water on the other side. It sounded very close. Much too close.

To drown out the menace of it she sang a melancholy air popular in the streets of Bristol.

> *"If any man or woman,*
> *in country or in city*
> *Can tell where liveth charity,*
> *or where abideth pity,*
> *Bring news unto the Cryer,*
> *and their reward shall be,*
> *The prayers of poor folks every day*
> *upon the humble knee."*

Chapter 6

If the ship were a cat stretching with forepaws extended and rump raised, the roundhouse would have been at the highest point just before the tail. It perched under the quarterdeck, above the master's cabin. The ship's carpenter had used wood and canvas to divide it into three parts, with the gentlemen's berths against the two hulls. Margaret and Mary occupied the space in the center. The stacks of goods lashed to cleats in the floor left room for one person to pass.

Apple and pear seedlings stood next to the high, narrow section of the oriel window still visible after the partitioning. Mary sat on a small cask of wine near the window. She had tucked her wide skirts around her and propped her feet on a tub of cooking oil. She was reading her missal by the morning light.

A sunbeam lit the wisps of pale, fine hair that framed her face and escaped from the coil set high on her head. The light in her hair made a sort of halo of it and threw her long, arched nose into profile. She was oblivious to the din outside and to the gentle, unsettling rock of the ship at anchor.

"Good morrow, dear sisters." Giles looked in. "How fare you?"

"Well enough." Margaret drew him into the corridor, wrinkling her nose at the odor. The gentlemen preferred to take care of their business here, rather than smelling up their cabin by using the privy stools provided for the purpose.

Margaret spoke into Giles's ear so he could hear her over the banging and shouting and damning on deck, but Mary couldn't.

" 'Tis a floating coffin, Giles. It leaks like a fish basket."

"Fret not, sister. 'Tis stoutly made."

" 'Twas stoutly made fifty years ago." Margaret crossed her arms over her stomacher. With her maids housed in the 'tween-decks, she and Mary had to help each other dress. Margaret's stays were not as tightly laced as usual and not containing the slow churn underneath them, in concert with the roll of the ship. "I saw a plank so rotted I might have pried it loose with my fingers."

"Master Skinner knows his business."

"Master Skinner was sufficiently in drink before he came aboard." Margaret could hear Skinner shouting orders from the half-deck. "He must make repairs before we sail."

"We're fortunate to have a freshening wind. If we don't leave now we shall miss the Portuguese trades. Delays have already diminished our stores."

Margaret had to concede that point. "Thou hast seen to the stowing of the provisions?"

"All is secure in the bottom." Giles smiled and Margaret relented. Even as a child he had been able to sweeten her sour moods with the warmth of his sleepy blue eyes and a display of his orderly teeth.

Giles doffed his plumed hat and bowed as gallantly as space permitted. "I shall see to the servants' quarters."

"They must be dreadful."

"No worse than expected, I'm sure." Giles hurried away.

Margaret returned to the cabin and sat on the bed. She leaned against the wall to relieve the pressure of her bodice stays and fanned herself with a thumbed copy of Hawley and Lewger's *Relation of Maryland*. She closed her eyes and tried not to listen to the hammering and crashing and shouting. The din was rising to a crescendo that signaled departure was near, but it wasn't too late. Margaret could still change her mind.

Mary sat beside her and took her hand. "We are but part of God's great design," she said softly.

Margaret smiled at her. "I fear I have led thee into terrible peril."

"God leads, dear sister. We can but follow."

They both jumped when the capstan began its ponderous ro-
tation with a loud shriek. In the small compartment under the
fo'c'sle, the anchor's great, wet hawser snaked through a hatch to
the hold where men coiled it.

"We must bid farewell to our native country," Mary said.

She and Margaret put on their cloaks and travel masks. They
climbed the steps to join Fulke and Giles at the railing of the quarterdeck. From there they could look back at the shore, out at the four
ships preparing to sail with them, and down into the ship's waist.
The crew was lining up along the main yard there, on a deck that
was miraculously cleared away and orderly. The pigs and sheep were
penned on the foredeck. Chickens no longer roosted in the ratlines.

When the anchor was catted in place along the bowsprit,
Skinner gave orders from the half-deck to the officers who bellowed them to the men of their crews.

"Two men to the foretop."

"Haul out the bowline."

"Hoist."

As the men heaved on the line, they sang.

> *"Tell 'em all, tell 'em all,*
> *Gallowsbirds all, gallowsbirds all,*
> *Great and small, great and small,*
> *One and all, one and all."*

Their chant was accented by the crack of canvas snapping
in the wind. The ship heeled to port. A shudder passed through it,
then a brief stillness, as though it were gathering itself for a leap.

" 'Od's blood, witness my trials," Skinner roared. "You sea
curs will be the death of me."

The shouting continued as the men unfurled and set the ranks of
sails on the masts. They flapped and swelled with the power of the
wind. The same wind billowed Margaret's skirts. Her heart surged

with the ship. She felt a sudden elation, as though she had cast into the water the silent pity of those dearest to her and the loud censure of strangers who would deprive her of her faith. Her brothers and the other Gentleman Adventurers planned to recreate England on a foreign shore, but Margaret had her own audacious plans.

She would make a home and a future for herself and for her sister. She and Mary would have their own manor. They too would have seigniory rights, as Lord Baltimore had promised those who ventured their fortunes with his. They would be beholden to no one. Answerable to no one. No silent pact would confine them to an upstairs room in someone else's house.

Fulke leaned over the railing and vomited into the restless chop far below. Mary lifted her mask and faced into the breeze.

"The strong airs are deleterious to health," Margaret reminded her. "Thou shouldst put on thy vizard."

"Is not this wind from the northeast?"

Margaret looked up at the pennant streaming in the wind's current. "Yes."

"Then mayhap the same breeze that touches our cheeks has blown across our fields and whistled about the chimneys of our house."

The fields and chimneys of our brother's house, Margaret thought. But she pictured the clouds of sheep drifting across the emerald-green hills of the upper reaches of the Severn. She remembered the peaceful villages of thatched stone cottages, the willows hanging over the watercourses, the nightingale that sang in the big ash outside her window.

She took off her mask and held up a hand to feel the stir of the air against her palm. She and Mary had said litanies to the Blessed Virgin asking for a fair wind. The Holy Mother had not failed them. Margaret watched the green cliffs recede behind the ship. Tears stung her eyes.

In the hot, fetid 'tweendecks, the creaking of the capstan vibrated in Anicah's bones. She heard the shouts and the slap of the sails, loud as the reports of cannon. She felt the shudder pass through the timbers. When the ship heeled suddenly she braced herself as best she could with her wrists shackled. Her heart jogged in her chest.

A woman screamed. Another sobbed. Somewhere in the gloom a man cursed bitterly.

Anicah began to sing. "Weep eyes, break heart . . ."

Next to her, Martin stared at the floor between his drawn-up knees, but he sang with her. Someone else joined in, and soon almost everyone did.

> "Weep eyes, break heart!
> My love and I must part.
> Cruel fates true love do sever,
> And I shall see you never, never."

On the quarterdeck Margaret and Mary heard the melody as it welled up from the planks of the deck. The sailors were walking on song. Music wrapped around them and rose to mingle with the wind in the sails. With the wind and Master Skinner's oaths it powered the ship.

When that song ended Anicah started another one. It had an author and a famous one, but the ballad mongers had given it to everyone.

> "Sweetest love, I do not go
> for weariness of thee,
> Nor in hopes the world can show
> a fitter love for me."

Tears stung Margaret's eyes and blurred the shoreline. The ship glided so smoothly past the tree-lined banks it seemed as though the land were moving, as though her country were leaving her.

Chapter 7

Everyone in the 'tweendecks watched the sunbeam's slow progress down the rough timbers of the companionway and into the gloom below. They all knew which knot in the beam marked noon and the time for the day's first meal. One person from each mess group crouched at the bottom of the ladder. Anicah waited with them and squinted up at the squares of sunlight framed by the grate over the hatch opening.

Harry was the leader of her group, but he wasn't the sort to wait in line, even if he were at the head of it. He had selected Anicah and Martin as his companions for meals, and assigned Anicah the task of fetching the food. If he suspected her true sex, he gave no indication of it. Martin had no idea, though he slept back to back with her every night. She had told him her name was Andrew, and Andrew she was.

The noon bell rang and the grate lifted. A seaman's toes and calves and the sagging hems of his canvas knee breeches appeared at the coaming. As the wooden bucket descended Anicah stepped forward to receive it. She took out the contents and balanced them in her arms while it rattled up again.

"Pease porridge?" Martin asked.

"Aye." She set the bottle of beer on the floor next to Harry's pallet and laid the chunks of bread and the wooden bowl on the coverlet.

No one spoke as they dug their fingers into the sticky lump of boiled peas and oats.

"The bread harbors weevils and worms." Martin began picking them out delicately with the blunt tips of his big fingers.

Harry uncorked the bottle and sniffed the beer. "I smell the stink of a nip cheese who's sold the master spoiled goods." He took a drink and passed the bottle to Martin. Martin grimaced at the sour smell of it.

" 'Twill be worse ere long." Harry rolled his dice onto the pallet that served him as cookhouse, tavern, parlor, gaming den and, thanks to Joan Parke, brothel. "Good folk, the afternoon lies longsome before us. Who desires to rattle Saint Hugh's bones?"

Stooped, and bracing her hands against the low ceiling, Anicah started toward the gloomy interior of the compartment. Most of the pallets had been dragged against the sides to make more room, but people were still packed like herrings and the heat was suffocating. No one had bathed or changed clothes since leaving Bristol three weeks ago. Anyone with enough belongings to fill a small chest sat on it. The others perched on whatever would raise them above the filth on the floor.

Just aft of the ladder was another locked wooden grate. A second ladder led to the bilge below. All the garbage and human waste on the ship eventually washed down there. The stench from the water that had soaked into the sand ballast grew worse each day.

"Meddle with me, ye priest's whores, and I will fling ye to the fishes." Joan was making another assault on the bed of the papist gentry's three maids. The bed was worth the effort.

The outer edges of the long wooden shelf were nailed to the hull. The other was fastened to legs that raised it a foot above the floor. The mattress was dry and relatively clean.

"Give way, ye pope's mutton." Joan grabbed a corner of the mattress and tried to heave the three occupants onto the floor.

"Leave off, or we shall joll thee about the ears." Bess Guest wasn't as tall as Joan, but she was broader and not wise enough to fear her.

Anicah ignored them all and sat on the edge of a nearby pallet. Bridget Murphy lay on her back with her arm over her eyes, as though even the dim light were too much for her. She shivered under her harsh coverlet.

"I be so cold," she said. "And there be no wood in the house."

Most of the transportees spoke with the sibilant burr of the west country, but Bridget spoke the dialect of the village where Anicah's mother was born. Anicah had first visited Bridget in hopes she might know something about her, but the girl was only sixteen and Anicah's mother had been dead almost eight years. She had roamed the countryside with Anicah before that. Bridget didn't remember her.

"She's burning with an evil humor, poor creature," Bess Guest said. "She says she aches in her joints, her head and her belly."

" 'Tis the Lord's judgment upon me for the killin' of me babe." Bridget sat up, her eyes wild, then fell back again. "They bade me wear the sheet and confess my sins in church. They rebuked me before the congregation." She trembled so hard her teeth rattled. She stiffened in convulsions, weeping with the pain they caused her.

"The Black Assizes. Ship's fever." Bess held her apron over her mouth and nose. "I saw the rash on her neck. We shall all perish."

"Rest easy, Bridget," Anicah said. "I'll bring ye water."

She hurried back to her pallet and picked up the broken hand spike she kept to discourage rats. She climbed the ladder and began pounding on the grate with it. She had no use for physicians who in her opinion killed people and were rewarded for it, but she made an exception in this case.

"We must have a piss prophet," she shouted. "Send us a doctor."

The blackness in the 'tweendecks was almost total. In spite of the wallowing of the ship Anicah could hear the rustle of Harry's covers and the muffled laughter, oaths and epithets that passed for affection with Joan. Anicah pulled the mildewed coverlet over her head. She was hardly under the cover when she heard the scratch of a rat's claws running over it.

She had a long and intimate acquaintance with rats, but those that swarmed here were as large as cats. They quarreled and chittered through the night. They gnawed shoes and ate clothes and bit people. Anicah was sure the fragrance and savor of Harry's greasy leather cap, which he wore even when taking a flourish with Joan, drew them in larger numbers to this part of the 'tweendecks.

The ship heeled, sending people sliding into each other. Joan shrieked with laughter, but others screamed. Anicah pitied poor Bridget. She was no better since the gentry's doctor had descended to poke and prod her.

The ship rolled to the other side.

"God strike me." Martin groaned. "God strike my father and my mother." He turned away from Anicah and retched onto the floor.

"Sold ye like a piece of goods, did they?" Anicah asked.

"They said 'twere to further my fortunes and that I would have high wages and little work in the western plantations."

When Martin lay on his back his arm brushed Anicah's and he drew it politely away. "My father's father and his before him farmed the commons, but when the fields were enclosed for sheep, he had nowhere to go." He sighed. "Did your parents bind you over too?"

"None was available to strike such a bargain. I been rented, but ne'er sold."

"Rented?"

"Aye. When I was a kidling. Beggars'd tip me mother a few pence to add me to their brood fer a day. They'd set themselves all about with brats, the better to gull the coneys. They'd pinch us to make us bawl."

"Where's your father?"

"Gone a-rogueing. He's the boldest pirate on the southern seas. Mayhap he'll board this tub and take me away. We'll rob the fat merchant ships and become rich and feared." It was an old fancy of hers and it cheered her.

"She's dead then, your mother?"

"Aye."

Anicah heard Martin sigh and knew he was probably sinking into sleep. As she lay next to him she tried to picture her mother's face, but she could recall only her aunt's description of her. "A wild and an airy girl," she would say when Anicah asked. "A lover of wakes and ales and dances on the green."

She did remember trudging with her mother along an endless rutted road, searching for the village where her father's sister lived. She had been seven and her mother large with child then. The tithingmen in each place had hurried them along, each determined that the baby not be born in his jurisdiction, to be maintained on his village's dole.

Anicah had been so exhausted and footsore, her mother had had to drag her. "Just another half league," she had said time and again. "His honor said 'tis but half a league."

Her mother had fallen, spent and starving, on the stones of the church dooryard in her husband's village just outside of Bristol. She had begged for a bit of straw to rest on and food for her daughter. She died before her sister-in-law arrived. Her unborn baby died with her.

Anicah remembered standing at the edge of a pit. Anicah's aunt had held her hand over her nose and mouth, but the smell was so strong Anicah could taste it anyway. She had watched while men tipped her mother's body from a barrow onto the heap of corpses in the Poor's Hole.

Anicah had held her aunt's hand tightly as they walked away. She had been afraid to look back. Afraid the dead would crawl up over the rim of the pit and follow her.

Martin was breathing in the slow, deep rhythm that had a soothing gentleness about it. Carefully, so as not to wake him, she found his arm under the covers. She put her small hand in his big one. She thought of that wild, airy girl dancing on the green. Tears rolled down her cheeks until she could taste the salt on her lips. They tasted like the sea.

Chapter 8

When Margaret left the gathering in Master Skinner's cabin a gout of tobacco smoke billowed out the door behind her. She could tell by the tone of the men's laughter that the conversation had already veered into profane territory. She had intended to return to her cabin, but instead she put on her cloak and mask and headed for the stairs to the quarterdeck. She was full of mutton and roast duck, boiled pudding and Madeira wine. A walk would help settle them.

She emerged into a night so flawless and spangled with stars it shook her with exaltation. The bellied sails spread outward in a pyramid of shimmering canvas. The gentle wind that filled them left no ripple on their taut surfaces. Far below her, small waves tipped silver with moonlight murmured in their rush along the hull.

Ferdinand Poulton, the Jesuit, stood silhouetted at the taffrail. She walked over and stood beside him.

"Methinks, Father Poulton, that had I been born a manchild I should have been a mariner, though before this voyage I had no more idea of the sea than a snail in its shell."

Poulton squinted at her in the dim glow from the lantern hanging off the stern. The crown of his sugarloaf hat barely reached the top of her hood. The breeze riffled the plume dangling over the edge of the broad brim.

"As a physician I would advise thee to shun the infectious airs,

47

but a night such as this belies medical wisdom." The slight Spanish inflection in his voice sounded exotic to Margaret.

"There are those who fear night's dark domino, but a mask allows one a certain liberty." Margaret lowered her own and smiled over it. "And we all travel masked, do we not, Father Poulton?"

"We're bound for a country where we'll have no need of masks." Poulton himself had to hide his identity as a priest. He was using his medical skills to pass as a doctor. "I long to reach that wild shore, to carry the word of God's salvation to the red children of the forest."

" 'Tis a most holy work."

"Your brother tells me you're a follower of Mary Ward, Mistress Margaret."

"My sister and I are two of Mother Ward's Galloping Girls. We studied with the Jesuits at Liège."

"And I in Spain, of course."

"The Archbishop of Canterbury opines that Mother Ward does more harm than six Jesuits." Margaret looked directly at him, her gray eyes sparkling with moonlight and mischief. They stood in a comfortable silence, united by their common persecution, he as a Jesuit priest, she as a lay nun schooled by Jesuits.

Poulton understood now what set the two Brent women apart from others of their class. Mary Ward's English ladies, as they called themselves, were a bold lot. They were of the world rather than cloistered and they scandalized even the Catholic hierarchy.

" 'Tis a valiant undertaking for a woman to sail over the horizon."

"I wonder at those who stay behind," Margaret said, "and content themselves with a thimbleful of the world."

"I think perhaps the Blessed Virgin led me to thee tonight."

Margaret turned to look at him, her face shaded by the hood.

"I have pondered how best to obtain an audience with thee," he said.

"With me?"

"Master Skinner has freighted the ship with more passengers than he ought. Many of them illegally obtained, I suspect. A grave peril festers belowdecks."

"Say on."

"The poor folk there are troubled by a throng of unruly distempers. 'Tis worse than a dog's kennel." The wind still blew from astern, but Poulton thought he smelled the terrible stench of the 'tweendecks. It had been in his nostrils since he visited Bridget the day before. "A man is loath to fetch breath for the funk that arises. The lice cracked under the soles of my boots."

"Thou hast gone below then?"

"I attended a young woman with a fever."

"One of our people?"

"Nay. An abandoned creature of addled wit. She was got with child by her master who then turned her out to perish. She was brought to bed under a hedge and stifled the issue. The magistrate gave her the choice of hanging or transporting."

"Is her infirmity contagious?"

"In those conditions, anything would be."

"Then we shall amend them."

"Surely there be little people in the new country." Bridget's fever made her restless. "How shall we know them?"

"Little people bedevil us the same, no matter the country." Anicah sat cross-legged on the edge of the pallet.

"Nay." Bridget half rose, supporting her thin frame on ulcered elbows. "Each country must have its own. How shall we speak to them?"

"Belike the salvages will know how to address them. We can ask them."

"Mayhap the salvages be little people themselves or worse. Raw Head and Bloody Bones, they will creep upon us whilst we sleep and suck the breath from us." Bridget began shivering so violently her teeth chattered. Anicah pulled the thin cover higher under her chin.

"The doctor did her no good," Bess Guest said. She sat on the bed while one of the other maids combed her head for lice.

"Bess has a potion," the maid confided.

"What simples I has I got at great pains."

Bess reached into her bodice and drew a leather satchel from between her breasts. She shook its contents into the valley of her skirt. Anicah leaned over to watch her sort through the bundles of dried herbs and the mummified mouse. She picked up a shriveled black lump, a human toe.

Anicah was impressed. "From a dangler?"

"Aye. The poor wight was gibbeted at the crossroads. He hung there like a caged lark, singing to be released from his misery. Took he days to die. And we all impatient. Some as stole parts in the dark, afore he was done, but I could ne'er be so heartless."

"Did ye fetch it yerself?"

"Aye. When he expired a neighbor brought a wagon and we climbed up. " 'Now mount who list,' " she recited,

> *"And close by the wrist,*
> *Sever me quickly the dead man's fist.*
> *Now climb who dares where he swings in the air,*
> *And pluck me five locks of the dead man's hair."*

"How shall ye give it?"

"In a 'fusion. Thus I can pluck it out ere she drinks and use it again."

A muffled voice sounded in the distance. "I charge you to halt."

The heavy tread of boots thudded on the planks overhead. Everyone turned to stare at the hatch.

"Who lays hands on my sisters forfeits his life." The rattle of Giles's sword echoed down the companionway.

Tiny black satin pumps, bone-thin ankles and the pitch-stained hem of a brown lawn skirt appeared. The hold was absolutely silent but for a cough and a moan from Bridget as Mary Brent descended the ladder. When she stooped and peered into the darkness the sunlight glowed in a diadem about her head. Anicah ducked into the shadows behind a broken cask. She recognized the papist she'd robbed at the Cocklorel.

Mary put one hand on the ceiling to brace herself against the ship's roll and held her skirts out of the filth with the other. Margaret followed her. Giles's oversized black boots, silk hose and baggy knee breeches came next. He held to his nose a hollowed orange with a vinegar-soaked rag inside. Father Poulton brought up the rear of the parade.

"They are a species of vagrants and felons," Master Skinner shouted down the companionway. "They are the scum of the country. Go you not among them, gentle ladies."

When Skinner paused for breath Fulke called down, "Giles. Margaret. Really. I say. This is unseemly."

Mary and her retinue made a slow progress past the silent transportees who knelt or crouched with heads bowed. The men took their caps off and crushed them to their chests. The women spread their aprons in attempts at curtsies. Only Harry, with his shiny leather cap still firmly planted on his head, lounged on his pallet and watched them through narrowed eyes.

Anicah was terrified to see the Brents heading straight toward her. They were coming to arrest her for stealing from them. She would hang. Her body would be meat for the fishes.

The three maids tucked errant strands of hair under their close-fitting white lawn caps. They shook their skirts, trying to dislodge the filth. Anicah scuttled farther behind the cask. She pressed her knit cap to her chest and bowed her head until the nape of her neck showed between the dark tangle of her curls and the blackened neck of her shirt. She waited for the sisters' accusations to fall on her like a butcher's blade.

"God keep ye, mistresses," Bess said.

"And may the Blessed Virgin hold you in her heart." Mary looked around at the pinched faces. "Had we known how hard it went with you . . ." Her voice trailed off.

"Do not concern yourselves, mistress. We be well here."

Margaret watched patiently. Other people thought Mary fragile, but Margaret knew better. During times of pestilence she and a few terrified servants burdened with hampers followed Mary into the nearby villages. They pried the locks off the doors of those quarantined and gave them food and solace.

"How fares she, Doctor?" Mary turned to Father Poulton who was holding his fingers to Bridget's neck to measure her pulse.

"Ship's fever belike. Or the Bridewell distemper."

"Mary . . ." Giles fidgeted. His sisters were a burden he did not always bear gracefully. "Come away. You can do naught here."

Mary gave the basket of food to Bess to share with the other maids and the family's servants. She closed her eyes and prayed for Bridget. When she finished she faced the silent crowd.

"You who have no means but your own merit to advance your fortunes, be consoled by the prospect of plowing ground purchased by your labor and courage. You shall erect in the wilderness a realm, fruitful and free of vice. Such joy will requite your present sufferings."

As Mary walked back the way she had come, she reached out to touch the bowed heads of those within reach. Some moved forward to receive her benediction.

Mary turned at the ladder to look around her. "You have endured worse. God will grant an end even to this." Then she and Margaret climbed up with Giles pressing at their heels.

Father Poulton did not escape so easily. The transportees flocked around him as he drew blood from Bridget to expel the evil humors. They held out the ulcered chilblains on their feet and hands. They bared their boils and sores and the discolored spots on shoulders, hips and gums. They hawked into their hands so he could examine their blood-flecked sputum. They regaled him with vivid descriptions of their excreta.

Still shaken, Anicah returned to her pallet. Martin was carving a slash mark next to the row of them in the plank at the head of the bed. He was keeping track of the days.

"They're kindly folk for being papists," he said.

"Belike they're fattening us to grace their board when the ra-

tions give out," Joan said. Her knowledge of theology was limited
to what she'd heard in the streets. What she'd heard about Roman Catholics and their belief in the transformation of bread into
the flesh of Christ was very unsettling.

Father Poulton finally shook free of his patients and hurried to
the ladder. Anicah watched his heels disappear up it, then she sat
brooding about the dreadful consequences the Brents' charity was
likely to have for her. When the good is gone, she thought, the
better seldom enters in its place.

At noon she lined up with the others for the buckets of pease
gruel and small beer. The slant of the sun crept below the knot of
wood that marked mealtime. Anicah was about to bang on the
grate with her hand spike when it slammed open. A face appeared
instead of the bucket.

"Get ye on deck and bring yer beds and fripperies."

One by one people handed up their mattress sacks, coverlets, chests
and bags. Then they climbed out of the hold. Martin carried Bridget
gently into the sunlight and returned for his things. When the last of
the passengers were waiting at the ladder, Martin neatly rolled up the
covers he shared with Anicah. Anicah herself sat on the bare pallet.

"Come along."

"I'm keeping here." Anicah's voice echoed in the hold,
empty now but for the debris. She imagined coming out of the
hatch and looking into Margaret's or Mary's eerie eyes.

"Don't be daft, lad."

Anicah turned away and ignored him until she felt the pallet
lurch forward.

"You great, hulking looby." She swung a fist at him as he
dragged the mattress with her aboard toward the companionway.
"The devil go with ye, for I shan't."

"Shall." He caught the back of her shirt as she tried to scramble away.

She struck out behind her. Martin wrapped his arms around
her from behind, immobilizing her, and began marching her toward the ladder.

"Ye cod's head." She went limp and slid out of his grasp. Still off balance she scuttled back to the pallet on her hands and feet, her rump high and undignified. Martin grabbed for her again.

When she felt him grip her crotch she collapsed into a spraddle-legged kneel and tried to roll away. Martin fell on top of her, forcing her onto the bed and pinning her there with his chest pressed against her back. His hand was firmly clasped where it shouldn't have been.

He groped around for the missing part and she was startled by the taut, tingling heat in the soft angle of her groin, as though someone had taken the delicate folds of skin there and pinched them. The amazing sensation spread outward from the center, making her dizzy with lust.

Martin leaped off her and hit his head on the ceiling.

Anicah began dragging the pallet toward the ladder. " 'Tis but a cunt and 'twill not bite ye, ye jinglebrains," she snarled.

Martin's cheeks glowed scarlet. He held his hand up, fingers splayed, as though he didn't know what to do with it now that it had had more experience than he.

"Ye be but a boy rattling about in a man's carcass," Anicah remarked. "A country boob grown great on neck beef and carrots."

"And who are you?"

"Andrew." Anicah knew better than to confuse him with another name.

She grabbed his ear and hauled his head close so no one would overhear. "I pray ye, Martin, do not discover me to them." She knew threats wouldn't shake him. He was too simple to believe she would harm him. She decided to appeal to his good nature. "If they find me out I shall have to bed in that black tomb with the dells." She put on her innocent waif's face and looked him in the eye. "I have a rare disorder. If deprived of the sun's light I shall die."

"Haul your arses aboveboard," a seaman shouted down the hatch.

Martin started up toward the main deck.

"Swear ye'll not betray me, Martin," Anicah called softly.

He looked back at her over his shoulder. "I swear."

Chapter 9

Clothing, mattress sacks and coverlets draped the rails and billowed from the shrouds and ratlines. Their owners hoped the sunlight would sweeten them. The sunlight did seem to sweeten Anicah's disposition. She sat with her head thrown back and eyes closed, letting the rays beat down on her face.

Martin had never seen her looking peaceful and innocent, and he couldn't stop staring at her. He studied the tilt of her nose, the curve of her wine-dark mouth, and the way her lashes brushed the delicate, lilac-veined skin under her eyes. How had he ever thought she was a boy? And how could he go on lying next to her each night?

Anicah and Martin sat with the other transportees among the goods heaped in the center of the main deck. From the height of the half-deck, Master Skinner watched them all as though he expected them to steal the bolts from the timbers. On the quarter-deck above him the mastiff was barking like heavy artillery at the rabble littering the main deck.

The cook's desperate threats and oaths, the smoke and uproar rising through the scuttle in the fo'c'sle resulted in a vat of thin gray broth. When Joan set down a bowl of it, the wizened turnips and salt herring, stiff as shingles, bobbed like detritus from a wrecked ship.

Harry had first use of the wooden spoon. Martin, Anicah and Joan waited while he trolled for bits of herring in the soup. Not much was left when he stretched out on his pallet and propped himself up on one elbow. He began filling his pipe with the cheap tobacco the swells had sent down. Anicah waited until he'd drawn in the first lungful of smoke before she spoke up.

"How came ye by the scar, squire?"

Harry ran his fingers along the livid red curve across his throat. "How think ye?"

"The gallows?"

"Aye." He seemed disinclined to go on, but Anicah and the others waited patiently. "The hempsman hauled me up and left me to dangle," he said finally. "All turned to darkness and a prickling commenced in me toes and spread through me body like a thousand stabbing shivs. When they reached me attic they blazed from me eyes like a pair of chimney fires."

Harry stared up at the mast, so like a high gallows hung about with lines. "Methinks," he said slowly, "that that fire were me spirit leaving me mortal husk the way rats will desert a doomed ship." Harry held the end of a hempen rope to his nose. "The stink of neck weed yet causes me guts to jig."

"His hanging was prime entertainment." Joan leered at him. "Part of him was so forward to reach heaven, it grew stiff before the rest." She waggled the spoon between her legs. "I ne'er before aspired to take a flourish with a corpse, but the way his yard stretched his breeches was an inspiration."

" 'Tis a prime scar," Anicah said.

And it was. It supposed a history of danger and courage and mischance. It declared that its bearer had cheated death. Harry ran his fingers along it.

"Lady Death was not done toying with me when she gave me this." He pulled up his shirt to show them a long, satiny welt that ran from his breastbone to his navel. "The sawbones laid me out for anatomizing. They had begun to carve me when I awoke. After much amazed discourse they sewed me together like a torn shirt. I entreated them to install laces so that I might inspect my guts at will, but they declined."

The tobacco had put Harry in such a mellow mood, Martin risked asking a question. "Why did they hang you?"

"If I tell ye, then ye'll know as much as I do, won't ye?"

" 'Twould take more than rope and blade to kill Harry Angell," Joan said.

Harry Angell. Anicah had heard of him. He was a cracksman, the best there was at the burglar's trade. When he cheated death on the gallows people began calling him Harry Angell after a gold coin of King Henry VIII's minting. It had a picture of a winged St. Michael on the obverse.

She leaned over to whisper the information to Martin. He looked stolidly ahead while her warm breath tickled his ear, but he could feel his cheeks grow hot. When her lips brushed against his lobe he knew she was doing it to bedevil him.

"Time to pump the hold." Anicah stood up. She glanced toward the quarterdeck to make sure the Brents weren't in sight, then set out toward the bow.

"Stand fast." The mate charged toward her, lash in hand. "Hie you back with the others."

"I must shit after such a splendid repast."

The mate looked annoyed at the consequences of feeding passengers. "Dally and I'll whip you till you shan't shit again."

Anicah climbed the short ladder to the deck atop the fo'c'sle. As the deck narrowed she held onto the ratlines and walked out onto the beakhead. She ducked her head against the spray that broke over the sides when the bow plunged into a trough between swells.

She lifted the trapdoor's iron ring and looked down at the foam-flecked water rushing far below. Using the seamen's privy hole had been her excuse to explore, but she would have preferred a corner of the deck. She lowered her breeches and clung to the stays while the ship's roll threw her from side to side. It caused her to wet her own feet, but the spray washed them clean. She pulled up her breeches and tied the drawstring.

She grabbed one of the fore topgallant stays overhead and

walked her hands along it as she moved farther forward. She felt the thrum of the taut line vibrating in her hands, forearms and chest. It made of her body a sounding box, resonating with the power of the wind coursing through the rigging. She half closed her eyes and leaned out into the cold salt spray.

The motion of the ship was exaggerated here where the bow took the full force of the swells. With its timbers creaking and groaning, the ship leaped and surged under Anicah's feet. It was a mythical steed, harnessed by the hemp lines and the iron and wooden collars about the bowsprit, masts and yards. It carried her along faster than she had thought possible.

The rush of wind and the roar of water crashing against the beakhead created a beguiling fantasy. For the moment she believed the winds blew for her. The ocean spoke to her. The ship had been built and launched and rigged to hurtle her toward the setting sun and a strange and wonderful life.

"Andrew!" Martin clung to the foremast. His black hair blew about his face.

Anicah motioned him forward. He advanced cautiously, not moving a hand or foot until the other three were anchored.

"This be bang-up prime!" Anicah had to shout to be heard. She flung out her arm to encompass the dark green sea, speckled with silver bubbles, and the huge orange globe of the sun hanging just above the horizon.

"They say we must go below." With his soaked clothes clinging to him and his wet hair lying flat against his forehead and ears, Martin looked thoroughly miserable. "The mate threatens to flay you."

Anicah guessed that he had volunteered to fetch her to save her from the mate's wrath. He was that sort of fool. "I care not a turd for the mate." Anicah stared at the seams where the sky and sea met. It was adorned now with a ribbon of gold tinsel from the setting sun. "How d'ye suppose it will be?"

"What?"

"America."

"I wot not." Martin started aft. "Hurry then, ere they close the hatch."

She made her way back to him. Instead of going on he leaned so close he almost touched her wet nose with his own. The dignity and command in his voice surprised her. "What is your real name?"

"Andrew serves me well."

"I have tried to be your friend, yet you trust me not."

"If ye do not know it ye cannot spill it by mischance."

He turned abruptly and left her.

He had disappeared when she reached the main deck. In spite of the overpowering smell of the vinegar and burning pitch used to clean the 'tweendecks, she was singing cheerfully when she dropped through the hatch and into the perpetual twilight below.

> "My father's dead and I am free,
> He left no children in the world but me.
> The devil drank him down to poverty,
> But I'll recline in fair luxury."

Martin handed her a bottle by way of reconciliation. She was startled by the smell of sherry wine.

"A dram," he said, "by the grace of the gentlefolk abovedecks."

"The papists do attempt to buy their consciences cheaply with it," Harry grumbled.

Anicah went to the ladder and looked up at the square of sky. She remembered the seamen moving high up in the lines as agile as rope walkers at a fair. She remembered the small clouds moving in a line like sheep grazing a bright blue meadow.

They gave us a time in the sun, she thought. And for that, papists or not, I do beseech God's blessings on them.

A long rectangle of morning sunlight flowed in through the narrow aft window of Master Skinner's cabin. Margaret stood at the chart table and traced the ship's route with her finger, south around Spain, past Madeira and the Canaries, then in a wide curve to avoid the bulge of Africa and the danger that lurked there.

"We're ready to start," Mary called.

Margaret sat opposite her at the small table. Giles and Henry Fleete faced each other from the sides. They had paired off for slam, and they played in silence for a while.

Margaret snapped her suit onto the table and fanned them out. "Trump!" She collected the cards and shuffled, her knobby fingers making a blur of them. "If thou persisteth in losing, Giles, Mary and I shall become like our uncle's poor sisters, following him to the alehouse and bowling green, crying for fear he should lose their portions."

"So long as I lose to thee, it matters not." Giles puffed on his pipe. "And I do believe you cheated, dear sister." He turned to Fleete. "Watch her closely, Henry. For such a saintly soul, Margaret sharks like the very devil."

"Did I tell you," Fleete said, "that China lies but ten days march from Maryland's western border, and that I myself went there?"

"You did tell us, Captain Fleete," Margaret said.

She dealt twelve cards to each. "And what of thy trucking expeditions among the salvages, Captain?"

"A dangerous business, but well worth the risk. The Indians besprinkle their bodies with powdered gold. They set precious stones on their ears and noses, and wear stoles of the silkiest ermine."

"And how fares the mutinous Assembly?" Giles asked.

"Mutinous?" Margaret looked up from her cards.

Fleete shrugged. "Rather than acknowledging Lord Baltimore's laws as instructed, the freemen of the first Assembly vetoed them and made their own."

"How impertinent and ungrateful." Margaret was shocked.

"I think," said Giles, "that like willful children, the freemen will behave badly while their elders are away. His lordship, as you know, sister, has been occupied with affairs at home and has yet to set the toe of his boot on the shores of his colony."

"Be that as it may," Margaret said, "those endowed with the ancient right, will and ability to rule will do so."

"One cannot expect the refuse of the 'tweendecks to rule." Giles gave a languid sigh. "Dids't thou mark the rogue in the leather hat, Margaret?"

"Aye." Margaret glanced at Mary over her cards, and Mary raised an eyebrow subtly in acknowledgment. "That hat would be a valuable item to own."

"How so?"

"If boiled it would yield enough grease for a bar of soap and a dozen tallow candles."

A knock sounded at the door and a seaman put his head in. "Asking your graces' pardon, but I'm to carry the master's brass optic glass to the half-deck." He took the telescope and vanished.

"Wherefore, think you, this sudden interest in the tele-scopium?" Giles asked.

"Mayhap one of the ships of the fleet is signaling for a visit." Margaret laid down her cards. "Some company would be a pleasant diversion."

Giles rose and stretched casually. "I think I shall see what transpires in the world."

"I'll go with thee," Margaret said.

When she reached the half-deck, she sensed that the oddly shaped sail far to the stern was not a friendly one. Skinner and the mate were grim-faced.

Margaret scanned the horizon, empty but for that angular sail. "Where are the other ships?"

"Our vessel is somewhat leewardly," the mate said. "They sailed away before us in the night."

"What think you?" Giles squinted east into the morning sun.

Skinner glanced at Margaret, then resumed his vigil with the telescope. "I think we had best bring the wind on the quarter and fly before the wind like a bat out of hell."

Chapter 10

The bare feet running across the planks above Anicah's head sounded like the flutter of quail started in flight. The low rumble of rolling cannon carriages and hogsheads vibrated through the timbers. Master Skinner roared over all of it.

"Salley rogues." Harry scooped up his dice and tumbled them out onto the coverlet again. "Or Algerines."

"Will they attack?" Anicah asked.

"Blood will run in the scuppers."

The hatch grate slammed open. A seaman lay on his stomach and hung over the edge of the opening.

"Men and boys report above," he called down. "If ye be shod, take 'em off."

People shifted and murmured, but no one came forward.

"Think ye the sea dogs'll not find ye cowering there like cockroaches in the bog pot?" he shouted. "Besides, the mate's tapped a cask of knock-me-down to top us off with courage."

The prospect of strong beer roused the men and they crowded toward the ladder.

"Not you," Martin whispered.

"Not yerself."

"Only we men must go."

"Get off! Ye're not me mother." Anicah gave him a pitying look, as though he were mad as well as stupid and annoying. "Above us there be more places to hide."

"We're to fight, not hide."

"Ye be such a howling great fool, Martin." Anicah scampered up the ladder and stepped into chaos.

While Master Skinner rained curses down on their heads from the half-deck, men bumped into each other and dropped things and tripped over tackle. They heaved crates and grain-filled sacks up from the hold and piled them into breastworks. They nailed canvas to the decks to keep incoming cannon balls from sending oak splinters flying like crossbow bolts. They hung the masts with chains to deflect shot.

" 'Zounds," Skinner roared. "Bear up, you curs, if we are to come off with our bacon."

The men of the 'tweendecks hurried away in search of the beer. A seaman lowered the grate over the hatch and dogged it down, sealing the women below. Joan pounded on it with the hand spike and screeched her assessment of the men who had locked her in and of mariners in general.

Martin and Anicah dodged as two seamen chased a squealing sow past them. They cornered her and heaved her overboard.

Anicah watched her land near the ship's tender where men were loading what animals they could retrieve. "They've taken yer sweetheart, Martin."

"I never." He blushed a rich crimson at the implication.

"Then ye prefer live mutton, de ye?" Bedeviling him had become her favorite form of entertainment.

"You!" The mate's voice boomed behind them. They turned to look into the dented bell of his speaking trumpet. "Hie thee to the powder stores ere you feel the lash."

As soon as the mate turned his back, Anicah veered away. Martin caught her arm as an avalanche of canvas dropped with a shriek of lines through wooden blocks. He pushed her down, threw himself on top of her and shielded his head with his arms.

The canvas covered them and they lay still for several heartbeats after they could reasonably expect to be crushed by the yard. Then Anicah became aware of Martin's warmth and weight and

his breath on her neck. The sudden desire for him created a churning in the pit of her stomach.

To hide her confusion she squirmed away and crawled out
from under the canvas. "Cease your pushing me about."

She looked up. A line of seamen balanced on the swaying foot
ropes of the foretop yard. They were bundling the canvas and tying
it in place.

Anicah cupped her hands and shouted at them. "Be ye lunatic?"

"Come below." Martin tried to coax her away before she got
into trouble.

"They're striking canvas." She shouted up at the men again.
"A sea dog sniffs at our breech and ye slow to let him mount us."

"Less canvas, less fuel for fires," one of them called down.

🌺 Clouds covered the moon and stars. The ship's lanterns
swung unlit on their gimbals. No lights shone as beacons for the
corsair, which by sunset had approached close enough for the oars
to be visible along its sides.

A few of the ship's defenders slept, but most would have said
they were keeping watch. What they were watching was the hogshead lashed to the rail. The level of the beer inside it had gone down
considerably. While the rest sang, a man danced on the hatch cover.

The same beer that set the others to celebrating made Martin
more taciturn than usual. Anicah dropped down next to him.

"Such foolery will lead the devils to us," he said.

"Nay, Martin. We must prove so rowdy a morsel in Death's
throat that he will cough us up."

Anicah figured Martin was such a large individual, he had
warmth to spare against the night's chill damps. She edged closer
until she touched him lightly from shoulder to hip. He flinched,
but didn't move. Something fragile and unseeable separated them
from the others, but Anicah had no experience with the fragile
and unseeable.

"The king's men pressed me father fer the low countries,"

Anicah said, to pass the time. "One of his mates cut off his fingers to keep from going. Another blinded himself with salt, but me father marched off proud."

Somewhere in Martin's beer-befuddled head he knew this story didn't tally with the ones Anicah had told before, but he couldn't marshal the wits to ask her about it.

Anicah elbowed him in the ribs. "Know ye why they call a woman's privities 'old hat'?"

"Nay," he said cautiously.

"Because they be so frequently felt." Suddenly the old joke was the funniest Anicah had ever heard. She collapsed on Martin's shoulder, shaking with mirth.

"Rats!" Martin leaped up and Anicah fell to the deck, still laughing. Martin agitated himself like a drenched dog. "I felt a rat on my leg."

"He felt one . . ." Anicah squeaked. A new spasm of hilarity swept her and she hugged her stomach to ease the ache of it.

Martin tried to stalk off into the night, but he tripped over the outstretched legs of a seaman. Mumbling to himself, he collected his feet under him again and reeled away.

Anicah stood up, intent on following him. She swayed and put out a hand to steady herself. The beer formed an eddy in her head that swirled faster when she moved. She churned through air that had suddenly turned thicker than water.

The craving for the touch of Martin's hands, for the smell and feel of him, sharpened. She followed him up the steps to the forbidden quarterdeck. She crept up behind him at the lee taffrail as he stood with feet braced well apart. He was relieving himself downwind, between the carved cherubs and ivy vines.

He jumped and yelped when Anicah half leaned, half fell against his back. His breeches fell down around his ankles, exposing bare buttocks, pale in the darkness. Anicah rested her cheek between his shoulder blades and encircled his waist with her arms.

When he tried to turn around he knocked her off balance. In an attempt to right herself she stepped between his feet and into the waist of his breeches, which wrapped around her ankle when he swiveled. The two of them fell in a tangle of legs and arms. Chest to chest they thrashed about until they lay on their sides with each other's arms pinioned under them or wound up in their clothes.

As Martin held Anicah tightly against him, or was held by her, he couldn't tell which, a tenderness suffused him. He searched in the dark for her mouth, the source of the yeasty zephyr that caressed his face. He kissed her ear by mistake, then her jaw and the side of her nose before he found her lips. But by then they were slack.

She belched a coy bubble of hops and went limp in his arms. She was soon breathing deeply, making small whiffling and smacking noises from time to time. Martin could feel the chill night air of late September on his bare rear end. He was vaguely aware of the potential for embarrassment in his position, but the task of freeing her feet from his breeches, pulling them up and retying the laces was beyond him. Nor had he the will or the inclination to disentangle himself from her softness and warmth.

He pulled her closer until her hand, which was resting on his waist under his shirt, dropped across his bare back. He fancied it was an embrace. He wandered off into sleep with his cheek against her tousled, salty hair and a smile on his lips.

Margaret sat by the window of her cabin. She held one of her two old snaphaunce pistols with the fish-tail grips, heavy and graceful, loaded and half cocked. She kept her expression calm, even though in the darkness Giles could see only her silhouette from where he stood in the doorway.

"I could have you both carried below," he said.

"And prithee, which of the worthies aboard shall you charge with laying hands on us?"

The shouts and singing on deck had gotten louder with nightfall. Even Giles was flushed with the wine he and the other gentlemen had shared with Master Skinner.

Giles persisted. "You are in peril here. If we cannot outrun them in the dark we must come about and have at them." He was about to broach a delicate subject, which was why he preferred conversing with milkmaids and ale wenches. Delicacy was irrelevant with them. "If they breech our defenses, consider your honor."

Margaret smiled wryly. "Those men are too cup-shotten to crack their own fleas. They could no more defend us below than here."

"We are in God's hands, dear brother," Mary said softly from the bed.

Giles sighed. "One last time, I pray you, get you below with the other women—"

"And the vermin and the ordure," Margaret interrupted. "I will not huckle our dignity for thy peace of mind."

"Then may God be tender of you." Giles gave a sardonic bow. "Rest well."

Margaret heard the door close behind him. She stroked the pistol and listened to one of the vulgar ditties the men had been singing for hours.

"I am not worthy of God's care." Mary's voice sounded small and far away in the darkness.

"I can name none worthier."

"Nay," Mary said sadly. "I should trust in Him, yet I'm afraid."

"As am I."

"Thou dost not seem so."

Margaret stared out the window, straining to see the chalky smudge of a sail against the carboned night.

A clink sounded above her and she leaned out into the window's bay and looked up. A faintly glowing object was descending on a line from the taffrail at the center of the ship's high stern. As she watched, the cloth that covered the lantern was lifted away by an unseen hand. A beam of light flashed outward to guide the corsair.

"Dear Mother of God!" Margaret threw on her cape.

"What is it, Maggie?"

"Someone means to betray us. He has hung a beacon from the stern."

Mary sat on the edge of the bed and searched with her stockinged feet for her pumps.

" 'Twere more prudent that thou keepest here, Mary."

" 'Woe unto them that are prudent . . .' " Mary spoke lightly, as though happy to escape from the cabin.

"Keep thee behind me, then."

When Margaret paused at the bottom of the companionway she heard the skitter of a rat's claws across the floor in front of her. With her heart thumping against the stays of her bodice she leveled the pistol's fifteen-inch barrel and steadied it with both hands.

She pushed open the door to Skinner's cabin and light spilled out, although the windows were prudently draped with heavy canvas. Skinner sat slouched in his big chair, surrounded by a litter of bottles. He lifted one in salute.

"I am an Englishman," he roared. "A prince of the seas. The proudest man in God's kingdom."

Margaret closed the door and climbed to the half-deck. On the main deck below, the crew sprawled in boozy companionship with the passengers they usually referred to as shifting ballast. They looked as though the pirates had already attacked and won the day.

"Is that not Father Poulton?" Mary pointed to the half-deck's rail where the Jesuit stood, his legs scissored at the knees and his arms crossed over his chest.

"Mistresses Margaret and Mary." He came to attention. "You really must go below."

"Some traitor hath hung a lantern from the stern, and Skinner lies thoroughly foxed."

Margaret headed for the quarterdeck and the high stern of the ship. Poulton followed with Mary trailing. Margaret stopped abruptly at the snarl of arms and legs pressed against the taffrail.

"A pair of bare-breeched cherubs seem to have fallen from the fretwork," she said.

"I say." Giles appeared suddenly beside her. He prodded Martin's taut, round nether cheek with the toe of his boot. "What have we here?"

Chapter 11

Martin and Anicah faced the rest of the transportees and the crew gathered on the main and fore decks. Between them stood the big capstan that weighed and lowered the anchor. Bars had been put through two of the holes in it and ropes draped over them. Martin stared at them and at the two buckets of lead shot. Anicah figured he was trying to imagine what forms of torture they represented.

"Bear up, mate," she whispered.

She had felt the lash and cudgels of Bridewell's turnkeys, but she had evaded public whippings at the cart tail. She had always thought herself invulnerable. Even now she felt as though she were acting a part in some ship's entertainment. Her main worry was that the old papist huddle and her brother would recognize and denounce her. She wished the corsair hadn't been lost in the night. She would have preferred the attack of pirates to Margaret Brent's wrath.

Giles and Margaret and the rest of the gentry had gathered on the quarterdeck above and behind her. The mate stood on the hatch cover. The tarred rawhide lashes of his whip dangled from his belt.

"You have been charged with treason, mutiny and sodomy," he announced. "The last will earn you two dozen strokes at the capstan. The crimes of mutiny and treason are punishable by hanging at the main yard or towing abaft the stern until dead. How do you plead?"

"I never." Anicah didn't know the meaning of either sodomy or treason and had only a vague notion of mutiny, but she was wise enough to deny any accusation emphatically and repeatedly.

"I too am innocent, your honor," Martin said.

"Then you shall be pressed at the capstan until you confess. Strip you naked from the middle upward."

Two seamen tied rope to the buckets of shot. Anicah knew they would hang them around her neck and Martin's and would add weight until the pain forced them to admit guilt.

"If I confess will ye reprieve me for the western plantations?" Anicah asked. The crew and passengers laughed.

Margaret leaned forward. She hadn't seen the culprits' faces by daylight, but the smaller boy's voice sounded familiar.

"Impudent knaves." The mate took his lash from his belt.

"Impudence merits not hanging," Anicah said. "Me only crime is that I be low in the world."

"Have a care," Martin whispered. He pulled off his shirt.

"They've done nothing for me. I'll not cringe for them." But she gave him a sad look as the seamen forced him to kneel. They stretched his arms along the length of one of the bars and tied them in place.

She pitied him the easy life that had left him unprepared for such a disastrous swing in his fortunes. Even in these wretched circumstances she was proud to have such a handsome, strapping companion in crime, though she wasn't sure what the crime was. "Martin," she whispered. "Me name is Anicah." He deserved to know that much about her.

The transportees had been carrying on a subdued discussion while the more educated explained the charges to the others.

"Buggery!" Joan Parke laughed out loud. "Whipped for buggery. That's prime, that is."

Anicah came to attention. She had a defense for buggery. She had yet to have a monthly flux and her chest was as flat as a boy's, so she untied the rope around her waist and let her breeches drop. She lifted her long shirttails.

"Be this a cove's breech?"

"The kidling lacks a prick," Joan shouted.

"The two of them were found near the lantern last night." The mate had to shout over the laughter. "The charges of treason and mutiny stand. Can anyone say why they should not hang?"

"Or be trawled at the ship's arse like so much dirty laundry," Joan sang out.

Anicah picked up her breeches and retied the rope.

Margaret looked at Giles. "You studied a smattering of the law, brother."

"Nay, sister," he muttered. "I'll not pettifog for the lower orders."

"But those two didn't signal the corsair."

"If they committed not that particular sin they're doubtless exquisite in all other manner of vice."

Margaret had expected a refusal. Giles disliked bother. She glanced over at Father Poulton and saw that he was about to step forward. She didn't have to do or say anything, but she headed for the stairs anyway.

"I say, Margaret, what foolishness are you about?" Giles sounded alarmed.

The soft leather soles of Margaret's pumps muffled the sound of her approach. When she and the smaller culprit saw each other, she couldn't have said which was more surprised, but the girl recovered fast. She raised her chin and stared calmly ahead, as though indifferent to her fate. Margaret's outrage at discovering the rogue who had robbed her gave way to mild amusement. The hoyden was a bold one.

"The defendants are not guilty of the charges." Margaret's own voice startled her. She heard Giles's groan of embarrassment.

"How say you, Mistress Margaret?"

"I wish to act as advocate for the accused."

The mate looked at Master Skinner who shrugged.

"The doctor, my brother, and I discovered them last night on the quarterdeck," Margaret went on. "If they had filled or lit the lantern the stench of whale oil would have lingered on their persons. The doctor examined them to see if they were alive or dead and he smelled no such, although the odor of barleycorn was much upon them."

She turned to include the spectators. "I am no expert at law, but I think an overindulgence in drink is no hanging matter. If it were, there would not be rope nor yards enough to accommodate the guilty, nor a man left unhung to do the hanging."

The crowd laughed again and Margaret was surprised by the satisfaction it gave her.

"The scoundrels were roosting where they oughtn't've been. They must be punished." The mate was annoyed. He'd gone to all this trouble and he intended to hang someone today. If he didn't, the passengers and crew would know a traitor still walked among them.

Margaret looked up at the half-deck and saw Father Poulton murmuring in Master Skinner's ear. Everyone waited expectantly while Skinner considered Poulton's proposal.

"We have been sorely pressed by vermin in the hold," Skinner said. "These two shall serve as ship's ratters. The wench can reach their nests where a man cannot."

As the seamen untied Martin's arms, Margaret started to protest. What was Poulton thinking, to suggest setting her sort loose among the ship's cargo? But then, he didn't know the girl was a thief, and Giles had been too drunk at the Cocklorel to remember her face. More puzzling to Margaret was why she hadn't denounced the wretch herself.

The crew and passengers dispersed, grumbling at such a sorry show. Martin rubbed his wrists where the ropes had chafed.

"Ratting is better than hanging." He grinned at Anicah.

"Nay, it is not," she said gloomily.

A pan of burning brimstone lit the ship's belly about as poorly as it fumigated it.

"A plague rot it!" Anicah's discontent issued from the cleft between two banks of hogsheads of salt beef. The smell of rotting flesh about them was too pungent for even the brimstone to affect. " 'Od's stones."

Martin squatted in the sandy, black ooze of the bilge so he could peer into the crevice. "If we abuse God's name He will lose interest in our welfare, Ani," he chided mildly.

"He lost interest in me welfare a long time gone." The soles of Anicah's feet appeared, then her ankles and calves as she wriggled from between the barrels. "Else He'd not have required me to crawl on me belly through this cesspit."

"I'll admit 'tis more troublesome than hunting rats in the fields."

Anicah sat wearily in the stinking, ankle-deep soup that washed lazily back and forth with the ship's roll. Her clothes clung to her in folds like a slick ebony skin. Her mahogany curls were japanned to her head. She held the long-handled iron spoon she used to deliver poisoned meal to the nests.

Her voice and Martin's echoed in the dark vault of the hold. It was crammed with crates and barrels of stores, most of which seemed to be empty. Stowed above and around them were the Gentleman Adventurers' tools, furniture and other lumber. While the vessel surged and rocked, tables, bedsteads and cupboards creaked and shifted in the webwork of hawsers that held them.

All the effluents of the ship's occupants mixed with sea water and seeped through water-logged timbers or rained between warped planks or ran down the limbers to end here. The malodorous stew bred scurrying packs of beetles, rodents and cockroaches. Anicah glowered at them, the whites of her eyes and teeth startling in a face as black as the rats she was hunting.

"Are you a papist, Anicah, to have friends amongst them?"

"Nay, I am not."

" 'Twere kind of the gentlewoman to defend us."

Anicah grunted. She was perplexed by Margaret Brent's behavior. The woman must have something dire planned for her, though this was dire enough.

She stood up so Martin could pour a bucket of cold saltwater over her. It sluiced down from the crown of her head, striping her faun's face black and brown. She shook water from her arms and legs and Martin handed her a bit of sacking. As she dried herself she sang the high, melancholy chant of Bristol's rat catchers.

> *"Have ye any rats, mice, polecats or weasels?*
> *Or have ye any old sows, sick of the measles?*
> *I can kill vermin and I can kill moles.*
> *I can kill aught that creepeth down holes."*

They climbed up the ladder to the 'tweendecks and found that night had fallen. A seaman was waiting there to lock down the hold's hatch. Anicah and Martin groped their way to their pallet. Anicah stepped quickly out of her soggy clothes and slid under the stiff, clammy covers. She was still wet and she quaked with the cold. Martin wrapped his arms around her and pulled her to him.

She brushed his lips with her own. "This morning," she whispered, "I thought I would not live to kiss ye, Martin. Not even once."

She lay so slight and fragile and shivering in his arms that Martin was terrified of doing something clumsy and hurting her. He cradled her with one arm and rubbed the palm of his big hand over her cold legs and haunch, back and shoulders, trying to coax warmth into them. She snuggled closer and he began to stroke her, feeling his hesitant way along her body in the darkness.

Anicah had put her hands into the side slits of many a man's breeches. She'd often brushed against what she called the soft goods, the three items men carried there besides their snuff boxes and purses, their watches and handkerchiefs. Her fingers were deft and subtle and skilled, and when she closed them gently around Martin's goods he thought he might faint.

Together they learned what they craved to know. The learning was awkward and painful, but never inept. Wherever they touched they left scintillant fire. Anicah drifted into sleep with Martin's arms around her. For the first time in her life she felt loved and happy and safe all at the same time.

Chapter 12

From the main deck Margaret heard shouts and firecrackers. This was November 5, 1638, the anniversary of the Gunpowder Treason. Thirty-three years ago Guy Fawkes and his fellow conspirators tried to further the Catholic cause by blowing up king and Parliament. It was not a good time for Catholics, even secret ones, to be on deck. Margaret and Mary had spent the day in their cabin.

Margaret watched Mary pick fat, black-headed weevil maggots from a biscuit the shape and heft of a cobblestone. Margaret remembered when Mary, as a child, would pick the raisins from her pudding and line them up in orderly rows to eat last.

Mary was so intent on the bread and its occupants she didn't notice that Margaret had closed her water-warped copy of *Good News from Virginia* and was staring fixedly at her. Margaret had been cooped up with Mary for two and a half months, but only recently had her sister's presence begun to annoy her.

She wanted to put her hands around Mary's pipe stem of a neck. She wanted to squeeze it and shake it until the mouse-brown hair flew from its neat little knot, until her wan face turned purple and her enigmatic eyes, pale and slippery as blue taffeta, bulged in the deep hollows of their sockets. Margaret loathed the odor of rue and lavender that clung to Mary's clothes. She loathed her treacly voice.

Margaret wondered if she were going mad. Her wide mouth

twitched in a rueful smile. If she was mad this was the place for her, a floating Bedlam freighted with lunatics and felons.

Giles opened the door and peered in. "Everything looks in proper order, dear sisters."

"Thou hast a strange notion of order, brother." Margaret glanced at her stained dress and the damp bedding, the broken furniture and chests and kegs of waterlogged belongings left from the last storm. But a fit of temper would remedy nothing. "Come in, Giles."

Giles looked as though he would rather not, but Margaret was glad for his company. With him to distract her she might make it through the afternoon without saying something to Mary that would cause them both grief later.

Most of the food and wine stored in the cabin had been consumed or ruined by sea water. Giles had room to perch on the padded lid of the privy stool with his long legs drawn up almost to his chin.

"Skinner invites us to dine with him tonight." Giles's hearty good humor had a dodging sound to it. His voice was a notch too loud.

Margaret moved to stand in front of the door so he couldn't escape. She regarded him through narrowed, steel-dust eyes.

"Didst thou inspect the stores?"

"I did." He rubbed at the biggest stain on his breeches.

"And in what condition didst thou find them?"

"Adequate, Maggie. Adequate."

Margaret held out a piece of cheese, green with mold.

"Beetles make of the bread their freehold, and the cheese abrades the skin from our mouths. Methinks, brother, that thy definition of 'adequate' is verily like thy definition of 'order.' "

"This biscuit is wholesome now." Mary held it out, a bright smile on her face. "I soaked it in water and brandy to soften it."

"I thank thee, but I'm not hungry." Remorse displaced Margaret's fury. How could she have harbored malice toward such a gentle soul? "Mayhap Father Poulton will hear thy confession, sweet sister. He and Fulke are in their cabin."

Mary looked relieved at the excuse to escape a certain quarrel. Margaret arranged the hood of Mary's cape to cover her head and handed her the mask. She kissed her lightly on the cheek and closed the door behind her. Then she sat on the bed, her knees almost touching Giles's.

"I apologize for my waspish tongue."

" 'Tis no rare new phenomenon." Giles smiled.

"I know 'tis thy tenderness of heart that compels thee to hide the truth. But I will discover the state of our supplies. If thou wilt not tell me, I'll descend to the hold to see for myself."

Giles shook his head. He looked bleaker than Margaret had ever seen him. His eyes reminded her more than ever of the hunting hound she had left behind.

"Nay, sister," he said. "Do not venture it."

"I've gone 'twixt decks."

" 'Tweendecks is a fair garden compared to the hold. It swarms with rats as big as piglets. Fifteen hogsheads of brew have gone dead and sour. In my life I have never known any like unto it for stink. And thou hast seen for thyself the bread and cheese."

Margaret felt a churn of fear in her stomach. "The meat?"

"The beef is blue and covered with a shiny verdigris."

"The pork?"

"I ordered several puncheons opened. They contained feet with hooves and hair still on them. Cheeks. Ears. Offal that should have been tossed on the dung heap. Pigs' heads with the rings in the noses." Giles laughed ruefully. "The seamen were pleased to make use of the iron in the rings."

"We have been imposed upon," Margaret said.

"We and the whole company. Victualed with musty bread, stinking beer, putrid meat, all the relics of former voyages. The only fresh meat in the hold has whiskers and runs about on four legs."

"Giles!" Margaret stared at him in horror, but he only shrugged, his sinuous lips undulating into a small, ironic smile.

Margaret crossed herself. "If ever we make a plantation," she murmured, "God works a miracle."

Martin pushed down on the hogshead's wooden lid. The ship's carpenter had cut it to Anicah's specifications, slightly smaller than the opening. A rod had been stapled across the center and threaded through holes on each side so it could swing freely. A peg set on the inside kept the left half of the lid from dropping below the barrel's rim. The right would tip downward if weight were placed on it, sending the object sliding into the trap.

Bits of bread soaked in rancid beef fat were nailed to it on that side. A frantic squealing and scratching rose from the depths.

Anicah unthreaded the lid's hinge and removed it. She stepped onto a box and hung by her waist over the barrel's edge. The pressure of the rim on her stomach eased the cramping ache of hunger. "Six here at least."

"The swells'll pay sixpence apiece."

"The swells may catch their own." When Anicah spit into the bilge the phlegm was pink with blood. "Fancy that, Martin, the squires holding a proper hunt in the hold. Tan-ta-ra! The gents in their fine togs and their hounds ripping through the bilge."

"You know about the gentry, then?"

"Me mother worked scullion in a house bigger than this boat. We ate all we wanted and then we ate some more. Puddings and roasts, bread and jams and cheeses as big as yer head."

"What happened to your mother?" Martin was curious. He had heard many versions of Anicah's father's history, but none about her mother. He didn't believe any of them anymore, but they seemed to make her happy and that was enough for him.

"Me mother was a beauty, but melancholic, what with me father three years gone, pressed to death for a highwayman. The young lord o' the manor became ravished quite by her." Anicah stirred the rats pensively with a cudgel.

"But his prancer stumbled whilst hallowing stags. Mashed him flat as a napkin, and we was turned out by his cruel kin." With a snap of her wrist and cudgel Anicah smashed a rat's head.

"Have you eaten rats before?" Martin asked.

"Aye. But none what partake of the dung heaps." How she knew where her past dinners had dined she didn't say.

Anicah and Martin skinned and gutted the rats on a barrel head. Anicah knew she and Martin could eat all six, but she saved three to give away. She wrapped them individually in sacking.

"I'll take one to Bridget," she said. "If she eats a morsel mayhap the fetch-life won't come for her."

The 'tweendecks hatch was open and the transportees were on deck, so Anicah was able to sneak aft to deliver one of the packages. By the time she returned to the main deck she saw she was too late to help Bridget. Bess Guest and the other two maids were sewing her body into her rotted coverlet. Joan was quarreling with Bess over the girl's meager possessions.

The gentry watched from the quarterdeck, but the doctor was with the transportees. He had just finished pronouncing Bridget dead. Anicah was pleased to find him.

"Beggin' your pardon . . ." She held out one of the packets. "Ye've been kindly to us, and to Bridget, squire. And even a physicker cannot live upon bones and crag ends. This be savory carbonadoed and braised."

When she grinned, her teeth flashed startling white against her brown skin, made darker by grime. Her doe's eyes were huge in her thin face, and famine gave them a deceptive glitter. The tatters of her clothes hung on her angular frame. She looked fragile, but Poulton knew she was tough and pliable as cat gut.

Poulton accepted the gift gingerly and noticed the dark purple bruises on her hands and arms, the swelling of her elbows and knees. Symptoms of scurvy had been appearing on those belowdecks and among the gentry too. He wiggled an eyetooth with his tongue. It was looser in his gums than the day before.

"Anicah," Bess called. "Will ye sing Bridget to her last sleep?"

Anicah bobbed in an ungraceful curtsy that was strange to see, with her in her boy's breeches and shirt. Then she joined her shipmates.

Four men lifted the body, hardly bigger than a child's, onto their shoulders. The seamen stood silently in the rigging or on the fo'c'sle and watched the transportees form a ragged line behind the corpse. The pallbearers balanced their burden on the railing and held it poised there, silhouetted against a sunset sky. Only sharks' fins, circling lazily, broke the tranquil surface of a sea tinted a pale lilac and gold.

No one volunteered to speak for Bridget, she being a Catholic and an infanticide as well. Anicah rapped a spike on the rail for attention.

"We have no sweet rosemary nor garlands of flowers to give ye, Bridget," Anicah said. "We pray the colors of the evening sky be garland enough. Ye have no family to weep ye to your rest. We pray we be family enough. May God bless ye."

Then she sang in her clear, piercing voice.

> "This sad night, this sad night;
>   ev'ry night and all:
> Fire and fleet and candlelight
>   and Christ receive thy soul.
>
> When thou from hence doth pass away,
>   ev'ry night and all;
> To heav'n above thous comest at last
>   and Christ receive thy pitiful poor soul."

Margaret and Mary waited until the song ended and the mourners dispersed. The sisters bowed their heads and, murderer or not, they murmured a prayer for Bridget's soul. Then they headed back to their quarters.

From below the floor of the companionway they could hear Master Skinner raving in the great cabin. His voice grew louder, then faded as he paced back and forth. Now and then a quieter voice broke in, too muted to distinguish the words or the speaker.

". . . will not submit my accounts," Skinner shouted. "You do ill to ask . . . Froward, mutinous . . . Never made any pact with the merchants."

"The gentlemen have finally collected courage enough among them to accuse him," Margaret said.

"Of what?"

"Fraud in the matter of supply. Perhaps collusion with the merchants."

"Surely he wouldn't starve his own men."

"Merchants and masters are prodigal of men's lives when money is to be had. If men die by ill-usage, Master Skinner has but to rummage the alehouses for more.

"Besides, Skinner suffers no ill effects from lack of food. In fact, I think he fattens. I suspect he has a private supply."

She stopped short at the door of their cabin. Lying in front of it was a small bundle wrapped in sacking stiff with dried blood. Flies crawled over it. Perplexed and a little frightened, they both stared down at it.

In their missions through plague-wracked villages the sisters had encountered grotesque talismans: Bones, skulls, animal entrails, crude effigies, the dessicated fingers and toes of some gibbeted criminal. They were the debris of subterranean pagan currents. Usually they were left before the door of the person thought to be a source of misfortune.

"A curse, do you think?" Mary asked.

"Mayhap." Margaret lifted her petticoats and nudged the bundle with the scuffed toe of her leather pump. It didn't nudge back.

A raving tosspot of a ship's master. An unknown renegado in league with pirates. Conniving merchants. And now this. All of it only confirmed Margaret's opinion that she and her sister were confined with lunatics and demons as well as felons and bawds.

She thought about going to look for Giles or Fulke, then decided this object didn't warrant it. At worst it was unsightly, and she would not succumb to foolish superstition. She used her shoe to worry the sacking away from its contents. She opened it enough to see the plump carcass inside.

"A piglet!" Mary exclaimed. "Dressed for cooking."

Margaret had overseen the slaughter of her family's swine and this did indeed look like a newborn pig; but it couldn't be one. The livestock that had begun the voyage had ended it as main courses weeks ago. It could be but one species. "The only fresh meat in the hold," Giles had said, "is running about on four legs." Margaret folded her arms and stared down at it as though she expected it to explain its presence here.

She started to kick it outside, then glanced sideways at Mary. Mary had always been thin, a delicate filigree of a woman. Now she was all edges and angles. The joints of her arms and legs were as sharp as folded reeds. Mary seemed to shrink along with the supply of spoiled food that the cook had been trying to make edible with various tricks involving vinegar marinades and a thorough charring of everything. Mary had acquired a translucence, as though light could pass through the skin stretched across the mullions of her bones.

"God hath worked a miracle." Mary crossed herself.

"Aye." With her nose wrinkled in distaste, Margaret picked up the gift. "I shall have the cook prepare a nourishing broth."

Maybe Mary knew exactly what this was and was making the best of it. Or maybe starvation had affected her mind. Margaret thought it possible. Margaret gave a fleeting, tight-lipped little smile. Maybe she and her sister were going mad in tandem.

But as Margaret laid the rat's carcass on the narrow shelf, she imagined a broth with a shiny rainbow of grease floating on top, and her mouth began to water. Maybe it was a miracle after all.

Chapter 13

Giles Brent and Henry Fleete rested their elbows on the taffrail and watched the slow progress of the Virginia shore. The mastiff and the whippet lay at their feet. Fulke Brent leaned over the rail, looking as though he were about to lose the contents of his stomach again.

"Ah, Jamaica." Henry Fleete stared wistfully astern and south, toward the island the ship had left ten days earlier. "I would that we had shipped aboard a few of its hot-blooded, lacquer-faced wenches." He grinned at Giles. "Did I not tell you they were the finest women a man can o'erset?"

"You did." Giles wasn't so enthusiastic. Father Poulton had been treating him all week for the clap.

"What smooching, what slobbering." Fleete turned away from the wind, lifted a fingernail of snuff to each nostril and sniffed loudly. "What rank, lewd folly!" he shouted before he sneezed.

"Good evening, gentlemen." Margaret noted that Fleete had at least enough breeding to look chagrined.

"Mistress Margaret." He doffed his hat and bowed.

"If Jamaica pleases thee so, Captain Fleete, I wonder that thou dost not establish thyself there."

"Though the women be comely, 'tis a haven for knaves, Mistress Margaret. The men of that a-cursed island will kill you most cordially for the buttons on your doublet."

"And 'tis hot as hell's kitchen besides," Giles added.

"Aye. But Maryland can rival Jamaica for marrow-stewing heat," Fleete said.

Margaret's left eyebrow lifted. This was the first she'd heard of it. " 'Tis advertised as a temperate, salubrious clime." In fact, Margaret remembered Fleete himself making that claim before they sailed.

He shrugged. "July and August arrive in such a swelter they're called the sickly season. Folks die like cats and dogs then, though I'm sure God will keep you and yours well." He bowed again. "If you'll be so kind as to excuse me, I shall ferret out some gentlemen to read the devil's books with me." He held up his cards and smiled amiably.

"I'll join you," Fulke said.

Margaret watched the two disappear down the stairs. "I should think Captain Fleete had already cheated every man Jack of his last shilling," she muttered. She looked over at Giles, her cool gray gaze sweeping him from head to toe. "Though in thy case the tailors of Port Royal left thee little to lose at gaming."

While the ship's crew took on water and food in Jamaica, Margaret and Mary had had their clothes washed and mended. Giles had ordered new ones made. His stylish breeches, slit to show the lining, were gathered at the knee by wide, red satin garters wound around several times and tied in big bows. Bright green silk stockings hung over the high tops of his polished boots. The brim of his hat shaded more territory than his narrow shoulders did.

Giles nodded toward the low-lying shoreline and changed the subject. "The standing timber is as plentiful as promised."

"That it is." In spite of late November's chill Margaret took off her mask and threw back the hood of her cape.

She stared at the faded shreds of autumn foliage. The trees seemed to form an unbroken wall, but they weren't a wall. Even the stoutest wall had limits, a front and a back. Whatever Henry Fleete might claim about visiting China, Margaret knew of no one who'd traveled far enough west to emerge from the other side of this forest.

"There's no sign of habitation," she murmured.

"Remember what the pamphlet said."

" 'When you are parted from England you shall meet with neither markets nor fairs to buy what you want,' " Margaret recited. " 'Nor taverns nor alehouses.' "

" 'Nor butchers, nor grocers, nor apothecary shops.' "

"I should not be surprised to discover this, what with the venture so recently begun, but . . ." Her voice trailed off at the prospect of a country whose boundaries and resources and perils no one could begin to assess.

"You expected fields and orchards. Flocks of grazing sheep. Hedgerows and stone cottages with smoke rising from the chimneys." Giles chuckled. "So did I, Maggie."

"Thanks be to God our people are in fair health." Margaret thanked God for that several times a day. Her fortunes depended on them for more than just the labor they would provide.

Lord Baltimore's formula for granting land in exchange for laborers was subject to change with the exigencies of his finances. The original twenty Adventurers received the most generous acreage, with the amount dropping in each succeeding year. But Baltimore had promised Margaret and her brothers land at the original rate, a manor of two thousand acres for every five men they transported.

He had also guaranteed her land in the town of St. Mary's, ten acres for herself, her sister, and for each of her two men and three maidservants. Margaret had calculated the numbers over and over in her head. As soon as she could arrange for the transport of three more men, she and Mary would have 2,070 acres to cultivate.

She was thinking about buying the term of one of the women belowdecks too, when she noticed something near shore.

"Look ye, Giles." Margaret pointed to a hollowed-out log, half hidden behind a tree that had fallen into the water.

A man occupied the canoe. At least he had the form of a man, and Margaret could see his form because he was naked. His head was shaven but for a tall, stiff crest of hair running from his forehead to his nape. Several feathers jutted from it. His face was painted half blue and half red. He sat so still Margaret could have believed him carved in dark wood with polished obsidian inlaid for eyes. Those eyes looked directly into hers as the ship sailed past.

Robert Vaughan stood on the high plateau overlooking the deep round bowl of St. Mary's harbor. He was of medium height and solidly built, short of leg, long of body. A scattering of old smallpox scars pitted his square face.

His eyes were green and the left one strayed slightly from its line of sight, giving him a reckless, slightly mad look. A tangle of reddish-brown hair poked from under the sagging brim of his felt hat. The wind fluttered his waist-length brown cape and drove through his threadbare woollen breeches. The accumulation of grease and dirt rubbed into his leather coat had lacquered it to a fine black sheen.

In spite of the cold wind that scoured the bluff, Vaughan preferred it to the landing. From here he could see down onto the ship's tiered decks. With his dented telescopium he could assess the latest shipment of lords and laborers, possibly the last to arrive in 1638. He wondered which of the newcomers would live to see the far side of the sickly season, or celebrate the Nativity in a month for that matter. Ships often arrived with more ill passengers than sound ones. Many never recovered.

Vaughan lowered his telescope and shook his head in amusement at the gentlemen-of-fashion milling about on the ship. Besides their plumes and laces and bows they wore fluttering ribbons in their long hair. Bedizened as any salvage, he thought.

Vaughan had long ago observed that the gentry took up more space than the common sort. These particular ones filled the upper decks with their wide hats and capes, their billowing petticoats and breeches, their padded doublets, cuffed bucket boots and swords and their beribboned dogs.

A few small boats and a dozen Indian canoes lined the shore.

The freemen who owned them crowded the crescent strip of pebbly beach. Most of them had paddled from their small holdings along the creeks. They'd been alerted by the ship's cannon. Skinner had ordered it fired off Point Lookout on the north bank of the Potomac's mouth and at intervals as the ship moved upriver.

Governor Leonard Calvert and the few members of St. Mary's social elite had been rowed out to welcome the arrivals. A wry smile played across Robert Vaughan's lumpy face as he watched the extravagant ritual of kissing and hugging and the flourishing of lace-edged cuffs and ivory snuff boxes.

Henry Fleete had abandoned ship when the gentle boarding party arrived. Now his canoe grated on the beach. His man jumped out and pulled it farther ashore so his master wouldn't get his boots wet. Fleete tied a twisted length of slow match around his arm above the elbow. He took his bandolier, match box and powder horn from the canoe. Carrying his old Dutch musket, its split stock patched with leather, he churned up the path to the top of the bluff.

Vaughan had known Fleete for four years, but he didn't waste time with greetings. They both embarked on so many trading expeditions that their comings and goings were nothing to remark. And given the unpredictable nature of the Indians with whom they trafficked, they always left knowing they might not see each other alive again. Neither did Vaughan bother asking about news from England. He had little interest in conditions there, and he knew that while Fleete's stories would be entertaining, they weren't likely to be factual.

"Sounds as though they're beating hemp on the quarterdeck." Vaughan nodded toward the Gentlemen Adventurers who, now that they had kissed all the women, were clapping each other on the back.

"Another cargo of popish live lumber." Fleete paused to catch his breath from the climb and look down into the ship.

"Anyone of skill or capability?"

"Simpering west-country dandies and priests abovedecks and

rogues and vagabonds below," Fleete said. "Skinner's no doubt embellished the manifest as always, to pass the riffraff off as carpenters and joiners, masons and blacksmiths."

"And the women?"

"The usual for the 'tweendecks. A few specimens ugly as toadfish who ne'er would find husbands at home. A nimble-fingered little Spaniard who finds things no one lost. And a pair of Bridewell tarts."

Fleete didn't bother mentioning Margaret and Mary. He and Vaughan both knew they would have meager chance of making a match with any unmarried gentlewoman. The few who traveled alone were of a higher station, and Catholic besides. Fleete and Vaughan were both Anglicans.

"Which one's Giles Brent?" Vaughan asked.

"The skinny gallant tethered to that furred flageolet and the devil's own bear hound." Fleete pointed with his pipe to the whippet and the mastiff who were hauling Giles around the deck.

"Were they mine, I would trade them both for a water spaniel." Vaughan shook his head at the fancies of the upper classes. "Why should a man of reason want a dog skin drawn over a bundle of kindling?"

"We thought at one point to eat them; but no one wanted to attempt the mastiff, and the rats carried more meat than the whippet."

"Think you Baltimore's wise to set so much store by Brent?"

Fleete grimaced and shook his head. "He's the sort of grasshopper killed with the first frost, and his brother Fulke won't last till then. His sister's a shrewd package though."

"Wintour's dead." Vaughan said. "Taken by a fever just after Bartholemewtide."

Fleete paused in tribute with his hand poised in the act of tying his powder flask to his belt. "He was witty company for a gentleman and a papist."

"Aye." Robert Vaughan already missed Wintour's small but excellent library, sold off with the rest of his estate to a Virginia merchant. He realized he would have to befriend the irascible Jesuit, Thomas Copley, if he wanted to borrow books.

The wind blew colder, driving the bloated, pewter-colored clouds faster overhead. Vaughan knew that even after the gentry reached shore they would waste time on their knees while their priests mumbled Latin over them. He debated between waiting here for them to finish their foolery or sitting by the fire at Smythe's ordinary, humble as it was.

He shouldered his old crossbow. "I'll stand you the first tankard at Smythe's, Henry."

"Done."

Chapter 14

The transportees had heaped the sodden, straw-stuffed sacks of their pallets against the sides of the 'tween-decks. Anicah and Martin sat on theirs and leaned against the hull. They held hands under the spread of Anicah's new skirts of coarsely spun russet-brown wool. They pressed against each other as though that would make them more difficult to separate.

Abovedecks they heard the laughter and chatter of the local gentry greeting the new arrivals. The highborn passengers had more than privilege and wealth and fine accommodations. They were welcomed here at the fag end of the earth. No one would welcome her, and she was about to be separated from the only person who cared about her.

"I shall persuade my master to buy your term." Martin put an arm around her shoulder and drew her closer.

She wanted to weep with affection for him, but she knew their love was doomed. He was a yeoman and far above her own poor station.

"Who bought ye, Martin?" she asked.

"A planter on an island three days' sail from here. A place called Kent."

"I would not serve a farmer except I be near you," Anicah said. "Field work mislikes me."

"There be but one type of work for yer sort," Harry observed.

"And that be field work. Some o' which ye'll do on yer back, I'll wager."

Martin gripped Anicah's hand so hard she feared he would crush her fingers. His calm, slate-blue eyes took on a wild look. Anicah stroked his hand to reassure him and gave Harry a disdainful glance.

Harry surveyed her as though appraising a ewe for market. "Yer skin be too olivaster fer the fashion, Spaniard, and ye're too meager for most. Yet wives are hard to be got here. Belike some dunghill dandy will take ye to wife."

Martin's fingers tightened again.

"Pay him no mind," Anicah said.

"I was bespoke in Bridewell." Joan joined in from her seat on the ladder where she was keeping watch at the hatch grate. "A rich swell sent fer me."

"Who d'ye think yer master'll be, Harry?" Anicah asked.

"I'll be no catch-fart, trailing behind some popish breast beater." Whatever Harry had in mind for himself he didn't say.

Anicah had no hope that she and Martin could serve their terms together. She tried not to think about what waited for her in the wild new country. Famine, pestilence and the whims and vagaries of the law had pitched her into worse circumstances than this, but at least she had been on familiar ground. She wondered what kind of city St. Mary's was. Did it have a marketplace and butchers' shambles? A theater? A bull-baiting arena or bear garden?

"Ye say there's no prison in Maryland, Harry?" she asked for the third time.

"Nay, nor wooden collar nor whipping post nor gibbet." Harry grinned at her. "They haven't even a cart-arse for lashing rabble like us through town."

Anicah still didn't believe it. The gallows were as much a part of Bristol as the church steeples. And she had seen them at each cross-roads when she had roamed the countryside with her mother.

She listened to the laughter overhead and the thump of heavy boots and the jingle of hawk bells. The noble passengers were making a grand exit.

"The doctor's a papist," Joan called from her station at the grate. She was indignant that Poulton had taken her in with his masquerade as a proper kind of Christian. "He's wearing a priest's gown as bold as brass."

The bells on the dogs' collars tinkled louder.

"We should've eaten the curs," Harry grumbled.

When the gentry had swept past, their indentured servants fell in behind them. First came a few younger sons of high birth and scant means who'd bound themselves as stewards or secretaries to pay their passage. They were followed by yeomen, then common laborers. Margaret and Mary Brent's maids brought up the rear. At the very last came another transportee from Bridewell. She wore the demure white cap and new skirt, bodice, chemise, and leather shoes just issued. Margaret Brent had bought her contract.

"A farewell to ye, Miss Mutton," Joan sang out.

"A pox on you, you filthy trug." The woman tried to stamp on Joan's fingers curled around the hatch grate.

"All keys fit yer lock, Mary Lawne." Laughing, Joan climbed down the ladder. "They've put ribbons on the dogs and clean duds on a bitch."

The mate's legs appeared at the hatch. "Martin Kirk."

"Aye."

"You're to be sold by the custom of the country."

"But I have papers."

"Your master's dead. He and his wife and babes and two bondsmen."

"Of what cause?"

"Salvages butchered them like so many hogs."

While the crew tumbled the last of the cargo into the ship's lighters, the mate positioned Master Skinner's wares on deck. He stood back to assess their newly issued finery of mildewed shoes, moth-gnawed stockings, stained linen shirts and bodices, horse-hide jerkins, and rumpled wool breeches and skirts.

"A damned brood of country lubbers, light-fingered knaves and bog-Irish." Shaking his head and muttering that no one would give a fart for such vermin, the mate climbed to the quarterdeck. He raised his battered speaking trumpet and shouted to the men waiting on shore. "A choice parcel of servants and a sprightly maid to be sold at outcry."

While he detailed the fine bargains to be had, Martin stood in a daze. What kind of country was this? He had known people to die of many causes, but never to be slaughtered by salvages.

Anicah tugged his sleeve to get his attention.

"When they ask yer age say sixteen," she whispered.

"But I'm thirteen."

"Say sixteen."

" 'Tis a sin to lie."

"Wights sixteen and older are bound for but four years. Those younger than fifteen must serve seven."

"I shall try, though I lack as a liar." He pulled her to him and held her. Desperation made him eloquent. "We have endured tempest and sea rovers, sickness and want," he murmured in her ear. "I pray it be God's will that we shall not be parted one from the other now, else I perish for love of thee."

"I will never wrong thee, Martin." Anicah's voice sounded strange in her ears, as though someone else's were rattling in her skull and tumbling off her tongue.

"Nor I you." He kissed her long and fiercely.

The feel of her lips remained on his own after he pulled away from her. He held her at arm's length trying to memorize her small face in its frame of curls. Her cheeks were soft as smoked kidskin, her lips were full and deep red as a new bruise. Her wide golden-brown eyes held his own soul's spark.

"Kirk." The mate prodded him with the butt of his lash. "Get you there with the rest of the riffraff."

As Martin joined the other men he heard Anicah hum an old tune. He knew the words.

> *"Had I as many hearts as hairs,*
> *As many loves as love has fears,*

As many lives as years have hours;
They should be all and only yours."

Anicah shared looks with him across the crowded deck. His
love astonished her. The wavery glimpses she had caught of herself in Bristol's windowpanes and muddy puddles had been of a
sooty-faced, ox-eyed urchin. That Martin considered her fair em-
boldened her to think she might use her gender to advantage.

She ran her fingers nervously through the thick curls that fell
over the tops of her ears now. She brushed a spot of mud from
her skirt and polished the toes of her lumpy new shoes on her
stockings. She had not worn a skirt in many years and she felt exposed and chilly under it.

The planters, eager to bid on servants, scrambled over the rail.
Even though Joan's indenture was already sold she couldn't resist
a performance. She raised her petticoats.

"Take a flourish here, sirs, if ye've the mettle for it." She
rubbed three fingers between her legs, and offered them to anyone who cared to sniff. "Ground not plowed and manur'd will
soon be o'erset with briars."

The men laughed.

"Pay her no mind," the mate shouted. "She's sold."

"Pity poor Hardige," someone said. "Cuckolded before he
beds the wench."

Calling out their bids the men moved on to Anicah. She looked
at Martin and smiled while the men pinched her arms and raised her
skirts to examine her legs. One bade her open her mouth so he could
inspect her teeth. One of them put his hands on his hips and leaned
forward onto the balls of his feet. His collar was frayed and his fingernails black with dirt. This was not the master she wanted.

"Wherefore decided you to emigrate?"

"I came abroad to discover if Mary's Land truly be the dunghill
of the universe."

"Impudent strumpet."

"I may be a strumpet, but me commodity's worth three hundred weight of tobacco," Anicah said. "And what do they pay to bugger the likes of you?"

"The devil take ye, then. I shall not."

The others crowded closer, laughing.

"How old be ye, wench?"

"As old as me tongue and older'n me teeth."

She stiffened when Skinner rapped her on the elbow with his truncheon. The blow shot bolts of pain into her arm and fingers before deadening them to sensation. She smelled the reek of soured wine as he leaned forward to hiss in her ear.

"Play the knave and I shall have you laid across the cannon's mouth and shall fire a salute that will make a sauce of your vitals." Skinner straightened and rapped the front of Anicah's skirts with the truncheon. "A stout wench, full of juice. All her parts below are firm and sound." He turned to her, smiling like a kind uncle. "Tell the gents your age, wench."

"Sixteen."

"I full doubt it." This was the man Harry had pointed out among those waiting on shore earlier.

Samuel Smythe was short and portly, with a belly that tested the laces of his greasy leather jerkin. His small blue eyes were merry in a face as round as a platter.

Harry said Smythe ran St. Mary's only ordinary, serving food and drink to anyone with credit. He would require no field work of her. Best of all, he was married. His advances would be furtive and easily turned away.

"She's a scrawny piece," Smythe said dubiously.

"Me spindle shanks be but the effects of sea tyranny, yer honor." Anicah lifted her petticoats, turned her foot and ankle beguilingly and bestowed a radiant smile on him. "I'm strong as an ox, lively as quicksilver and honest as a corpse."

Chapter 15

Margaret wore wooden platforms tied onto the soles of her leather shoes. Even so, she had to lift her skirts with one hand to keep mud from splashing the hems. Her other hand lay lightly on Governor Leonard Calvert's forearm as he led her across what he called the village common. Hogs had rooted it into a bog, though, and a stubble of Indian corn covered part of it.

Behind Margaret, the newcomers were regaling St. Mary's gentry with stories of the crossing. They laughed gaily when anyone made a misstep and dirtied their boots. After three months at sea, even mud was a delight.

Margaret was used to the motion of the ship under her feet, and the unyielding earth beneath the mud felt like iron. Her legs wobbled with the impact of each step. Calvert steadied her.

"My bones have turned to seawater," she said solemnly.

Leonard Calvert laughed and Margaret was struck again by how young he was, how out of place here. Of course, they were all out of place, but Calvert especially so. He looked the quintessence of what a cavalier should be. Had he not been a Catholic he would have been studying law in the inns of court with the other young rakes or setting noble maidens' hearts to fluttering at Windsor.

The upturned ends of his moustache extended beyond his hollowed cheeks. His brown hair hung in shiny waves to his shoulders. His sharp little beard disguised a chin somewhat in retreat. His pale brown eyes looked tired.

His man carried his master's damascened, double-barreled flintlock and five-foot-long gun rest. Besides his sword, Leonard wore a leather bandolier a-dangle with powder flask, shot bag, and wooden cartridges that clattered at each step. Margaret noticed, in fact, that all the freemen were armed with guns and festooned with the necessities for firing them.

When they crossed the common, the Indian corn gave way to another sort of plant, the woody stems broken and dry now. They flowed in a stubbly brown sea around hundreds of ragged tree stumps and out to the edges of the towering forest that surrounded them. Leonard Calvert led the party among them.

"Is this the most notable sot weed, Governor?" She waved her kerchief at the stalks and breathed in the aroma of tobacco.

"It is, Mistress Margaret."

In makeshift sheds servants stood in front of chest-high piles of it and stripped the big brown leaves from the stems. They were surrounded by hogsheads and bundles of the sot weed strung on poles and racked on scaffolding.

The laborers wore the same brown homespun rags of the lower sort at home. They watched the parade rattle by in a clanking of guns and swords and wooden cartridges. Many of them didn't bother to curtsy or take off their caps.

"Be not offended by the folks' forwardness, Mistress Margaret." Leonard Calvert nodded gravely to the spectators. "They see so few strangers. Your arrival is like a fair or a raree for them."

"What are those?" Margaret nodded to a scattering of long, domed, bark-covered structures rising from the tobacco stubble. Most of them were falling to ruins among dead brush and dry leaves, split shingles and barrel staves.

"They are the dwellings of the heathen folk who lived here, the Yoacomico. They gave us their fields and homes and shared their stores of Indian corn. Without them, we would have suffered greatly that first winter. And many more would have perished . . ." He didn't elaborate on just how many had perished.

"When will we reach the town?" Margaret looked for a house, a road, a proper sort of manor.

"Ah, well." Calvert cleared his throat. "You see, the gentlemen are seating their townlands at some little distance from the city's center." He gestured vaguely at the trees. "But several still reside at the fort. And their servants tend their crops here when they aren't clearing their masters' fields."

Calvert gestured to his left and his long face lit up. "There is where we shall raise our government house. At the far end of town shall be our cathedral, a glory to God and an inspiration to man. The shops of smiths and joiners, merchants' houses and tobacco factories will be built there." He made a sideways cast of his lace-draped hand as though dealing out buildings in a neat row through the tobacco-sown swamp.

A cold wind rattled the dry stalks, and Margaret saw the desolate landscape through a mist of tears. For this she had left the cropped green hills and willow-lined streams of northern Gloucestershire, reckoned the most beautiful county in England even by those not bred of it.

Calvert took a tighter grip on Margaret's arm when a hog led her brood at an amble toward them. With a practiced eye, Margaret measured the sow's sunken sides for chops and bacon, and the sow reciprocated. She wore the fractious look of an animal hungry enough to try to eat something large and inappropriate.

"With your permission, Governor." Margaret took the gun rest from Calvert's servant.

"What are you about, Margaret?" Giles called warily from behind her.

"I shall turn highwayman, and charge yon goodwife to yield the road."

Margaret advanced holding the rod like a pike with the sharpened end leveled. The sow lowered her head and gave her a baleful look. Margaret rapped her sharply on the tender tip of her snout. The sow squealed, but she stood her ground.

Margaret took off her hat and flapped its wide brim in the animal's face. "Begone!"

The sow backed up, stepping on a piglet as she went. When she wheeled and ran, her offspring scattered then reconverged behind her. The gentlemen applauded.

"Governor, mayhap you should appoint her muster master," someone said from behind her.

Margaret knew they were indulging her as they would a child, but she was accustomed to it. She had used it to her advantage before. She turned so they could all hear her. "Swine forget their station and take on airs now and then, like merchants' wives who've been to London."

The men laughed.

"Women love themselves best and London next." The speaker was short and wiry and taut with an energy that Margaret suspected was often misspent.

"Quite so, Secretary Lewger." She gave him a sardonic smile. "And certain men would be far down on the list of things women love."

St. Mary's gentry laughed again. Lord Baltimore had sent John Lewger to Maryland to act as his secretary in his absence. The man wasn't popular.

"Who dwells in yon hut, Governor Calvert?" Margaret nodded toward one of the Yoacomico houses.

Bark, brush, sacking, and shreds of old canvas sails covered the bowed framework of saplings. Someone had draped it with pieces of fishnet, lengths of twine, animal pelts and jawbones.

"Original Brown, late of Virginia, has recently finished his term of indenture here." Leonard speeded his pace, but not enough.

"Good morrow, yer honor, and may God keep ye in his tender care." An old man threw aside the deerskin door and bustled to intercept them. "I've caught the red bird his lordship desires."

Calvert's eyes brightened and he stopped to look. Brown held out the treasure.

"His lordship requires that the bird be alive, Goodman Brown."

"Alive?" Brown jiggled the mangled corpse in his palm as though he could shake breath back into it. "Alive, ye say?"

"Yes." Calvert started away, but Margaret lingered.

"I would sell it ye fer a keepsake, mistress, else I shall stew it," Brown said. "I'm asking but a penny, though it cost me great labor to snare it."

Margaret stared at it, fascinated. It was a deep, rich scarlet with a black mask around its eyes and stubby red beak. "Is this creature rare, Governor?"

"They fly about as thick as sparrows," Calvert said. "But so far they've eluded capture."

"What is it called?"

"It hath no name but that of red bird."

Margaret gave the old man a penny. She wrapped the bird in a handkerchief and put it into the pouch hanging from her belt. "I'll take it to my sister. We've n'er seen its like before. I can understand why his lordship would want one."

"Aye." Leonard started walking again and lowered his voice so only Margaret could hear. "But my brother's importunings in the matter are a great distraction. Every ship brings another request for a live specimen of this bird or that beast. Frankly, Mistress Margaret, we have more to do here than supply his menagerie."

"Well, it is lovely."

It was more than lovely, it was exquisite. It gave Margaret a sudden hope in her future here. She was elated to think this new country sheltered a creature so beautiful. What other wonderful surprises might it hold? She hurried her pace. Mary had been feeling ill, and two of Calvert's men had carried her ahead in a makeshift litter. Margaret was eager to see her reaction to the red bird.

They approached the only real dwelling that Margaret could see, a two-story clapboard house being raised in the middle of the tobacco. Across from it stood a dilapidated hovel. The ivy bush raised on a pole outside the shack declared it a tavern or ordinary. Margaret wasn't surprised to see it. Taverns sprouted in the most barren of soils.

Beyond the house and the ordinary stood a palisade, but the vertical logs of the wall had obviously been set up while still green. They had warped where they stood and leaned drunkenly. Smoke rose above the palings.

Margaret sniffed the air. Each place had its own signature of smells, and she would be breathing this one from now on. The emanation from the fort was the usual mix of excrement, decay, livestock, and smoke, except for two features. The smoke wasn't sulfurous coal or musty turf, not dried dung or leaves, but the aroma of burning oak, maple, ash. Such smoke was rare in England these days, and Margaret breathed in great lungfuls of it.

The second difference was tobacco. The place reeked of it.

"And here is the house I'm a-building." Calvert stared intently at the two-story building. "Master Skinner hath brought glass quarrels so I shall have proper windows."

"It's quite handsome."

"We have roofed the kitchen and the central passage as well as the great hall and upper chamber to the right of it. The parlor will be to the left." Leonard cocked a critical eye at his mansion, searching for flaws and finding them.

The planters had heard the governor's complaints before. They steered the newcomers inside for a drink and the meal Calvert's servants had laid out.

"Giles says thou hast transported a carpenter," Calvert said. "Mayhap we could come to some agreement for the hire of him. At least until thou'rt ready to begin building."

Margaret opened her mouth to ask just when that might be, but he headed her off.

"We suffer a great want of skilled joiners and carpenters." He pointed to the eaves. "See there, how the windows run not parallel to the roof? It hath an abundance of such faults."

"I'm sure we can come to an arrangement."

"Good day, gentlefolk." Vaughan had left the ordinary and ambled over to join them. He bowed and saluted Margaret with the leather flask he had detached from his belt. "I must beg your pardon, gentle mistress, for my rude, country manners. My name is Robert Vaughan, known by my friends as Sir Lack-Latin."

The wild look in his errant green eyes startled Margaret, but he was oddly attractive for one so ugly. She recognized the type. He was one of those dangerous rogues who could make a woman feel on first meeting as though she had known him all her life.

She gave a curt nod. "Mr. Vaughan."

"Sergeant Vaughan," Calvert amended. "He is sheriff here and a leader of our militia. When the Virginia knaves on the Isle of Kent refused to take the oath of allegiance to Lord Baltimore, Sergeant Vaughan helped win the day against them."

From the glint in Vaughan's eyes and the blush under the dark stubble on his cheeks he looked to be losing the battle with his flask. Margaret was annoyed to see that Giles had attached himself to Vaughan's elbow. Giles could be counted on to befriend the worst possible companions in any given place.

Vaughan drained the last drops from his flask and retied it to his belt. "Our new friends must be exhausted by their travels. I propose we avail ourselves of the hospitality of Goodman Smythe's house." Vaughan angled toward the ordinary, trying to start a general movement in that direction.

"We shall repair to my chambers for refreshment," said Calvert, "and thence to the chapel to give thanks."

Vaughan flourished his hat. "You papists will mumble and chant a long while. I'll amuse myself until you finish."

He smiled broadly to blunt the offense. He bowed, then strode away, jumping the smaller puddles and splashing through the bigger ones. He disappeared into the ramshackle building and Giles looked longingly after him.

Chapter 16

One of the first houses built in St. Mary's now served as its ordinary. The hearth took up most of the rear wall. The public room was only sixteen by twenty-four feet, yet the murk of tobacco fumes and wood smoke obscured the tiny barred counter at the other side of it. Huge logs blazed in the fireplace and torches of fat pine flared in iron sconces on the walls. Their light glinted off the vitreous coat of soot covering the hewn beams and planks of the ceiling. Shadows danced on the flaking plastered walls.

Men from the ship's crew added to the local drinkers, and Goodman Smythe had had to crowd in more sections of logs to serve as chairs at the trestle tables.

"Welcome, welcome, my fine gallant." Smythe bowed to Giles and led him to the table near the fire where Robert Vaughan and Henry Fleete were sitting. Smythe bowed again and hustled off, looking busy but only managing to get in the way.

"A merry, round knave," Giles observed.

"A merry knave indeed," Vaughan said. "But usually Smythe must know your history, destination and business before he leaves you to get drunk in peace." He waved a large, scarred hand to summon the new maid. "Here, wench, with the usual."

"In a pissing while, sir." Anicah had to hold the leather tankards above her head to squeeze through the noisy crowd.

She had tied her skirts up, baring her thin brown calves and ankles. She had taken off her shoes and stockings to preserve them from wear. Besides, she could maneuver better barefoot on the sanded floor, although she had to step nimbly to keep her feet from being stepped on.

She swiveled to avoid a hand trying to reach up under her petticoats. "Away with ye, Sir Knight." She pirouetted and set the tankards on the table board with a flourish and not a dark drop spilled.

"Fetch me a beer," shouted one of the Irishmen sitting near Vaughan.

"Our brew be smooth as oil, sweet as milk, clear as amber, strong as brandy," Anicah said.

"And expensive as the devil," he grumbled. "Bring me double, then. And a pipe and a twist of sot weed. And let it be sweet scent, not the Orinoke."

"Aye."

"A cool tankard for me," added his companion.

"Aye."

"Know ye the makings of it?"

"Nay, me lord." She leaned close, as though to impart a secret that everyone didn't already know. "The tide just washed me ashore and I be new to this rig."

"Three parts wine and one part water, with lemon, sugar and a pinch of borage."

"Water we have, sir, in great store, and wine, thanks to yon ship in the harbor. But we lack lemon, sugar and borage."

Smythe's wife Patience sat behind the wooden bars that reached from the tall counter to the low ceiling. She guarded the kegs of home-brewed beer and hard cider around her and the potbellied, long-necked bottles of wine on the shelf above. Anicah thought Goody Smythe resembled the kegs she kept such close company with.

"Score up twin beers and a cool tankard for the Irishmen," Anicah shouted.

Only this afternoon she had listened intently as Smythe and

Skinner arrived at a price for her; 250 pounds of tobacco for four years of her life. But weeks seemed to have passed since she watched Skinner tear a copy of her contract of indenture in two and give half to her and half to Samuel Smythe. She had folded it, put it into the stolen tin snuff box with her father's will, then into the cloth bag tied under her skirt. She had given Martin a kiss and a smile before she followed Smythe here and into the gale of his wife's rage.

Patience Smythe had instructed her husband to purchase a manservant or at the very least a strapping country wench who could do heavy lifting and hard work. She was furious that he had chosen instead this tawny wisp of a girl with shifty Spanish eyes. She divided the blame for Smythe's bad bargain equally between him and Anicah. Only after she had made certain that Anicah wasn't a Spaniard or a papist or a Gypsy did she allow her to stay.

Except for a hasty meal of Goody Smythe's small beer and the Indian corn porridge called samp, Anicah had been working ever since. She should have been exhausted, but she was too happy for exhaustion. Captain Fleete had told her that the papist doctor, Poulton, had bought Martin's contract, which meant he wouldn't be sailing to the far-off Isle of Kent. Also, she'd discovered a career as suited to her talents as picking pockets. The noise and smoke and confusion of the public room soaked into her skin and invigorated her as sunlight nurtured flowers.

She remembered every order shouted at her. She retrieved the smoking tongs and brazier of embers, the clay pipes and braids of tobacco from the shelf. She jollied the guests and made a lively jig of her rounds among the tables.

Whenever Goodwife Smythe looked away Anicah drained the lees from the cups, but that wasn't why she was giddy. The town of St. Mary's had disappointed her, but in her most extravagant dreams she had never envisioned a life as grand as this. New clothes, shelter, a roaring fire to chase the winter's cold, all the food and wine she could filch. Goodwife Smythe's ill-temper was a small enough price for it.

She cast a professional glance around the room. Best of all, here was a score of tippling gamesters in a country that didn't have a hangman or a gallows or a prison. She could find a way to profit from them.

She stepped lightly over the dogs and one old man who had fallen asleep on the ale bench with his legs sprawled in her path. The motion of her passing created blue eddies of tobacco smoke spiraling lazily in the light of the fireplace and the torches.

The hour was past nine, which was when Goodman Smythe was supposed to usher his guests out and bar the door behind them. But Smythe had seated himself comfortably on the ale bench. He was regaling the men there with stories they'd probably heard before but were too drunk to remember. Now and then he beamed broadly at Anicah, as if she were an unexpected inheritance. At the very least, paying for her passage would get Smythe ten acres of town land to plant in tobacco, and the wench herself to cultivate it.

Smythe had cause to be happy. St. Mary's meager, overworked population couldn't support a public house except at certain times of the year. Business was always brisk during court sessions or muster days or when the legislative Assembly met. The ordinary also filled up when a ship arrived, but tonight was different. The new maid's jaunty style had infected the place. The usual noise and confusion crackled with a frantic gaiety. The laughter was heartier, the shouting more good-natured.

"Mind you, baggage, tope not," Goody Smythe scolded. "And if a customer slips you a penny, you're to give it to me."

"Aye, mistress." Anicah gathered up the tankards on the counter. As she crossed the room she muttered, "I'll gi' it ye when sows bear saddles."

From the corner of her eye she saw Goody Smythe add charcoal marks to those that covered the whitewashed wall behind her. Anicah could tell she was scoring drinks twice on the accounts of men too fuddled to remember how much they had had.

Robert Vaughan seemed absorbed in his game of cards with Captain Fleete and the papist, Giles Brent, but Anicah approached

his table cautiously. She had discovered that Vaughan was a bois-
terous and unpredictable man. She tiptoed up behind him. She set
his Faial wine down quickly and tried to dart away, but he caught
a handful of her petticoats and pulled her onto his lap. She juggled
the remaining mugs to keep from spilling the contents.

"Mark the wench's waggish eyes and little roguish nose, her
fritter ears and pouty little paps." Vaughan stuffed a length of
green ribbon into the low neckline of her bodice, between breasts
not big enough to pout yet. He nuzzled her neck, huffing loud
explosions of air as he did it. "A cup o' cheer is well worth the
kissing, me pullet."

The hot blasts of Vaughan's breath and his unshaven cheek tickled Anicah's bare breastbone and shoulders. She threw her head back
and laughed so loud, so without care, that for a moment conversations hushed and everyone looked at her. Goody Smythe glowered,
but she dared not leave her kegs unattended to thrash her.

Anicah swiveled at the waist and handed the other mugs to
the Irishmen sitting behind her. Then she grabbed Vaughan's big
ears and twisted them hard as she yanked his head back.

"Ye shall have a kiss when all false knaves prove honest men,
sir," she said.

"You would take my kindness, yet say me nay?"

She held him painfully by the ear with one hand and with the
other made a show of drawing the ribbon from her bodice.
" 'Love, sir,' " she recited, " 'Be like a fisher's angle, which oft hath
golden baits, silly maidens to entangle.' "

She gave him a demure peck on his broad forehead and
slipped off his lap. She heard his laughter behind her as she tied
the ribbon in her short hair. She sang as she wove a path back to
the source of beer.

> "Fresh fish and news grow quickly stale.
> Some say good wine can ne'er want sale.
> But God sends poor folks beer and ale
>   enough until they die."

"She'd make a Saracen smile." Vaughan rubbed his reddened ears.

" 'Twas rumored on the crossing that her fingers possess a peculiar quality," said Fleete. "Small objects of value stick to them like iron filings to lodestone. We feared that if she strayed too near the poop she would hinder the compass's reckoning."

Vaughan laughed. "Magnetic fingers or no, a score of such wenches would bring in more profit than a hundred acres of the sot weed."

"Indeed." Giles frowned at the collection of stiffened leather rectangles in his hand. Stare as he might at them, not a single honor card appeared among them. "Wenches succumb not to drought nor locusts," he said.

Even with his spirits buoyed by wine, Giles was ill at ease among so many Protestants. Servants weren't allowed to drink in here, but many of those who had arrived in 1634 had completed their four-year terms. Most of them held with the Church of England.

"Prime!" Vaughan laid out his winning hand and added charcoal marks to his score on the table board.

"Damn me!" As Giles gathered up the scattered cards he fingered the edges of the pack. He was trying to discover if Vaughan had trimmed them so the honor cards could be distinguished, making it possible for him to deliberately pull prime.

"If only Lord Baltimore had persuaded Madam Hollandia to transport herself and her laced legion." Vaughan sounded almost melancholy. "Imagine an establishment like Holland's Leaguer here." He waved his tankard to include the sleeping hamlet outside and the endless, brooding forest beyond. "A house inhabited by whores of exceptional wit and limberness."

"I was present at Madam Hollandia's during the beleaguering, although as a noncombatant," said Giles.

"Were you now?" Vaughan regarded Giles with new interest. Fresh stories were valuable goods here.

"The jealousies of high-placed investors in other such dens finally gathered in a storm around her enterprise." Giles paused to light his pipe and increase the drama. "When the sheriff's halberdiers appeared on the drawbridge, General Hollandia, by a devilishly clever device, dropped them into the moat."

"Which I remember served both as a means of defense and a sewer," said Fleete.

"Aye. 'Twas the stench of it that occasioned the complaints and drew official ire. The putrefying corpse of the third horse proved more than the delicate noses of the neighbors could abide." Giles got back to the story. "Whilst the sheriff's army flapped about like smelts in a privy basin, the stalwart whores pelted them with pretty words from the upstairs windows. And with chamber pots full-charged, of course."

"I knew Dame Hollandia well in the old days," said Fleete. "Just after she had ascended from common whore to bawd. Her house was the finest in the stews then, and I a member of the Half-Crown Chuck Office there."

"And I the Groom Porter in charge of all gaming in the kingdom." Vaughan winked. "As you know, Squire Brent, in matters of fact Captain Fleete is much given to embellishment."

" 'S'truth," Fleete insisted. "One of her agile Dutch whores, naked of course, would upend and balance with her head pointed toward hell and her soles to heaven. She'd spread her legs and we pitched half-crowns till her nether vessel filled to overflowing." He drew a penny from his pocket and shied it with a sideways flick of his wrist. It landed with a plop in Vaughan's tankard. "My aim was always true."

Vaughan drained his cup, leaving the penny for Anicah. He belched loudly and held the vessel over his head. Anicah snatched it from his hand as she hurried past, turning sideways to present less of a target.

On the other side of the room several Virginians from the Isle of Kent had been talking louder and louder. Finally their voices rose above the others in the room.

"We are already plagued with paternosters, and now another has arrived. Priests are o'rruning the country."

Giles kept discreetly silent. He had expected the talk to turn to this subject eventually.

"Which country, Knight?" Vaughan asked.

"All countries. But particularly this one." Knight had trouble enunciating "particularly."

" 'This one,' as you call it, is but an extension of England," Giles said in a reasonable tone. "Its inhabitants may take direction from Lord Baltimore, but damn me, we are all subject to his majesty, King Charles."

"Subject to the anti-Christ in Rome, more like," Knight shouted. "Those devil priests would establish a most wicked and pernicious tyranny over us."

"Not a fortnight gone a Christian lad was slaughtered at Mattapany where the priests have planted their manor," Vaughan said loudly. "Mayhap the priests and salvages conspire with you Kentish swine to murder us in our beds."

The men of Kent were too drunk to recognize the irony in his voice. "Knavish piss-vinegar!" In a scraping of keg rims and stool legs they stood as one. "We do not conspire with papists."

"Kiss my freckled arse, you hog-stealing rogues!" Vaughan stood up too, the better to bellow across the room.

Goodman Smythe looked distressed and Anicah hugged herself happily. A fight would crown the evening's entertainment. Then misgivings struck her. As far as she could see, this was the only public house in the entire miserable village. If the authorities closed it she would have no job but field work.

"Sergeant Vaughan," she called into the silence. "Be it in truth freckled?"

"What?" He squinted at her through the smoke and his own haze of alcohol. Drink had exaggerated the wanderings of his eyes.

"Yer arse. Be it freckled?"

"Certes, wench."

"May I see it?"

Vaughan grinned at her. He climbed onto the table, untied the points and laces of his breeches, and let them fall with his hose about his ankles. He bent at the waist to present her with the furry magnificence of his buttocks.

He was still doubled in half when the front door swung open behind him. He peered between his knees at the slender man silhouetted there. The room grew still.

"Secretary Lewger, good ev'ning to you," he shouted. "You spider-shanked lolpoop," he added in a slightly lower voice.

Then the effects of the wine and the blood draining into his temples upset his balance. He toppled forward onto Giles and the two of them crashed to the floor. Fleete, laughing, tried to help them up.

" 'Tis past the hour for closing." Lewger had to raise his voice to be heard over the commotion. "Anyone here when I return shall be fined. If there is a falling out with noise, disturbing the peace, the culprits will be whipped."

When the door closed behind him Vaughan leaned forward to confide in Giles. "Some say that Secretary Lewger is too rigid in his opinions, and too quick to forward his own enterprises. But I say he is a dissembling varlet."

Fleete helped Vaughan reassemble his clothes. He was having trouble with the metal-tipped points that fastened his hose to his breeches. When they were more or less secure Fleete and Giles steered him across the room, trying to avoid his affectionate, rib-crushing embrace. They effected a general swap of hats at the door, ending up with each other's.

Anicah handed Giles a blazing pine knot in a metal basket suspended from a pole. She giggled at the sight of Vaughan's big hat hanging loose over Giles's ears. She gave Vaughan a kiss on the cheek, thanks for the penny in the bottom of his mug.

"Do lodge at my humble house this night, Brent," Vaughan offered. "I have a bottle of fine Madeira. And you can regain in a few games what you have lost here. On our way there we can serenade the governor."

Vaughan began singing in a booming baritone, and Giles had to speak loudly to be heard.

"I should not like to be fined for tipsification."

"None o' that for the likes of you, Squire Brent." Vaughan stopped in the middle of a note. "We all know that when Lord Baltimore grants your patent of land, you shall pull prime. Aye. You and your kin are the honor cards in his pack."

Chapter 17

Margaret and Leonard Calvert sat inside his huge, plastered fireplace, sharing it with the dangling carcasses of two hogs and a pile of blazing logs as long as a man. When Margaret looked up she could see sparks joining the stars at the other end of the broad chimney. She settled deeper into the cushions of the oversized chair and held her feet closer to the flames. She shut her eyes, enjoying the amiable crackle and roar of the fire and letting its warmth soak into her weary bones.

In the shadowy chamber beyond the hearthstones loomed pale, hulking shapes. Calvert's servants had shrouded his furniture in canvas to protect it from the sawdust and powdered plaster of construction. Stacks of oaken wainscoting rose here and there like headlands in the night. The aroma of freshly sawn wood filled the room.

Fulke slept on a pallet near the fire. The murmur of Mary's nightly devotions no longer emanated from behind the green baize curtains surrounding Leonard Calvert's bedstead. Her quiet snores played counterpoint to Fulke's. Faint gusts of laughter and song blew through the cracks in the shutters. Giles had disappeared a couple of hours ago. Margaret assumed he was reveling with his inferiors at the ordinary.

The welter of the day's conversations echoed in her head. Questions, stories, suggestions, jests, cautions, opinions. Everyone here had advice for her and she had listened intently to all of it. She was beginning to realize how much she didn't know.

She was pleased to find that she liked Lord Baltimore's younger brother, and she had the feeling he liked her too.

She glanced at the steel helmets and potbellied breastplates hanging by the door. Two matchlocks and a snaphaunce leaned against each other in the corner nearby.

"May I inspect thy piece, Governor?"

"Certes." Calvert took his arquebus from its pegs on the wall by the hearth and handed it to her.

" 'Tis most unusual." She ran her hand along the twin barrels and into the graceful open scrollwork curves of the skeletal stock. She admired its heft and balance. "Seventy caliber?"

"Seventy-five. It's French, of course." Calvert perked up at her interest. "The barrels are mounted on a central axis and rotated by hand into firing position."

"And the range?" Then she added, "If one actually intends to hit something."

"Forty yards." Calvert reconsidered. "Thirty-five."

"Beautiful work." Margaret held it to the light to look at the lock, damascened in gold and silver. The Calvert coat-of-arms was inlaid with mother-of-pearl and staghorn in the polished pearwood stock. She returned it to him. "Father Poulton tells me a servant of the Jesuits was killed by Indians."

Calvert sighed. "The Jesuits insisted on seating one of their manors ten miles north at a place called Mattapany, the better to exhort the Indians who live there. The mission being so far removed, they put themselves and their servants in peril."

"Then every man carries his long-piece as protection against salvages as well as wild animals?"

"I require it." Calvert swirled his peach brandy in its goblet. "Should an alarum be sounded I will accompany thee and thy sister to the fort. I've ordered everyone to repair there if hostiles are sighted."

Margaret remembered the sagging line of rotting tree trunks. She wanted to point out that the palings wouldn't thwart a mob of Bristol street urchins. "Why was it built so far inland?" she asked instead.

"We expected attack from the forest, not the water." Calvert took a sip of his brandy. "Yet the folk who inhabited this place greeted us amicably. Their children ran and played among us, their women cooked for us. Without them we might have perished that first winter, as those in Virginia did. Belike 'twere God's hand at work, to turn such barb'rous men to good intent. Men of more remote tribes are the ones attacking us now. Some of them travel great distances for the sport."

They both sat in silence, Calvert remembering what had been, Margaret wondering what would be.

Leonard Calvert was handsome in the fire's light, but Margaret could detect the languor bred of privilege. It hovered about his eyes and blurred the line of his mouth. He had a fastidious softness in his face that made Margaret wonder how he had held his brother's fragile endeavor together for four years against so much privation and adversity.

Margaret went on to the next subject that had been bothering her. "I take it Giles hath told thee of the conditions aboard Master Skinner's ship."

"Yes."

"Skinner was insolent and reckless and provisioned us with moldy bread and stinking beef. He transported known felons, masquerading them as honest citizens. He crowded the ship with a score more souls than the 'tweendecks would accommodate." Margaret paused. " 'Tis said that many die here before a season passes. I believe the mortality is caused by those like him. I wish to bring charges against him."

Calvert lifted his goblet to the fire's light and seemed, for a few long moments, lost in its amber glow. "To begin with, Mistress Margaret, our courts hold no jurisdiction over the conduct of a ship's master at sea."

"Then he must be banned from commerce here."

"Whatever his faults, Richard Skinner and the other mariners are our life's blood. They carry our beaver pelts and wainscoting, our Indian corn and tobacco to England. They bring us cloth and iron, tools, wine, letters from home, the communications of our factors. They bring us laborers. We cannot exist without them."

"Skinner must kill as many men as he delivers."

Calvert held his goblet by the stem and flicked the bowl with his fingernail. A single crystalline note hung quavering in the air. "You mentioned that you would send for the Murano glassware you left behind. Whom do you think will fetch it?"

"But surely there are others . . ."

"Ships disappear without a trace, yet Skinner hath yet to lose a cargo. We can ill-afford to alienate him." He gave her a conciliatory smile. "Before he departs I wager you yourself will tender an order of English goods for his next voyage."

Calvert stretched his thin legs and stifled a yawn. "I have been most discourteous keeping you awake when you must be weary."

"I'm too a-roil with thoughts to sleep, Governor."

"Then I shall bid thee a good night and leave thee in their company and in God's."

Calvert went to the door and called softly to the man wrapped in a blanket on the floor of the central passage. The servant lit a stick of resinous pine before he banked the fire. He helped his master drape his short cape stylishly over his left shoulder and tied it under Calvert's right arm. Then he set the torch in an iron cresset and suspended it from the end of a long pole. Calvert bowed and put on his hat before following the servant out.

Margaret couldn't bring herself to call Bess Guest downstairs. She unlaced her bodice herself and struggled out of her stays and stomacher and skirts and laid them across a trunk. She unpinned her fine brown hair and let it tumble down her back. She knelt and recited the paternoster, the Lord's Prayer, then crossed herself.

Shivering in her long shift and gartered wool stockings, she pulled back the bed curtains and slipped in next to Mary. Her head was so full of plans and fears and speculations she thought she would never sleep, but the two mattresses were stuffed with down. She sank into them as though falling into clouds. Before she could finish her prayers to the Virgin Mary, she was asleep.

She didn't awaken until almost dawn. She sat up so suddenly she grew dizzy. She couldn't see anything in the dark, but she knew she wasn't at home. Her heart thumped like a drum.

Had she only dreamed she heard someone shout "Salvages"?

"Didst thou hear it, sister?" Mary gripped Margaret's arm.

"Yes." She pulled her pistol from behind the bolster and aimed it at a rustling on the other side of the bed curtain. It was a reflexive action. The pistol wasn't loaded. "Giles?"

"He's not here." Fulke groped toward the fireplace and stubbed his toe against the big sideboard. " 'Od's blood!"

More shouting came from the street. This time Margaret definitely heard "Salvages." She threw back the curtain and fumbled for her shoes.

With Calvert in the lead and Fulke guarding their backs, Margaret and Mary and their maids approached the fort. Margaret clutched her wet cloak more tightly about her. Underneath she wore only her long wool shift with her pistol stuck in her narrow girdle. Bess carried her powder flask and shot pouch.

The buff-colored mud sucked at Margaret's pattens as she made her way among them. The freemen leaned on their gun rests. The women and a few children sat despondent and shivering on whatever they could find. Their wet hair clung to their faces and shoulders.

Joan Parke straddled an upturned log in the dooryard of a tiny house just inside the fort's gate. Her new master stood to one side as though trying to put distance between them. He looked stunned by the flame-haired folly he had bought.

"Be it heathens, your lordship?" Joan called out. "Come to murder us Christians in our sleep?"

"Someone hath raised the cry of salvages," Calvert answered.

"Knowest thou who saw them?" Margaret asked.

"Nay."

Henry Fleete and Robert Vaughan angled toward them. Giles, looking wretched from too much Madeira and too little sleep, trudged behind. His fowling piece rode horizontally across his shoulders. One wrist rested halfway along the barrel, the other just in front of the lock. His hands dangled in their wide, soiled cuffs. The gun was six feet long, and Giles was unconcerned that people had to step lively to avoid being hit by it.

Henry Fleete carried his old matchlock on his shoulder. He held it just above its swamped muzzle with the patched stock projecting over his back. Protruding from his belt was a plug bayonet fashioned from a broken sword blade. It was the sort used to stand off a charging boar or stag, but he obviously intended to employ it against two-footed prey. As he walked he stuck a feather-bedecked hatchet into his belt at the small of his back. Fleete wore muddy Indian shoes and he had adorned his sweat-stained, sugar-loaf hat with additional turkey feathers.

Vaughan's hat was at least as disreputable as Fleete's. A partisan knife with a twelve-inch blade and steel cheeks rode in a fringed case at his belt. Next to it hung the goat's-foot lever for the crossbow he carried. He had stowed the steel-tipped quarrels for the bow in a shaggy quiver made from a wolf's pelt with the paws dangling.

Vaughan and Fleete looked as outlandish to Margaret as any red child of the forest. Did this barbarous place turn civilized men wild or did it attract uncivilized men to begin with?

"Good morrow, mistresses." Vaughan grinned, as though Indian raids were a fine form of entertainment.

"God keep thee." Margaret regarded him aloofly. His good humor soured her own mood even more. She could tell from Giles's expression that he had lost at cards, no doubt to this ginger-haired wastrel.

Giles saw her scrutinizing him. He mumbled something about manning the flanks and went off after Calvert.

"Thinkst thou the salvages will attack, Captain Fleete?" Margaret asked. Fleete's shipboard romances of Indians had taken on relevance.

"Nay. Not here, Mistress Margaret. The red man is cunning and circumspect. He would rather surprise some isolate husbandman at work in his fields than face an enemy armed to oppose him."

"God be praised, because this . . ." With a wave of her hand she included both the rickety fortifications and Vaughan and his crossbow. ". . . appears scant protection."

"You do not place faith in my aim then?" Vaughan asked.

Margaret tried to detect mockery in his tone or his unnerving bottle-green eyes, but couldn't. "Archery has been quite abandoned in England these days, Sergeant Vaughan. Men have found noisier and more inventive ways to kill."

"That's true for pheasants and deer and such as do not return fire. But against the most elusive of animals, there is no better weapon than a bow."

"The salvages?"

"Some call them so, but they represent diverse nations. Nanticoke and Patuxent, Potomacks, Yoacomicos, Susquehannocks, Piscataway." He seemed to relish the shape of the words rolling about his lips and tongue.

" 'Tis a barbaric and uncivilized sort of warfare."

"*Silent enim leges inter arma,*" Vaughan said. " 'Laws are mute in times of war.' "

"Then thou'rt familiar with Cicero, Sir Lack-Latin. I scarce would have thought it."

Vaughan held open the door of the blockhouse and bowed to Margaret's rigid back as she strode inside. He was amused by her disapproval. He'd been disapproved of before by women of her class.

"Have you plans to court her, Rob?" Fleete asked.

"I think not."

"Then you have designs on her sister's estate? She is the more comely of the two."

"Heady wine can be found in homely casks, Henry." Vaughan

caught Anicah by the skirts as she tried to slip by him and into the blockhouse. "Only gentlefolk may enter here, me romp."

"I be looking for me sweetheart."

"Will I do?" He crowded her against the wall.

"Fie, sir. Away with ye." She put her hands on his leather coat and pushed. She was strong for her size, but she couldn't budge him. He laughed and she tried another tack.

"I like not splinters in me arse."

"I can recommend a sturdy log in another place."

"Nay, sir, I would find me friend."

"How looks your friend?"

"Tall, he be, and strong. And comely. Not like some." She cast him a slant-eyed look of disdain.

"Hot in the breech, are you?"

"Nay, kind sir. I wish to pray with him for the salvation of our souls."

"Praying with your knees heavenward, I'll warrant." Vaughan laughed. "And do you find our town exciting, Maid Anicah, what with attacks of red Indians?"

"It hasn't much to commend it. No proper bear garden nor theater, nor even a market cross." Anicah peered around him. "Martin!"

Martin broke into a run when he saw Vaughan looming over her. Anicah slipped under Vaughan's arm and bobbed in a hasty curtsy. She lifted her petticoats and hurried to meet Martin. He picked her up, bare, muddy feet and all and swung her in a wide arc. She threw her arms around his neck and kissed him.

"I searched for you everywhere." He set her down, but kept his arms around her. "I feared the salvages had stolen you."

"No need to fear that." She stood on tiptoe to murmur in his ear. " 'Twas me what raised the alarum."

"Anicah! They'll whip you if they find out."

"I wanted to kiss and hug ye, but me mistress watches me close." She waved at the miserable crowd huddled near the gate. "They'll all troop home anon and none the worse for it."

"Who's your mistress?"

"The alewife. I've been busy as a rat in a cheese loft at yon bousing ken." She took his hand and started toward the ordinary. "We can kiss care away by the embers whilst the alewife awaits the red men here."

"I cannot leave my master."

"Ye'll abide with the papist doctor then?"

"Aye. His plantation is at Mattapany, half a day's walk north of here."

Anicah dragged him toward a distant building sitting alone in a trampled yard.

"Where are we going?"

"I would lie with ye, bulkin, but I be no stargazer."

"Stargazer?"

"Hedge whore."

"My sweet Ani, you're no whore of any stripe."

Chapter 18

Anicah pushed the door open and peered inside. Martin looked over her head. In the pale predawn light they could see that the walls were the usual plastered timber and wickerwork. Rushes covered the earthern floor. A small table stood in front of the screen separating the low platform of the chancel from the nave.

Beyond the ranks of crude benches in the rear, Governor Calvert's pair of enclosed pews rose like fortified keeps. Four years ago they had arrived in sections with Maryland's first Gentleman Adventurers. Chin-high wainscoting enclosed the two narrow stalls, one on the women's side of the nave and one on the men's. Each had a gate and a wide, hinged seat folded up against the back. They represented the authority of Lord Baltimore and the Calvert family, but they looked ridiculously out of place in such rude surroundings.

" 'Tis a church house," Martin whispered.

"Aye." Anicah pulled him inside and shut the door. The wooden shutters were closed and the room became pitch-black. As they fumbled along the rough wall, dry straw rustled underfoot.

"We must not profane God's house." Martin felt doomed and helpless to do anything about it.

" 'Twere raised by breast-beaters. It counts not as holy."

"Even so . . ."

"Halloo, Your Honor. Good morrow t' Ye." Anicah's voice

sounded hollow in the empty building. She cocked her head, listening for God's reply. "He be not at home."

"We'll burn—" Martin tried to object, but Anicah slid her arms around his neck and pressed her soft lips against his.

Martin's muscles and sinews went limp, but his yard grew quite durable and nudged Anicah's hip. He sagged, pinning her against the wall. He felt her heart beating in rhythm with his as he fumbled at her skirts.

Still kissing him, she slid her hands down, untied the drawstring of his breeches and pushed them around his ankles. He managed to hook one side of her muddy hems and lift them. The hard shield of her pubic bone was pushing against his cock when they heard voices.

While he struggled with his breeches, Anicah dropped to the floor. She yanked him down beside her as the door creaked open and a robed silhouette loomed in the opening.

Anicah scrambled to the nearest pew. She opened the gate and crawled into the narrow stall, hauling Martin along by the collar. She closed the gate behind him.

"They'll find us." Martin was on his hands and knees with his head hanging disconsolately between his elbows. As much as he loved Anicah, he was beginning to realize that she tempted ruin in ways that would never have occurred to him.

Anicah knelt over him. She put both hands on the small of his back and threw her weight onto them, forcing him to sprawl full-length on the dirt floor. She braced her shoulder blades on the front partition, planted her feet in his side and shoved him under the pew. Then she rolled over to lie with her back pressed against his chest.

Light cavorted with shadow as pine torches were set in their iron cressets on the walls. Anicah and Martin heard the hubbub of voices and the rustle of straw as the chapel filled with people.

" 'Tisn't the Sabbath." Anicah was vexed at the Catholics. She counted on people being tediously predictable.

The murmur and the rustling grew into a low roar as though

a mob were converging. Anicah glanced up and saw that the shelflike seat was folded up. She eased it down and pushed harder against Martin.

Several men sat on the bench behind Calvert's pew. When they stuck the toes of their shoes into the narrow opening under the pew wall, they poked Martin in the back. The gate swung open and four pairs of mud-caked boots and eight paws shuffled past just beyond their noses. Anicah recognized the red ribbon rosettes on Giles Brent's boots. The seat creaked and shifted on its frame as Giles, Fulke and Leonard Calvert settled in. Anicah held her breath, waiting for the whole affair to break under their weight and dump them on top of her and Martin.

Giles's two dogs sank to the ground at his feet. The mastiff looked around his master's boots and seemed astonished to find the pew's cellar occupied. Anicah and Martin sucked in their stomachs to add an inch or so to the space separating them. When the mastiff opened his mouth it gaped wide enough to take in her head at a gulp. He curled back lips like slices of raw liver and exposed yellow teeth as long as Anicah's thumbs. He growled.

Giles nudged the dog with his boot, but he hardly noticed. With his head still at a right angle to his body he reared his hindquarters as though he'd run a badger to ground. He couldn't squeeze his broad shoulders between the columns of the men's legs, but he started barking.

"Damn me! Be quiet!" Giles's head was still throbbing from his celebration of the night before. He dug the toe of his boot into the dog's ribs and shoved. The mastiff lay back down, but he continued to watch Anicah and Martin, his lip twitching in an occasional snarl.

Behind the rood screen two priests began the morning litany in Latin. Martin didn't know who the first one was, but he was horrified to recognize Father Poulton's voice. Most of the Catholics prayed aloud or read their missals. Their Protestant servants gossiped at the rear of the church. Giles and Calvert discussed tobacco and beaver pelts sotto voce. In the second pew

Mary and Margaret clicked the beads of their rosaries and recited their Ave Marias and paternosters. The dogs fell asleep.

Anicah hadn't attended a religious service since her mother and aunt had sneaked her inside churches for warmth. She had never seen Catholics worship. She hadn't expected it to be so boring.

The curves of Anicah's body pressed against Martin finally seduced his misgivings. With the subtlest of touches they tantalized each other into pleasure that seemed to go on forever.

At last the urgency crested and drained away, leaving a blissful lassitude. Martin lay his head on the crook of his arm. With his other hand he picked the bits of straw from the tangle of Anicah's hair. He kissed the nape of her neck, then fell asleep.

He slept through the sermon. In it the priest thanked God for preserving the flock from the arrows of the heathens. He asked Him to bless the enterprises of the newly arrived Adventurers. He took up quite a lot of God's time, and His flock's too. The sun was well up now and everyone had a great deal to do. They stirred restlessly.

Anicah took her knife from her belt and cut the threads that fastened the rosette onto Giles's right boot. She wanted to take its twin, but knew that would be too suspicious. When he discovered one was missing he would think it merely lost.

Ye should've watched as well as prayed, Squire Brent, she thought. She tucked the ornament into her bodice. Lulled by the drone of the priest's voice she joined Martin in a nap.

Robert Vaughan jiggled his crotch to settle himself more comfortably in his baggy breeches. Then he continued his saunter around the mud holes of St. Mary's street. John Cockshott was likely to be away for a fortnight and his young wife had been in need of a physic for the green sickness, the malaise caused by chastity. Vaughan was always happy to provide it.

As he neared Smythe's ordinary, shrieks emanated from inside.

"Murder! The death of o' me!"

Vaughan pounded on the front door. He could hear running feet, the crash of furniture and more screaming. John Lewger came hustling up the street and the two men dashed around the house and burst through the back door. They hurried through the attached shed that served as the kitchen and into the common room.

Table boards and trestles lay strewn about. Goodwife Smythe made the air whistle with her hickory rod as she chased Anicah through the wreckage. Anicah's short doublet hung open. The drawstring that gathered the neck of her linen shift had come untied, allowing it to slide off one bony shoulder. A large bruise, bisected by a welt from the rod, was already darkening there. Another welt ran across her cheek.

"Kind sirs, I am kilt." Anicah collapsed in a heap at Vaughan's feet and wrapped her arms around his ankles. She shook all over as though with the ague, gave a piteous groan and sprawled in a swoon.

"Dissembling little scut." Goodwife Smythe drew back a foot to kick her but Lewger grabbed her around the waist and dragged her away.

Vaughan disengaged his feet and crouched to see if Anicah was alive. "Prithee, alewife, how came the wench to merit such ill use?"

"I am the one ill-used." Goody Smythe panted with exertion and rage. "The lazy trollop traipsed in halfway to noon with her clothes awry and the stench of lust about her."

Anicah moaned and fluttered her eyelids. She looked beseechingly up at Vaughan, her huge dark eyes brimming with tears. "I am dead," she sighed.

"Not yet." He helped her to her feet and guided her, limping and crying out in pain, to the ale bench.

"Goodwife Smythe," Lewger said. "We will not tolerate thy breaking of his lordship's peace, either in the conduct of thy business or in the chastisement of thy household."

"The saucy wretch is shamming." Goodwife Smythe was outraged. "I hardly laid wood to her."

Lewger took Goody Smythe aside, so as not to reproach her in front of her inferior. "Thou hast been warned before about keeping a disorderly house." He excelled at being stern. "Discipline thy maid as her faults merit, but do not think to injure her unduly."

Goody Smythe could barely swallow the retort quivering on her tongue. Her round, taut body looked about to explode with her outrage. She wound her hands into her apron, as though to keep from strangling whichever of the three of them came within reach.

"Aye, Squire Lewger."

"I trust neither Sheriff Vaughan nor I will have occasion to remonstrate with thee again."

"Nay, squire." She knew Lewger thought her establishment a nest of Protestant rebellion. He would relish an excuse to revoke her license to run it. She curtsied perfunctorily. "Let the gentlemen out, wench."

Anicah moved gingerly to lift the latch. She opened the door and stood aside, clinging to it for support. "God keep ye, kind sirs," she murmured.

"What is thy name?" Lewger asked.

"Anicah, yer honor."

"We tolerate no lewd or licentious behavior here, Maid Anicah."

"I'd never—"

Lewger held up an admonishing hand. "Thou must work hard and obey thy mistress's orders, else she is within her rights to strike thee to teach thee proper behavior."

"Aye, sir."

The men left and Anicah leaned against the door, pushing it closed with her weight. She was ready to bolt if her mistress came after her again. Goodwife Smythe glowered at her.

"No matter what that chicken-hammed lobcock Lewger says . . ." When Smythe shook the rod at Anicah it made an ominous whir. ". . . the next time you steal away or disobey or play the impudent knave with me, I shall whip you till you bleed at the nose and ears."

The door opened, bumping Anicah in the back. Robert Vaughan poked his head inside. "I have a spark in my throat, Goodwife. . . ."

"We can extinguish no sparks until ten of the clock, Sergeant Vaughan." Goody Smythe smirked at him. "By order of the governor and Secretary Lewger."

Vaughan withdrew his head and closed the door behind him.

Still watching her mistress warily, Anicah edged around the room, picking up fallen table boards and trestles as she went.

"When thou hast set things to right here," Goody Smythe said, "grind the guinea wheat as I instructed thee yesterday."

"Guinea wheat?"

"Indian corn, thou ignorant heathen." Smythe shook the rod again. "Thou'rt good for nothing, but if a wench be but comely, men will cavil before her."

Still grumbling, she put on her cloak and left. As soon as she had gone, Anicah began singing cheerfully. She had discovered another marvelous advantage of her position here. The ordinary was not situated like a planter's house at the head of some isolated creek where a mistress could beat her servants to death and no one the wiser.

Chapter 19

Margaret, Mary, and Leonard Calvert stood on a high bluff a mile or so south of St. Mary's. They were enjoying the day, mild for December. Below them the St. George's River glittered like quicksilver. The late afternoon sun ignited incandescent spikes on the water's surface.

"Methinks they resemble fallen stars," Margaret said.

"Such a lovely form for angels to take," Mary murmured.

"Angels, Mistress Mary?" Calvert asked.

"This would make a splendid site for the manor house." Margaret had developed the knack of diverting attention from her sister's strange remarks.

"I would suggest farther inland, Mistress Margaret."

"Why, prithee?"

Calvert put a finger to his lips and nodded toward the jut of land to the south. Margaret listened and heard a faint noise like the creaking axles on a farm wagon. Then several dozen axles. Then a multitude of them. The first of the birds appeared above the trees in the distance. Before long the sky was dark with them. They circled before settling in a strident, restless raft.

"Ducks." Calvert raised his voice to be heard. "And geese."

The cacophony made conversation difficult.

"We shall resume our tour on the morrow," Margaret shouted.

She was tired. Rather than trust Calvert's wobbly canoe, she had insisted on walking to the Jesuits' plantation at St. Inigoes, five miles to the south. The path through the forest and bramble-filled ravines had been marked only by chips hewn from trees as big around as a castle's tower. Even then they had had to cross St. Inigoes Creek in a smaller canoe than Calvert's, while Margaret clung to the gunwales and Mary recited her rosary.

Margaret and Mary followed Calvert toward the small house Calvert had offered them until their own was built on the eighty acres due them. The house stood at the edge of a hastily cleared field, the girdled trees rising gaunt from the stubble. From the dooryard Margaret could hear dissension inside. Bess Guest was at odds with Mary Lawne, the wench whose term of indenture Margaret had bought.

Margaret expected trouble from her. She was Protestant to begin with and impertinent besides. She had pale yellow hair, a plump pair of breasts always poised to leap from her low-cut bodice, and a pugnacious set to her wide jaw.

Margaret pushed the door open and the quarreling stopped abruptly. She walked into a cloud of dust from the mattress sacks the maids had been beating.

"God keep you." The four maids curtsied. Bess sneezed into her apron.

Margaret glared at them. "Take the pallets outside to shake them. And do not drag them on the wet ground."

"Aye, mistress." They paired off, each lifting an end of a sack and wrestling it toward the door.

Calvert's people had cleared out most of the lumber and tools stored here, but the odor of mildew and dust and carelessly tanned beaver pelts remained. Margaret turned slowly, inspecting the room that would be her home for the next few months.

Calvert had ordered fresh rushes laid on the earthen floor, but blackened spiderwebs hung from the log rafters. Dust had already begun to settle on Margaret's furniture.

Her old curtained bedstead took up one side of the room. Even stacked on top of each other, the chests and benches, stools, table boards, trestles, and a carved sideboard filled the rest.

"What of the freeman who lived here, Governor? Did he claim his landright and build his own house?"

"Nay." Calvert let a few moments pass. "He did not survive the seasoning, but died of a fever."

The maids tussled the mattress sacks up the ladder to the cockloft. The split logs laid across the rafters shifted as they walked on them, and dirt drifted down through the wide cracks.

Mary Lawne backed down the ladder first. "Mistress, I shall fetch some wood." She hurried out.

"I must apologize again for the disorder," Calvert said. "The want of laborers and the exigencies of the sot weed . . ." He sighed. "It's like no other crop for the labor required."

"We expected inconveniences, Governor."

Bess began ransacking the trunks in search of bed linens while the two younger maids tilted at the cobwebs with their brooms. Mary Lawne's offer to haul wood suddenly struck Margaret as odd. It wasn't like the wench to volunteer for work.

She threw her cloak over her shoulders and went outside. She wasn't surprised to hear voices from behind the woodpile. Mary Lawne gave a squeak of alarm when she saw her and darted away, snatching up kindling on the run.

"I shall deal with thee later," Margaret called after her. "You!" She pointed at the man who was trying to sneak away. "Who are you and what brings you here?"

"James Courtney, freeman and planter." Courtney was presentable enough in a shabby, sorrowful way. He was the sort whose middling good looks made a promise of prosperity that he probably would not keep. "I was searching for a lost hog and stopped to ask your maid if she had seen it."

"If thou hast business here, Goodman Courtney, it shall be with me."

"As you wish, mistress." He touched his hat brim and walked quickly away.

In spite of the gathering darkness the noise of the ducks and geese drew Margaret to the edge of the bluff. The view stunned

her. Birds filled the river from bank to bank. Behind the black
lacework of bare branches across the river, the sky glowed orange.
She stared at it until the color faded to a muddy yellow.

When she turned back toward the house an Indian emerged
silent as a ghost from the trees not twenty feet away. She wanted
to call for help, but the word lodged in her throat like a bone.

He was slender and taller than an Englishman. His black hair
was knotted over his right ear and decorated with feathers and
beads. He wore a mantle of animal pelts and a leather breechclout.
He carried an old Dutch matchlock of the sort called a bastard because of its shorter barrel length and smaller bore.

He held out a pair of furred gray ears linked by a strip of hide.
He looked young behind his fierce dark scowl, and maybe even
comely. Margaret jumped when someone spoke and the boy's
mouth didn't move.

"Ah, my dear Margaret, thou hast met Anansine." In his black
robe, the tiny, gray-haired priest blended with the night that had
already collected among the trees. He finally freed his sleeve from
the bramble that held it.

"Father White." Margaret had met the Jesuit that morning at
St. Inigoes. She wanted to weep with relief. "I didn't know he
was one of thine."

"He is not yet, though we have hopes of bringing him to the
light. However, he hath agreed to hunt for thee, if thou so desirest."

Only then did Margaret notice that the boy was wearing the
plaid Scottish stockings Captain Fleete said were so popular in the
Indian trade. Beaded garters with red yarn tassels held them in
place below his knees.

"What does he hunt?"

"Red deer and bear for thy table. Hares and turkeys and diverse other creatures equally savory."

"In what currency is he paid?"

"He accepts as wages any of the fripperies supplied for the
trade with his people. The reward for the killing of a wolf is two
yards of duffel for a matchcoat, however."

"Are these a wolf's ears?"

"Yes." Father White bowed and smiled apologetically. "I would like to visit, but we must hurry to reach St. Mary's before the light is completely gone." He made the sign of the cross. "God keep you in His care." He picked up the skirts of his cassock, the better to navigate the dark, uneven ground. He left, with Anansine leading the way.

The great sagging gulley in the center of the bed annoyed Margaret. She wanted to roust her sleeping sister, find the wooden bed screw hidden somewhere among the contents of the chests, fling back the mattresses and tighten the rope mesh underneath.

Patience, she thought. Patience is the virtue I most lack.

Plans and lists of tasks churned in her mind. This journey had disrupted the rhythm of the seasons. By this time in the fall her men should be laying down straw and dung that would change into a rich dressing for the fields in the spring. She should be mixing medicinal cordials and herbals in the still room. The new cider should be singing in the cellar, bubbling and hissing as it fermented.

But there was no cellar here. No barn or brew house, no wash house, bake house, kitchen or stable. No great hall, littered with sleeping hounds and squirming piles of kittens, where as a child she had played at shovel board on rainy days.

She thought the sense of loss, of abandonment and hopelessness that swept over her would carry away her will to persevere in this mad endeavor. She stared into the darkness, her lids and the inside of her nostrils burning.

"Raphael watches over us," Mary said softly.

"The Archangel?"

"Yes. He says that the good spirits here are more numerous than the bad."

From the loft overhead came the chime of the maids' metal-tipped points being unlaced from their bodices. The dry corn husks in their mattresses rustled as they settled under their covers. They whispered to each other and laughed softly.

"Maids to bed and cover coal," Bess sang.

> *"Let the mouse out of her hole;*
> *Crickets in the chimney sing*
> *Whilst the little bell doth ring.*
> *If fast asleep, who can tell,*
> *When the clapper hits the bell?"*

The wolves' song woke Margaret much later. She lay rigid with fright, listening to the eerie keening, the call and response. They sounded so close. She didn't sleep again that night.

Chapter 20

Outside, a chill wind moaned around the splintery corners of Smythe's ordinary. Inside, a few of St. Mary's middling sort sat on the bench against the wall. A rank steam rose from their wool breeches and leather jerkins. Most of them were laborers who had only recently completed their four-year terms of indenture.

Even in January the work of clearing fields and building fences and shelter continued, but at least the tobacco crop had been cut, cured, stripped and packed into hogsheads. The meager celebrations of the Nativity season had ended. The men were taking their morning pint and pipe with the grim resolution of those who knew that months of bitter weather were just beginning and there was nothing they could do to speed them along.

In the kitchen Dina the cook was preparing hominy gruel. The sausage-shaped turnspit dog had been trotting for two hours inside the wheel-like cage on the public room's hearth. He was flagging in spite of the live coals Goody Smythe put inside to keep him moving. As the roast revolved drops of fat sizzled in the flames.

Anicah pushed open the kitchen door with her foot and walked into the taunting aroma of roasting meat, something she didn't often smell here. She carried a stack of firewood so high she held the top faggot in place with her chin. Flakes of snow sparkled in her hair. Robert Vaughan followed her in. He palmed two great handfuls of her petticoats and squeezed the taut pair of haunches underneath.

"Fie, sirrah, away." She laughed and shook her hips to dislodge him. "Ye wrong me."

He squeezed her waist with his hands and nibbled her earlobe. "I would wrong you till you warbled like a lark, sweet maid."

"What kept you, you lazy baggage?" Goody Smythe thundered.

"The wood was frozen, mistress." Anicah dropped the kindling on the hearth with a loud rattle. "Like yer own black heart," she muttered.

Her ear tingled where Robert's teeth had nipped it. The throbbing repeated itself in the cleft where her thighs met. The lingering pressure of his fingers made her long for Martin. She thought she would die if she could not wrap her legs and arms around him and press hard against him.

When she went into the public room she recognized the greasy leather cap of the man sitting in the shadow of the chimney corner.

"Harry! Bondsmen aren't allowed here."

"I drink where I will." Harry's mouth gave the twitch that served him as a smile. "I be a freeman."

"And I the Virgin Mary!"

"So must ye be then."

"Ye bought yer convenant?"

"Aye."

"How?"

He merely glanced up at her from the corner of his yellow eye, and she knew she would get no more information from him.

She laid a few logs on the fire. The turnspit dog, his short legs churning furiously, whined and stared at her. She pried a bit of beef off the roast with her fingernail and fed it to him while Goody Smythe was looking the other way.

"Before the papists arrive allow me to stand a bumper for all true believers here." A man rose up from his seat near the fire.

He looked not yet thirty and he wore his yellow hair longer

than the bowl-shaped Puritan style. He was fashionably dressed, broad-shouldered, narrow-hipped and fair of face, except for watery blue eyes set close together under a brow that hung a trifle too low.

"He's Richard Ingle," Smythe murmured to Vaughan. "Master of the pinnace riding at anchor in the harbor."

Robert Vaughan sat down across from Master Ingle while Smythe made the introductions.

"This is my first visit to your fair province," Ingle confided, "and I see 'twould be an Eden were it not for the heretic snakes that rule it."

From across the room Goodwife Smythe grunted in agreement. If she had her way no papist posterior would warm a seat in her establishment. But she saw more business after the Catholics' monthly service than the rest of the days combined, so she tolerated them, but with ill grace.

"I am drinking with those who hold for the restoration of Parliament," Ingle said. "Wilt thou share a bowl with me, Sergeant Vaughan?"

"I'll drink with the devil if he pays the score."

"A health to the foes of tyranny and false religion." Ingle held up his bowl.

"Drinking with the devil and drinking to the devil are different propositions," Vaughan said. "It has been my experience that those who rail loudest against tyrants would replace them with their own tyranny."

"Truth is no tyranny."

"Truth is the greatest tyrant and a mummer besides, wearing many masks." Vaughan blew a kiss to Anicah when she delivered his pipe. "You have trucked in New England, where the Puritans hold sway, have you not, Master Ingle?"

"Aye."

"Is it true a man may be whipped for kissing a wench on the street there?"

"Certes. But the maidens kiss the kinder behind doors."

"Give me none of a religion that forbids kissing."

"And how canst thou, a Protestant, consort with popish sinners and heretics?" Ingle asked.

"As our dear and departed virgin queen Bess so aptly observed," Vaughan said cordially, " 'There is only one Jesus Christ. The rest is but a dispute over trifles.' "

Anicah stood on tiptoe and peered through the crack in the shutter. "The swells approach," she called out.

As she watched the Catholic gentry and their servants approach, her feet danced a little jig all on their own. She was about to begin acquiring the means to buy her indenture and Martin's. She had arranged with Henry Fleete to help him cheat Giles Brent by signaling the cards Brent held. Fleete said Brent was a fool and easily gulled, but sharking gentry was quite a career advance for her. She ran her fingers through the tangles of her hair.

Goodman Smythe tugged his waistcoat over his paunch. He hawked and spit onto the floor. When the door opened he made an elaborate spiral with his hand and arm, as though doffing and twirling a plumed hat.

"Welcome, kind sirs and gentle ladies. We have beef on the spit and stories to spice it."

The gentlewomen and their maids laughed and exclaimed as they warmed their hands at the fire. They sipped the mulled wine Anicah brought them and showered Richard Ingle with questions about affairs in England. After devouring trenchers of beef and hominy gruel, they collected their cloaks and hats and muffs. Margaret Brent stared at Anicah before she followed the others toward the door.

Mistress Margaret's unwavering gaze always unnerved Anicah. She turned away from it with a bounce of her petticoat tails and gathered up the empty bottles and bowls from the table they had just abandoned.

As she passed Robert Vaughan he put an arm around her waist. "When shall we enjoy a flourish together, my roaring girl?"

"On St. Geoffrey's Day." She relished his teasing and his

kisses and the rough caress of his big, callused hands, but as she had reminded him many times, she was betrothed to another.

"Brent!" Fleete waved his cards. "What do you say to a game of two-handed put?"

"I say aye if I deal first."

Fleete handed him the deck with a bow. As Giles shuffled he made sure the high cards weren't marked.

"Shall I turn out my clothes to discover fugitive honors concealed within?" Fleete pretended to be aggrieved at his lack of trust.

"Nay, Henry, but I shall watch you well."

"Shall we wager beaver skins, shells, the sot weed or the king's portrait?" Fleete held up a half-crown, useful for pocket expenses, but more of a keepsake here than a form of currency. The same coins passed back and forth so often that people recognized them individually by their nicks and wear.

"Silver." Giles dealt them each three cards. He settled back to enjoy the game and Henry's usual performance.

" 'Od's wounds!" Henry's eyes flew wide open. "Damn me! Who'd not put at such cards!" He leaned across the table. "What will ye lay on the game?"

"What you dare." Giles's sardonic smiled never flickered.

"A shilling," Henry said finally.

"Two."

"You'll stay then?"

"Aye."

The two of them laid out their cards. Giles's were worth more. Henry groaned and chalked his loss onto the tabletop.

"What shall ye pour down yer bores, squires?" Anicah smiled down at Giles.

"Did yon ship's master deliver Madeira?" Giles nodded toward Richard Ingle.

"Aye."

"I'll have that."

Anicah leaned down to whisper loudly in Giles's ear. "Be ye

fly to St. Giles's Greek, squire?" She asked it even though she knew from her encounter with him in Bristol that he spoke the thieves' cant.

"I'm awake to the flash."

"Cap'n Fleete's a cozening cove," she said, loudly enough for Fleete to hear. "He'll shark ye if ye hug not your books to yer brisket." She put a hand around Giles's and pushed his cards closer to his chest.

"Away with you, trollop." Fleete lobbed an empty bowl at her but she sidestepped and caught it neatly.

For the next hour Anicah hovered solicitously near Giles. While she surreptitiously held up fingers signifying the value of his cards, he volleyed jests with her. He squeezed whatever part of her was closest and watched Henry Fleete's clumsy attempts at subterfuge. Giles lost steadily.

On the ale bench the old man, Original Brown, had taken advantage of Ingle's generosity. He'd been downing pints of cider as fast as Anicah brought them to him.

"I shall catch a red bird for his lordship," he announced. "And he shall pay me handsomely. I'll fart a gentleman's farts."

Brown's voice rose along with the cider in his belly, until Giles turned to stare at him. Anicah bent down to whisper in Giles's ear.

"Be ye easy with him, squire, for his wits be moon-raking." She rolled her big dark eyes and tapped her temple. "In Virginia, in the starving time, he did slay and boil a salvage with roots and herbs. 'Tis said the taste of it so liked him he butchered his wife and cured her parts."

Giles cocked one agile brow but didn't raise his eyes from his cards. "Supping on pottage of salvage and salting a wife are but pecadillos compared with interrupting a gentleman's game."

Robert Vaughan stood up and collected his hat and cloak. "Brent, we're retiring to the governor's house to mix business with brandy. Do join us."

Giles smiled graciously in defeat as he gathered up the cards.

"Being so recently arrived, Henry, my commercial ventures are but newly set in motion—"

Fleete waved his hand. "Vowel me the sum."

"I.O.U. six shillings." Giles repeated it loudly enough for witnesses to hear.

He and Vaughan, Fleete and Ingle, went out as a black man in tobacco-brown breeches and doublet and cloak entered.

"What will ye have, Sir Blueskin?" Anicah was fascinated by Mathias DaSousa's wide, flat nose, flaring nostrils, swollen lips and the satiny sheen of his dark skin.

"Ale." He hooked his cloak and sugarloaf hat on a peg and warmed his hands at the fire. "I come from the Jesuits' plantation at Mattapany, Maid Anicah."

"Ye've seen Martin there?"

"Aye."

"How fares he?"

"His heart is in his hose, so all in despair is he."

"Fie, and why would that be?"

"For love of a maid, I'll wager."

For the rest of the day Anicah daydreamed about buying passage with Martin on Ingle's ship and returning to Bristol. She had no idea of what they would do there, but she pictured herself sitting happily with him in front of their own fire.

Night had arrived early and bitter cold when Goody Smythe sent Anicah out for one last armload of wood. The full moon shone like an old pewter platter. Anicah stared north, at the vast forest lying between St. Mary's and Mattapany. The path through it had been only faintly worn by Indian feet. The blazes that Englishmen cut on the trunks were often scratched over by bears. Panthers screamed in the depths from time to time. Much as Anicah longed to see Martin, she dared not attempt the journey.

A wolf howled and Anicah hurried in the kitchen door and slid the bolt behind her. Using the faint glow of coals for light, she stacked the wood on the hearth. She ran her hand around the bottom of the big kettle in search of congealed hominy. She unlaced her shoes, laid her thin wool cloak in the warm ashes, and rolled up in it. The turnspit dog curled tight against the hollow of her chest. A cold wind blew through the wide crack under the door and across the floor. Shivering, Anicah longed for Martin's warmth until she fell asleep.

Night lifted like a heavy black cloth pulled slowly from a lark's domed cage, leaving a band of carnelian light at the horizon. At the base of the bluff a great wedge of shadow stretched almost to the water's edge. Margaret and Mary and their maid, Mary Lawne, picked their way across St. Mary's landing. A crust of dirty ice munched under their feet.

"Sergeant Vaughan!"

"Good morrow, Mistress Margaret." Vaughan held the stern of a battered, thirty-foot-long hollowed log. John Price, the muster master of the fort at St. Inigoes, sat in the bow. Mildewed canvas covered the heap of goods in the waist of the boat.

Margaret noted, again, how extravagantly unkempt Robert Vaughan was. The slight misalignment of his eyes gave him such a roguish look she could easily imagine him at the helm of a pillaging corsair.

"We shall accompany thee to St. Inigoes, Sergeant. I will pay thee for thy services."

"If I remember a-right, mistress, you have referred to the canoe as a swine trough."

"I did, and it is." Margaret peered at the black slime in the bottom. A trick of the predawn light made it look as though the canoe had no bottom, and that to step into it would be to disappear into a fetid abyss. "I must ask the gunsmith to put sights on my pistols. And my sister and I wish an interview with Father White." Margaret still couldn't bring herself to utter aloud the word "confession," the deed had been proscribed for so long.

Margaret gestured for Mary Lawne to hand Robert the cush-

ions of waxed cloth. "There . . ." She pointed with the butt of
her pistol. "Set two behind Captain Price and one astern."

"Your brothers would not approve." Vaughan smiled wryly.

"I do not always approve of their activities either."

Vaughan climbed back out to lift the two Marys aboard. Mary
Lawne tried to resist, but Margaret held her firmly and gave her a
look more terrifying than the prospect of drowning. The women
lowered themselves cautiously onto the cushions, trying to keep
their petticoat hems from the bilge.

Margaret sat in front of Vaughan. She had been looking for a
chance to talk with him in private. Vaughan and Price paddled in
silence while the light of the unrisen sun tinted the trees a silvery
beige. Beyond the harbor's mouth, floating birds covered the
river. Margaret gripped the gunwales tightly, dropped her chin to
her chest and squeezed her eyes shut. Mary Lawne screamed.

The canoe nosed into the flock, and the ducks and geese rose
in a roar of wings, like an army of muskets firing at once. A column of birds took to the air in the boat's path. They circled in a
noisy cloud, then settled back behind the canoe in a vortex that
flapped Margaret's hood about her face.

The men paddled steadily, and finally the noise and wind re-
ceded, like a tempest passing. Margaret opened her eyes.

"What goods doth thou carry?" she asked.

"Provisions for Inigoes Fort and the Jesuit plantation there,"
Vaughan said. "Indian corn, several flitches of bacon. Powder and
shot from Virginia. Also trucking goods for the priests' trade with
the Indians."

"What sorts of items do the salvages desire?"

"Stroud cloth. The color red strikes their fancy most. Axes,
hatchets, knives, hoes. Fripperies such as horn combs, glass beads
and hawk bells." Vaughan paddled in silence a few moments.
"Eventually, too many English traders will involve us in some fa-
tal quarrel with the Indians."

"Why thinkest thou so?"

"Some men introduce spiritous liquors amongst them. They take advantage of the salvages' appetite for it to cheat them."

"The colonies do attract idlers and odd-job men," Margaret said. "Felons and wild youths sent here for taming. Some who've lost their credit and others who've lost their wits."

"I count myself among the latter." Vaughan laughed ruefully.

"I'm told that March begins the trucking season," Margaret said. "I'm prepared to put up surety with the governor for a license to trade with the Indians. I would engage you as factor."

"My own affairs greatly occupy me."

"I would provide the goods and fathoms of shell beads . . . how is it called?"

"Wampum. The purple is called peak, the white roanoke."

"We would divide the profits after his lordship's percentage is subtracted."

"I prefer a fee to a share." Vaughan didn't mention that so far the Indian trade had yielded almost no profits to divide.

"A fee it is then."

"My fee is glassware."

"I beg pardon?"

"Master Skinner said that you contracted with him to transport glassware on his next voyage."

"You jest." She turned again to study him with those eyes gray as a gathering storm.

"No, madam. I ask only the hollow-ware."

Margaret pictured the hovel that he called Vaughan's Vanity. During every high wind it shed shingles and clapboards as a hen molted feathers. Giles had described the disorder inside, and Giles hardly recognized disorder when he saw it. Certainly Vaughan would not be hosting a banquet of the sort that required goblets.

"Two pieces," she said.

"Two dozen."

"They were given to my grandmother by the virgin queen herself."

"My fee is but the loan of them."

"I cannot have you arriving at my door demanding glassware when it suits you."

"May I suggest Captain Fleete as a candidate for factoring."

"I would not trust him, with his tales of a cock and a bull." The silence that followed pulsed with Margaret's irritation. "Twelve pieces," she said finally. "And you must give me notice."

"Twenty-four. And I shall ask the use of them but once."

Margaret brooded awhile longer. "Done," she said.

Vaughan grinned and held out his palm. "Strike me."

She looked at his hand, then glowered up at him. She was insulted, but amused too at such a common and distinctly masculine gesture. At last she slapped his hand much harder than she needed to strike the bargain.

"Squire Cornwaleys is the best man to supply trucking goods." Vaughan's voice held no hint of triumph.

"Some have dubbed Thomas Cornwaleys a most unconscionable extortioner for the price he puts on his goods." Margaret turned to look at Vaughan again. One corner of her wide, thin mouth hitched up into an ironic smile. "But I see that another rogue deserves the title."

"The Lord of Misrule, at your service." Vaughan managed a gallant bow while still paddling.

Chapter 21

In early February, during the longest, blackest nights of winter, the Catholics celebrated light. Dozens of pine torches flared along the rough walls of the chapel. People owned few candles to be blessed at Candlemas, but they brought the fat pine slivers and peeled rushes they would burn to brighten the darkness. Baskets and bundles of them were stacked around the altar table.

In spite of the torches and the braziers and muffs and foot warmers, the gentlefolk shivered beneath their wool cloaks and lap robes. The servants and common sort quaked under thin blankets and sacking. Margaret's breath formed clouds in the icy air, but she hardly noticed the cold.

In the altar lamp burned the last of the perfumed oil the Brents had brought on the ship. From behind the rood screen the chanted Latin of the mass mingled with the murmur of prayers and muted coughs and rustlings of the congregation. The women's voices provided a descant to the men's, and all combined in a drone behind Margaret's thoughts.

On the communion table stood the silver chalice and paten. Inside a small wooden tabernacle lay the splinter of the true cross that the Jesuit Thomas Copley had brought from Spain. A plaster angel adorned the rood screen. Its face was serene, only its chipped nose hinted at the abuse it had survived. All the sacred relics had been rescued from theft and destruction and hidden, sometimes for generations.

For a hundred years the English government had deemed the looting and defacing of Catholic churches an act of piety. Protestants bought estates, titles and lucrative offices with stolen Catholic gold and silver plate. They converted monasteries and convents to manor houses.

Margaret remembered the abandoned Catholic church near her family's manor house. Her parents said it had been beautiful once, with stained-glass windows, a carved chancel rail and ornate rood screen and pews. Margaret had seen only the ruins. Weeds grew from the crumbling blocks of limestone. Creepers covered the south wall. Sheep cropped the grass around it, hogs rooted up the dead in the adjacent cemetery, and a huge dung heap rose in the yard.

This was the first time Margaret had openly celebrated Candlemas and the purification of the Virgin Mary since she had studied in Liège twenty-five years ago. In spite of this chapel's crudely plastered walls, dusty beams and simple benches, it looked as grand as a cathedral to her.

She closed her eyes, but the glow of the torches passed through the delicate skin of her eyelids. She felt as though the light were radiating from within her. Her voice and Mary's entwined in the soaring polyphony of the psalm, the harmony raw and untrained and magnificent. The song of adoration enveloped her, permeated her. For this privilege she would have endured that terrible voyage here again and again. She swayed as she sang and tears ran down her cheeks.

The Smythes' cook, Dina, stood in the fireplace stirring the corn and water and wood ashes. The stars burned cold in the black square of sky capping the chimney above her. In spite of February outside, sweat glistened on her round face, dark as molasses. Her husband was a former indentured servant, one of the few freemen able to pay the fees to acquire the land due him. Dina wore his cast-off woollen doublet over her patched linen blouse. Layers of tattered wool skirts enlarged her sturdy frame. Her oversized men's shoes were gray with ashes.

She hummed a melancholy tune that resembled none Anicah had ever heard. She wrapped a rag around her chapped hand and pulled the iron trammel and soot-enameled kettle over the coals. Goodwife Smythe had not asked her to cook for weeks and Anicah was happy to see her back now.

The winter had pushed the Smythes to the brink of ruin and Anicah with them. The freemen's elected representatives, the burgesses, would gather soon for the February sitting of the Assembly. Some of them at least would be forced to rent Goody Smythe's filthy pallets and pay for her meager meals. Dina's presence gave Anicah hope of more food to filch and of a better quality.

In the public room Goodman Smythe lay on the ale bench, his girth overhanging the bench's sides. He snored like an ox being throttled. He was one of the reasons the bottles of wine and the barrels of beer and hard cider were empty.

While Dina scrubbed the utensils with ashes, Anicah crouched in the hearth with a piece of sacking over her shoulders. She stared into the flames and scratched the mangy back of the turnspit. The dog's back leg jittered madly. A large brown rat scuttled behind the water barrel. Anicah eyed it hungrily.

On one meal a day of samp and crumbly corn cakes cooked in the ashes, Anicah hauled wood and water and buckets of river sand for the floors. Driven by Goody Smythe's hickory stick she scrubbed and swept and scoured, but she could see no use in it. Dust drifted from the rafters and blew through the cracks in the shutters. Men tracked in mud and dung. Soot formed a gritty coating on everything.

Anicah tilted her face closer to the heat and shut her eyes so that even her lids could absorb the warmth. "I ne'er thought to pass a winter next to a hearth nor under a roof."

"In Jamaica we needed no fire to warm ourselves. The sun burned like a furnace."

"Be that where ye're from?"

"Aye."

"I be out of Bristol."

"Is it a fair country?"

"Wondrous fair." Anicah felt a gust of nostalgia for the foul streets her memory had refurbished considerably. "Me and me mates went to baitings and revels every day. And every fortnight a market or ale." She sighed.

"But had ye gentlemen a-wooin' of ye such as here?"

"I count not running up on the serving wenches as wooing."

A loud thudding on the street door sent the turnspit dog into a frenzy of yipping. Anicah picked up Goody Smythe's cudgel and carried it through the dark public room. Dina followed, holding the big skillet in both hands. The dog, with his tail between his legs, slunk after them. Goodman Smythe went on snoring.

Anicah peered through the latch hole but could see only the midsection of a leather doublet so greasy it reflected the light from a pine torch. "Who be ye?"

"Those two most excellent friends, Phintias and Damon."

"We brave English spirits have a burning in our bores that only beer will quench," a second voice added. Both men giggled.

"Sergeant Vaughan and Squire Brent be foxed again," Anicah muttered to Dina. She called through the latch hole. " 'Tis late and we know no Damon here, nor Phintias neither."

Vaughan started singing.

> *"To make good sport,*
> *I fart and snort,*
> *And blow the candles out so.*
> *The maids I kiss,*
> *They shriek, 'Who's this?'*
> *I answer naught, but 'Ho, ho, ho.' "*

He bellowed the "Ho, ho, ho."

"Ye'll roust the village and bring old spider-shanks Lewger down on us as a hawk on a hare."

"Secretary Lewger is a shapeless pile of excrement," Vaughan said enthusiastically.

Anicah lifted the bolt, opened the door a crack and glared around it. She had been looking forward to pulling her coarse coverlet close to the hearth and falling asleep with the dog before the embers cooled.

"Damn me. 'Tis cold as a whore's heart." Vaughan pushed his way in, stamping mud and exhaling clouds of alcohol fumes. "Ah, my nut-brown wench and my ebony doll." He doffed his hat with extravagant courtesy, although Dina had already gone to the fireplace and was blowing up the coals.

"Great hogen-mogen, I'm drunk," Giles roared. "I'm porterly drunk."

Anicah stood with her hands on her hips.

"Such a dark and tempesty look," Vaughan said.

"Intent on wakin' the dead, were ye?" she growled.

As Giles went by, he put an arm around her waist and kissed her quickly on the mouth. The kiss left a whiff of the rosewater in his beard and the brandy on his breath.

Vaughan kicked a chair from under the table by the hearth and dropped onto it. Anicah tried to sidle away, but he caught her skirts and hauled her closer. "Deliver us bumpers of the alewife's cider."

"Only lees to be had."

"Don't tweak me, my pullet. Your mistress brewed forty barrels."

"Mayhap. Yet none remains. 'Twere drunk during Twelfth-night or spilled or hocussed. Pissed away in any case."

"Passing strange." Vaughan rose and wandered into the kitchen in search of the vanished cider. Anicah could hear his rumble of a voice and Dina's husky laugh.

Anicah circled to put the table between herself and Giles, but he leaped from the chair onto and across it and crashed down on the other side. For a man in high boots with such enormous cuffs he was surprisingly agile. He overturned benches and stools until he cornered her by the chimney.

"You know you want to be doing, wench."

"Have pity, sirrah," she said. "Me master'll beat me fer a drab."

Giles glanced over at Smythe who grunted, mumbled in his sleep and turned onto his side so he faced the wall.

"I think not." He fumbled with the knots of his breeches' points. "I will have some Spanish tail this night."

"Brent." Robert supported himself on the door frame and peered into the dark room. "For once the wench tells the truth. The barrel's dry." He caught Giles by the skirt of his doublet and hauled him backward toward the door. "We'll knock up Squire Cornwaleys. He always has apple brandy hidden away."

"Thomas Cornwaleys is so refined," Giles giggled, "he probably pisses brandy."

Anicah closed the door behind them and barred it hastily. All was silent outside except for a barking dog and the sound of Giles's laughter and Vaughan's shouts of "Ho, ho, ho." She draped a blanket over the tapster before she banked the fire. She had had to use a fire tong to break the ice in the water barrel this morning and it was colder than that now. Smythe might freeze where he lay.

Chapter 22

A skull-rattling din jolted Margaret awake. She sat bolt upright in bed, certain that the house's single room was full of turkeys. The bedlam started as it had since the beginning of March. About an hour before dawn the first tom gargled out a challenge from his roost on the chimney. The chimney amplified the call and funneled it into the room. In the forest to the east a second bird started, then a third, and then thousands, until the noise made thought difficult and conversation impossible.

Margaret glanced at the other half of the bed. The covers were neatly pulled up. Mary had already risen to perform her morning devotions to the Blessed Virgin. Margaret crossed herself and hastily recited the paternoster.

She threw aside the bed curtain and stepped into her old shoes, neatly lined up on the dirt floor. Draping her cloak around her shoulders, she picked up one of her pistols. She hurried out into the clamor and peered up at the hunched form, black against the gray sky.

She measured powder from her brass flask, poured it into the pistol's flared muzzle, dropped the ball in and rammed a wad of cloth on top of it. She poured priming powder into the flash pan, slid the cover in place, and blew off the excess grains. She drew back the cock until the catch clicked, then adjusted the frizzen so its lower edge hovered over the pan. If all went as it should, the arms and levers of the trigger mechanism would drop the flint onto the steel frizzen and send a shower of sparks into the pan, igniting the powder and exploding it into the touchhole.

Usually the gun fired once every two or three tries, but today it went off with a loud report. The tom pitched forward into the chimney. The other turkeys leaped for the sky with a great shout and an explosion of wings, then plummeted to the ground.

When Margaret went back inside the house, one of the maids was dressing Mary's hair by the light of a burning rush and another sweeping the stone slab of the hearth. Bess was retrieving the carcass from the ashes so she could build the morning fire. She had to hold the forty-pound bird off the ground with both hands. She muttered about the misfortune of having to eat turkey again.

"Where is Mary Lawne?" Margaret asked.

Bess looked reproachfully up at the planks laid across the rafters. Margaret thumped the loft floor with the butt of the broom handle. She received in return a cascade of dirt through the cracks and Mary Lawne's grumbling.

"If I come up there thou wilt rue it," Margaret called up to her.

Bess lowered her voice so Mary Lawne wouldn't hear her. "She said she would hang her Ave Maria beads from the new heifer's neck with a bell, that they might serve some purpose."

Margaret banged again with the broom, this time under the pallet the maid shared with the youngest one. She didn't hold with whipping servants, but Mary Lawne could make her change her mind. An old pair of shoes, their soles worn thin, appeared on the ladder.

"The sun almost risen whilst she lazes a-bed." Bess fanned the fire furiously with her apron.

"Now gather we all for prayers." Mary Brent smiled brightly. "Tomorrow is Lady Day, when the angel Gabriel appeared to the Virgin to announce that God had chosen her to bear His most blessed Son."

Mary rang the Angelus bell and three of the maids knelt for devotions. Mary Lawne went to the hearth and vomited in the ashes.

"I am disordered in my belly, mistress," she said wanly.

Looking as though she were about to breathe her painful last, Mary Lawne headed for the loft ladder again, but Margaret blocked her path. Scowling, the maid kneeled, but she sat defiantly back on her heels, and when Margaret looked away she pinched Bess hard on the arm. When the menservants had filed in and taken their positions behind the women, Mary led them in the recitation of the rosary.

Margaret's lips murmured the Ave Marias, but her mind wandered. The twenty-fifth of March had finally arrived, the first Lady Day celebrated in this new country. The Annunciation of the Virgin Mary was the first of the rosary's five joyful mysteries, but Lady Day also marked the beginning of the growing season and the new year. The willows were sheathed in green already. Among the bare branches of the oaks and beeches and maples hovered clouds of tiny pink blossoms on slender trees Margaret had never seen in England.

So much needed to be done to finish the house before Margaret must divert the men to plant tobacco and corn. Construction inched along as delays and mistakes multiplied. She suspected that the carpenter had exaggerated his skill in order to reduce his term of indenture from five years to four.

She tried to concentrate on the comforting words of the prayer. "Hail, Mary, full of grace . . ." But an irreverent thought intruded. The Virgin Mary had indeed been blessed to have a husband and a son who were carpenters.

Margaret and her new steward, Edward Packer, stared at the massive oak beside her unfinished home. Three men with arms outstretched could barely span its furrowed trunk. Its canopy would shut out the sun and make of the house a damp and gloomy place. Its branches would fall on the roof. Its leaves would cover the garden and make the soil unfit for growing vegetables and herbs.

"Your servants have little learning with axes," Packer said.

"They cry 'Oh, Lord,' to see the number and size of trees to be felled."

Margaret knew that. She had anointed and plastered their torn and bloody hands. Her youngest man sobbed while he hacked at the trees and his ax bounced off the tough wood. The older one cursed steadily as he worked.

"We shall leave the oak, Mr. Packer."

"You won't regret it, Mistress Margaret." Packer looked relieved. "It will provide a cooling shade over the parlor in the heat of summer."

Margaret gestured at the forest covering most of her new freehold. "Still, so many trees stifle folk and are the cause of great sickness."

"Aye, mistress."

Packer followed her through the litter of wood chips, broken shingles and dirty white peaks of hardened plaster. At the seven-foot-high sawyer's trestle Margaret fretted that the boards weren't being sawed with the grain. She fretted that half a dozen laborers wandered back and forth, aimlessly as far as she could tell.

She crossed the small porch and stepped over the threshold. She would have to instruct the joiner to build the doors of ash for her maids' peace of mind. Bess insisted that the wood of the ash tree kept away evil spirits.

Leonard Calvert's servants had delivered a hundredweight of slaked lime made from burned oyster shells. In the great hall two men stood poised to dump a bucket of water into a tub of it to make whitewash for the mud-packed walls.

"Have a care." Margaret was appalled at their carelessness. "Lime agitates greatly and gives off quantities of heat."

She could hear the carpenter swearing upstairs. With her arms folded across her chest she surveyed the mess. The house looked as though it were being razed rather than built, and Father White intended to bless it tomorrow afternoon.

"I fear I have been ill-used in the matter of a carpenter," she said.

"He has but rude stuff for assistants." Edward Packer was new

to the prestigious job of steward and eager to please. He was small
and thin, with hair like a chick's down. "We lack artificers and
many are ailing from winter's ill effects."

"Maryland's populace seems divided between those who can't
work and those who won't."

Margaret strode to the narrow stairway that wrapped around
behind the chimney. When she bounced on the bottom step it
creaked but held firm. She walked into the big open hearth and
peered up at the freshly laid plaster of the chimney's walls. Margaret worried about everything, but the two chimneys worried
her the most. If the plaster wasn't properly applied a spark could
ignite the stacked framework of sticks underneath and send the
whole house up in flames.

The men rolled their eyes heavenward in thanks when she
marched off to inspect the tobacco beds. Edward Packer looked
grateful too. He knew more about raising sot weed than houses.

Three months ago, in December, Margaret's two servants had
cut the bark in a ring around each tree to kill it. Now they were
burning the dead trunks. Margaret coughed as she walked into the
shroud of smoke rolling from the newly cleared land.

Logs framed the long, raised beds set out among the stumps of
the old Indian fields. Piled around them was the brush that covered them at night and protected them from frost. She leaned
down, scooped up a handful of soil from one of them, and rubbed
it between her thumb and fingers. "What is the mixture?"

"Three parts loam, one part wood ashes, and one part manure," Packer said. "Though when the seedlings are transplanted
to the fields we will not manure, of course."

"Why is that?"

"It taints the taste of the leaf. And besides, such dressing is
hard to obtain. As you've probably noticed, the livestock is not
penned, but roams the forests freely."

"Requiring us to fence every acre." Margaret didn't want to
think about how much fence her men still had to build. " 'Tis a
barbarous form of husbandry they practice here."

Still rubbing the soil between her fingers she turned slowly in a circle. She surveyed the disheveled fields, the rotting stumps nearby, and the more distant trees with flames licking up their charred trunks and out onto the bare branches. Huge piles of brush smoldered here and there. No plow or harrow could be found in all of Maryland, nor horses or oxen to pull them. No proper roads, but only the paths beaten into the forest floor by the brown feet of pagans.

"I want to see the fence on the back field," Margaret said at last. "Against my better judgment I hired the tavern keeper to build it, and I suspect he shirked in labor and materials."

Margaret's temples were throbbing and the sun marking midafternoon by the time she pushed open the gate in the brush fence enclosing the kitchen garden. Mary looked up from hacking with a hoe at the roots and forest underbrush. She pushed her old felt hat back on her head and smiled a welcome. Laying a spidery, dirt-blackened finger to her lips, she nodded to the far side of the garden. Dozens of birds hopped about looking for insects and seeds in the rich dirt. Among them were four of the beautiful, crested red birds Lord Baltimore so coveted.

"So many kinds," Mary murmured. "Mary's Land is a wondrous fair place, Maggie."

Margaret pulled a small cloth sack from the pocket of her old wool skirt. She opened it and laid it in the palm of her hand. Mary bent down to look at the heap of tiny black seeds.

"Tobacco?"

"Aye." Margaret stirred them with the tip of her finger.

"They're no bigger than nits."

"Aye." Margaret replaced the seeds and picked up a shovel that was leaning against the fence. Our fortunes depend, she thought, on a speck the size of a louse's offspring. And on smoke.

She began shoveling dirt into a raised bed near the kitchen door. Here she would plant the herbs and vegetables most often used. The work was familiar, soothing. She and Mary had always tended the garden together. What grew here would be eaten, not burned and inhaled as smoke.

She picked up one of the shiny oak leaves. "We shall have to lime the soil."

"Squire Cornwaleys offered us some. And Mistress Lewger brought lavender and rue." Mary nodded to a basket filled with packets of seeds, each labeled in a neat, feminine script.

"Secretary Lewger is displeased with us for patenting our own land," Margaret said.

"Did he say so?"

"He complained of a disaffection for high-handed women." Margaret flashed her wry smile. "I can't imagine who else he had in mind."

"Father White's Indian lad brought us game for the table." Mary grinned. "A brace of turkeys."

"Mary Lawne can make a succotash of them to feed the workmen."

Mary looked dubious. Most of the freemen and bondsmen alike had survived the winter on turkey and oysters and Goody Smythe's watery gruel. They were working for the Brents for food alone, and would expect better than their usual fare.

"Sergeant Vaughan passed by," Mary said. "He says he is experimenting with distilling spirits from Indian corn."

Margaret felt a disquieting twinge of disappointment that he hadn't stopped to speak to her. He had a way of making her laugh. " 'Tis no surprise," she said. "He being so frequently unbuttoned with drink." She sang softly and Mary joined her.

> *"Oh, we can make liquor to sweeten our lips.*
> *Of pumpkins and parsnips and walnut tree chips."*

Leonard Calvert looked over the fence. "God smiles on your endeavors." He glanced up at the clear blue sky. "Methinks you shall have fine weather for the blessing of Sisters' Freehold on the morrow."

Giles appeared next to him. "There is some grumbling though, dear sister, that all the able men in the province are at work here."

"God keep thee." The doctor's wife, Susannah Gerard, opened the gate so that two of her servants could trundle in a cart heaped high with pig manure mixed with straw and bracken and aged over the winter.

"What a fine gift." Mary scooped up a handful, crumbled some in her fingers and inhaled deeply of its fragrance. She touched the tip of her tongue to it. "It seems an exceptionally good blend, Mistress Gerard. And where did you get the manure?"

Mistress Gerard was about to elaborate on her recipe when Giles's mastiff bounded through the open gate and almost knocked her down. The dog was accompanied by a stench like none Margaret had ever smelled. It had the bite of brimstone and the cloying odor of something dead too long. The women hurried through the gate and Margaret closed it on the mastiff's nose.

"What is it?" Margaret looked back over the fence.

"The Indians call it 'skunk,' " Calvert said. " 'Tis a beast about as big as a cat, black with a patch of white diverging into two stripes along its back. It moves about at night and when disturbed it sprays the perfume you smell."

" 'Tis a most disgusting stink," Margaret said.

"Yes." Calvert looked wistful. "Would that I could send a pair to my brother for his menagerie."

Chapter 23

Robert Vaughan clamped his legs around the sow's neck. Her hindquarters thrashed and vaulted, flinging the foul stew of Joan Parke's monumental midden over him and spattering Giles and Anicah too.

"Thirty weight o' sot weed fer the hire of her, squire," Joan said.

"Agreed," Vaughan panted.

Ignoring her sow's squeals, Joan reached into her basket and separated a pale, translucent tube from the heap of them there. The section of pig's intestine had been gathered and tied closed with thread at one end. Joan inserted two fingers into the sheath and spread them, stretching the filmy tissue.

"This should encompass yer mighty sausage, yer lor'ship." She flopped the gathered end at Giles. "I'll warrant me engines against the pox. Tuck yer prick into one and ye need not dread shankers nor yer maid's belly grown great of a May Day brat."

"Mayhap later."

" 'Tis Maying time. Me wares will quickly sell." She dangled the intestine temptingly.

Anicah grinned. "I misdoubt ye'll have done selling the commodity that ne'r leaves yer basket."

"Ye cannot give yers away, ye Spaniard's get—"

"We are much occupied here, kind ladies." Vaughan grabbed the sow's floppy ears to keep her from wriggling out of his grasp.

"And a good day to ye, then," Joan said.

Giles waited until her skirts and her basket had swayed out of hearing. "Methinks the goodwife and her swine doth resemble one the other in body and temperament."

Vaughan chuckled. The sow was a great, mangy, smelly, bristly, barrel-shaped beast. She possessed tiny, red-rimmed eyes, a vinegary disposition, snout hairs that would puncture leather, and hooves like chisel blades.

"Hold fast her pins," Vaughan shouted.

"Damn me!" Giles caught the back legs just above the slicing hooves, but he had to fall onto his knees to hold them. What had seemed a capital jest when discussed over wine last night had lost much of its appeal today.

Anicah pulled a round-bellied brown bottle of ale from the gaggle of them, their long necks craning above the hamper like geese. She uncorked it and passed it in front of the pig's nose. The sow ceased hopping and her squeals turned to hungry grunts. Anicah poured the ale into a wooden bowl and held it out. The animal plunged her mud-crusted snout in and sucked her way to the bottom. Anicah passed a second bottle to Robert and Giles.

Giles, however, must have realized that the fort's sagging palisades gave scant cover, and drinking in public with a pig and a tavern wench would set tongues to wagging.

"It saddens me to leave such amusing company." He bowed and gave a sweep of his plumed hat with the brim folded up like a swan's wing. He smiled at Anicah. "Mayhap we will take a flourish, thou and I, ere the revels end."

"Me mistress requires me to carry beer to the tosspots all day." Anicah didn't bother to remind Giles that she was betrothed. It had never discouraged him before.

She left after Vaughan decanted the fourth bottle and the sow had become not only tractable, but affectionate. On her way back to the ordinary Anicah stopped to watch the raising of the maypole.

Leonard Calvert's reeve shouted to the men holding the ropes, but the forty-foot-long pine trunk still looked as tipsy as those trying to position it. The rack of garland-draped antlers on top described

ever-widening circles, then dipped suddenly. Flowers shaken loose
by its careen drifted down. Anicah dropped the hamper and pushed
into the laughing crowd. She found a grip among the other hands
easing it into its hole. Once it was steady she continued her trudge
toward the ordinary.

"Make way for the King o' the May," Original Brown shouted.

Anicah paused at the door to watch the parade. Brown
pounded on the town drum and Leonard Calvert's huntsman
bleated on his horn. For his duties as the May Day shrive,
Vaughan wore a robe of ragged leather strips. He rode the sow on
a weaving course, or at least he trotted along with the pig between his legs. He held the reins with one hand, and in the other
he waved a revel staff.

The ordinary's door opened suddenly and Goody Smythe
yanked Anicah inside. "The devil's work," she muttered. "A very
nursery of unthrift and inconvenience."

While her mistress watered the wine and cider in the kitchen,
Anicah stood at the window. She couldn't see the dancing, but
she could hear the music well enough. She imagined her mother,
her hair fanned out behind her as she whirled, laughing. "A wild
and airy girl, a lover of wakes and ales and merry nights, when
music and dancing abounded," Anicah's aunt had said. "With
only her dark copper hair and her smile for her portion."

Grief burned in Anicah's eyes and high up inside her nose.
Death was as familiar to her as lice, but she had never thought
much about either. Now, for an instant, she understood death.

Death was the Great Cracksman, the supreme burglar. It crept
inside people, as a picklock entered another's house, and it robbed
them of their breath and souls. It left their kin and sweethearts
weeping, consoled only by the sad distortions of memory. It left
Anicah a glimpse of the feathery wilderness of her mother's hair
and the haunting fragments of a lullaby.

Dead, she thought. Dead and gone.

She was only partly right. Her mother was dead, but she wasn't
gone. The lovely curves of her nose and lips, chin and brow had

become Anicah's. The mother looked out at the world through her daughter's eyes.

"Step lively, thou lazy wench," Goody Smythe called from the kitchen. "The priest's boy waits on a charge from his master."

Anicah left the window reluctantly. What would the unctuous Thomas Copley want?

"Thou'rt to carry this pot of stew and bottle of ale to the papist," Goody Smythe said.

"And cannot the paternoster's catamite fetch it himself?" Anicah had heard the ale-bench talk about Thomas Copley and his young acolyte.

She took the basket and went out the back door. The torn hat brim hid the boy's face, but she recognized his broad shoulders and long, sturdy legs. She dropped the basket and flung herself at him. He untangled her long enough to collect the basket and lead her away from her watchful mistress.

"I've missed ye, me dear marrow," she said.

The pink in Martin's cheeks deepened. He handed her a garland of dusty gray leaves and long clusters of tiny purple flowers. She inhaled its pungency before she set it among her auburn curls.

"What is it?" she asked.

"You ne'er saw lavender before?"

"Nay."

Martin's cheeks grew redder, intensifying the dark blue of his eyes in contrast. "They say lavender is for lovers."

"Let's deliver the victuals and sneak away." Anicah quivered at the prospect.

"The repast is for us. My master, Father Poulton, said to enjoy it as a Maying feast."

Anicah closed her eyes and pressed her cheek against Martin's chest. She had something else for which to thank the priest. She took Martin's hand and led him toward the path down the side of the bluff.

"Will ye tarry awhile?" she asked.

"My master is mounting a mission among the Indians and desires me to go along." He saw the alarm in her eyes. "I can't refuse him."

"Dina says the salvages eat Christians."

"Father Poulton holds them to be honorable folk. I'll return with tales to amuse you."

Anicah was disappointed to see that the small crescent of river beach was occupied. Mary Brent sat on a gnarled root exposed by the constant gnaw of the water. She graced them with her wraithy smile, put a finger to her lips and beckoned them closer.

A flowering bush grew from the embankment, and Mary had put a spray of its fragrant pink blooms in her pale hair. An aura of iridescent color shimmered and hummed around her head. It consisted of fairies, sprites, imps maybe, hovering on blurred wings. Anicah moved closer and saw that the tiny beings were birds no longer than her little finger.

"Of all the forms His angels take, this must be the loveliest." Mary spoke softly, but the birds darted away so fast Anicah wondered if she had imagined them.

Mary stood up and took the flowers from her hair. She leaned close to weave them into the garland Martin had given Anicah. Anicah could smell the scent Mary wore and she recognized it now as lavender. The odor brought back a memory of the night in the garret room at the Cocklorel. She wanted to beg forgiveness for stealing Mary's things, but she couldn't say the words.

"May God bless you both and may you cherish each other always." Mary made the sign of the cross over them and started up the path.

"She's thin as a coat of paint," Anicah whispered, "but fair withal. I wonder that she has no dearling to chase the night's sad darks."

One of the tiny birds appeared in front of her nose, as though formed spontaneously of rainbow and sunlight. She could hear the hum of his wings. She could see his shimmering ruby-red throat and emerald-green sides. Then he vanished.

"Did ye see that, Martin?"

"Aye. Father Poulton calls it a hummingbird. 'Tis not half so lovely a creature as thee." Martin drew her to him and held her close. Using Anicah's cloak as pallet and coverlet, they celebrated May.

Margaret tapped her foot, but not in time to the music. She was impatient for the dancing to stop so her people could go home. They must all wake early tomorrow to continue raising thousands of hills for planting tobacco and corn. April and May were the busiest months of the year and no time for foolery.

She had tried to forbid her servants their celebration, but even Bess had rebelled, so she had compromised. They had gone to the fields before dawn this morning and worked until midday. Now they were dancing, with none of the fatigue they'd complained so bitterly about when Margaret roused them from their beds.

Off to one side Mary was teaching Father Andrew White's Indian lad, Anansine, the steps to the dance. He was dressed in his breechclout and moccasins and his head was shaved on one side. He stared at his feet as he danced and his look of concentration bordered on ferocious.

Margaret surveyed the rest of the merrymakers. She had been counting her maids all afternoon. As always on May first, lust hung in the warm air as much as the scent of flowers. Ancient, nameless rites of fertility and increase ruled here, not reason and piety. "Ta-ran, ta-ray, the first of May," the vulgar commons sang. "Fucking outdoors begins today."

"A capital revel, is it not, Mistress Margaret?" The planter touched his hat brim. Mary Lawne waited at a distance, her plump arms crossed at her waist, her hands clasping her elbows.

"If thou hast not her price, Goodman Courtney, the answer is no." Margaret wasn't in a mood for pleasantries.

"I can pledge tobacco from my next crop."

"I will not let her go for the warmed air of a pledge," Margaret said. "I must have coin in hand or tobacco to hire someone to take her place."

"Jack's in the box already, mistress." Courtney blurted it out and reddened at the corners of his jaw.

"And you put him there, I suppose." Margaret wanted to slap his large, red ears. That would explain the maid's morning crop sickness. Margaret was furious that she had wasted time dosing her for a stomach ailment. She beckoned to Mary Lawne. "When is it due?"

"Toward Michaelmas, mistress." The maid looked at her shoes, but Margaret detected the defiance and the triumph in the plant of her feet.

"We have not the wherewithall to maintain an infant," she said.

"Goodman Courtney and I shall maintain it."

"And who shalt do the work thou'rt bound for?"

"I know not."

Courtney and Mary Lawne studied the ground. Margaret allowed the silence to lengthen and harden and chill before she relented. There was nothing else she could do.

"Publish the banns, then," she said. "And at the cutting, Goodman Courtney, thou must remit five hundred pounds of sweet-scented leaf, half that in the cask."

Courtney bowed as he backed away. Mary curtsied, then turned and bolted.

Giles ambled up beside his sister. "Due to launch a merry-begotten, is she?"

"Nature will out." Margaret kept her voice even.

"I say, Margaret, lend us the use of your man a fortnight. The raising of my manse goes slowly for want of hands."

"His price is forty weight per diem."

" 'Tis dear."

"He claims to be a carpenter and others have asked for the hire of him."

"Add it to my score then."

"Thy score is so considerable that were I a tavern keeper, I should have denied thee credit long since."

"Thou art not a tavern keeper, but my own beloved sister." Giles kissed her on the cheek. "I shall pay thee when the cutting's done." He sauntered off to cadge a dram of Thomas Cornwaleys's brandy and seek a dance partner among the gentlewomen.

Margaret knew that later he'd likely solicit favors of a different sort from the serving maids, although so far he had skirted scandal.

The muscles of Margaret's angular jaw relaxed as she watched Anicah and Martin weave in and out among the dancers. They parted reluctantly when the dance demanded it. When it brought them together again, they kissed and clung to each other. They laughed as they whirled, their hair and clothes flying out around them.

Margaret couldn't imagine loving someone as they seemed to. When she was eleven or twelve, before she dedicated her life to God, she had become enamored with an older youth. He had radiated wit and elegance, and she had thought she would die if he didn't notice her. She couldn't remember his name now.

Only faith in God and the love of the Holy Mother was constant. Watching Anicah and Martin, she doubted their infatuation would last. Belike the boy would become besotted with another pretty face, or a man with more prospects would lure away the wench.

Robert Vaughan interrupted her thoughts. "This rout shall dance up the dawn, I'll wager." He flashed her his brandy-and-ale grin. Leaves and twigs poked from the wiry tangle of his cinnamon-colored hair. A wilted garland had slipped to a jaunty angle over his left eye.

Margaret laughed. "How very like Bacchus thou seemst."

"Bacchus would not attend such a sorry show. I fear this will be the last May revel we shall see."

The frolic did have a shabby air about it. There weren't many folk to celebrate, nor time to do the celebrating. And people had come from so many districts in England, they disagreed as to which customs to follow or what songs to sing. Only the maypole and the dancing and the flirting were constant.

"It isn't as it was," she said.

"Do you miss those times?" Vaughan asked.

"Nay, Sergeant. They were a shameful debauchery."

"You talk very like a Puritan, Mistress Margaret."

"Not so!" She was horrified at the thought. "In my youth I loved riding and dancing and mumming and all manner of sports. I was what the graver sort call a hoyting girl."

"In truth, 'tis not the Puritans will put an end to revelry here, but the deceivable weed."

"Tobacco?"

"Aye. The sot weed is not a gentle mistress like wheat or barley. I have known a planter to force his dying servant to dig his own grave because he had not the hands to spare."

"I did not realize you grew the weed."

"I haven't the resources to transport men and so gain a manor. A piddling hundred acres yields not enough to provide a man more than the barest sustinence." Vaughan had obviously forgotten that Margaret's new freehold was only eighty acres.

Margaret picked a long, feathery frond from the fern at her feet and tapped him lightly on the shoulder with it. "The Lord of Misrule must be merry, sir."

"Secretary Lewger would have the Assembly enact a law," he said abruptly, "whereby a woman must marry in seven years or forfeit her manor to the next of kin."

Margaret was startled by the sudden shift in the conversation. "A woman who marries loses all," she said. "Would you consent to forfeit your affairs and your property, your person, liberty and prerogatives to some man for as long as you live?"

Vaughan looked confused. "Nay. But I'm not a woman."

"Lewger's proposition is a foolish one." Margaret dismissed it with a wave of the fern. "His lordship will not allow it."

Robert took a deep breath, as though about to plunge into an icy stream. "Mistress Margaret, would you accept my hand in marriage?" He rushed on while Margaret stared at him, her mouth half open. "I assure you, I hold you in the highest esteem and ask it only with regard for your virtue. 'Twould be solely for your protection and to further our mutual economic interests."

She couldn't even be irritated with him. At least he had asked her directly and not gone to her brothers, as though she were a child or a simpleton.

Maybe it was the wreath perched a-tilt in the melee of Robert's hair that started her laughing. She laughed so hard she had to hold her stomacher for fear of bursting the laces. She leaned against a tree and shook while tears ran down her cheeks.

Vaughan's sheepish smile widened into a grin, then broke into a deep, rolling guffaw. The two of them laughed until they were out of breath and their sides ached.

"Thou wouldst take a whither-go-ye? A wife?" She wiped her eyes and blew her nose on the handkerchief in her sleeve. " 'Tis no wonder you looked like a man about to be hung."

"Marriage and hanging come by destiny."

"Then thou shalt be a free man and a quick one yet a while longer, Sir Lack-Latin."

Chapter 24

osquitoes hovered like smoke at the bottom of the ravine where Margaret crouched. She had tied a dish clout over her face to keep them out of her nose and mouth, but she thought their constant whine might drive her mad. While she waited for the leather bucket to fill with spring-water, she waved her apron to scatter them, but she only stirred them up a bit.

The late King James called tobacco an abomination of the devil and the herb from hell. Margaret decided that if he was right, then this was the most fitting place to grow it. Hell could not hold a candle to Maryland in the summertime.

Margaret's scalp prickled. Sweat soaked the linen kerchief wrapped around her hair and knotted at the nape of her neck. It stained the flat-brimmed felt hat she wore over it. It saturated her long cotton chemise and laced linen bodice. Under her wool skirt and petticoat it collected in the creases behind her knees and trickled down her bare legs.

The only breeze was the riffle created by the apron she flapped methodically. Perspiring like a dray horse and squatting in the mud like the lowliest crofter, this was not how she had imagined life as one of Maryland's landed gentry. Next year, she vowed, she would have men enough for such work. Healthy men.

She hung the second bucket on the wooden yoke and hoisted it onto her shoulders. She shifted it for balance and started up the side of the ravine. Rocks bruised her feet through the thin soles of her Indian shoes. The mosquitoes settled on her hands and ankles until they looked as though fur had sprouted there. The buckets grew heavier with each step. At the top she set them down and rested. In the distance she could see the river sparkling in the sunlight. So much water, and all of it too salty for drinking or irrigation.

She trudged past the well that had gone dry. At the bottom of it one of her men swore feebly while he dug. The other hauled up the buckets of dirt. Both were weak with the bloody flux and covered with the livid rash that had plagued everyone all summer. The same open sores covered Margaret's own hands and arms, and the itch drove her to a frenzy.

Margaret's new house rose stolidly from the litter of shingles, barrel staves and stacks of firewood. The dairy shed was only half completed and no other outbuildings even begun. In the stifling heat Mary's rooster and three hens stood motionless, their dusty wings and tails drooping. The stench from the midden by the kitchen door floated beyond the unfinished palisade.

Sisters' Freehold was not the efficient, neatly laid out manor Margaret had dreamed of, but she had come to an accommodation with it. She thought of it as a beloved but recalcitrant and slovenly child who would improve with age and a lot of effort on her part.

She wanted to weep at the sight of the fields, though. The tobacco drooped under the sun's relentless glare. The corn stalks were stunted and brittle. The maids had made a scarecrow of bundled reeds and dressed it in a suit of tobacco leaves yellowed by the drought. It dangled on its pole, its head lolling like an inept godling brooding over the ruin of its kingdom.

Margaret had heard stories of the starving time in Virginia years ago. People had eaten vermin then, and stewed shoes and tree bark and finally each other. The Virginians were suffering from this drought too, and Margaret knew she could not expect help from them. The season's few ships had sailed for England, their holds bulging with hogsheads of tobacco. None were expected back be-

fore fall. Margaret looked down at her moccasins, dusty and stained
and cracked, and wondered how they would taste.

She walked through the Indian corn to reach Mary and the
maids working in the tobacco. By this time in July the tassels
should have waved over her head, but they barely reached her
chest. Their ears were small and few, but she took some consolation in the brush of the leaves against her as she passed. Such slender stalks to support life.

She was staggering with fatigue by the time she reached the
only living tree in the fields. A cow's stomach paunch hung from
a low limb so that evaporation would cool the contents. Mary
held it open while Margaret ladled the water into it.

Mary had rolled back her sleeves and pinned up her woollen
skirts. Above her moccasins her thin ankles were scarred by scratches
and mosquito bites. She and the maids had tied their hair back in
kerchiefs. Their felt hats, their shoes, their skirts were all snuff-
colored with dust.

Mary bent over a tobacco plant, searching for fat, green
worms as long as her little finger. She picked each one off using
the curved horn at the rear end as a handle, and crushed it underfoot. Bess Guest straightened from her hoeing. She swayed, then
pitched forward, crushing the tobacco when she fell onto it.

"Dear God," Margaret murmured.

She and Mary half carried her to the shade and sat her down
with her back against the trunk. Bess's round face looked like a
peeled beet. Mary took the maid's hat off and fanned her with it.

She held a ladleful of water to Bess's lips, then she looked up
at Margaret. "Rest thyself, sister. Thou too look'st ready to fall."

"I am that."

Mary held the ladle to one side and her lips moved in a silent
exchange before she passed it to the other maids who waited patiently. They'd become used to Mary's invisible companion. His
unsubstantial presence comforted them. Margaret encouraged their
belief in Mary's angel. A celestial reeve might keep them from
committing as many indiscretions as they would otherwise.

Margaret wiped her face on her apron. She rubbed her arms with it, trying to ease the tormenting itch of the sores without causing them to bleed more. What she wanted to do was scream and claw at them, to tear them from her body.

With her hat she waved away the swarms of midges while she squinted up at the sky. It was cloudless, bright as new-dyed indigo silk with the sun burning a hole in it.

"Dost Raphael say 'twill rain?" she asked.

Mary listened, her head cocked to one side. "Nay," she said sadly. "He does not."

Margaret took Mary's slender hands in her big ones. They were swollen and torn from the hoe handle. She was looking in her pouch for woundwort leaves to bind around them when Bess cried out.

An Indian had appeared among the thigh-high tobacco plants. The youngest maid threw her apron over her head and ran behind the tree. Margaret squinted into the sun, trying to make out his features.

Mary held out the ladle. "Dost thou thirst, Anansine?"

The Piscataway boy was dressed as usual in breechclout, moccasins, feathers and bear fat, though he had abandoned his plaid wool stockings and wore just the tasseled garters. Behind him Mathias DaSousa carried one end of a blanket litter with Father Andrew White on it. Martin held the other end. Father Poulton hobbled after them leaning on his cane. His toes had become frozen while staying with the Patuxent Indians during the winter.

Mathias and Martin set the litter down in the shade.

"I fear Father White hath succumbed to the fever," Poulton said. His own hands shook as though palsied.

Margaret put her hand on White's forehead. It was so hot it burned her. The Jesuit's hair had turned from gray to the color of new snow.

"Martin and Goodman DaSousa and I were at St. Inigoes this morning," Poulton said, "when the Indian lad arrived with Andrew insensible in the bottom of his canoe. He had brought him the hundred and twenty miles from Piscataway."

"Edward." Father White could barely be heard.

"How say'st thou, Andrew?"

"The Piscataway boy . . . baptismal name Edward . . . I promised him a shirt." White closed his eyes and seemed to fall back into sleep.

Using his cane and Martin's arm, Ferdinand Poulton eased himself down and leaned against the maple.

"We have need of the curative distillations of your still room, gentle sisters, and of the apothecary of your garden. The demands of the spiritual sowing have been such that I have not had time to plant herbs." When Poulton smiled and shrugged, the twin knurls of his shoulders lifted the thin material of his frayed and faded cassock.

"Thou could'st use some psychic thyself," Margaret said, "though we have but few conceits and simples." She thought of the pitiful state of the kitchen garden.

"Edward says he'll hunt game for you while he's here."

"We would be grateful."

Edward had gone ranging among the weeds at the edge of the field. As Margaret watched him she envied him. He and his people must have no problem finding food. The forest was their larder, their marketplace, butchers' shambles and apothecary.

He returned with two handfuls of leaves. He held up the narrow dark green one and spoke in a soft, musical tone at odds with his ferocious appearance.

"What does he want, Martin?" Poulton asked.

"He says this is called the sweating plant." Martin leaned forward, intent on understanding the words. "Boil it in water and drink the infusion to drive out fever."

Edward caught hold of Margaret's wrist. She pulled back, offended that he would lay hands on someone of her rank. And vaguely afraid too.

"He means thee no harm, Mistress Margaret," Poulton said.

The boy crushed a handful of different leaves and stems and rubbed the juice on the sores on Margaret's hand. The itching eased and Margaret stared intently at him. What other knowledge lay behind those enigmatic black eyes?

Mary was reaching for the leaves when she collapsed. Margaret knelt by her and touched the papery skin of her forehead.

"She hath the fever." Margaret's hands shook with panic as she held Mary's head. "I should never have allowed her to work the ground." She fought back the sobs that rose in her throat. No matter what happened, the servants must not see her cry.

With the doors and shutters closed the air inside the house felt thick enough to suffocate any who breathed it. The heat upstairs under the eaves was unbearable. The maids had moved their pallets into the kitchen. Martin and Edward and the two men servants lay in the stillroom where Margaret and Mary mixed their remedies.

Father White groaned on the big bed and Mary whimpered now and then on a mattress in the corner. Either the infusion of Edward's leaves had broken their fevers or they had abated of their own accord. Their soaked nightgowns clung to them.

In spite of the heat Margaret and Father Poulton sat in the smoke of the green pine needles smoldering to discourage the mosquitoes. Poulton had just returned from a trip up the Patuxent River in search of heathen souls. He had stories to tell in his elegant and faintly Spanish accent.

"They have a strange and barbarous notion of Heaven, Mistress Margaret," he said. "Paradise is for them an eternal bacchanal of sensual pleasures. Yet we have made some humble progress in leading them to the truth."

"Still, you must have a care, that you perish not in the endeavor," Margaret said.

"I would rather die on the bare ground than abandon this holy work." When he smiled his dark eyes glittered the way Margaret had seen crofters' do in times of famine. "Since Lord Baltimore gave permission for us to go among them, Andrew White has won the affections of the Piscataway king." He paused. "Know'st thou how fares the young Bristol wench? The one bound to the tapster?"

"She hath found her own kind among the riffraff there."

"Yet methinks she hath a gallant soul withal. She fed me when I was hungry."

"How so?"

"She gave me a fresh-killed rat, dressed for the pot." He smiled at the memory of it. " 'Twas her gift of life when we were without bread on the ship."

Margaret had an instant's image of the mysterious pink carcass lying in front of her cabin door. She never would have guessed the little thief had left it there.

"God will judge both her good deeds and her bad." She changed the subject. "What hast thou learned of the Indians' language, Ferdinand?"

"Not so much as young Martin Kirk. My own efforts have oft been the cause of chagrin." Poulton laughed. "Thou wilt find this tale droll, I wot. . . ."

In spite of the heat, Margaret felt a sweet contentment with the gentle and learned priest. She could almost imagine what it would be like to have such a man as a life's companion. She talked and laughed softly with him until cock crow.

" 'Od's ballocks!" Anicah slapped at the fly stinging her arm. She waved away the gnats trying to crawl into her eyes. "The devil take this plaguey country."

With a heavy wooden mattock she chopped at the weeds smothering the drooping tobacco plant. A fine gray mix of dust and ashes swirled up. She sneezed and wiped her nose with the bloodstained rag wrapped around her hand. She thought surely such heat as this would simmer the marrow in her bones. "I have swallowed dirt enough to grow tobacco in me belly."

In the next row over Original Brown cackled. "Dirt may be

all ye'll find in yer belly this season." He went back to pinching off the tops of the plants to keep them from flowering.

Anicah shielded her eyes and looked up at the sun. It still hung just above the western horizon, stopped in its path to prolong her misery. The Smythes' ten charred, stump-filled acres stretched around her as vast as a county.

"Get ye off me ground, ye trug." Joan Parke's voice carried through the openings in the nearby palisade.

"I go where it pleases me, you poxy jade."

Anicah rolled her eyes at Original. Mary Lawne Courtney and Joan were at odds again.

"I would have the petticoat ye stole from me," Joan shouted.

"I would not touch such a filthy clout."

"Return it or I shall give ye a blow on the chops."

"I did not take it, ye sluice-cunt."

Goodwife Courtney yelped. Joan must have fired a few volleys from the dung heap that served as her source of ammunition. Flouncing her skirts like an angry hen, Mary Courtney fluttered out of the front gate. Large with child, she waddled away through the crops and clutter that surrounded the fort.

Anicah winked at Brown. He gave her his look of befuddled innocence, but she knew he had taken Joan's petticoat from the fence where it was drying. He had spent the winter on Smythe's ale bench unraveling it and knotting it into his net. The net had grown to cover his lap, then the burls of his knees, and finally to lie in folds at his feet. He had draped it over the bushes near his hut, but so far he had not caught a red bird in it.

Anicah unwrapped the sacking around her hands and stared at her palms. The mattock had rubbed away the skin there and the gentlest touch caused fiery agony. She wanted to cry from rage at fate's treachery. She thought she had arranged life so she wouldn't have to grub in the dirt like some simple rustic.

"I would top the tobacco whilst you weed, Goodman Brown." She tried to hand him the mattock, but he shook his head.

"Ye haven't the tools." He held up his thumbnail. It was long and brown, hardened in the flame of the ordinary's rushlights. Even so, blood had dried black around the quick of it.

"I'll pull off the suckers then."

"Nay." He waggled a finger at her. "Leave them for a second crop."

"The governor said sucker leaf is inferior and forbidden." Anicah didn't care about legality, she just couldn't bear the mattock anymore.

"His lordship also said to plant three acres in corn for the sustenance of the household." Brown waved a skinny arm over the despondent rows of tobacco. "D'ye see corn here?"

Anicah didn't answer. She was busy trying to uproot the weeds with the heel of her bare foot. When she stepped on a dry tobacco stalk instead, it snapped with a lovely crack. She stomped on several more just to hear the sound again. She could claim Joan's hogs had done the damage.

The destruction improved her mood. She worked along, holding the mattock between her wrists and swinging it gingerly until the sun had set and the first tiny light winked in the forbidding stand of trees at the edge of the field. Then she threw it down and stalked toward the ordinary and Goody Smythe's certain wrath.

"The goodwife said we must work till dark," Brown called after her.

"I'll not stay without doors when fairies or imps are about."

"They're but fireflies, ye silly wench."

"They're sprites and they may be evil. I'll have naught to do with them."

She hurried her pace as more of the ghostly lights flickered in the bushes around her. She slammed the door behind her, shutting out the only source of fresh air in the ordinary's stifling kitchen.

She was so weary she endured in silence Goody Smythe's lecture about the sin of sloth. She scoured the crusted hominy kettle with ashes and shelled a pile of corn for the morning bread.

The Smythes retired early to their bed in the taproom. Even

though Anicah dreaded the night airs, she laid her cloak near the kitchen door in case a breeze might blunder under the wide crack between it and the sill. She stripped to her chemise and lay on her back with her arms and legs outspread so that no part of her touched another. Drenched in sweat she panted and stared up at the sooty ceiling, invisible in the darkness.

When she heard the soft tapping at the door, she scrambled away from it, dragging her cloak after her. She half expected to see a forest troll's arm snake through the crack and make a grab for her.

"Ani," Martin whispered into the latch hole.

"Martin!" Anicah rushed to open the door. Martin stood in a pool of moonlight and Anicah threw herself into his arms. "I feared the salvages had made hash of ye!"

"Nay, love. They treated me courteously, but I languished for the sight of you." He held her face in his hands and kissed her gently.

"Will ye tarry long, bulkin?"

"My master thinks me asleep with the servants at Mistress Margaret's house. We return to Mattapany on the morrow. But Edward knows the forest paths even in the dark, and he brought me to see you." Martin turned to introduce his new friend, but the Piscataway boy had tactfully vanished.

"Who's there?" Goody Smythe called from the taproom.

"No one, mistress."

"I heard voices."

Martin tried to draw away but Anicah hung onto him. "I was but saying my prayers, mistress." She stood on tiptoe to kiss him again.

"That I know to be a lie." The bed frame creaked as the goodwife sat up.

Martin pried his shirtfront from Anicah's grasp. He opened her palms and ran the tips of his fingers across the blood-stiff sacking that bandaged them. He put a strand of beads over her head, enclosed her small fists in his hands so that she couldn't hold onto him, and leaned down and kissed her good-bye.

When Goody Smythe shuffled into the kitchen with her hickory switch and a rushlight, Anicah was sliding the bolt home.

"Thou slut! Thou wast entertaining some lecherous knave."
But the goodwife was too enervated by the heat to give Anicah a
lashing. Mumbling about Anicah's bottomless iniquity, she turned
and shuffled back the way she came.

Anicah took off the necklace and put it into her pouch with
her father's will, her paper of indenture and the sprig of lavender.
She knew if her mistress saw it she would accuse her of stealing it
and would confiscate it for herself.

Chapter 25

Seething with anger, Margaret strode into a late October wind. Bess had to break into a lumbering trot to keep from falling too far behind her as she strode past Cornwaleys's mill and along the path paralleling the garbage-strewn ravine of Mill Creek. Margaret had just come from Secretary Lewger's house, but she wasn't any more vexed with him than usual. He had observed that the dispensing of herbs and simples was the proper activity for women, but she was used to that.

His wife had caused Margaret's ire. Mistress Lewger had sent her servant to ask Margaret to bring some of her coltsfoot-and-honey electuary for her ailing son. She could have consulted with the chirurgeon, but Margaret suspected the Lewgers were loath to part with his fee.

Margaret would have preferred to be overseeing the construction of her barn and drying house, but she didn't mind walking the mile and a half to help the Lewger scion, imperious brat that he was. What incensed her were the angry welts and purple bruises on the young serving maid's arms, back, and buttocks. She'd found them because Mistress Lewger had asked her, as though in an afterthought, to examine the girl. She didn't look more than twelve, but she was so emaciated her age was difficult to guess.

"The lazy wretch doth pretend illness to avoid her duties," Mistress Lewger had said.

"It appears someone hath beaten her sorely."

Anne Lewger dismissed the bruises with a wave of her hand. "The saucy wench offered to oppose me, for which I gave her conversation with a stick."

"I recommend kitchen physic for her." Margaret leveled her flinty gaze at the woman, but she didn't seem to notice. "A thick broth of mutton or beef with onions and quantities of cheese and bread, until she puts flesh on her bones." But even as Margaret said it she knew from the set of Mistress Lewger's thin mouth that her maid would not be dining on beef broth and cheese.

She stayed as long as courtesy dictated. She accepted a glass of wine, which rumor said Mistress Lewger took quite frequently these days. She discussed the scion's course of treatment and left a salve of ground horseradish root mixed with grease for the maid's bruises. Then she said good-bye in a voice as chilly as the wind blowing around the house.

Once Margaret passed through the palisade gate she heard a clucking noise behind her. It was the one Bess usually made when about to tell tales.

"What is it?"

Bess tightened her lips, as though to contain the information trying to tumble out. Margaret cocked one eyebrow at her.

"Prudence says her mistress beats her with the fire tongs and locks her in the root cellar with the rats."

"Prudence is the serving maid?"

"Aye," Bess answered. "She says she fears the darkness in the cellar."

Margaret knew that servants often required discipline, especially here where so many came from a class unsuited to work of any kind. Prudence, however, hardly looked like the troublesome type.

She was so preoccupied by the thought of that starved, frightened child that she almost passed the narrow track leading into the trees. She slowed, hesitated, then turned onto it.

"Will we be gettin' some of Mary Lawne's cheeses, mistress?"

"Aye."

"She has the best hand in the dairy, Mary does."

At the end of the lane sat the small house and stump-littered fields of James Courtney's freehold. Bundles of tobacco leaves, pegged together at the stalks, hung on the worm fence around the house. As Margaret and Bess made their way through the clutter of the dooryard, a pair of hounds barked. Margaret had her knuckles raised to rap them on the door when it opened.

"God's blessings, Mary."

Mary Courtney curtsied. She looked harried, unwilling to invite her former mistress inside, yet unable to leave her standing on the threshold. From behind her came the feeble wail of an infant.

"We cannot stay, Goodwife Courtney." Margaret took pity on her. "We were on our way from the Lewgers' and thought to buy half a dozen of thy cheeses."

"Ah, Mistress Margaret, this being so late in the season the pasturage is used up and I have only hay cheese. Even in summer the milk wants the sweet flavor the mousetail grass imparted at home." Mary looked relieved to have her dairy house to talk about. "Goodman Courtney has made a fine press. I'll show it thee."

Mary reached for her cloak. She was eager to show off her press and her skimming pans, scoured and neatly stacked and her shelves of round cheeses. She was also frantic to steer them away from her sickly son and her own house, which she knew was not up to Margaret Brent's strict standards.

"Do not trouble thyself, Mary. Bring them later."

The baby had stopped crying and the silence was more alarming than his wails.

"I have some simples in the basket," she said. "Mint and purslane for the stomach."

Tears filled Mary's eyes and rolled down her cheeks. "I know not what to do, mistress. He cries and cries and will not suck."

She stood aside so Margaret could lift the baby from his nest of rags on the Courtneys' corn-husk mattress. As Margaret looked at the wizened little creature she wanted to cry too. She would leave the herbs here and she would send parched cornmeal and dried pumpkin to make into a nourishing gruel. But she knew the child would have little chance of living even until the anniversary of the birth of the Christ child.

She murmured a prayer over the baby and handed him back.

"May God grant him health." Margaret gave Mary Courtney instructions for the herbs' preparation and dosage. Then she wrapped her cloak around her. "May the blessed Virgin Mother keep thee and thine in her care."

"Thank you, mistress." Mary Courtney curtsied again. She was crooning to her child as Margaret and Bess walked away.

> *"Sing lullaby, my little boy.*
> *Sing lullaby, my only joy."*

Margaret followed the main path back to the Mattapany road and turned right along the north wall of the fort. Giles hailed her from the street in front of the governor's house.

"Brother, back from the Isle of Kent at last."

"Look what I've brought thee." He held the bridle of a wiry dapple gray with a white blaze and a hogged mane.

"Giles!" Margaret picked up her skirts and hurried so fast she almost broke into a run. She peered into the mare's eyes, lifted her lip to inspect her teeth and ran a hand over her shaggy winter coat. "Where didst thou get her?"

"She's part of the rebellious Billy Claiborne's forfeited chattel. I shipped her and a bald-faced cow on the pinnace."

"Pinnace?"

"Once Claiborne's pinnace, now mine." Giles waved airily toward the harbor. "The cow is named Old Motley, but the mare is thine to christen."

Margaret was incredulous. Kent Island lay three days' sail north from the mouth of the Potomac. The Virginian, William Claiborne, had settled it three years before Leonard Calvert declared it part of Maryland. And he had ferociously contested the Calverts' claim until driven out a year and a half ago.

"Baltimore granted thee Kent Fort Manor?" she asked.

"Aye." Giles lowered his voice. Attracted by the sight of the first horse in St. Mary's, people were converging on them. "The governor, as thou knowest, is in Virginia. Baltimore's letter arrived on a ship that anchored there, and Leonard sent word directly to me at Kent."

"Two thousand acres?"

"Aye. And Clairborne's manse and mill, swine, kine and mutton, tobacco houses, forge, barn, and wood lots." His grin displayed every tobacco-yellowed tooth in his head. "I am lord of the manor. Leonard says it's the greatest privilege of seigniory conferred since the first Gentleman Adventurers arrived."

Margaret suffered a twinge of envy so intense it almost caused her physical pain around her heart. Giles had been given a manor intact, the results of another man's labor. Margaret now understood exactly how much labor that entailed.

She leaned close so only he could hear. "Then thou canst finally pay me what thou owest."

"Alas . . ." His smile drooped. "The enterprise on Kent has fallen into disarray. The tenants are a surly and unruly lot who have elevated that rogue Claiborne to sainthood, though he's still alive in Virginia, more's the pity. They are in arrears with their rents and careless of the ownership of my livestock, which they seize whenever they feel hungry. I shall have to borrow a small sum to set things running in proper order." Giles hesitated. "I was hoping thou would'st forgive some of my debt in exchange for the mare."

The horse drew the bandy-legged Irishman, Baltasar Codd, like a lodestone attracted filings. Across each shoulder he carried a long pole draped with bundled tobacco leaves. He set them down, and while Giles and Margaret dickered, he lifted the mare's tail and felt her hind legs, knees and pasterns.

Giles donned the bland look he used for gaming. "She's worth at least eight hundred weight, half in cask, wouldn't you say, Margaret?"

"I would not." Margaret glanced warily at Codd who was working his way forward along the mare's body, probing every inch of her. Knowing him, he planned to steal her at the first opportunity. "I shall give thee one hundredweight."

"Dear sister! One hundredweight buys a pair of wretched Virginia shoes."

"Mayhap ya should be makin' shoes of her yerself, squoire." When Codd stepped back to assess the mare from a distance, he almost tripped over Bess Guest who, with a look of enchantment on her plain, full face, was treading on his shadow.

Codd was about twenty-five, with a burry Irish accent, a shock of red-gold hair and faded blue eyes in a lantern-shaped face burned red by the sun.

Margaret suspected that Codd was trying to ingratiate himself so he could ask her for another loan. He had appealed to her before as a fellow Catholic and he had as silken a tongue as any Irishman Margaret had ever met. Whatever his motives, she wasn't one to turn away expert advice.

Margaret lifted the mare's lip to look for marks burned in the teeth to simulate youth. "She hath not been bishoped."

"Margaret, how could'st thou suggest . . . !" Giles sputtered in genuine outrage.

"Nay, nor feagued." Codd had looked first for evidence of someone putting ginger up the mare's anus to make her spry. "But she c'd be a bone-setter, Mistress Margaret, a hard-trotter and a bit of a coquette."

"Damn me, man." Giles rounded on him.

" 'Tis but the opinion of a humble horse courser, yer honor."

"When I want your opinions, Codd, I'll solicit them."

Margaret took the reins. "We shall discuss the price later, Giles."

She beckoned to Bess. She'd noted that Bess's wits had gone moon-raking as soon as Codd had appeared. She would have to lecture her again about the wiles of men. Margaret led the mare through a crowd that murmured as if the horse had been a unicorn. Bess followed reluctantly, casting wistful glances back at Codd, though only his bowed legs were visible now below the poles of tobacco leaves he'd hoisted onto his shoulders.

As Margaret approached the ordinary she was astonished to hear her sister singing a vulgar ditty with the thieving ale wench. Margaret dreaded to think how many verses of it they had sung already.

> "A master of music came with an intent,
> To give me a lesson on my instrument,
> I thank't him for nothing and bid him be gone,
> For my little fiddle should not be played on."

The two of them gaily launched into the chorus.

> "My Thing is my own, and I'll keep it so still,
> Yet other young lasses may do what they will."

Margaret was mortified, but it wouldn't do to march inside and fetch her sister from a public house as though she were a wastrel wagering the family's fortune at the gaming table.

She stroked the mare's nose. "Bess, hie thee inside and tell Mistress Mary that a surprise awaits her here."

Chapter 26

"Hip, hip, huzzah!" A ragged rank of men vaulted the knee-deep holes hogs had rooted in Governor's Field. "God save the king!"

About half of them wielded eighteen-foot saplings with fire-hardened points. The rest brandished mattocks and pitchforks. Over their loose breeches they wore an assortment of coats—quilted jackets leaking tufts of wool from the seams, leather buff-coats, rusty iron breastplates and moth-eaten wool jerkins. Their headgear included helmets, wide-brimmed felt hats and knitted caps. Some wore scuffed, mud-caked boots or laced pumps. Others ran barefoot even in late October.

"Halt!" the sergeant shouted. "Face about."

The line broke as some men took longer to skid to a stop than the others. They swiveled this way and that in a clash of metal and wood that knocked one helmet off and almost skewered an eye. In spite of the cool air of late October, agitation created pink blotches on Giles's cheeks. Shoving and jostling, the foot soldiers reformed into their wavery rank. Giles slogged along it, taking care not to trip over his dogs or the wide cuffs of his own boots.

He wore a long leather coat and bandolier a-clatter with the usual paraphernalia. He carried his tattered copy of *English Military Discipline* under one arm.

"To salute your superior you must pull off your hats." The wind carried his reedy voice the length of the line.

The men, most of whom were servants to one gentleman or another, hastened to remove their caps and bend their right knees in a low bow.

"Damn me! Do it without making a leg," Giles shouted. "Stand upright and keep your hats off, thusly, until the person has passed." He held his own hat over his chest. The wind wrapped the wide brim around him and blew the plume into his mouth.

For some of the pikemen, presenting their weapons and doffing their hats without bowing was one maneuver too many and one too few. They dropped their poles and bumped their heads trying to collect them again. Giles clamped his hat back on and stood with his fists on his narrow hips. The subtlest skill in managing a muster was knowing how much hard cider would make his men enthusiastic and how much would make them even clumsier than they already were.

Robert Vaughan and John Price watched from the cider barrel near the well sweep. The other musketeers, freemen all, squatted on their heels or hung on their gun rests. Vaughan's crossbow and his old matchlock musket leaned against a tree.

"I endeavored to advise him on how to train the country vulgar, but he would not heed." As muster master at St. Inigoes, Price was offended by the poor show. He raised his chin and sighted imperiously down the length of his nose at Vaughan. " 'Damn me, my good fellow!' " He gave a rather good imitation of Giles's west country affectation of a London dandy. " 'I know the business, Price. 'Tis as simple as farting, really. Damn me!' "

"A pity his sister were not in charge." Vaughan upended his leather flask and drank the last of the peach brandy.

Vaughan had seen Margaret Brent marshal her servants and he didn't doubt she could manage troops. She had been friendlier since his proposal of marriage, smiling impishly at him now and then, as though they shared a secret jest at someone else's expense rather than their own. An impish smile on Margaret Brent's craggy face was a vision worth seeing.

As for Giles, Vaughan was more impressed with him than

Price was, maybe because he had expected so little of him at the start. Vaughan was also one of the few not astonished by Lord Baltimore's conferring Kent Fort Manor on Squire Brent. Giles was a wealthy ally, and a fervent Catholic. The two thousand acres would buy his loyalty rather cheaply. Besides, unlike Thomas Cornwaleys, who was also wealthy and devout, Giles was too incompetent to threaten Leonard Calvert's authority.

Vaughan had already decided to throw in with Brent. For five years he had been the gentry's man when risks were to be taken. Anglicans like him were good enough to serve as sheriff to police the riffraff, or sergeants to lead the charge into arrows or bullets, but important positions and rank went to Catholics. Even though Vaughan could read and cipher as well as any gentleman in the province, Giles was the only one to offer him a position as steward, engaging him for his new manor on the Isle of Kent.

"Mistress Brent engaged the cooper last winter before anyone else," Price said. "Now he's behind in his other orders, which makes the gents peevish."

"More than that," Vaughan said. "She loaned him one of her servants at no fee. Now she has a man with at least the rudiments of the cooper's art." Actually, Robert knew of men who resented the fact that Margaret Brent could concentrate on building and planting while they must appear for muster or the sessions of court and the elected Assembly.

"Copley doth recruit among the thwack-coats for his popish legion." Price nodded toward the cudgel and billhook men.

They had slung their weapons across their shoulders and gathered at the second cider cask. Father Copley's black cassock moved among them. He approached one surly individual and Vaughan watched as though waiting for a pair of overloaded dray carts to collide in a narrow ally. The man resented just about everything, but he especially resented being passed over for the rank of sergeant. He considered it a popish plot. He swayed where he stood and swore steadily.

Copley fixed him with a baleful stare. "Any who blasphemes the holy Trinity shall burn in hell when he dies."

"By God's guts." The man rounded on him. "Go to the devil, you petticoated son of a bachelor, and be well disposed of."

Giles's look of irritation sharpened into fury. He had troubles enough without Copley stirring up religious controversy. Robert Vaughan picked up his weapons and sauntered over. He caught Copley's elbow in mid-gesture.

"Thomas, come tip a bowl with me in yon public house."

"Methinks we shall find there much heresy and drunkenness and mispence of time," Copley snapped.

"I do hope so." Vaughan winked at Giles and led the priest gently but firmly toward the ordinary. Behind him he heard the man muttering about priests who heretofore had been obliged to hide in the walls of papish manor houses but now were free to scuttle about in daylight, bold as cockroaches.

"In any case," Vaughan said, "we can wash the dust from our intellects and resume our discussion of Bacon's theories."

"Nunc scripsi totum pro Cristo da mihi potum," Copley recited dryly.

Robert Vaughan chuckled. Copley was quoting what monks wrote when they finished transcribing a manuscript. " 'Now I have written so much for Christ, give me a drink.' " Thomas Copley's wit was usually expressed in Latin which was why most people thought he had none at all.

Price trailed along. He didn't care about Latin wit or Bacon's opinion of the four causes of human error. He also knew that the talk would probably develop into Copley's usual list of grievances against Lord Baltimore; but Vaughan was likely to buy at least one round of drinks in the interest of religious harmony. As for Vaughan, he assumed he would listen yet again to Price tell of how he saved Squire Cornwaleys's patrician arse from the irritable Susquehannocks four years ago.

The ordinary's walls seemed hardly able to contain the stir and noise inside. Tobacco smoke eddied like turbulent water. With a brace of tankards held high over her head, Anicah emerged from it like a graceful shallop under sail. She rolled her eyes at Vaughan as she tacked and jibed around the outstretched feet of her customers.

The loud talk and the clamor of wooden spoons scraping wooden trenchers hushed briefly when Thomas Copley entered holding a pomander delicately to his nose. Even here where fashions were plain, Copley's cassock was conspicuous.

Vaughan went to his table near the fire and nodded pleasantly to the four mariners sitting there. They picked up their cups and moved, with sour looks, to the ale bench where everyone had to shift closer together to accommodate them.

In the center of the room Goodman Smythe had set the turn-spit dog on a table. He sang a bawdy ditty while the dog danced on his singed hind legs for bits of gristle. The gunsmith John Dandy and Harry Angell sat with their heads together.

"There sits a brace of poxy rogues I would not pay a turd for," Price muttered.

Dandy, however, seemed delighted to see Copley. He pushed back his stool and came over. When he leaned close Copley drew away in distaste.

"Have we a bargain?" Dandy asked. "A thousand pounds of weed for the boy?"

"In the cask, all inspected and stamped with the governor's seal," Copley muttered. "I will accept no seconds, nor bruised nor burnt nor worm-eaten leaf mixed in among the good. No wet leaves or stones nested in the shipment."

"Certes, padre, albeit a dear price for a bumpkin."

Copley flinched when Dandy clapped him jovially on the back. The gunsmith returned to his companion and Copley's tension eased back to its usual level.

"Which man's papers are you selling, Thomas?"

"Kirk, Martin Kirk."

"What of Martin Kirk?" Anicah appeared at Vaughan's shoulder with their drinks.

"It concerns not the likes of thee," Copley said.

She rested her knuckles on the table board and stared into the priest's gloomy eyes. "Martin Kirk be me betrothed, yer reverence, and I will know the what-for and whereabouts of 'im."

"Your dearling shall sleep closer to you, Ani," Vaughan said. "He is to be bound to the gunsmith at St. Inigoes."

Anicah's smile turned radiant. She swooped suddenly and kissed Copley on his high forehead. A deep blush stained the pallor of his cheeks. Then for good measure she kissed Vaughan and Price.

"I've a song of a religious nature, and it please yer lordships." She curtsied prettily.

> *"To save a maid, St. George, the dragon slew.*
> *A pretty tale, if all that's told be true;*
> *Most say there are no dragons, and 'tis said*
> *There was no George;*
> *Pray God there was a maid."*

She winked slyly, and was surprised to see Copley's thin lips flicker in a smile.

Vaughan smacked Anicah playfully on the bottom. "Shall we have one of Dina's eel pies today?"

"I shall ask her."

"Ani." Harry beckoned to her, but he was watching the door.

The chirugeon, Thomas Gerard, filled the doorway. He paused to let his eyes adjust to the gloom so he could survey the customers. When he saw Harry he started toward him, pushing people aside to clear a path.

Harry pressed into Anicah's hand a piece of bloody sacking. She slipped it into the pouch hanging under the slit in her skirt. As she hurried into the kitchen she heard Gerard's voice boom out behind her.

"Damn me, Angell, you rogue. You've kil't a boar of my known mark, butchered it where it lay and made away with the bloody ears. Turn out your pockets."

" 'Tis the salvages that steal our cattle and hogs, squire," Harry said. "I espied one skulking about the forest only today."

"Turn out your clothes, you larcenous puppy!"

The ensuing uproar made no difference to Anicah. Gerard wouldn't find the ears he was looking for, at least not until Harry had altered the mark to make it look like those of Joan's. She grabbed Dina's hands, one of which held a cleaver, and danced a few steps of the trenchmore with her.

"Martin's to serve out his term with the spoil-iron at the fort on Priests' Hill."

"John Dandy?"

"Aye."

Dina looked dubious. Both she and Anicah had seen the gun-smith's rages when in his cups.

"Dandy's an easily kindled little chimney," Anicah said, "But Martin gives offense to no one. And he shall be less than a league away."

The kitchen was too small to contain Anicah's joy. She wanted to run outside and shout to the trees and the heavens. She threw open the back door and charged straight into a Potomack Indian, naked but for some beads and feathers, a strategically placed fox skin and a coat of old bear grease. He was so tall her nose hit the middle of his breastbone. She yelped and backed away.

"He'll do ye no harm." Dina rummaged among the heap of bottles and boxes in a corner.

"I know that." Peevishly, she used her apron to wipe the grease off her face.

"Take the hamper from him," Dina said.

When he held it out an ominous rustle and hiss came from inside.

Anicah shuddered. "He always leaves some alive."

" 'Tis but a jest."

"A plaguey odd way he has of jesting."

Dina took the creel and handed him another one in exchange. Inside she'd placed a bottle of ale and a lump of sorghum sugar as dark brown as he was. Without a sound he disappeared. The smell of rancid fat he left behind blended with the kitchen aroma of venerable garbage and spoiled meat.

Anicah hung the kettle on the hook, filled it with water and swung the trammel over the flames. Dina opened the creel's lid and pulled out a wriggling black snake as long as her arm. She gripped it just behind the jaws, laid it on the block and with formidible grace severed its head with her cleaver.

She deftly separated out the backbone and cut away the jaws and teeth. She would boil the flesh from them later and put them to use. The skins she would tan and sell for hatbands and belts. She had persuaded the more gullible men that wearing strips of the hides tied around their members added to their sexual potency.

Not only Indians and tradesmen and goodwives with produce and cheese and eggs called at the back door. Dina received other visitors there. They conferred with her, handed her some small payment for a packet of powdered snake bone or a grotesquery of chicken feathers and delicate vertebrae and teeth strung like beads. Sometimes they stayed to gossip, but most often they hurried away.

Anicah once had asked her if she had magical powers. Dina had laughed. "Only the power fools give me," she'd said.

"Where's the wench?" Goodwife Smythe shouted from the common room.

Anicah hurried out and slipped the wrapped hog's ears to Harry as she passed. She put an arm around Robert Vaughan's shoulders and leaned close.

"Ye shall have yer eel pie," she whispered. "Cooked very savory, with butter and parsley."

"Splendid." He beamed at her and ran a hand up the inside of her skirt to squeeze her thigh affectionately. "For I am as hungry as a wolf."

Chapter 27

March's full moon hung low in the western sky. The sun wouldn't rise for another hour. Harry Angell stumbled in the dark and lost his grip on the rope harness around the cask of hard cider. Goodman Smythe had been letting Harry do most of the work, and the keg escaped him too. It bounced and careened down the steep path along the face of the bluff behind the ordinary.

Harry's oaths floated up from the darkness as he crashed through the thorny brush after it. "The devil take it!"

"Meseems the devil hath done so," Anicah called softly after him.

"Have a care, ye clumsy loobies." Goody Smythe held up the shrouded lantern and peered into the blackness. She handed the lantern to Anicah. "When the goods are laded, hie thee here directly or I'll whip thee as ne'er a dog was whipped."

Anicah picked her way down the rocky incline. "A fine black night for owlin'," she called softly to Harry.

She was pleased at being included in the enterprise, if only as lantern bearer. The owling trade was highly regarded and smugglers were as admired as Robin Hood by the common folk. They provided goods often not obtainable otherwise, and cheaper too, without the high tariffs the king's customs men demanded.

"Lift the devilish light aloft." Harry's tone was exasperated but subdued. Voices traveled on the still night air.

Anicah was amused at the sight of him with his leather cap missing and his greasy hair awry. He was trying to wrestle the barrel back
onto the path while Goodman Smythe leaned against a tree and
panted. Smythe's round cheeks glowed red with exertion.

Anicah found Harry's hat, but when she picked it up it felt
heavier than it should be. She pulled out an object as big as a nutmeg, wrapped in paper, and unwrapped it while Harry was occupied with the barrel. It was a hard ball of wax. She ran her fingers
over it in the lantern's light. One side was flattened, and im-
printed in it was the Calvert family coat of arms. She smiled to
herself. Harry was up to something, no doubt about it.

She replaced the wax mold in the cap and handed it to him.
Then she lit the way as the men maneuvered the barrel down to
the tangle of vines and snags along the river. They rolled it onto a
crude raft beached there. Smythe bent over and panted.

The water lapped at the pink sand. Anicah and Harry sat on a
fallen tree trunk and stared out at the black river.

"Do ye intend to float spirits to the salvages on that bit o'
flotsam?"

"Nay. When the priests go out amongst the heathens, they'll
deliver it fer us."

"Why would the paternosters help ye debauch the Indians?"

"They'll not know." Harry grinned. "We'll float it to the harbor and hide it aboard their shallop. Their man Lewis'll transport
it to St. Inigoes."

"Is Lewis in on the rig?"

"He knows naught of't, but I'm to sail with him. John
Dandy'll help me unload it when we get to St. Inigoes. We'll
ghost it back aboard the shallop when their servants stow the
goods to trade with the salvages." A travesty of piety played across
his gaunt, vulture's face. "I've realized the shipwreck I've made of
me soul," he said solemnly. "I'm to be catechized in the true faith.
As a devout convert I shall go along to hunt game for the priests'
maintenance. And truck spirits on the sly."

"Ye'll find Lewis standing sentry in the boat," Anicah said.

"Certes?"

"Aye. He was toping at the alehouse and I heard him swear he would lie atop the goods that they not grow legs during the night and run away."

Harry pondered that complication.

"I c'd distract him, fer two fees," Anicah said.

"What might they be?"

"First, tell me how ye bought yer covenant."

Harry tossed a pebble into the liquid night of the river. He waited for the hollow splash before he spoke. "Ere I left Bristol I sewed a stolen bill of exchange into me hat, charged upon one Samuel Moody, banker. A figure dancer, another of the king's guests at Newgate, converted the sum of twenty shillings on it to two hundred."

"Who would honor such here?"

"A few rascals and several fools; but I sold it to the mate on Richard Ingle's ship for half the new value. From the look of him, he wrung something from the misfortunate Mr. Moody when he docked at Bristol."

"Harry, ye're prime, ye are. Bang-up prime."

"I hung the lantern, ye know."

"Lantern?"

"On the ship."

"Ye flashed the sea curs and almost got me hung?"

"Aye. I thought to join 'em should they catch us. Ye being dressed as a boy, ye could've come along. Ye'd've fancied the life, I wager."

For an instant Anicah saw herself and Martin on the tossing forepeak of a corsair, free to roam the wide world and pillage at will. Then, though more than a year had passed since that voyage, she remembered the seasickness and storms, the turned beer and weeviled biscuits hard as cobblestones. "A voyage to St. Inigoes be sea career enow."

"Then your second fee would be passage to the priests' hill?"

"Aye." Anicah wrapped her arms around her legs and rested her chin on her knees.

Mathias DaSousa had brought her messages from Martin for a while. But he had sailed for Virginia to trade, and Martin had sent no word through anyone else for more than two months, since before Christmas.

Jealousy gnawed at her. Dina said Dandy's maid servant was comely and Anicah feared Martin's affections had strayed. She would find out today, though, and Goodwife Smythe and her rod could go to the devil.

"What ho!" The sky had faded to gray but the sun still hadn't risen when Anicah stood on the landing. She peered at the shallop pushed low in the water by the weight of its cargo. "What ho!" she called again.

One long, canvas-wrapped bundle stirred.

"Good morrow, your honor."

The bundle rolled over. A hand peeled back the canvas and the priests' steward, William Lewis, squinted at Anicah. Aside from his watery blue eyes, the only color in his pale face was the scarlet tip of his long nose and the red rims around his eyes.

"Methinks I found the paternosters' bit o' the True Cross." Anicah held up a sliver of wood. She waited for Lewis to gather his wits from wherever sleep had strewn them.

"The true cross?"

"Aye."

" 'Tis not missing."

"After ye left the tavern yesternight Goodman Brown boasted of lifting it. Methinks he believes it'll stiffen his yard again. But he foundered in his cups and I discovered it on the floor when I swept this morn."

"Why bring you it here?"

"Copley's such a shite-fire I fear he'll charge me with filching it."

"Likely ye did." Lewis crawled out of his cocoon and shivered. The stiff canvas retained the shape of his body a long moment before slowly collapsing.

"Nay, sir. I'd not risk my immortal soul thus. I pray ye go with me to the priest's house. 'Twere whacking bad luck to lose such a relic."

"And leave my goods for your friends to steal? I think not."

"Surely ye'll want to return this holy piece of the rood to the black robes. If the heretics get their daddles on it they might visit disaster on us all."

"Protestants be minions of the devil." Lewis settled his knitted cap more firmly on his narrow head and arched his back to ease the ache there. "Gi'it me and I'll return it to Copley."

"And tell him I stole it? Nay. I'll find some other wight to share in the glory of its recovery. Mayhap they'll reward me fer its finding." She turned and trotted across the beach. Lewis climbed off the boat, splashed ashore and hurried after her.

Harry was waiting for them when they returned.

"The wench led me on a wild goose chase." Lewis was furious. Father Copley had sniffed the pale wood, gouged it with his thumbnail. He remarked that the tulip tree didn't grow in the Holy Land and only a ninny would think this a part of the True Cross. "She said Christ's rood was purloined, yet it lies in its proper place."

" 'Tis no fault o' mine that Brown's a flimflammer." Anicah winked at Harry.

Harry Angell was as good as his word. Anicah was sitting in the prow with her back against alewife Smythe's shrouded barrel of cider when St. Inigoes creek hove into sight. Fort St. Inigoes sat on a rise with a view of the confluence of the St. George's River and the Potomac River to the south. From the open shed that housed his crude forge John Dandy had a view of the river. He was waiting at the landing. Anicah noticed Harry take off his cap and give the packet to Dandy.

Then she saw Martin standing well behind him. He kept his

hat pulled low and his head down. If he saw Anicah he didn't acknowledge it. In fact, he acted as though he didn't know her. Anicah's greeting died in her throat. Dandy's serving wench must have made a conquest of him after all.

As soon as Lewis trudged away, Harry and Dandy uncovered the cask and heaved it onto Martin's broad shoulders. Staggering under its weight, he started toward the smithy without a glance at Anicah. Dandy followed him.

"Yer faithless swain left ye wearin' the willow did he?" Harry said.

"Mayhap."

"Jealousy works on the brain like fleas and lice."

"Nay." Anicah thought she would die from grief and rage and longing. " 'Tis no such gentle thing, but a starved rat gnawing at the heart."

She saw no purpose in staying here. She would not cavil after Martin's affections. She studied the dense forest beyond the charred tree stumps and corn stubble. "Whereat lies the path to the village?"

"A faint heart ne'er wins field."

"I can scorn as well as he."

"As you will." Harry headed for the forest fringe and the blazed trail to St. Mary's.

Anicah started to follow him. Then she stopped. She turned toward the shed. She swiveled back toward Harry who was growing smaller as the distance lengthened between them. If she didn't go with him, she would have to make her way alone through the forest.

" 'Faint heart,' " she muttered. "Go to, Harry. I own not a faint heart."

She took an oblique course around behind the smithy and sat on a low heap of firewood amid the towering stacks of it. Charcoal was hard to get here and a smith needed a lot of wood. Martin would appear eventually to fetch it. Grief stung Anicah's eyes and caught in her throat, but her hands trembled with fury. She considered picking up a length of kindling and rattling his ears with it. She was so preoccupied she didn't hear him approach from behind.

"Anicah."

She leaped up and whirled on him. "Thou heartless wretch, thou—" Then she saw his face.

A mask of deep lavender and green surrounded his eyes and connected across the bridge of his nose. His upper lip was cut and swollen. His cheeks were hollow below the arched bones that defined them. His shirt and filthy leather jerkin hung in tatters.

"What happened to ye?"

"Better my parents had kilt me than sent me here." He looked so desolate Anicah threw her arms around him, but he winced and eased her away.

"Yer master beats ye?"

"Aye." He sat wearily on a log. "Have you any bread about you?"

Anicah reached into the slit in her skirt for the bag that hung there. She had spent most of her life hungry. Now that she had access to a kettle, she always sneaked extra food to save for future want. She gave him the bread and the cheese she'd stolen. When Martin took it she saw that the palms of his hands and insides of his fingers were covered with unhealed sores, blisters that had burst and been rubbed raw. He wolfed down the food.

"What happened to yer daddles?"

Still chewing, he nodded at the piles of split logs around him.

"Ye chopped all this wood?"

"Every faggot." He paused. "How came you here? Will not they raise a hue and cry for you?"

"The gentry haven't time to hunt such small game as an errant serving wench. Me mistress will rage but she needs me labor too much to beat me seriously."

"I would've sneaked away to see you, Ani, but at night he hangs a horse lock upon my leg."

"Then ye're twice a prisoner." Her voice softened, lost the harsh tones of the streets. "For thou art locked within my heart."

Martin rested his elbows across his knees. He laid his head on his forearms and sobbed.

Anicah put an arm around his shoulders to comfort him. "I'm sharking chink from the swells to redeem our terms."

Martin looked up, the despair plain in his big dark eyes. "I fear there won't be time."

"What mean ye?"

"I shall kill my master if he murders me not first."

Chapter 28

Governor Calvert had convened the court session for March 1640. It would continue for weeks, and men from farms as far away as the Isle of Kent had arrived to bring suit or defend themselves against charges. The majority of them headed directly for Smythe's ordinary while they waited for their cases to be heard. Many had not tasted hard drink nor disputed politics or religion for months. They were eager to make up for the time lost.

In the resulting tumult Goody Smythe ran nervous hands through her brittle hair until it stood out in rattails around her doughy face. Exasperated, she kicked the turnspit dog away from the fire. With his tail between his legs he leaped onto the ale bench. He scrambled up Goodman Smythe's sprawled thighs to lie precariously balanced atop his great berm of a belly.

"Have I told you of the droll mischance that happened in London during the time of pestilence many years since?" Smythe asked to the congregation at large.

"Aye," said Goodman Brown.

"Aye," Anicah muttered, but Smythe proceeded anyway.

"A certain gentleman had several servants who were ill. Loath to have his house quarantined, he made a compact with the men of the pest cart to haul away in the night any that might die."

Anicah had heard the story of the drunk taken away on the pest cart long before Smythe told it the first time. It had circulated in Bristol as far back as she could remember. She had small patience for it or for the men who shouted orders and proposals at her as she hurried back and forth. She was almost fifteen now and her breasts had begun to make taut curves under her low-cut bodice. She received a lot of proposals.

All she could think of was Martin's bruised and swollen face and, inexplicably, Mary Brent's hands. Mistress Mary had helped Anicah prepare apples for cider back last November until her sister sent the maid Bess to fetch her. The image of the russet peel reeling in a sinuous ribbon from the gentlewoman's spidery hands still haunted Anicah. They looked like hands that could cure pestilence or spin out a miracle as easily as a skein of yarn. That they were as callused as her own had astonished Anicah.

Mistress Mary would intercede with her sister to redeem Martin from the gunsmith, Anicah was sure of it. Anicah was also sure that Mary knew she had stolen from her in Bristol, but she didn't seem to care. Margaret Brent cared, though. Her glare delivered a reproach and a threat every time she looked at her. And so Anicah argued with herself as she balanced the bowls and tankards and dodged her admirers' hands.

Ask Mistress Mary. I dare not. Ask her. I cannot.

She was so preoccupied she passed close to a Kent Island man she usually avoided. He was to be presented in court for slandering Governor Calvert and Calvert's officer on Kent, Giles Brent. He was scowling into his bowl of cider as though he had found a cockroach there. "I hate them as hold with popish folleries," he muttered. "And I hate that scurfy puppy, Leonard Lack-wit."

Anicah thought he might be so engrossed in his ire she could pass unnoticed, but he caught her skirts in a filthy hand. "When will ye marry me, Ani?"

"When pigs take wing, Ned."

"I'll buy yer covenant from the alewife." He tugged her toward him.

"Ye've not chink enough to pay yer score here. And ye stink like a bog pot, besides." She said it airily to show she held him no malice and swiveled her hips to yank her skirt from his grasp.

She passed Henry Fleete who was sitting alone. She leaned down and murmured in his ear, "I must have me portion now, Cap'n."

"Portion?" He looked blandly up at her. "Of what?"

"Do not think to deceive me."

"If you think I owe you, present me in court." He winked at her.

Anicah wasn't surprised. She had half expected Fleete to renege on his promise to share his card winnings with her. But his duplicity now in her time of desperate need made her furious.

"Step to, wench." Goodwife Smythe emerged from the kitchen. "Deliver this peck and booze to Squire Cornwaleys at the Hawley house." She shoved a big, cloth-covered basket at Anicah. "Don't dawdle."

Anicah curtsied in a rare display of social grace that made Goody Smythe stare at her suspiciously. She was suddenly elated. Everyone said Squire Cornwaleys was rich as Croesus. He could buy Martin's term from Dandy.

Anicah grabbed her threadbare cloak from its peg by the door and threw it around her shoulders. She took a fat-pine splinter to use as a torch on the return trip and stepped into a cold dusk. Carrying the heavy basket in her arms, she set off toward the uncertain track through the trees that covered much of the deceased Squire Hawley's land.

She dreaded the forest with its dangling webwork of vines, thick and shaggy as ships' hawsers. More than the little people, she feared the wolves that howled in the depths, the salvages gliding through the shadows, the snakes rustling along the forest floor. Even the colonists' roving hogs were a menace.

When she reached the frame house she pounded on the heavy door.

"Enter," called out Cornwaleys.

Anicah pushed the door open, shoved the basket through and slipped in after it. She picked up the basket and bumped the door closed with her hip.

"Ah, the romp from the tipling house," Cornwaleys said.

" 'Od's codpiece." Anicah stared open-mouthed around her. She had never been under the same roof with so much wealth.

Two chairs and several stools, a cupboard, sideboard and a stocky table draped with a Turkey carpet crowded one half of the twenty-by-twenty-foot room. On the other side, a big flock bed and feather bolster stood next to a hearth. The lids of two hulking chests were open. Clothing hung over their rims. The bed was piled with neatly folded linens.

"Set out the spirits on the table and warm the sausages in yon skillet." Cornwaleys stood at a tall desk with a ledger open in front of him.

He wore a black velvet doublet whose wide shoulders and fitted stays emphasized his slim waist. His brown hair, streaked with gray at the temples, fell in waves to his shoulders. He had handsome features, but pared too fine for Anicah's taste.

Anicah unpacked the basket on the carpet that covered the table. An assortment of pokers, tongs, cheese toasters, ladles and bread paddles hung next to the fireplace and she tried to decide which one she should use for the sausage. Cooking utensils put her uneasily in mind of a torturer's kit.

Cornwaleys had the brooding look of a man beset by too many sorrows and too little brandy. Anicah set a pewter noggin and a bottle of brandy next to the desk. She wanted to lighten his mood before she made her request of him. Cornwaleys looked askance at the noggin, but he poured the brandy into it anyway.

"Countin' yer money, are ye, squire?"

"Nay, another man's. A dead man's." He rubbed his eyes. "So many of us dead." He said it more to himself than to her. "I am the Reaper's accountant. I am like a battlefield whore, counting the possessions of corpses."

"Well, ye're alive, and have all yer fingers and toes to do the countin' on, don't ye?"

Cornwaleys smiled and looked vaguely surprised to be doing it. He waved an arm at the ledger. "My friend left his affairs in such a tangle, and even the lawyers for other dead men are suing him. I dare say there are quarterly sessions in heaven."

"Nay, sir, there are not." With a long-handled spoon Anicah chased the plump sausages around the skillet. "Bloody hell." She jumped back when one popped and spit sizzling grease onto her hand.

"I beg pardon?" Cornwaleys stared at her.

She impaled the first sausage on the point of a cheese toaster and held up the string of them. Grease dripped on the floor while she considered dropping them onto the table carpet. She thought better of it and pushed them off onto a trencher.

" 'Tis a known fact that green bags do not go to heaven," she said. "Therefore, 'tis certain no court session may be held there."

"Green bags?" he asked.

Anicah licked the grease from her fingers. "Lawyers are called so fer the bags of green baize they carry, which they stuff with old clothes to make themselves look prosperous."

Cornwaleys started to laugh. He moved books from a chair so he could collapse into it. He laughed until he had to wipe his eyes on his lace cuff. Anicah knew she wasn't that funny, but Cornwaleys looked like a man in need of even a poor jest.

Anicah took a knife, a spoon and a bowl from the sideboard. She dipped the bowl into the pot of cold samp, wiped the drippings off the rim with her finger and licked it. She set it next to the bread and cheese and the trencher of sausages.

"Is that yer lady, squire?" She nodded to a portrait of a gray-eyed beauty leaning against the wall.

"Nay. Ill health forbids my wife from attempting the voyage."

"Could I marry my sweetheart I nevermore would leave him." She kicked a stool close to Cornwaleys's chair, sat on it and prepared to wade boldly into her proposal while he ate.

Over their Sabbath wine in the ordinary the gentry complained about the lack of laborers for their planting. Everyone said Cornwaleys was the richest man in Maryland, and for a papist, uncommonly fair to Protestants. He was lord of more land than anyone except Governor Calvert and Lord Baltimore himself. She'd heard that on the other side of St. Inigoes Creek he was building a house even finer than the governor's.

"Squire, ye c'd use a strong pair o' hands."

"Yours?"

"Nay. Martin Kirk's. The gunsmith holds his covenant."

"My debts and miseries have multiplied beyond reckoning and 'tis all I can do to keep from sinking myself."

Anicah dared not contradict him, but she was sure he was lying. No one who dressed so fine and sat his satin-clad arse on a chair ornamented with balusters and bobbins could be poor. For once, though, she kept her thoughts to herself.

"The smith abuses him, sire."

"I've seen your Martin. He's a strapping lad."

"Strong as a drayman's prancer, and honest too." A wave of hope lifted Anicah onto its crest.

"The chirurgeon offered to buy the boy," Cornwaleys said.

"Did he?"

"Dandy said he would be the death of the man that tried to fetch him."

Anicah shrugged. "He roars when he's drunk, yet he's a coward withal." But she knew Cornwaleys would deny her.

Sergeant Vaughan had explained it to her. A simple mechanic, even a strong, young yeoman, wasn't worth making an enemy of the gunsmith. Everyone's life depended on Dandy, no matter that his temperament could be as hot and as cold as the steel he shaped.

"I cannot buy his covenant," Cornwaleys said.

"Ye must, sire." Anicah dropped to her knees and caught his smooth hand in both her small, hard ones. "He'll be kilt."

"Anicah, the sovereignty of law rules us here. Your swain will not be . . . kilt."

Anicah thought of Henry Fleete's taunt that she sue him for the money he owed her. She wanted to laugh at Cornwaleys's foolish prattling about law. The law would never work for her. She would always be on the wrong end of it.

She released his hand and stood up. She was furious at herself for thinking someone of his rank would help her.

"Me mistress said to return as soon as I'm done here. Will ye be wantin' anything else?"

"No."

Anicah put the cloth and the emptied brandy bottle into the basket. Cornwaleys would send one of his people with the samp pot and the second bottle in the morning. She put on her cloak.

"I bid ye a good night." She curtsied perfunctorily and picked up the basket.

"Anicah."

"Sire?" She paused with her hand on the latch.

"Know you the meaning of stealth of oneself?"

"Running away."

"It is a servant's unlawful departure out of service or out of the colony without consent of master or mistress."

Aye, Anicah thought. Running away. Cornwaleys was about to deliver a warning to Martin through her.

"Stealth of oneself is a felony. Know you the punishment for a felon?"

"He twists."

"If the offender can read he preserves his life, but loses his hand or is burned in the forehead with a hot iron."

Anicah didn't tell him that she was quite familiar with the punishments for a felony. She curtsied again, opened the door and walked out into the moonlight.

Chapter 29

Martin ached as though he had tumbled down a long slope of rocks. Pain stabbed his side where John Dandy had beaten him with his heavy leather strap after hanging him up by his wrists. He tried to wet his lips, but his swollen tongue stuck to them.

He pissed where he sat, fouling his breeches again. He hadn't enough moisture left in him to produce much urine. He would have drunk what little there was, but he couldn't. The chain that attached the manacles to an iron ring in the woodshed wall was too short.

He regretted that there was no cleric to intercede with God for his soul. He tried to remember a prayer for the dead, but hunger and a tearing thirst, pain and humiliation and a sense that he somehow deserved this punishment made it impossible. The only clear thought he could muster was that when he died Anicah might see his battered, filthy, rank remains and be repulsed by them.

Finally the words of the burial service came to him. "I am the resurrection and the life." Tears left burning tracks on his cheeks. The ringing in his ears was so loud he didn't hear the rattle of the lock on the door.

"Mah-teen?"

"Edward?" Martin peered into the darkness.

The Indian lad was wearing the linen shirt Father White had given him for being baptized. His legs were bare under the shirt-tail. Bags dangled from the belts and straps that crisscrossed his slender waist and chest.

He squatted in front of Martin and held a water pouch to his lips. Most of the contents ran off Martin's chin and soaked into his shirt, but the rest tasted better than anything he had ever known. Edward fumbled for the key to the manacles among those on Dandy's ring. After two or three tries the shackles fell away with a clatter.

Martin rubbed his torn wrists. The blackness inside the shed whirled around him. He felt Edward tugging at his arm.

"No." He tried to push his friend's hands away. "Mustn't help me. Seven years servitude."

Edward hauled him to his feet, a difficult task given Martin's size, even half starved.

"You stink," Edward observed.

"*Ha ho.*" They were the words of agreement that punctuated most Piscataway conversations.

Edward propelled him outside, through the clutter of the smithy's yard and toward the low bluff. As they passed Dandy's one-room house Martin noticed the door standing open. He could see by the moonlight that Edward's shirt was black with soot and so was he. He had done what all the English feared some hostile Indian would.

"You climbed down the chimney, didn't you?" Martin imagined him creeping silently among the sleeping figures, taking the ring of keys from the nail stuck into the wall near Dandy's pallet, then lifting the bolt and letting himself out the front door.

"*Ha ho,* damn me. Too right." Edward's teeth flashed in a tobacco-yellow grin as he opened the biggest sack hanging from his belt. It bulged with goods that Edward had scooped up in the dark house on his way from the chimney to the door. A knife and a pewter spoon lay on top of a wadded up linsey-woolsey petticoat. Smaller items probably lurked under it.

"You mustn't steal, Edward. 'Tis a wicked sin."

"Payment for hurt." Edward's fingers barely brushed Martin's ribs but he winced in pain. "And gifts."

"Gifts?"

"For *tayac* and Uncle and First Wife." Edward lobbed the keys over the low bluff and a few seconds later they splashed into the river. "Canoa, that way." Edward started toward the black wall of the forest to the south.

Martin looked back at the moonlit clearing, at the tree stumps in the bare fields, the bulk of the fort's earthenworks, the tobacco barn and smithy. He knew that if he stayed, Dandy would get drunk and beat him again. He knew hunger would continue to ravage his belly and his teeth would grow looser in his mouth from the diet of corn bread and watery soup. On top of that, he would be accused of breaking into Dandy's house and stealing his goods.

He trotted after Edward, but stopped where the huge trees bordered the corn stubble. Martin could spread his arms wide at the trunk of one of them and it would extend past his fingertips. Beyond it the forest loomed dark and ominous. No one went there at night if they could avoid it. Father Poulton said even the Indians feared Hobbamoco, the evil spirit who wandered about then. Edward had been courageous to come here.

Edward had darkened into a shadowy figure among the trees and bushes, a faun dappled with moonlight. He beckoned. With heart pounding Martin took a deep breath and followed. The forest closed around him as though he had never existed.

Goody Smythe stood in her usual stance with her oversized leather shoes planted about a foot's length apart. In her bulky apron, petticoats and skirt of gray-brown wool, she seemed to sprout like a very solid mushroom from the debris on the kitchen floor. She grabbed the low-cut neck of Anicah's bodice and pulled it so she could look down it.

Satisfied that Anicah had hidden nothing between her sleek

brown breasts except the small sack with her indenture paper, she stood back and wedged her fists in the fold of her thick waist and wide hips. Her hickory rod nodded from one hand.

"Up tails, ye baggage."

Anicah caught up the sides of her skirts and raised them over her head. From behind them she crossed her eyes and stuck out her tongue. Dina chuckled.

Goody Smythe walked around Anicah, looking for packets of food she might have stowed under her skirts.

"Do ye want to peep inside Venus's glove too?" Anicah swiveled her groin tauntingly and braced for the whistle of the rod through the air and the sting of it. It raised a curved red welt across her bare right nate.

"I'm not a fool." Patience Smythe glared at her from narrowed eyes. "I know you steal bread and cheese daily."

"Mayhap the rats ate it." Anicah dropped her skirts so they tangled with the switch and blunted the second blow.

Goody Smythe contented herself with one stroke well delivered. Disciplining Anicah was an exhausting undertaking. The wench was so nimble at dodging that the few blows the goodwife landed hardly merited the indignity of chasing her. Smythe always ended up huffing and panting, her arms aching from the exertion.

Goody Smythe and Anicah had arrived at an unspoken pact. Anicah continued to leave more weeds in the fields than she hoed up and more worms on the tobacco than she picked off. She forgot the samp until it boiled over and burned. She still dumped refuse behind the water barrel in the corner instead of carrying it to the midden by the door, and she frequently let the stack of firewood on the hearth dwindle to a few sticks before replenishing it. But she stopped mocking her mistress in her hearing. In turn Goodwife Smythe only boxed her ears or gave her a few strokes with the rod.

"Deliver the eel pie to Sergeant Vaughan." Goody Smythe waved the switch at her. "He shall discover if thou didst eat of it."

Anicah rearranged her skirts, picked up the basket with what the goodwife called eel pie, though Anicah knew it was snake. She went out into an early spring. The din of birdsong wasn't as entertaining as the music of Bristol's roving ballad mongers but it was pleasant enough.

As soon as she was out of sight she turned into a lane that led to a tumbledown cottage. The rear of it had been dug into a hillside. Smoke rose from a hole in the thatch that roofed the part above ground. A torn piece of sail served as a door.

"Good morrow, Goodman DaSousa," Anicah called. "God keep ye."

"What brings you out so early, Ani?" Mathias dug for lice in the felted mass of his hair as he pulled aside the canvas and squinted into the sunlight.

"I bring a charge fer ye." Anicah ran her hand up under her skirt.

She had promised Dina ten pounds of Fleete's debt of tobacco to sew two long, narrow pouches. She had tied them to a cord around her waist so they hung suspended at her sides between her ragged skirt and petticoat. She kept her snuff box with her father's will in one and filled the other with food. When Goody Smythe ordered her to raise her skirts she caught up the bags and their contents and lifted them with the petticoats. It was an old pickpockets' trick, but so far the goodwife hadn't tumbled to it.

The bag contained several pieces of stale bread, a fist-sized lump of cheese and a bit of boiled pork Anicah had sneaked off a trencher before she returned it to the kitchen the night before. She wrapped the food in a piece of sacking and held them out to Mathias.

"Ye'll take these to Martin then? I can gi' ye tuppence now fer yer trouble, and thirty-weight o' the sot weed when Captain Fleete pays me what he owes."

A look of melancholy skimmed across Mathias's dark face. He was remembering his own debts accumulating in Secretary Lewger's ledger. Ownership of a freehold seemed further away now than when he had agreed to come to the colony as Father White's servant six years before.

Anicah mistook the look for annoyance and she tensed. Lewger had sent DaSousa on a trading expedition and he'd been gone a fortnight. Anicah hadn't been able to find anyone willing to risk Dandy's ire and take food to Martin nor bring word back.

Cornwaleys had already declined to help her. Robert Vaughan and Giles Brent had been away at the Isle of Kent until recently. As for the rest, some had refused her more politely than others. They had given her bemused or irritated looks, as though she were gibbering at them in Dutch or French. She wanted to twist their ears and thump their noses.

Now she feared she'd be thwarted again, but Mathias took the food with a slight bow.

"God bless ye, Master DaSousa." She curtsied and gave him a brilliant smile. "Give it not to another, but set it square in his daddles."

"I shall endeavor to do that."

"Endeavor don't fit. Ye must do it, and no endeavor to it."

"Aye." He smiled back at her, and she stood on tiptoe and kissed him on the cheek.

"Backgammon is like a coquette's play with a lover." Robert Vaughan moved his piece. "All open at first, then one is backed into a corner and deprived of everything."

"I should be going." Father Copley studied the board and stroked his pointed black beard. "Mistress Mary Brent desireth that I hear her confession."

"Mistress Mary doth confess more sins and commit fewer than anyone in America." Vaughan took a drink of sack.

He sat on a stool with his knees spread to encompass half the small keg on which the backgammon board sat. He had draped his belt around his neck and his shirt hung loose outside his breeches. The russet rebellion of his hair and beard had snagged bits of dried corn husk from his pillow and ticking. He was puffing on the first pipe of the day.

Father Copley perched on the edge of Vaughan's single chair, dragged outside to take advantage of the light. With his black pin-feather hair and high hooked nose, he seemed to hover like a hawk over the board. His woollen cassock was cleaned and starched and pressed as always. It once had been black, but after each boiling and scrubbing and pounding, it emerged a rustier brown. The collar was frayed and the material over the elbows and knees worn thin as tissue.

Copley might look the part of an impoverished priest, and he sometimes used the name Philip Fisher to confuse the English authorities as to his identity, but Vaughan knew that his father had been a knight of the realm.

"I envy you priests," Vaughan said.

Copley looked more animated, or at least his usual expression of ironic disdain blurred. "If thou desirest to accept the true faith I shall instruct thee in the catechism."

"You know me better than that, Thomas. I'm freighted with too many sins to confess." Vaughan put on his battered hat to shield his eyes from the sun climbing higher in the morning sky.

"Then thy supposed envy were but more of your quibbles and carriwitchets?"

"Consider this . . ." Vaughan enjoyed tweaking the Jesuit. "You're God's secretary, are you not, perched outside his office door. You collect his fees and screen petitioners and pass down the Lord's judgment, assuring a sinner he will be forgiven. 'Tis an office to excite envy among the rabble, but that is not the end of it.

"You priests are a species of sanctified magician. With a wave of your hand and a mumble of Latin, you hocus oil, water, a shaving of wood, a tatter of cloth into holy fripperies from God's own pocket. You imbue them with the power to pass the possessor into heaven, or banish his warts, or make his prick to stand. You can even transform the Son of God into a piece of bread. Surely God must be a sort of celestial Baker."

"And I the Baker's boy?" Copley smiled indulgently. Vaughan was good company. He might entertain intense antipathies, but no malice. Copley liked him for it. He was also one of the few

Adventurers, even the Catholic ones, who didn't have a crow to
pluck with the Jesuits.

"I am a devout Anglican, one of King Harry's own . . ."
Vaughan leaned forward, all earnestness. "But I will tell you this, the
Church of England has banished magic from religion. Stripped it of
its pomp and abracadabra and left us a plain, humdrum thing."
Vaughan sighed. "Printing and gunpowder have conspired with religious reformers to fright away Robin Goodfellow and the fairies and
your faith's pantheon of friendly demiurges."

"I believe your eel pie approaches." Copley decided not to
enter into a discussion that would be interrupted by breakfast.

"Lost you the way, Ani?"

"Nay, sir." Anicah's good spirits vanished at the sight of Copley. She hated him for selling Martin to Dandy and she had hoped
to find Vaughan alone so she could cajole his aid. "I had only to
follow me smeller to this swine's ken ye style a cottage."

"Such fine sensibilities you're acquiring." Vaughan turned to
Copley. "She thinks that rooking a gentleman elevates her own rank."

Vaughan held no grudge against Anicah for helping Henry
Fleete cheat Giles at cards. Cheating was expected and skill at it
was admired. He could have warned Giles, but he enjoyed watching Anicah operate. Giles could take care of himself.

"Ye must be no gentleman then, because I've not sharked ye,
have I?" She winked as she disappeared into the chaos of his house.

She returned with his second stool and set the pie on it. "What
means rictus and *alias dictus*?"

"The first is a gape-mouthed grin, the second means 'otherwise called.' " Robert looked up at her in mild surprise. "Wherefore decided you to con Latin?"

"I was only curious."

"Impudent more like." Copley glared at her.

"Your long jaw has turned red as rhubarb, Thomas."

"Someone posted a libel on the chapel door last night." Copley
grumbled. "A libelous, heretical doggerel."

"Do say it."

Copley flapped his long hand, as though to wave the subject away. Anicah recited it instead.

"His swarthy phiz, a lowering rictus;
Fisher and Copley, alias dictus.
A Spanish Janus, an impious mope,
An odious rogue who worships the pope.
In heretic zeal, with fervor enow,
He falls on his knees and rogers his sow. "

Vaughan threw back his head and laughed until his hat fell off. Copley took the spoon from his hand so he could help himself to the pie.

" 'Tis the work of some *caca-fuego*," he muttered. "A shite-fire."

"Surely you know who framed it, Ani." Vaughan was still chuckling.

"I do not peach." She looked down at him with great dignity. "But his muse sets her breech on the ale bench amongst the other wags. The rhyme was all the cackle there." She didn't mention that she had helped Henry Fleete with the last two lines.

A faint cry echoed from St. Mary's. "Out! Out!" It was followed by a blat from Leonard Calvert's hunting horn.

"*Hutesio et clamore,* hue and cry," Father Copley said. "Some wastor or draw-latch on the run."

Anicah danced from one foot to the other. "Will ye be needing me?"

The villagers were turning out to chase some felon over the countryside. Nothing this exciting had happened since Anicah's arrival. It couldn't rival a bear baiting or a riot, but it would serve.

Vaughan waved her on her way. "They'll raise a great breeze, I shouldn't wonder." He untied his drawstring and began tucking his shirttails into his breeches. "I'd best go along. The new sheriff can't find his pego in the bog house."

He was still pulling on his old doublet as he ran down the path. Father Copley lifted the hem of his cassock and hurried after him.

A noisy crowd churned at the crossroads near where the new chapel was a-building. Everyone would have been shouting anyway, but they had no choice if they wanted to be heard over Calvert's reeve-cum-huntmaster blasting on the horn. The two Brent hounds barked incessantly and galloped in circles, winding their leashes around Giles's legs like top strings. The freemen carried their muskets. The rest brandished picks, shovels and cudgels.

Anicah picked up a pair of stones. "Beggars' bullets." She grinned at Vaughan.

He could see he would get no reliable information in the confusion, so he pushed his way through the people gathered around the old mulberry. Even those who couldn't read were studying the notice posted there.

"What says it?" Anicah asked.

"It concerns a runaway servant. His master is offering a reward of two hundred pounds of tobacco to the man who takes him up."

"Two hundred pounds! I shall go along, and to the devil with me mistress."

"Anicah." Robert took her by the arm and led her away from the mob. "The runaway is Martin."

Chapter 30

The seedlings surrounded Margaret in brilliant green carpets. With her skirts gathered up to keep them from trailing in the buff-colored mud, she squatted beside one of the beds. She hardly noticed the warm April rain falling on her wide-brimmed hat and shoulders and back. She cradled the tobacco leaves, big as half-crown pieces, in her knobby fingers.

"They look well." She glanced at her steward, Edward Packer.

"Aye, mistress. We'll begin transplanting tomorrow as soon as the rain stops."

"With the hire of James Courtney we count four men able to work the ground, do we not?"

"Aye."

Packer held out his arm to steady Margaret as she stood up. In her high wooden pattens she could have rested her chin on the top of his bright pink scalp. Unmindful of the rain and the mud that sucked at her platform shoes, she walked slowly among the beds, studying each one. From the forest to the east came shouts and the barking of dogs. The hue and cry was still afoot.

When Margaret entered the house Bess was in the kitchen berating the youngest maid. Their taciturn Piscataway hunter, Edward, had delivered another of his strange beasts this morning, tossing its stiffening corpse onto the table. The maids were arguing about how to prepare it.

It was one of those badgerlike creatures with the dark rings around their gray tails and the black fur masks across their eyes. Like portly little highwaymen they swarmed over the refuse heaps at night. Bess and the others were too terrified of them to relieve themselves by the back door after dark.

Bess was peevish anyway and Margaret blamed the Irishman, Baltasar Codd. All day men had been hallooing about the countryside instead of doing honest work. Their pursuit of the runaway servant, Martin Kirk, and Dandy's reward, had degenerated into a general rowdiness.

Codd had taken advantage of the confusion to try to lure Bess into the buttery. Just this morning Margaret had shot Codd's wool cap off as he weaseled through the dairy yard, and had smiled to see the worn soles of his shoes when he fled. She hung the cap, with a neat pair of holes through it, alongside her old snaphaunces. It would serve as a trophy and a caution.

Margaret shuffled through the expresses that the gentry's servants had delivered that morning. The stack of them contained invitations and promissory notes, petitions for loans or the hire of a man or a maid. She reread the letter her youngest sister had sent on the ship now at anchor in the harbor. It was cheerful, with no mention of the political and religious turmoil Margaret knew was building in England.

Packer appeared in the doorway and cleared his throat politely. "Goodman Angell would have a word with thee, mistress."

"Tell him I'll be without directly." But not too directly, she thought. Sisters' Freehold had a reputation for hospitality, but Harry Angell would wait in the yard. In the rain.

Margaret wrote out a bill of exchange to return with the ship. It was a draw on her account in London, but most of her business transactions now were enmeshed in the complicated web of local barter and credit. She had become adept at figuring the rates of exchange in currency that ran from hard metal to airy hopes—English sterling, Spanish coin, doubloons, wampum, beaver pelts, labor, tobacco, and corn, most often from crops not even planted yet.

When Margaret finally did go out onto the small, covered

porch, she was not surprised to see Harry in the garter bows, welted doublet and plumed felt hat of an ambitious yeoman. No more wool jerkin and breeches open at the knees for Goodman Angell, nor that leather cap that looked like a dog run over by a dray sledge. A heavy pewter cross hung at his neck and a kerchief hid the long curved scar there, but his eyes were still the color of singed fingernails.

"Good morrow, Harry."

"Mistress Brent." Harry doffed his new hat and dove into a deep bow. He gestured with the hat to the pigs in a corner sty and the three cows in the close. "I see by the increase of your estate that God in His goodness hath vouchsafed to bless you and your enterprises." He crossed himself solemnly.

"What brings you, Harry?"

"A business proposition, mistress."

Margaret stood with her arms crossed at the laces of her old linen bodice and her chin raised so she could sight down her long nose at him. He seemed neither daunted nor offended by her silence.

"I am prepared to offer you a fair price for your seconds."

"The sot weed I could not ship?"

"Aye. My associates and I—"

"My seconds have not Baltimore's seal and cannot be sold abroad."

"You speak the facts of the case, mistress. Yet we can vend the leaf here to those who are content with an inferior grade. Or to mariners, of course, who will smoke anything."

"I think not."

"If you reconsider, you may contact me at the gunsmith's—"

"Good day."

Harry bowed and turned. On his way out he passed Mathias DaSousa, who strode through the palisade door with the long, easy gait that people used to cover distances here.

"Mistress Margaret." He bowed.

"Good morrow and God keep thee, Goodman DaSousa."

"Governor Calvert said to tell you they've arrested a salvage," DaSousa said. "He murdered a servant at Snow Hill. The governor thought you would want to take precautions."

"Thou art as familiar with the salvages as any, Mathias. What makest thou of it?"

"I think you would be wise to go armed and in company."

"Why would the salvages wish to harm us?"

"They require no reason, Mistress Margaret." DaSousa tipped his hat and hurried to carry the word to Margaret's neighbors to the south.

Margaret remembered standing at her kitchen door one evening, listening, horrified, to the story Robert Vaughan told the men gathered in the great hall. Many years ago Indians had murdered 350 men, women and children in Virginia. The massacre had been the worst, but not the last.

The salvages had been so friendly, Vaughan said, they had lulled the colonists into thinking them harmless, until they could enter houses at will and sit down to sup with them. Then one morning, with knives and hatchets and clubs, they killed and mutilated everyone they could find.

Margaret thought of Edward appearing silent as a shadow in the kitchen with game or joining the household at mealtimes. An instant's terror almost took her breath away. She didn't think Edward would murder them. But she feared the mob had caught Edward and would hang him, or worse.

"Mr. Packer, have Jack bring the mare around." She started toward the garden. "Mary!"

Mary looked out over the palings.

"We're going to the village, sister," Margaret called. "They've taken an Indian suspected of murder."

"I shall go with you," Packer said.

"Thou shalt not."

"Squire Brent ordered me, whilst he's on the Isle of Kent, to accompany you if danger be about."

"Thou must keep watch here. Salvages have a fondness for other people's pork, and so do certain Englishmen." She thought of the men ranging through the woods after Martin Kirk.

"But Squire Brent said—"

"Thou art my man, Mr. Packer, not my brother's."

Margaret moved calmly so as not to panic the maids, but her heart raced. Even as she tarried the drunken rout might be slaughtering Edward for the sport of it. Nothing would amuse them more than the spectacle of a drawing and quartering. Some of them complained about the lack of such entertainments here.

Still in her old work clothes she snugged her pistols into their leather cases on the saddle, next to the dangling water pouch. Her ring of keys hung at her waist so no one would get into the cider cellar or buttery while she was gone.

She stepped onto the mounting block and put her foot into the stirrup. With a hop she sat sideways in the saddle. She arranged her petticoats and gathered the reins as Bess helped Mary up behind her.

"Mistress, do send a man to inquire." Edward Packer tried once more to object.

"God will watch over us." Margaret hit the mare's flank with her crop.

"Mr. Packer," she called over her shoulder. "Set a man to burn the seconds from the tobacco crop. Be thou certain he destroys them all."

When Margaret and Mary arrived at Governor's Field they found a small crowd around the man tied to the post there. He was tall and brown and naked but for a breechclout, strands of wampum at his neck and a single black-and-white striped turkey feather in his hair.

"Thanks be to God, he's not Edward." Margaret rode the mare into the crowd, scattering it. The Indian looked past her as though he had no interest in any of this, even when Joan tossed a handful of filth at him.

Furious, Margaret pointed her crop like an admonitory finger and fixed her with a hard look. Joan gave ground and backed away, holding up crossed fingers and muttering about popish witchery.

Margaret cantered to the governor's house and left the mare with a servant. Mary went to the garden to see what Calvert's maids were planting. Calvert himself was standing at his desk in the great hall. He put the quill into his silver penholder and rubbed his eyes.

"I'm just now writing to my brother of the affair," he said when Margaret entered.

Margaret didn't bother mentioning that months would pass before he received a reply. No one knew that better than Leonard Calvert.

"Thinkst thou the salvages mean to attack us?"

"Nay." Calvert shook his head. "John Dandy accuses him of getting drunk and killing Lewger's man. As they will do," he muttered. "No matter how White and Poulton defend them and their fratricidal king, Kittamaquund."

"Thinkst thou Dandy speaks the truth?"

"The salvage says that if Dandy swears he killed the man he must have done it. He claims he has no memory of it."

"Hast thou spoken to the accused?"

"I know not enough of their language to ask his name of him. Fleete and Vaughan could question him, but they're away." Leonard rubbed his eyes. "In any case, the man shall have a fair trial by jury."

Margaret believed Leonard's sincerity but she doubted that a jury would acquit an Indian accused of killing a white man. She walked to the cage sitting on a shelf. "Leonard, where is thy red bird?"

"The maid allowed it to escape this morning." Calvert looked through the pile of letters until he found the one with Baltimore's coat of arms in the red wax seal. "And my brother continues importuning me for one. I thought finally to silence him on that score at least."

He regarded his correspondence morosely. "So much paper

passes back and forth and so few goods. We would be better served to put these in our worn-out shoes to block the cold and damp."

"Doth his lordship send news?"

"Very little. He complains of the difficulties he's enduring at court and warns of the Jesuit conspiracy to unseat him." Calvert held up the pages, covered with his brother's rambling script. "With each ship I receive new conditions of plantation to present to the Assembly. Laws, policies, questions, rebuttals."

"Decrees, memorials." Margaret continued the list, turning it into a game. "Arguments, notanda, oaths."

"Commissions, discourses, concordants." Leonard smiled wearily at her.

"And libels." Margaret looked mischievous.

"About me?"

"Nay." Margaret lowered her voice. "His lordship's secretary."

Leonard brightened, as Margaret knew he would. John Lewger's interference and spying were a continual annoyance.

Margaret sang softly so the servants wouldn't hear, though they undoubtedly knew the song already. With her riding crop she tapped a sprightly syncopated rhythm on the edge of the desk.

> "At back-biting he doth not stick
> Nor moldy lies nor slander,
> Our errant consciences to prick,
> This spindly salamander.
>
> "He pokes and pries with fervent zeal
> From First Night to December.
> How can he serve the public weal?
> He's but a privy member."

Calvert laughed. He looked relieved that the wag had chosen someone else to label a prick, but he seemed wistful too. Margaret understood why. No one was likely to share with him verses crit-

ical of his brother's appointee, nor could Leonard encourage them
to. Only with Margaret could he be himself.

A mist chilled Anicah as she left the ordinary at dusk. St.
Mary's looked sodden and raw and dreary. It matched her despair.
She knew Martin hadn't run away. She knew he was dead. Her
head ached and her eyes burned from crying through the night
and all day too.

She approached the eel seller warily, even though his hands
were tied to the post.

"Dina sends ye peck and booze." She held up the basket.

"Hot waters?" he asked hopefully. It was one of the few English phrases he knew besides "Damn me."

"Aye." She pushed a jar within his reach and stood back.

By crouching and pulling the rope taut around his wrist he managed to get the beer to his mouth. When he finished it she gave him
some bread and a hunk of cheese. She left the water jug where he
could reach it. And she wondered, suddenly, if he had a sweetheart
and if she was crying because he hadn't returned to her.

She saw the sisters leave the governor's house. "Mistress
Brent." She ran to catch up with the mare. "A word, please."

"Yes?" Margaret looked down at her.

"Good evening, mistress." Anicah curtsied.

"Good evening."

"Will he dance the Tyburn jig?"

Margaret stared at the tall shape stark against a darkening sky.
" 'Tis likely."

"Dina and me, we say he ne'er settled the cove."

"Then who did kill him?"

"The gunsmith."

"John Dandy?"

"Aye." Anicah went on in a rush, fighting to keep her voice
from breaking. "He kilt Martin too and only claims he's scoured
off. As God is my witness, I know it."

"To call on God's name, and thou an unbeliever in His true Church, imperils your immortal soul," Margaret said. "Hast thou proof?"

"Nay." Margaret's steady gaze made her as uneasy as always.

"Hast thou lost thy dearling?" Mary asked.

"Aye, Mistress Mary." Anicah looked up at her, misery plain in her wide, dark eyes.

Anicah's hair stood out in a wild auburn mass around her face. The tiny drops of water trapped in the fine ends glittered like diamonds. Mary reached down and touched them with the tips of her fingers. The caress, light as spider legs, sent a thrill through Anicah.

"He is not dead, child," Mary said.

"It grows dark." Margaret flicked the mare with her crop.

As the horse trotted away Mary looked back over her shoulder. "His angel will care for him," she called out. "Trust in God and His sainted Mother and His holy messengers. 'For He hath given His angels charge over thee, to keep thee in all thy ways.' "

"I would that He keep her not in her thieving ways." Margaret said it loudly.

"She looks an angel, think thee not, sister? If angels could look so grieved."

Margaret only grunted, but a sudden and inexplicable pity tugged at her heart.

Chapter 31

T he tattoo of hammers seemed to echo off the dark clouds hanging low over St. Mary's City. From the ordinary's yard Anicah and Dina watched the gallows rise on Governor's Field. The gaunt silhouette revived Anicah's old fear of a catchpole's cold hand on her shoulder, but it also promised the fun of watching someone else hang.

Pickpockets had always favored Collar Day, though this would be a paltry affair compared with some she'd seen. In Bristol, merry throngs lined the road from Newgate prison to the scaffold. On a good day six or more prisoners sat on their own coffins in the tumbrels and vollied jests with the spectators. The mob cheered them as they passed by and rated their courage and style after the job was done.

Anicah was in the mood for an execution-day frolic, now that Mistress Mary had assured her Martin was alive. She regretted that the Indian would die instead of John Dandy. But in spite of his frequent appearances at the ordinary's back door, he was still a stranger to her. People had been debating whether he even had a soul or was merely another beast of the forest.

The scaffold filled a lack Anicah had felt since she arrived. Real cities, with theaters and market shambles and well-fed merchants, also had gallows trees. Anicah expected to see storehouses, alehouses, brothels and shops rise along the harbor. Instead, the ships anchored long enough to receive Governor Calvert's letter of approval. Then they sailed back down the St. George's River, nosing into the deeper creeks to sell their cargoes at individual landings and take on the hogheads of tobacco.

Except for the new chapel being built, St. Mary's had hardly changed since Anicah arrived a year and a half ago. Not even a permanent pillory or stocks adorned Governor's Field to provide amusement. No ducking stool hung out over the river to rinse the soil of slander out of gossips. Raising a gallows before prosperity and the criminal element arrived might be the cart pulling the horse, but it was something.

"Now they have a Tyburn tree they'll be building a bear garden next." She smiled at Dina.

"I much doubt it."

Dina went back into the dank gloom of the ordinary. Anicah hurried toward Governor's Field where a few of the common sort were playing at cudgels. She was urging them to draw blood when she felt a light hand on her shoulder. She turned to look up into Father Poulton's sad blue eyes.

"Good morrow to ye, sire." She gave a small curtsy.

"God keep thee, Maid Anicah." He paused. "I want to tell thee how sorry I am about thy Martin."

" 'Tis kind of ye, yer honor." She curtsied again. *Thy Martin.* She repeated the words silently to herself. *Thy Martin.*

"Had it been my decision, I would not have sold his term, but I could not gainsay Father Copley."

"I thank ye fer yer care."

He made the sign of the cross over her and walked away.

Margaret took Mary's hand as the procession approached. She held it tightly, sharing with touch a joy too powerful for words. She had never thought she would live to witness such a sight on English soil. In fact, Father Copley was putting on a show the likes of which had not even been seen in England since King Henry banned the Roman Catholic religion a hundred years ago.

Copley's young servant carried the standard of the Society of Jesus on a tall pole. Lewger's son held up a large wooden crucifix. Mathias DaSousa followed, holding the reliquary with the sacred splinter of the True Cross inside. A servant carried a stoppered jar of blessed water.

Over his ankle-length white linen alb Father Copley wore a stole encrusted with gold braid. Over that hung a heavy wool chasuble with a cross embroidered in crimson and gold from the neckline to the hem. With his long hands peaked in front of him, he chanted the Agnes Dei as he marched slowly along.

Leonard Calvert and Father Poulton brought up the rear along with the six members of the governor's council. The Gentlemen Adventurers had had their servants unpack their best clothes and shake the rue and wormwood from them for the occasion, but hardly anyone noticed them. All eyes followed the six Piscataway walking in the center of the parade. Their lithe grace made the bedizened cavaliers look like boys floundering about in their fathers' fripperies.

In his tattered cassock Father Andrew White shuffled along with the Indians, his worn sandals flapping rhythmically. The white wisps of his hair stood out around his pink bald spot like a tonsure. Beside him walked a shorter Indian wearing a new linen shirt and a loose-fitting matchcoat of blue duffel. His strong, bowed brown legs were bare though.

"That would be Kittamaquund," Margaret murmured to Mary. "They call him *tayac* or emperor."

Kittamaquund would be dining at Sisters' Freehold, and Margaret wondered what sort of guest he would be.

He looked about thirty-five years old. The right side of his head had been shaved, but on the left a hank of black hair hung to his waist. Strings of wampum beads strung with talons and a hawk's beak lay in concentric loops across the throat of the shirt.

The condemned man had allowed Father White to baptize him, but Kittamaquund was the real cause of all this pomp. The

Jesuits believed that if they could convert the *tayac*, he would deliver his entire nation to them.

The feathers in the hair of Kittamaquund's warriors waved above the tall crowns of the gentlemen's hats. The designs painted on their faces and chests had the look of sorcery. They carried long bows and wickerwork quivers full of arrows tipped with turkey feathers. They wore rawhide belts with hatchets stuck into them and small aprons of trade cloth or fox skins hanging to their knees. Their mantles of wolf and panther and bear hides trailed in the dust. They stared straight ahead as though unaware of the stir they were causing.

Behind them walked the prisoner with his hands bound. He wore only his breechclout and a pewter crucifix on a thong. He was taller than any of them.

When Father Copley reached the gallows, he looked up at the sky and raised his arms. At that moment the sun broke through the clouds and washed the scene in a golden light that sparkled on the gilt braid of Copley's robes. The crowd closed in as though to contain the priests' heaven and hell in its center. Even some non-Catholics sank to their knees. They were so awed that the gallows wit and laughter was subdued and confined to the rear ranks of the common vulgar.

After half an hour of chanting Father Copley dipped his fingers into the basin of holy water and signed the cross on the eel seller's forehead. The Indian mounted the low platform and stood quietly while the sheriff put the noose around his neck. Copley administered the communal wafer and the chalice of wine, which the condemned man drained. He chanted the rite of extreme unction. He commended the new convert's soul to God Almighty, to Jesus Christ, and His Blessed Mother Mary, and all the other saints of heaven. Then he stepped away and Secretary Lewger motioned to the sheriff.

He had a hard time hauling up such a large individual, and Vaughan grabbed the end of the rope and helped him. The Indian's eyes bulged and his tongue extruded. His face turned purple, his legs jerked and he soiled himself. A final spasm shook him like a marionette on a wire and then he hung limp.

Margaret and Mary began praying for his soul, but some in the crowd cheered.

"One less hog thief," Joan Parke said loudly enough for Margaret to hear. "The papists may dunk salvages to the ears in hocussed water, yet they will have naught of humanity but form."

The funeral cortege formed behind Original Brown who kept mournful cadence on the town drum all the way to the consecrated cemetery at the chapel. Servants and freemen fell in at the rear, where they loudly discussed the hanging, the weather, crops, livestock, and a deformed piglet newly born. They enjoyed the fine spring day and an hour's respite from labor.

As Copley's eulogy droned on, Margaret tried not to fret about the thousands of tobacco seedlings left to transplant. She wondered why she had agreed when Leonard Calvert asked her to prepare a feast for the Piscataway emperor. He had tried to make it sound as though it were an honor, but she knew very well he merely disliked the bother of entertaining.

She worried that she shouldn't have ordered the servants to lay extra rushes in the corners and upper chambers at Sisters' Freehold. As the sack and cider flowed this evening, a thick layer of reeds would invite guests to relieve themselves there rather than in the dooryard. But they might do it anyway, and then the floors would require extra scrubbing with sand in the morning. She didn't want to even think about what the Indians' habits were.

She wondered if Mary Courtney and Bess had come to blows in the kitchen. She had hired Goody Courtney to help cook the shoulder feast, the meal for the pallbearers. Or rather, the goodwife was working to pay off some of her husband's debt. Her son had died, but she was high with child again.

The ringing of the sanctus bell recalled Margaret from her worries. Father Poulton shook a few drops of holy water over the body before the coffin lid was nailed down. After a final hymn Margaret and Mary led the way along the path through the woods and across Giles's tobacco fields. The black-gowned priests, the feathered Indians, plumed cavaliers and their cloaked ladies and a retinue of servants, with Giles's dogs casting through the bushes, made an odd parade.

When they reached Sisters' Freehold Kittamaquund stopped to stare out over the broad river. He said something to Father White but Robert Vaughan gave his own translation.

"He says his people once roamed happily here. They fished in these waters and hunted in these forests. He says they stole their neighbors' wives and corn here," Vaughan said solemnly.

"Why did they leave?" Margaret was used to his foolishness.

"Susquehannocks. Seneca. Other marauders from the north. Year after year they raided his villages, killed his people. That's why they were so quick to welcome the English and their guns. We're but bully boys defending them from their enemies."

"I prefer to think, Sergeant Vaughan, that they recognized the light of God's love."

"They recognize the range of English musketry, Mistress Margaret."

Margaret's steward waited at the door and Kittamaquund made straight for him. He pumped his hand and thwacked him so hard on the back in the English fashion that he almost knocked the breath out of him. Father White took Margaret's arm and hurried over to correct his error.

"Mistress Margaret is the . . ." He fumbled for words his friend would understand. ". . . the *tayac* of this village." With its palisade and house and collection of new outbuildings, Sisters' Freehold was beginning to resemble a village.

Kittamaquund grabbed her hand and shook it. All the while he jerked her arm in its socket he spoke in that soft, guttural tongue. As Margaret ushered him into the parlor, steeped in the odor of roasted meat and Mary Courtney's mysterious mélange of herbs, she nodded gravely at him.

Up close, the dark, weathered promontories and steep ravines of his features were even more fearsome than at a distance. Margaret had little trouble believing him capable of killing his brother for his throne. She had none at all imagining him killing Englishmen. He was solid and powerful. A quick intelligence glinted behind a veil of shrewdness in dark eyes set close to a massive slab of a nose. She judged him to be a generous man and a self-serving one.

Margaret was adept at entertaining, but for once she was at a loss. Her great hall measured only fifteen feet by twenty-four. It was hardly large enough for the trestle tables already set up, and extra people had invited themselves along. Seating was always a delicate art when hosting gentry. Today's meal would be especially so, what with six of the guests being naked and smeared with bear fat, and a seventh bare on the bottom.

The Piscataway saved her the trouble. With their bearskin mantles sweeping the rushes behind them, they stalked through the great hall and parlor. They inspected everything while the women held aside their flounced petticoats to let them pass. They climbed the narrow stairs and peered into the upper chambers. They stood in the hearth and looked up the chimneys. They poked their heads into the kitchen, but withdrew quickly when Mary Courtney screamed and threw a pan that bounced off the door frame.

Margaret tried to apologize, but they seemed unperturbed by the crochets of women in the throes of cooking. They filled her house with their imposing, alien presence. Then they filed outside with the dignity of those unable to speak their hostess's language and thus lacking the means to embarrass themselves.

Their departure left only the problem of Kittamaquund. Father White was determined to treat him as an honored guest, which meant that he must be invited to set his unclothed buttocks in the best chair. Her merry gang of guests pretended to be unaware of the dilemma as they swirled around her.

"I have tried to persuade him to wear breeches, Margaret," Father White murmured while the *tayac* took one of her pistols from the wall and sighted down its barrel. "He says wool chafes his tender parts."

Margaret found it hard to imagine any tender part on him. His dark brown skin looked tough as boiled leather. She decided to tell Bess to drape a sheet over the chair as though it were a throne.

A crash came from the kitchen, followed by a maid's wail.

"Simpleton!" Mary Courtney shouted. "Dishclout!"

"Heaven sends meat . . ." Margaret nodded toward the disturbance. ". . . but the devil sends cooks."

She closed the door quietly behind her. When she returned silence pulsed at her back. Kittamaquund rumbled something and Father White smiled.

"He says he wishes he could govern his wives thus."

"Wives?"

"He has three at present, but I am lecturing him on the error of his ways."

Kittamaquund said something else but Father White seemed inclined to ignore it. Robert Vaughan translated.

"He asks why you have no husband, Mistress Margaret."

"Tell him, Sergeant, that I have chosen to devote myself to God."

Vaughan interpreted Kittamaquund's reply.

"He says you're very wise. Mates are a great distraction."

Kittamaquund held up Baltasar Codd's cap with his finger through the two holes.

"He wants to know if thou did'st make these holes with the small thunder stick," Father White said.

"Yes, though the ball only routed the rogue."

Kittamaquund opened the front door. He held up the hat with his finger still through the holes and brandished the pistol. Whatever he said started his men to laughing.

"He says if you ever decide to quit the English, he shall give you a place with his warriors," Father White said.

"The table is laid, mistress." Mary Courtney, red in the face and glistening with perspiration and greasy soot, curtsied in the doorway.

The guests ranged themselves along the tables. They proposed healths first to King Charles, then to all and sundry, before laying waste to the beef and venison, the squirrel pie, roasted pigeons and baked sweet potatoes sopped in wine. Robert Vaughan sighed happily and loosened his belt when the huge basin of Mary Courtney's salmagundi appeared.

After the steamed corn pudding even Vaughan admitted defeat and the party retired to the parlor for more sack and peach brandy. Vaughan entertained them with the story of the Welshman's first sight of seeing a man taking tobacco.

" 'O Jhesu, Jhesu, man!' " Vaughan's Welsh dialect was clumsy but his delivery was ebullient. " 'Py God's plud ty snout's afire.' And he throws a bowl of beer in the poor wight's face."

Vaughan pretended to heave the contents of the wine bowl he had just emptied. The women squealed and ducked.

Margaret laughed with the rest. "Oft have I wished to do the same."

Anne Lewger leaned over to murmur in Margaret's ear. "Sergeant Vaughan doth wear stockings of two parishes. They are not fellows."

"Nay, but he is polished above the yeomanry." Margaret had noticed Vaughan's mismatched hosiery, but she was irritated that Mistress Lewger would insult a guest in her house.

Margaret had had her doubts about inviting Vaughan and his hat with the tail of one of those raccoon creatures dangling from the brim. He was sure to grow disorderly with drink. He was also a Protestant and not of gentle breeding. But Giles couldn't manage his manor on the Isle of Kent without him, and Margaret could hardly exclude him. Besides, he had a marvelous singing voice, even if all his songs were vulgar, and he made her laugh.

The company passed the afternoon in music and dancing and

games. At dusk Kittamaquund stood and waited for silence. Father White, his lined face lit with a smile, translated.

"Kittamaquund declares that he will receive the sacrament of holy baptism and become a child of the true faith. He will renounce his sins and live content with one wife, that he may have more leisure to pray to God."

The company applauded and then the Lewgers gathered their cloaks and hats, anxious to be gone before dark. The other guests followed. Kittamaquund and the Jesuits retired to the great hall to begin the emperor's catechizing.

Night had fallen before Vaughan decided to leave. Margaret stood in the doorway and watched him and Giles stagger off arm in arm toward Giles's house. When they reached the gate in the palisade Vaughan turned and waved.

"A prime affair, Mistress Margaret," he shouted. "Your cider is better than a thump on the back with a stone."

"May God be with you." Before Margaret closed the door and drew in the latch, she looked out at the Piscataway men sitting under the oak.

The light from their fire illuminated details of their faces and feathers, their fur mantles and their long tobacco pipes. It lit up the underside of the oak's vast canopy. The scene was so tranquil, yet so unearthly. Margaret wondered what her brothers and sisters, comfortable in their English houses, would make of it.

Chapter 32

To a fanfare of barking dogs, Kittamaquund led his guests among the domed houses and heaps of oyster shells, the racks of drying fish and garden fences of his palisaded town. Most of the Piscataway nation surged around the procession. People had traveled from distant villages for the annual feast of the new corn and the initiation of their leader into the black robes' religion. They had also come to see the pale, hairy strangers, bulbous and misshapen in their peculiar costumes.

The English didn't disappoint them. Leonard Calvert and the members of the governor's council were arrayed as though headed for a coronation at Westminster. As they clomped along in their big boots, the wide cuffs drooped to show off their brightly colored hosiery. The brims of their big hats flopped like wounded vultures.

Martin pressed his back against the rough log wall at the rear of the throng and kept his head down to hide his dark blue eyes. In four months he had almost gotten used to wearing moccasins and a loincloth, but he felt suddenly naked and conspicuous, hulking and pale. He stood no taller than the average Piscataway man though, and the sun had darkened his skin to the color of burnt sugar. His hair had been long and shaggy when he ran away from John Dandy. Now it was streaked with copper and hung in loose waves almost to his shoulders.

Martin expected the Englishmen to turn, point and bellow,

"Seize that rogue. Hang him for a felon." But they entered Kitta-maquund's new house, a bark-covered half cylinder eighty feet long, fifteen wide and twelve high, and they stayed there. All morning messengers sprinted back and forth, bringing food, drink, tobacco and turkey wing fans. Kittamaquund sent for a lot of fans. In their clothing the English did not cavil to nature, and the air was as torrid as usual for July.

By late morning people got bored waiting for a glimpse of them and scattered to their own houses to prepare for the ceremony. As Martin trotted across the dance ground where Kittamaquund's baptism would be held, a crowd of children chased after him.

"Mah-teen," they shouted. "We want to fly."

Hardly slowing his pace he picked them up, one at a time, and whirled them around. He set them down and hurried away, but they ran after him, holding onto his hands and legs.

Their laughter made him realize how desolate St. Mary's was. Servants were forbidden to have children, and even married freemen begrudged the time and effort to care for them. Most died anyway before they had a name to remember them by. The ones who survived infancy worked along with the adults and had little time to play.

With the children still clinging to him, Martin made his way among the longhouses. When he reached the one belonging to the wife of Edward's maternal uncle, he stopped to pick them off like burs.

"Did my brother have the tobacco, nephew?" Edward's uncle sat in the doorway with three of his friends.

"Yes, Uncle." Martin gave him the pouch and went inside.

Uncle's wife's house was ten feet high along the top of the domed roof. It was fifteen feet wide and forty feet long. Shafts of light poured through the three holes in the roof. Wisps of smoke from the hearth fires undulated upward inside them, as though lazily testing the confines of a narrow cage.

The sunlight illuminated the blankets on the sleeping benches along the walls. It spilled like honey down the curved sides of the earthen jugs and baskets. It gilded the hoes made of the shoulder blades of bison.

It was stifling hot, but Martin didn't dare join Uncle outside where he might be seen by the English. He sat on one of the mats covering the dirt floor and picked up the ash limb he'd cut to make into a cudgel. He went back to carving the bole at the end into a basket-shaped hand guard. The men's conversation flowed over him, punctuated with frequent explosions of *Ha ho!* "That's right!" At times like this Martin thought of himself as a puppy, leaping up to snatch at scraps of talk when they flew by. He fell into a reverie about Anicah. He was trying to remember, exactly, the timbre of her laugh, the light in her eyes, the tilt of her nose, when Uncle's voice disturbed him.

A smile rarely deepened the gullies around Uncle's slash of a mouth, his lumpy nose and bulging brown eyes, but his friends laughed a lot. Detecting Uncle's wit was like realizing the earth was trembling far beneath the surface when pottery danced on the shelves.

"Nephew, will a country be set aside for us in the blackcoats' heaven or will we have to live with smelly Englishmen?"

"I know not, Uncle," said Martin.

"Will the blackcoats drip water on the Senecas and the Susquehannocks and make them holy so they can go to heaven too?" Wolf was a bony, droopy-eyed individual.

"I suppose so."

"Then what's to stop them from driving us out of heaven as they drove us from our ancient hunting grounds?"

"There is no war in heaven." Martin could tell they weren't convinced.

"I wouldn't travel to the blackcoats' heaven anyway," Uncle said. "They say we cannot tickle our women there."

As though on cue, Second Wife and her cousins sauntered in laughing. They had just come from bathing at the river and their long black hair hung shiny and wet down their bare backs. Aside from their short skirts of soft leather, they wore strands of blue glass and copper beads. Necklaces of bear claws curved across their brown chests to lie cool and grasping between their breasts.

From where he sat, he had a startling view of the tops of their thighs. He concentrated on his carving, but he could hear their laughter as they passed by him. He could feel their eyes coquetting at him from behind the dark fringes of their hair. He still amused them for reasons he couldn't fathom.

From the corner of his eye he watched them lift aside the mat partitions hanging from the curved framework of the roof. Martin knew every item of the clutter around him, but the area behind the last set of mats was as mysterious and unexplored as China. Second Wife, First Wife's sister, lived there. The melody of the women's conversation floated through the woven reeds as though up from underground. Martin would have sooner crawled into a bear's cave than venture to the other side.

"Itah," Edward said. "Good be to you, Uncle."

Before he entered the house he turned and threw several walnuts at the child following him. She ran, but not far. Since Edward's baptism, Kittamaquund had taken a liking to him. Being singled out by the *tayac* had its advantages, but becoming a favorite of his ungovernable daughter wasn't one of them.

"Nephew, did you see the blackcoats perform feats of magic in the *tayac*'s house just now? Did they perchance conjure his third wife to keep silent?"

"No, Uncle." Edward was patient. His uncle's constant questions about the Jesuits' powers weren't trivial. If what they claimed was true, they could give their followers the spiritual advantage they needed to feed and protect their families.

"The white-haired blackcoat tells of his God turning a man's wife to salt," Wolf said. "That would be useful magic to have."

Behind the mats the whispering and giggling turned into laughter. The noise grew loud enough to interrupt Uncle's conversation just as First Wife walked in, her large, sturdy breasts marching ahead of her like an honor guard.

She was not in a good mood. She had spent most of the day keeping watch at her garden so no one broke the plants in the hurly-burly. With a wave of her hand she signaled several of the boys who regularly wandered in and out of the house.

The two smaller ones climbed on the others' backs. They untied the mats and lowered them silently. They worked their way toward the rear, revealing more of the interior, as though peeling away layers of an onion. The women were making so much noise they didn't notice the silence in the rest of the house.

The last mats fell away and they froze, faces turned toward the front, dark eyes blinking. They tried to look contrite but couldn't manage it. One started to laugh, then another, until they were all helpless.

Second Wife and Edward's cousin had sneaked two of the men's trade shirts and put them on. They had turned under the collars to form low necklines, and knotted thongs above their elbows and ballooned the sleeves. Over the shirts they had draped and tied blankets, shawls and lengths of trade cloth. They had added every piece of ribbon and trim and bead necklace they owned or could borrow. They had even formed stomachers out of pieces of bark.

First Wife threw back her head and laughed, her breasts quivering. The men chuckled. Martin had never paid much attention to fashions, but as far as he could tell they had imitated with astonishing accuracy an English woman's costume.

First Wife ordered the mats hung back in place. She commanded the lower mats covering the house to be rolled up to let in air, and she scolded the younger women for not doing it before.

She sat with her heels drawn in and her knees up and murmured in Uncle's ear, staring in Martin's direction the while. The attention made Martin nervous. The precarious way First Wife's thong belt and short skirt hung on her hips made him more nervous. She was wide from side to side, and except for those breasts, as flat fore and aft as a sideboard.

"Come." She gestured to the doorway and the bright sunlight.

First Wife gave orders as though she had no doubts about them being carried out. Men built the houses, but the women owned them. First Wife had the air of command that came with proprietorship. He imagined she and Mistress Margaret Brent would get on well together discussing their households and their fields and the problems of getting others to perform to their standards.

Uncle and his friends arranged themselves for a good view of Martin as he sat where First Wife indicated.

"She's going to cut your hair," Edward said.

"But I'm not a warrior. I haven't been in battle."

"Aunt and Uncle think it would be a good disguise." Edward didn't mention that Kittamaquund had suggested the haircut to him that morning, while his English guests smoked their pipes nearby.

Everyone knew the *tayac* approved sheltering Martin. Edward was of the opinion that Kittamaquund enjoyed depriving John Dandy in particular of a servant, and the English in general. Dandy cheated in his trade with the Piscataway and he sold them adulterated spirits. As for the rest of the English, they were always trying to buy the strongest young men to work in their fields.

First Wife sorted through a basket of clamshells, testing the edges with her thumb. The dry rattle from the basket stirred the hair on Martin's arms. He had a vivid memory of a rabbit's pink carcass, its fur matted with blood, its skin peeling back under the short, quick strokes of one of those shells.

"How shall she cut it?" he asked.

"Like mine. Neither of us has killed an enemy yet." Edward turned so Martin could get the full effect of his skull shaved on the right side with the hair tied up in a club over his left ear.

Uncle leaned over and used the slender stem of his pipe to lift the mass of dark curls away from Martin's right ear. He shook his head sorrowfully and let them fall. The other men, solemn as owls, nodded in agreement.

"What?" Martin asked.

"Nothing." Edward shot Uncle an oblique look.

"What?"

"Blue Wing's wife's blade slipped once," Uncle said. "It left his ear hanging by a flap of skin. She sewed it back on with a bone needle and deer sinew." The description implied that Blue Wing's wife would have nothing to do with those effete steel trade needles and thin silk thread. "The ear turned red as a raspberry, then green and purple and black and soft as a rotted toadstool."

"Did he die?"

"Of course."

First Wife wound a fistful of Martin's hair around her hand and jerked his head hard to the left as though she intended to yank the hair out by the handful. Agony stabbed into his scalp like slivers of bone. His eyes watered and he wanted to cry out when the clam-shell began scraping and sawing at the tender skin of his skull.

"She means to take my scalp and save the Seneca the long trip south," he said.

The men laughed. Martin blinked away the tears and realized he was staring straight at First Wife's breasts, pliant and wobbly and congenial as a pair of half-cooked suet puddings. In fact, his nose was in danger of being pressed between them while she worked. He inhaled the smoky musk of her. He shut his eyes and tried to ignore the rake and drag of the clamshell across his head.

Second Wife and the cousins gathered to watch the barbering and murmur and laugh softly behind their hands. The blush that spread from Martin's cheeks to his ears and neck made them laugh more. When First Wife finished they squatted around him and ran their fingers over his head. They marveled at its silky texture and exclaimed over the way it sprang back into curls when they pulled it out taut and let it go.

Martin felt as though he were being smothered by fragrant, glistening female bodies. Breasts in shades from honey to molasses filled his line of vision—small and taut and button-tipped, wide and soft and pendulous. One of the firm, round ones brushed his shoulder and he flinched as though it had scorched him.

First Wife mixed brown pigment into a salve and rubbed it onto his scalp. It eased the sting and blended the paler shaven area with his sun-bronzed neck and broad shoulders and chest. She tied his hair in a club and poked a turkey feather into the knot.

Uncle dipped his thumbs in a clamshell of red clay mixed with bear grease. He placed them under the inner corners of Martin's eyes and pressed hard down and outward. He paralleled the diagonals, beginning at the outer corners of the eyes. He added a horizontal swipe across the chin and sat back to admire the effect.

Edward's cousin held up a trade mirror. Martin's gentle, deep blue eyes peered from it as though imprisoned in the bones, flesh, skin and sinew of a ferocious stranger.

Cousin brought a basket of the elongated corn cakes called pone. They were still warm from the flat stones of Second Wife's fire, and the indentations of her fingers were baked into the hard bread. Cousin sat back on her heels to stare at him. Martin's capacity for food amazed everyone.

Martin had joined the Piscataway during early March when game was scarce and the corn supply low. He had known hungry times with them. But now, even though food was plentiful, he was still astonished by the luxury of eating until his stomach would not accommodate another crumb. Of having his own bowl to dip into the pot whenever he wanted. He was halfway certain it was a mistake that would be rectified. That he would return to going to sleep with an empty belly as he had most of his life.

His last full meal among the English had been the May Day feast Father Poulton had provided for him and Anicah more than a year ago. He thought he would weep at the memory of it.

Uncle's friends left to make their preparations for the black robes' ceremony, and the rest of the family returned to theirs. Martin sat in a daze and fingered the knot of hair over his ear. As he chewed the ashy lump of corn bread he wondered what would become of him.

Chapter 33

The Piscataway were as able as the English at speech-making. Through the hot shimmer of the July afternoon, Kittamaquund and the lesser leaders gave ornate assurances of friendship and peace with their English guests. A low platform of mat-covered logs lifted the dignitaries from the choking dust. A chapel in the form of a bark-covered arbor shaded them. The thousands of spectators sat in the sun. The steady wag of turkey- and heron-wing fans created the only breeze.

Martin shifted in his place at the rear of the assembly of seated men and older boys. He tried to sight between the dark, knobby skulls, the bobbing feathers and elaborate crests and knots of hair. Edward stood on the dais, translating, but the only face Martin could see was Father Poulton's, gaunt and serene.

Behind Martin came an occasional cough from one of the women or the brief squall of a baby. In spite of the heat and the tedium of listening to everything twice, first in English, then in Piscataway, no one fidgeted or spoke. Martin could imagine the noise and stir among a like number of England's common sort. By this time they would have been rattling dice boxes, hawking up oysters, farting merrily and cracking jests with their neighbors.

The English had become as foreign to Martin as the Indians had been when he first came among them as Father Poulton's servant. Two years ago, bedizened in paint, dressed in feathers and animal skins, the Piscataway had seemed not real men at all, but glyphs of savagery. Now he wondered how he ever could have thought they all looked alike.

One of Uncle's favorite recreations was to ask Martin about his people. The questions were always direct and perceptive, and in truth Martin was at a loss to answer them. The English's reasons for acting as they did seemed more outlandish to him each day he was apart from them.

The pale-eyed folk paid little attention to dreams. Uncle considered that the most perplexing of their ways. How could anyone ignore dreams? he would ask Martin. Without the wisdom the spirits pass on in them men were as blind as eyeless salamanders slithering through the eternal night of caves.

For his part, Martin could no longer understand the English distaste for bathing. He had been doing it almost every day with Edward and the other men. He enjoyed it, and so far it hadn't ruined his health or anyone else's. The Piscataway, in fact, were remarkably fit.

Since Martin had stared into the familiar blue eyes of the stranger in the mirror that morning, a change had settled into his bones and joints. He held himself more erect, his shoulders relaxed, his chin at a higher tilt than before. He walked with more grace. Instead of reaching clumsily for something he paused first and considered. It was an extraordinary transformation and he was unaware of it.

Eventually, Leonard Calvert's shrill voice blended with the shrill buzz of the insects. Martin looked straight ahead. He narrowed his eyes and set his mouth in the same cryptic expression as the men around him. The shaved skulls became a field of shaggy gourds, then they blurred as though a fog had settled. Martin saw images that he couldn't have if he had tried to focus on them. He wandered among the shades of his memories.

He tried to imagine what his mother and father were doing at that moment, but they eluded him. He knew they would be horrified by the sight of him, but he didn't care. They had condemned him to slavery in a far country. They had sold him as they would a bawling calf or a sack of barley.

Then he saw the ghost of Anicah's smile and heard the echo

of her laugh. Grief at the loss of her tore at his heart. His fingers twitched, aching to twine with hers.

Martin sat stoic as a tree blasted by lightning while emotions collided around him. He felt bereft, forsaken, lost, frightened, desperate. In spite of the kindness of Edward's people, he knew he didn't belong here.

Every day some small incident reminded him that they shared a past he couldn't ever know. He didn't even understand how the individuals who wandered in and out of First Wife's house were related to each other. Edward had tried to explain it, but had given up in the face of Martin's bewilderment. The Piscataway were worse than Scotsmen with their clans and their titles, their feuds, private jokes and alliances that endured through generations.

Martin had not felt so alone since that moment when he was locked in the cellar in Bristol and he knew, with the certainty of a blow from a maul, that he would never hear his mother's unhappy voice again. He would never watch the dancing on the green with his friends or duck to enter the doorway of his family's squat stone cottage.

"The light shines in the darkness, though the darkness comprehends it not." Andrew White spoke the words in Algonkian, the language of the Piscataway. Martin understood them perfectly, not in his head, but in his marrow. He came alert.

The speeches had ended, the rite of baptism was about to begin. Kittamaquund stepped forward. He wore breeches and stiff, laced shoes, a white linen shirt and a velvet waistcoat. He seemed smaller in them, less imposing than in the breechclout and leggings, the feathers, the necklaces of wolf teeth and bear claws and the wolfskin mantle he had always worn. He looked not so much lost in the new clothes as misplaced.

To satisfy the God of his dear friend, Father White, he had given up two of his three wives, though not without a clamor of recrimination. Now Kittamaquund and his first wife and several of his counselors knelt, bare-headed, in front of the three Jesuits. Father White raised his arms, weighted by the heavy vestments.

He held up the sacred relic, the sliver of wood from the holy rood. He made an elaborate show of floating it in a basin of water held by Father Copley's boy. White made the sign of the cross over the wood. He retrieved it, dried it on a linen cloth, wrapped it in a square of red velvet, and replaced it in its painted rosewood reliquary.

The crowd drew in its breath and tilted forward. Even those from the remotest villages had heard that the blackcoats' bit of tinder possessed enormous power. Water in which it had been dipped had cured the *tayac*'s daughter of a stomach ailment. Everyone agreed that the illness must have been a serious one. It was the first time anyone had ever seen her quiet.

Uncle's friend Wolf stood abruptly and made his way among the tightly-packed spectators. He sank to his knees in front of the bark chapel. Others rose and moved forward to join him. The fear and bitterness, longing and despair that had been roiling in Martin merged and crested. He felt dizzy, possessed by the sensation of drowning and of salvation, both in one.

"Jesus Christ is in each of you," Father White's frail voice soothed and compelled. "The power of His love enwraps you. The light that is the Savior and Creator shines on His red children and His white children alike. You who are lost in the wilderness, He welcomes you home. Let His light lead you out of darkness and despair."

You who are lost in the wilderness. Martin sat wrapped in a love so vast it filled the universe. Tears stung his eyes. The top of his head grew hot, as though someone had focused a burning glass there. Splinters of light exploded around him. He struggled to breathe and his heart thrummed erratically.

He looked up. Through the shimmer of his tears he saw rays radiating from a cross suspended in front of a ragged hole in the clouds. He saw the shadowy outline of a body, arms outstretched, legs bent, head fallen forward.

A shudder rolled through Martin. His legs raised him up without conscious will. His feet moved him forward. The men parted in front of him. He sensed, vaguely, that he was walking toward the English, toward captivity, pain and maybe death on the gallows. He reached Kittamaquund's chapel without being aware of how he got there. He knelt with a score or more men and women and bowed his head while Father Copley's sonorous Latin rained down on him. When Copley stopped, Martin waited in the silence.

Then Father White began chanting, his voice quavering but growing louder, like a wind approaching through trees. Finally Martin could distinguish the words he repeated as he moved among the converts.

"Ego te baptiso en nomine patris, filius et espiritu sanctu." I baptize you in the name of the Father, the Son and the Holy Ghost.

Martin saw the hem of White's heavy white surplice, darkened by dust. He closed his eyes and raised his head to receive the blessing. The gentle pressure of White's thumb signing the cross on his forehead was a caress, the coolness of the water a blessing. White didn't move on, though, as he had with the others. Martin knew he had been discovered.

He felt the trembling touch of Father White's hand on the crown of his newly shaved head. Heat radiated from his palm and fingers. Too much heat. The priest had a fever. The hand rested there for what seemed an eternity, then White moved on to the next man.

"Ego te baptiso en nomine patris, filius et espiritu sanctu."

Chapter 34

Even over the loud conversation in the ordinary, Anicah could hear the rumble of hogsheads rolling toward the harbor. By now, in late November, most of the leaf had been pressed into the big casks, but the essence of tobacco still clung to those who did the packing. As the fire in the hearth warmed the men's woollen breeches and jerkins, the rich, sweet aroma filled the room.

A shifty-eyed, jovial rogue in the corner waved the wood slab that served as a plate. "Wench! Where's the hash?"

He wore a mariner's shaggy knit cap pulled down to the single dark eyebrow that overhung his veined carbuncle of a nose. Anicah scowled. She didn't like William Howkins anyway, but he had had his head together with John Dandy most of the morning. Any friend of Dandy's was doubly detestable to her.

She had been eavesdropping, in hopes Dandy would let slip some word about Martin. Instead he had boasted about his thievery of the Jesuits' trade goods and supplies. Howkins had agreed to fence them to his employer, ship's master Richard Ingle. Ingle would then sell the loot at the landings of outlying planters.

Anicah snatched the dirty trencher from Howkins's hand and stalked into the kitchen.

"More hash for Howkins." She held the plate out for Dina to spoon diced venison onto it. "I saw the alewife and Howkins the other night," Anicah confided. "She with her skirts up and he against her at the garden fence. The gate made a whackin' great rattle. D'ye reckon Goodman Smythe knows Howkins has made a cuckold of him?"

Dina shrugged. " 'Twould be Smythe's good fortune if his old woman ran off with the cur."

As though to prove Dina right, Goody Smythe's shrill voice rose in the common room. "Fie on thee, thou grout-head!" It was followed by the sound of a hard slap and Goodman Smythe's yelp. "Thou extendest credit to rogues and mumpers."

Anicah winked at Dina. "If the husband gave not credit to rogues and mumpers, the wife would see no business at all."

She hurried out and dropped the trencher with a clatter in front of Howkins who was enjoying the scene with his boots on the table. Smythe cowered in a corner, rubbing his bruised ear, his dog skulking between his legs.

His wife thrust a piece of charcoal into Anicah's hand. "I must go aboard Ingle's ship to see to the wine casks. Mark thou the score honestly, ye trollop, or I shall beat thee when I return."

Anicah knew it must gall the alewife to realize she could trust her nimble-fingered serving wench to keep stricter accounts than her husband. Anicah was given to frolic and profanity, contention and base heresy, but she was stern with the men who wheedled her for a pint off the score.

Goody Smythe stared at her customers' accounts, the ranks of black strokes on the rough plaster yellowed by tobacco smoke. Tapster Smythe's were bold and generous and given to straying from their lines. Hers were crabbed and neat.

"No more sense than a cheese mite," she muttered. She yanked her cloak from the peg by the door. She curtsied perfunctorily to Robert Vaughan, ship's master Richard Ingle, and the rest of the courtgoers who were arriving for the noon recess. Then she bustled, head bowed, into the autumn wind.

While the newcomers distracted the others Anicah delivered a mug of hot cider with a dash of brandy to Original Brown who sat frail and shivering in the chimney corner. He gave her a befuddled smile as she surreptitiously added a mark to John Dandy's score.

Brown had stood in the cold wind just after dawn, drumming the judges, witnesses, plaintiffs, defendants and gawkers to the benches set up in the great hall of Leonard Calvert's house. He would earn thirty pounds of tobacco a day, or at least a promissory note for them, while court was in session. He was drinking up his illusory salary before fire, flood, pestilence, drought, or Indian raid deprived him of it. He was also fortifying himself to stand in the wind and drum everyone back to court after the noon recess.

As Anicah took orders she sang loudly enough for Howkins to hear.

> *"She had a trick that in some wives is rife,*
> *She kept a sheath for another man's knife."*

"Make way, me fine cull." Anicah bumped Vaughan with her hip to move him from her path.

As she passed he kissed her on one cheek and reached down and fondled another. Laughing, she shook him off.

"Be this the draggle-tail little sewer rat I saw here two years gone?" Ingle surveyed her from top to bottom and back again.

Anicah had caught her mane of auburn curls up in two tortoiseshell combs. Robert Vaughan had given her the combs not as a bribe for her favors, but more as a patron's contribution to a work of art. Tendrils escaped them and curled around her face.

Her cropped hair had grown out, but some aspects of her hadn't changed. She had always had the sly gleam in her wide, dark amber eyes. Her full lips had been the same bruised shade of red two years before. Her skin was still dark and satiny against the rough linen of her chemise. The bones of jaw and cheeks were still prominent, but her face had lost the pinched look of famine. And her breasts swelled taut and round above the tight lacings of her bodice.

"Her tawny pompions have ripened and her nature sweetened." Vaughan put an arm around her slender waist and gently squeezed each breast in turn. She wound her fingers into his thick, wiry hair and gave it an affectionate tug that pulled the skin of his temples and the corners of his eyes sharply up toward the crown of his head. He grimaced in pain. "Though not so sweet as some might wish," he added.

Vaughan smiled, watching Anicah's skirts twitch and sway as she moved among the tables, a teasing mix of business and pleasure.

"I hear that Parliament doth consider the impeachment of the king's bishop," Vaughan said.

"They have considered it and done it already." Ingle smiled.

"Belike the king's guts will spill in the street," Dandy muttered. "And his head adorn a pike."

"God save his majesty." Anicah blurted it reflexively. She cherished a fierce and elemental loyalty to King Charles, though she could not name any kindness he had ever done her.

Anicah knew there would be no singing or foolish fun now that people had news of England, or at least news that was fresh when Ingle left Gravesend two months ago. The ordinary hummed with schemes of commerce or complaints about tobacco prices, taxes and politics. Before long men grew quite hot. They pounded the table boards, making the trenchers and spoons and flagons dance over the excesses of the king's archbishop and his anti-Puritan policies. They denounced Charles's habit of summoning Parliament then dissolving it again when it refused to levy his exorbitant new taxes.

The Catholics in the ordinary considered those not of their faith as heretics. Those with Puritan leanings thought themselves the elect and all others damned before birth. The Anglicans viewed both factions with alarm. Like a dog with a scrap of untanned hide, they worried the merits of Arminius's teachings, the dogma of predestination and the efficacy of spontaneous prayer.

When they wearied of that they began on the king and his taxes again. Propelled from their seats by righteous outrage, they stood nose-to-nose and shouted until their faces turned red as raw beef. In their excitement they sloshed their drinks onto the table, each other, and the sand on the floor. They inhaled snuff and sneezed and spluttered in their agitation.

Anicah enjoyed the noise and the ferment, and she was sorry when they returned to court after the noon hour. Ingle and Vaughan, John Dandy and several others stayed, though. As soon as the Catholic gentry left the mood changed.

"What was Calvert's grandfather but a grazier," Ingle said. "And what was Leonard Calvert himself as a lad but a dunce and a blockhead. How can such a looby be governor of a province and flout such airs?"

"The Calverts have treated me well and I hold no quarrel with them." Vaughan had long since grown weary of this debate.

"The Calverts hold with popery which is a most wicked and insolent tyranny." Ingle leaned across the table in his fervor. "But Parliament is about to get the papists on the hop." He lowered his voice, "And the king as well, I'll wager."

"May he founder who foments sedition." Vaughan found Ingle's attempts to recruit him for rebellion irritating. He sensed beneath Ingle's pious cant and convivial air an abiding and ominous self-interest.

As Vaughan stared at the pattern of stains on the scarred table board he felt a sudden longing for the familiar liturgy of the small Anglican church where he had worshiped all his life. He longed to smell the odor of the dank stones of the wall next to his family's pew, to feel the stickiness of the communion wafer on his tongue, to chant in unison with the rest of the congregation, *Almighty God, unto whom all hearts are open, all desires known and from whom no secrets are hid . . .*

" 'Tis that loggerhead Brent I would see hung." Dandy kicked a stool from under the table and dropped onto it. "He and his chicken-hearted pack of rascals haven't the courage to defend what they steal and so must make laws." He seemed to have forgotten that Robert Vaughan was Giles Brent's lieutenant.

Vaughan decided the company no longer suited him. He stood up, kissed Anicah lightly on the mouth, and went to settle his score in the kitchen. He would rather deal with the tapster than his wife.

Ingle gathered a handful of Anicah's skirt and tugged it. "Sing for us, wench."

"What ditty would ye have of me?"

"Ye would warble most sweetly under my caresses."

"Fie, sir. I be forespoken."

"To a dead man." John Dandy smiled evilly. "If salvages have not slain the rogue nor lions eaten him, I shall be the death of him when I catch him. Then I shall fuck his doxy, will she or no."

He grabbed Anicah's arm in a grip so tight it sent pain into her shoulder and down into the tips of her fingers. He reached his other hand up under her petticoat, groping between her legs, but he yanked it away as though he'd been burned. While he wiped it on his breeches Anicah retreated to a safer distance.

"She pissed on me!" Dandy leaped up, sending the stool flying. "The whore befouled me."

"Would that I'd shit a turd for ye, ye trendle-tailed cur," Anicah shouted.

The rest of the men watched. Anicah's quarrels were always entertaining.

She pointed at him with her middle two fingers folded down and her index and little finger extended in the sign of the cuckold. " 'Tis yer own wife ye must cajole after all the town has had the use of her, ye whoreson." She circled the room with him after her.

" 'Od's blood, I will not abide such impudence from a two-penny whore." Dandy lunged toward her, knocking table boards awry.

"A pox on you, wench." Goodman Smythe rushed in from the kitchen. "Fie, sir, fie, calm yourself." He looked to Vaughan for help, but Robert just watched with an amused smile.

People scattered when Anicah picked up a quart-sized wooden tankard and heaved it at Dandy. It showered him with cider and missed his head by less than two fingers' breadth. It felt so good she grabbed Howkins's trencher and threw that. It crashed against a wall and left a crust of hash there.

"Your whore of a mother begot ye atop a hay cart when she was hot in her breech," she screamed at him. The rage pent up inside her exploded. She grabbed the iron poker from the hearth and swung it so hard it whistled through the air.

Robert Vaughan ducked under it and caught it on the backswing. He held it effortlessly with one hand while Anicah kicked at his shins and tugged on it.

"Death and the devil take you, you draw-latch hoyden!" Dandy shouted. Now that she was helpless he started toward her, but Vaughan pointed at the door with his free hand. Dandy hesitated, then whirled on his heels and stamped out, leaving a string of oaths behind him.

"Think you it well-done to chuck a pot at his head?" Robert pried the poker from Anicah's rigid fingers.

"Nay, sire." She smiled up at him and curtsied. " 'Twere badly done that I missed him." She ran to the door. "Lobcock!" she screamed after him. "Codshead! May yer bum-gut fall out and ye trip over it and land snout down in a dung heap."

She returned humming contentedly. She smiled cheerfully at the men who stared back at her.

"Me prime gents and rufflers, what would ye tope?"

Chapter 35

Margaret dismounted and hoisted her petticoats out of the malodorous spring mud of her dooryard. She handed the reins to her servant and hurried into the house. She looked into the kitchen first, perfumed with toasted cornmeal. With a deft jerk of her wrist Bess slid a weighty, yellow-brown disk of corn bread off the long wooden baker's peel and onto the table. She curtsied and crossed herself.

"God keep thee, mistress. How fares Mistress Greene?"

"Better, by God's grace. I gave her a vomit and a dose of honey-leaf balm steeped with borage."

"For melancholy?"

"And the vapors. I pray God restores her to health." Distracted by the memory of her neighbor's dry, hot skin, mumbled speech and frightened eyes, she searched the house. Then she went to the garden and stared over the gate.

May of 1641 marked the garden's third spring. Each year Margaret and Mary extended the beds. In spite of the hard winter just past, the perennials were unfolding bright green shoots. They were meekly observing the long borders of their beds now, although they would soon grow in a riot over the paths and fences.

Mary wasn't in the garden and without her it seemed empty and incomplete. The quiver of fear in Margaret's viscera expanded into a slow churn. Her visit to nurse her fevered neighbor had started it. Margaret had sat by the bed while Mistress Greene stared past her as though looking at something horrifying that no one else could see. Margaret had to stop herself from glancing over her shoulder to catch an enemy sneaking up on her.

The fear was caused by more than Mistress Greene's fever. Word had reached St. Mary's that a band of northern Indians, Iroquois probably, had attacked an outlying farm on the Isle of Kent. They had slaughtered the family, burned the house and outbuildings, and butchered the cattle. Giles and Fulke were at Kent Fort Manor, and Margaret was worried about them.

The fierce Iroquois and Seneca, the Oneida and Susquehannocks, reminded Margaret of the stories of ravaging Norsemen the servants had told her when she was a child. Centuries ago they too had traveled far from their countries in the north to murder and rape and pillage. When Margaret grew up she dismissed them as bugbears invented to frighten her and her noisy crowd of sisters and brothers into obedience.

She thought about the illnesses, the deliriums, and depredations she had encountered here. She was used to disease and madness, and even persecution. She had lived through plague and the nighttime visitations from gangs of men hunting Catholics and their priests. But the incursions of warriors who lived only for war and conquest, those unnerved her.

She put a hand on one of the two pistols she carried in holsters, even to the dairy shed and the garden. She had always hung a pocket from her belt with keys and other oddments, but back in England she had never thought she would carry a powder flask and a bag of shot as well.

As she stared over the gate the individual plants blurred into a mottling of green leaves and dark loam. The hum of her neighbor's treasured bees in the garden and the flies on the dunghill resonated in her skull. The doubts and forebodings that lurked in the darker corners of her mind at night assailed her in sunlight and made her dizzy with fear.

Were Giles and Fulke being murdered even as she stood here? Had Mary's pretty delusions, as Robert Vaughan called them, finally developed into insanity? Had she drowned in the river or wandered into the forest? Had she tried to tell a bear or a catamount about the blessings of the true Church? Did she lie, insensible, in the bottom of a ravine?

Margaret wanted to hike her skirts up and run through the fields and cow close and wood lot shouting Mary's name; but that would alarm the servants. Worse, it would be undignified.

She found Mim in the dairy shed. "Hast thou seen Mistress Mary?"

"Nay, mistress. Methought she went to town."

Margaret could see the men hoeing up hills for tobacco. Mary wasn't with them. She started down the steep path to the river.

A marshy creek to the south marked the line where Sisters' Freehold met the town lands of Thomas Greene. The tall sedge there made her particularly uneasy. Sergeant Vaughan said the Indians waged war by treacheries and surprisals from among reeds or behind trees.

Then she heard Mary's laugh and found her and Edward sitting by the river. Edward wore his tow linen baptismal shirt, his deerskin breechclout, moccasins and purple wampum necklace.

"Sister!" Mary smiled up at her. "Edward has been amusing me with droll stories."

Margaret controlled her temper. "I have searched for thee everywhere."

"And thou hast found me." Mary closed the Bible. "Edward will have his little jest. He has asked me to teach him to read, though of course he knows how already." She smiled at him. "He knows everything, yet would fain amuse me by pretending ignorance. In return he teaches me the language spoken in heaven."

Margaret let that pass, although Mary's linking Edward and heaven were becoming more frequent and disquieting.

"These are perilous times, sister. Do not wander away with none for company."

"But I am in company."

And that, Margaret thought, is the problem. Before Calvert sailed for a visit to Virginia he had passed an edict. Knowing that few Englishmen could tell a friendly Indian from a hostile one, he had forbidden contact with any of them. He prohibited colonists from entertaining or arming them. He had also authorized the people on the eastern shore to kill any Indian they saw there. Edward's presence was a danger for him, and for Mary and Margaret too.

Margaret tried not to stare at Edward's dark, impassive face. She could not imagine him telling droll stories. As far as she could tell, his eyes were black wells, letting no light out from his soul. She realized she knew nothing about him.

She wanted to ask him whether he had parents living. And did he have a wife or did he court the maids of his village? How did he spend his days? What did he think of the English, and what went through his mind as he sat in the kitchen eating the samp and ash cakes that Bess gave him?

Mostly she wanted to ask him one very uncivil question. She had a brief, silent argument with herself, decided it was too impolite, then blurted it anyway.

"I wonder if he hath ever killed anyone?"

Mary interpreted as best she could. The musical, incomprehensible sounds coming from her lips astonished and disoriented Margaret, as though she had crushed a spray of purple lavender and smelled musty sage. When, how, had Mary learned the Indian tongue?

Edward's stoic expression shifted ever so slightly, no more than a twitch of skin around the eyes, but it looked like remorse.

"He says he's ashamed," Mary translated. "He hath been in battle, but he hath yet to slay an enemy and win honor."

Naked and brown, Martin waded chest high in the water. On either side of him and Edward the line of men stretched from one bank to the other. May was just beginning and the water was still so cold it numbed Martin's legs and feet. The wet muscles in his shoulders and back and arms rippled and gleamed as he steadily pounded the surface with the palms of his hands.

He was doing it as much to keep warm as to drive the fish into the angled fence of twigs in the shallows. Here where the river bluffs curved to embrace the head of the creek, the oaks and maples, beeches and walnuts spread their massive branches high above it. The quivering tiers of leaves shut out what little heat the sun could have provided.

Martin shivered and his stomach cramped and growled. As he pushed his way through the water he scooped up handfuls of it to ease the hunger. May was earlier than they usually fished the creeks, but everyone's stomach was as empty as Martin's and they needed the food.

As the line of beaters approached the weir the water in front of them roiled. Fins and tails and the silvery arcs of spines flashed above the surface. The palisade quivered as fish were pushed against it by those crowding them from behind. They slipped through the narrow opening in the middle of the funnel and darted into the fenced area on the other side.

The younger boys grabbed them and tossed them into the big baskets lining the shore. Some of the fish missed their mark and flapped in the reeds while the boys scrambled after them. Dissension broke out between two of the children. They fell in the mire, fighting for the biggest fish.

"Little sister." Edward called to the smaller one, a naked, mud-covered elf of about six, Kittamaquund's daughter. She made a hideous face at him and went back to pummeling the boy.

"Do not behave like a quarrelsome mink." Edward waved his arms at her, but she not only stood her ground, she threw it at him. The mud spattered her and her young foe more than Edward, but he waded ashore and gave chase.

"She doesn't act like a princess," Martin observed.

"You've known a great many princesses then?" Edward called over his shoulder.

"None well enough to borrow money from." As usual, Martin couldn't tell if Edward was jesting with him or asking a serious question.

Edward caught the child by an arm and a leg and tossed her in a high arc. She landed in the middle of the stream with a squeal. When she scrambled out he threw walnuts at her to drive her away.

She disappeared over the top of the embankment. Over the splashing and shouting they could hear her calling to the women. Martin eased ashore and began looking for his small heap of clothes among the items strewn along the sand and flung over bushes. The lilt of approaching voices had no noticeable effect on his naked companions who now were helping the boys catch and sort the fish.

Martin was left with the choice of being the only one dressed when the women and girls arrived or having them see all of him. At sixteen he was muscular as well as tall. The time he had spent working in John Dandy's forge and fields had filled out his solid frame. He had also become the best wrestler in the village, which lent him a certain amount of notoriety. Even after a year the young women eyed him, usually in flocks, which was how they traveled. Maybe they were wondering if the part of him they couldn't see was proportional to his height and breadth.

More than one young woman had slid him that upslanted glance from a demurely downcast face. It was the same look he'd seen at markets and festivals in England. He couldn't consider coupling with anyone but Anicah, but two or three of the bolder women reminded him of her. A flash of dark eye, a bounce of black hair, a laugh, a brown curve of breast or hip would start the longing up in him.

Only yesterday Martin had awakened from a beguiling dream of Anicah to find Edward's tittering female cousins clustered at his sleeping platform. Martin was mortified to discover that his member was not only standing erect, but saluting under the thin blanket that covered him.

His face burned now at the memory of it. With cold-stiffened fingers he fumbled at the knot in the thong that served as a belt. Even after he straightened the doeskin breechclout it bunched and clung to his wet body in a most aggravating way.

The women talked and laughed as they scaled and gutted the fish. Their clamshells and knife blades sliced too fast for the eye to follow. They tossed the fillets into the baskets for drying later, while the dogs quarreled over the offal. Edward and the others took their time dressing, and the women made ambiguous comments in their direction.

The men collected their weapons, but even naked they kept a vigil for the Seneca or Susquehannock raiders who slipped like the shadows of hawks through the forest. Martin settled the strap of his quiver diagonally across his chest. He had made it from the pelt of a wolf caught in one of his snares. He stuck his small stone ax into the rear of his belt where it rode in the curve at the small of his back. He picked up his bow and cudgel.

He had won the bow and the ax in a wrestling match. He had been the best wrestler among the boys of his parish in Dorset, and he had won most of his belongings in bouts here, including his latest pair of deerskin moccasins. He had challenged that particular opponent because of the size of his feet. Kittamaquund was happily planning to pit him against the Delawares' champion on their next trading visit.

While the women worked, the men walked along the high ground to where the small creek met the larger one that flowed past Kittamaquund's walled town. From the height they had a view of the spangled maze of waterways and tree-crowned bluffs all the way to the broad Potomac. The majesty of forest canopy, sun-silvered water and buff-colored cliffs repeated itself at each of the thousands of creeks and streams splaying out along the river. It was a country remote and aloof and unmeasurable.

The men settled themselves on an oak's gnarled roots, hard and polished as gray flint heaved up from the earth by frost. Under the tree's green eaves they took out their tobacco and pipes. They were completely at ease in what to an Englishman was a howling wilderness. They lounged about as though this were a deer park on some gentleman's manor.

Even now Martin found it difficult to relax as thoroughly as they did. Sloth was one of the seven great sins, and idleness was sloth, no mistake about it. The Piscataway, however, saw no purpose in counting hours like strands of wampum or filling every day with hard labor. On mornings after a dance the members of Edward's family slept past sunrise. It was a moral lapse that would have scandalized anyone of Martin's yeoman class.

Martin drew Edward aside. "Tell me again how she looked."

"Has love so addled your brains you don't remember what I've told you ten times already?" Edward grinned at Martin and mischief danced in his dark eyes. Martin would have given his soul to see Anicah as those eyes had only days ago.

"Did she look well?"

"With all the clothes the English wear it's hard to judge how they look."

"Tell me again what she was doing."

Edward patiently repeated the part of his trip to St. Mary's that interested Martin. "I watched from the forest as she made mounds for the tobacco. She didn't put a fish in each hill." He said it with just a hint of disapproval.

"Did you hear her speak?"

"There was no one for her to speak to." Edward tamped a pinch of tobacco into his small clay pipe. "She looked lonely there by herself, brother. Why do the English tend their fields separate from each other instead of all together?"

Martin was about to try to explain once more the concept of freeholds and tenant farmers and manors when he saw the shallop round a bend in the river. Edward too watched its oars rise and fall in rhythm.

"Would that I had a long piece," Martin muttered.

"If you killed them, more would come. There is no dearth of Englishmen."

"Your people almost starved because of them."

"They did not have to give their corn for beer, or for those blankets that fell apart as soon as the traders left."

No, Martin thought. Nor did the rest of the village have to share what little they had after the stores in the communal warehouse were depleted. But they did. It had been a hard winter. Martin thought bitterly of Second Wife's baby, dead of starvation.

The other men had seen the boat by now. They trotted down the narrow trail to the sandy strip of beach while Martin watched from the laurel thicket above.

The women must have spotted the Englishmen too because they chose this time to saunter past with their baskets of cleaned fish. If any goods were to be traded, they wanted to see them. As usual they wore only short aprons of cloth or fox skin. The swaying cascades of black hair covered their backs as far as their thighs, but hid little in front.

Martin had grown used to their nakedness. He knew that even unclothed they were more modest than English maids at a husking or ale. To dress them would have been like laying paint on a tree or putting a ball gown on the Jesuits' statue of the Virgin Mary.

Most of his countrymen thought differently about the matter, though. Martin didn't recognize these particular individuals, but he knew what schemes and lusts and opinions they harbored. He wanted to shout at the women to hide themselves. Instead they gathered, whispering and laughing, behind the Piscataway men.

Martin knew that Edward would refer all offers to the *tayac*. That didn't stop the English from trying to strike a deal here and now, offering the adulterated beer they undoubtedly had in the boat. Martin could only watch as they tried to barter for the prettiest and sturdiest of the women.

Chapter 36

Anicah looked gloomily at her hands. In spite of the thick calluses, they were raw from days of topping and weeding the tobacco in the July sun. Scouring the table boards now with moist sand pained them.

"A bit o' soil ne'r hurt anyone," Anicah grumbled.

"They look as though a sow farrowed on them," Dina said.

She carried a sack of meal from Cornwaleys's mill and another with a few stunted cabbages and turnips from a goodwife who sold produce. The winter had howled long around the corners of the houses and whistled through the chinks. A late frost killed the first shoots in most of the gardens, and no one had much to sell this spring.

Soon she was banging lids and trivots as she began preparing the pease porridge she would serve the Smythes and anyone who ventured in that day. Goodwife Smythe had bought no pork from Harry's purloined stock, so the turnspit dog could sleep undisturbed by the fire. He whimpered and twitched, his toenails clicking on the hearthstones as he chased some rabbit in his dreams.

"May God keep you."

A shadow fell across the sanded floor. The doorway framed Father Poulton's lean silhouette framed with the early morning sun streaming around him. He signed the cross and leaning on his cane, stepped into the room.

"G'd morrow to ye, sire." Anicah curtsied self-consciously.

She never knew how to address the priests. She liked Father Poulton, but all the Jesuits were incomprehensible to her. She could not imagine a man willingly giving up the pleasure of coupling with a woman, though the knowledge was common that some priests liked boys well enough.

"I thought to see how you fared." Poulton looked around at the spare table boards and trestles stacked against the wall, the rickety stools, the ale bench, the smoke-darkened rafters and the rows of black marks on the yellowed walls. He breathed in the smell of smoke, spirits, vomit and garbage.

Anicah brought a stool and dusted it off with her apron. She set it down with a flourish at the table she had just scrubbed, then she fetched a pewter spoon and a mug from the sideboard. She had the proprietary air of a goodwife welcoming the parson to her cottage for a Sabbath supper.

"Dina and I saved some cheese and pone and a bit o' turkey hash against rank famine." She winked at him and hurried into the kitchen.

She returned with a wooden bowl. Poulton looked stooped and forlorn, sitting by himself in the gloom of the empty taproom. He was staring out the window and gave a start when Anicah set the bowl with a bang in front of him.

"You needn't trouble yourself," he said. But he ate as though he sheltered a starved wolf in his maw.

" 'Tis no trouble."

He waved vaguely toward the marks on the wall. "I have no account here nor coin to pay."

"Ye're but skin and bones, yer honor." Anicah crossed her arms on her chest and studied him. "Thin as a shotten herring."

"Many of my red children traded their winter store of corn for spirits, and our own supplies have been stolen. We are in straitened circumstances to find food for them." He pulled a long sigh up from the depths of his being. "So many needy souls famish there daily for want of the bread of life, and of the spirit."

Anicah felt a pang of guilt at her own small part in smuggling whiskey. "Some cove's priggin' yer swag?"

Poulton stuck a moment on the meaning of prigging. "Is someone stealing from us? Aye, I fear they are." He looked at his food as though wishing he could re-create the miracle of the Mount and turn it into loaves and fishes. "The Indians are content with little and mind their bellies less than any people on earth, yet now their bellies begin to mind them."

He reached into the sack hanging from the belt of his old brown cassock. "I almost forgot the other reason for coming here." He handed her a sprig of lavender with a small purple plume of flowers. "Master DaSousa sailed with Governor Calvert to Virginia. Before he went he asked me to give it thee. I trust thou knowst the import of it."

Anicah held it to her nose. Martin had sent her a token, a pledge of love. Tears ran down her cheeks. The flowers' sweet aroma brought back the Maying, two years before, when she and Martin had held each other amid the flowers by the river. It had been the happiest day of Anicah's life.

"Aye, sir." She wiped the tears away. "I do know the meaning of it."

She wanted to ask about Martin, but didn't dare. As soon as Goodman DaSousa returned she would wheedle the information from him. Then she would slip away and join Martin.

"Father Copley awaits me at the chapel." Even with his cane Father Poulton had trouble rising, and Anicah took him by the elbow to help him. His arm felt like a chicken's leg.

"I thank ye, yer honor. From the bottom-most hold of me heart and soul, I thank ye."

He recognized her gratitude with a sad but affectionate smile. "Thou hast a name popular among the Spanish, my child. It means 'graceful' in Hebrew, the language of our Lord Jesus."

Anicah shrugged. "Meaning no offense, yer honor, but I be no Hebrew nor Spaniard nor papist neither."

"Someday God will vouchsafe to blind thee with His light, that thou mayest see." The deprecatory wave of his hand elaborated into a sign of the cross above her head. "May God bless thee and keep thee well, my child." He hobbled toward the door, his thin shoulders rounded and his head down, as though leaning into a high wind.

As Anicah watched him go she realized that another such winter would likely kill him. It would certainly kill him if John Dandy continued stealing his food and trade goods.

Anicah had never informed on anyone. She didn't relish the idea of doing it now. But if any rogue deserved to be discovered, Dandy was the one. She hesitated until Poulton had almost reached the first curve in the Mattapany path, then ran after him. He had to know who was stealing from him, and she was the only one who could tell him.

"One less priest to plague us." Goodwife Smythe stopped by the garden to check on Anicah. The news of murder had dredged up her sense of humor from wherever it usually lurked. "Gone to the Diet of Worms, and good riddance, I say."

Anicah looked up from her hoeing and wiped the sweat from her forehead before it rolled into her eyes. "Which priest?"

"The spoony-shanked cripple."

Poulton. Somehow she had known Poulton would be the one. Dread soured in her gut until her gorge rose and left its bitter taste.

"This very morning some devout soul shot him from the foreland whilst he rode in a boat. Picked him off like a fish in a weir. Would that he had killed all the paternosters."

Anicah picked up the basket of onions she had just dug and followed her into the kitchen. Goody Smythe held up brown bottles to the sunlight from the open door to check the level of beer, certain there had been pilferage in her absence.

She nosed around the kitchen, getting in Anicah's way and grumbling about the heretical burial the papists would give Father Poulton and the warm reception awaiting him in hell. Anicah hardly heard her. The priest must have confronted John Dandy with his thievery and it had proved the death of him. If Anicah hadn't told Poulton about it, he would be alive.

I've kilt him, she thought. I've surely kilt him.

For a few terrible moments she believed she had caused the death or vanishment of everyone who had ever been kind to her—her mother, her aunt, Martin, the priest, even her father, though she had no memory of him. Then she started worrying about a more practical problem.

Did Dandy know she had told the priest about his theft? Would he kill her next?

She was skittish all day and spent most of the night sorting through plans and discarding them. She could stay close to the ordinary and wait to see what happened. She could run away, she could accuse Dandy of the crime, or she could ask someone for help. But whom? Sergeant Vaughan and Goodman DaSousa were away. Her only other friend with any influence had just been buried in the ever-expanding cemetery before the heat caused his remains to stink like last night's boiled tripe.

The next morning Anicah awoke wrestling with the same quandary that had gone to bed with her. As she wandered outside for her morning office, she heard the uncommon sound of a horse's hooves. It rattled above the cackle and grunt of the chickens and pigs and the hammering of St. Mary's few cottagers trying to hold their roofs over their heads another season. The Brent women were about.

Anicah went to the road to watch Margaret Brent pass by alone on her mare. The mare turned onto the path to the chapel.

Anicah hurried inside. "Mistress." She curtsied to Goody Smythe. "Squire Brent bade me fetch the bottles I delivered there yesterday."

"Make haste then. Thou must needs weed the near field." Then as an afterthought, "And commit no sin with him, though he will certainly importune thee."

Anicah hurried along the path to Sisters' Freehold but stopped

at the edge of the field closest to the house. Standing in the angle
of the worm fence, she studied the house and rear dooryard. Heat
shimmered off the hard-packed earth. A few dispirited chickens
moved among the scattered stacks of boards and barrel hoops. The
shrill whir of cicadas rose and fell.

Mistress Margaret's house was one of the few within the borders of St. Mary's town lands that Anicah hadn't entered on some
errand or another. She tried to imagine life inside it. From what
she knew of Margaret Brent, she thought it must be a joyless place,
austere as a convent, cold as a prison.

She hurried across the yard to the garden and looked over the
palings. Mary sat on a stool at the far corner. Her skirt was pinned
up at her waist, leaving her petticoats hanging about her bare ankles. She had caught her fine, pale hair up in a white cloth tied at
the nape of her neck. Over that she wore a wide-brimmed hat
woven of reeds.

Keeping her head low Anicah opened the gate, slipped inside
and made her way along the paths between the rectangular beds.

"G'd day to ye, mistress."

"Maid Anicah." Mary looked up from under her hat brim and
smiled. Then she went back to tying the hop vine to a stake. "May
the Holy Virgin keep thee well and all those thou lovest."

"It seems, mistress, that one I love—" The word "love" kindled
a grief so intense that Anicah couldn't continue. It scalded her eyelids and the inside of her nose and tightened the back of her throat.

The realization that she had loved the Jesuit as a father was a
blow to her heart. She started to cry. Mary stood and gathered her
into her arms. Anicah laid her head on Mary's thin shoulder and
surrendered to great, shuddering sobs.

"Grieve not, child." Mary stroked her wild hair. "The body is
but the prison of the divine spark. He's in heaven, sitting in glory
before the throne of his loving Father."

"He was kilt." Anicah wiped her noise on her sleeve, then
saw the embroidered cambric handkerchief Mary held out, blew

her nose on it and gave it back, much dampened. She was too distraught to even consider lifting it.

" 'Twas a tragic mischance, a hunter's ball gone astray."

"Nay, mistress, he was murdered." Anicah's head ached from the battering of her grief and guilt and the flood of tears that had been a decade building inside her. "And I know who kilt him."

Anicah had to use all her skills at persuasion to cajole Mary into telling the governor about the murder. As they walked along the path Anicah expected Margaret Brent to canter around each curve. When they arrived without meeting anyone on the way, she refused to go inside.

"Please, mistress," she pleaded. "Ye mustn't tell a soul who peached on the spoil-iron. He'll kill me too."

Mary knocked and entered and Anicah trotted around to the rain barrel at the side of the house. She hiked up her skirts and sat back on her heels in its shade, as though she were a serving maid waiting for her mistress. Just above her head was an open window through which she could hear Mary and Calvert talking. Calvert was obviously bemused by the appearance of Mary alone, without her sister or a manservant. But he launched gallantly into the usual pleasantries while Anicah chewed the calluses on her palm and endured the heat and the suspense.

After what seemed an eternity, Mary broached the subject.

"Leonard, Father Poulton was murdered by the gunsmith, John Dandy."

"The sheriff will conduct an inquiry, of course, but evidence and witnesses indicate it was but an unfortunate mishap."

"I have it on good authority that murder was committed."

"What authority would that be, Mistress Mary?"

Mary hardly paused. "My angel's, of course."

"Thy angel's?"

"Certes, Leonard."

"What did thy angel tell thee?"

"That John Dandy is the perpetrator of the deed."

"Why would Dandy kill him?"

"Because Father Poulton knew he was stealing the supplies meant for God's holy work among the heathens."

"Thy angel told thee this too?"

"Yes."

"When did he tell thee?" Leonard asked. He had heard Mary talk about her angel before.

"This morning. She appeared to me in the garden, whilst I was tying up the hop vines."

"She? I thought thy heavenly guardian was of the masculine persuasion."

"Leonard . . ." Mary laughed brightly. "Angels can assume any shape at their pleasure. This morning she appeared as a comely maiden, of radiant locks and lambent glances. She wept most piteously for the soul of the murderer lost to sin."

Anicah realized with a start that Mistress Mary was referring to her. She also worried that with all this talk of angels, Governor Calvert would not likely credit her charges.

"We shall look into the matter, Mistress Mary. And I thank thee for thy concern."

"Leonard, hast thou seen the Holy Mother's legions when the air fills with their radiance, and they are as many as snowflakes falling from the skies?"

"Alas, I cannot say that I have."

" 'Tis a glorious sight. Mayhap thou wilt witness it someday."

"My man shall accompany thee home. 'Tis not safe to wander alone." From the diminishing volume of Calvert's voice Anicah could tell he was guiding Mary toward the door.

"No need, Leonard. Margaret is nearby."

Anicah met Mary on the road and fell into step behind her.

"D'ye think he believed ye, mistress?"

"God alone knows, Ani."

The affectionate name from one of Mary's station touched

Anicah. They walked in silence until they came to the ordinary. Anicah paused on the doorstep.

"I shall walk with thee, mistress, to keep thee company."

"No need, child. I shall stop at the chapel to pray for Father Poulton's soul."

"I thank ye for not saying I told ye about the spoil-iron."

"Angels speak through unlikely channels. I do not discount that thou art an angel guised as a tavern wench." Mary's fey, compelling smile lit her thin face. "Many will not believe that God's holy messengers can be seen by mortal eyes. And though the most judicious of persons may swear he hath seen them, they account him a fool, a dreamer, a madman."

"I have never seen one, mistress, yet I do not think ye mad."

"God bless thee, child. And may the Blessed Virgin return thy dear Martin to thee." Mary smiled again, turned and walked down the path toward the chapel.

Chapter 37

By mid-October the amber-colored tobacco leaves were strung in tiers from a scaffolding of poles that rose to the roof peak of the drying house. They hung like the folded wings of huge bats sleeping in their thousands on a cave ceiling. Margaret's steward, Edward Packer, stood by while she turned slowly to survey the crop and calculate. So many pounds on a pole. So many poles to a cask. So many casks.

Margaret reckoned that this leaf should bring enough extra profit in London to transport five more servants. That would qualify her for a thousand-acre patent under Lord Baltimore's latest conditions of plantation. She had already selected a stretch of hilly country on St. Inigoes Creek, well-watered and with rich, dark bottomland for growing the choice sweet-scent leaf.

Standing in the aromatic brown gloom, Margaret imagined herself as lady of the manor, presiding at the manorial court for scores of servants. Her fields would reach farther than she could see. Hundreds of cattle and sheep would graze the green pasture. She would grow proper crops—barley and wheat and fragrant hay to put up in the barns.

She thought of the clean smell of new-mown hay, of the men and maids laughing and teasing as they pitched it onto the lumbering wagons. She remembered the huge horses that pulled the wagons, and how she used to perch on their backs when she was a child.

This year's tobacco cutting could make the dream real, if too much or too little rain didn't spoil the leaf before it was packed. If seawater didn't breach the casks in the ship's hold. If the ship didn't sink or fall prey to sea rovers. If the bitter contention in England between king and Parliament, Puritan and Anglican, didn't explode into war.

Margaret wrapped a leaf, big as a kerchief, around her finger. When she pulled it taut across her knuckle it stretched and clung like the softest, thinnest kidskin.

"Methinks the weed is ready to strike and strip, mistress," Packer said. "Yesterday's rain raised the humidity sufficiently."

"Aye." Margaret put her hand among the leaves to judge the distance between them. "Have the men set the bundles not so nigh each other, Mr. Packer, lest mold be the ruin of them."

"Maggie." Mary stood in the doorway. "Do come see the sunset."

"I have work to do before dark, sister."

But Mary took her hand and pulled with a gentle, irresistible insistence. They walked to the bluff above the river and stared at the bands of clouds, stacked in rose and gold striations above the orange, red and gold-leafed trees on the far bank. Geese slanted noisily down to the water to float in their vast rafts.

Margaret looked south toward the point of land that reached into the river. Three months had passed since the last time she and Mary had stood here together. They had waved to Father Poulton as the Jesuits' shallop headed for St. Inigoes. When the boat reached the foreland a hunter's bullet found him in all that expanse of water and killed him. A haphazard, misshapen lump of lead had stopped his valiant heart. Margaret would not hear his soft voice again nor see God's love in his eyes. She squeezed her own eyes shut against the burning grief.

Mary took her hand. " 'The Lord gave,' " she recited, " 'and the Lord hath taken away: as it hath pleased the Lord, so it is done.' "

" 'Blessed be the name of the Lord.' " Margaret finished the verse from Job.

When she saw a boat rounding the point she thought for an irrational instant that Father Poulton was being returned as suddenly and inexplicably as he had been taken away. Then she realized it was a canoe and it was filled with Indians and it was heading for her landing. The sight of their feathers and rough fur mantles and dark faces raised a reflexive alarm. She put one hand on her pistol and the other on the rosary hanging from her belt.

" 'Tis Father White." Mary waved and the Jesuit waved back. She and Margaret hurried down the slope to the beach.

Edward carried White ashore while Margaret and Mary stood with heads bowed for his benediction. Edward waded into the cold water again and lifted a small girl from the canoe.

She looked about eight years old. Shoulder-length black hair arced in parentheses around a delicate oval face and a mouth formed with the deep double curves of a Cupid's bow. She wore moccasins, an ankle-length white wool shift and a brown wool cape.

She curtsied and murmured, "Gah kip dee, midress," which Margaret could only surmise was, "God keep thee, mistress." She obviously had been coached and had no notion of what the sounds meant. She stared up at Margaret and Mary with an unreadable expression in eyes the color of jet and the elegant shape of pumpkin seeds.

None of the other Piscataway left the canoe. When Edward had deposited several leather pouches and Father White's small chest on the shore, he pushed the bow off the sand and jumped in. The men paddled away without a word or a glance back. The girl gave a small start as though to follow them, then stood still.

Father White laid a hand on her head. "This is the emperor Kittamaquund's daughter. He desires her to be educated among the English. When she understands all the Christian mysteries she is to be washed in the sacred font of baptism. Kittamaquund asked that you and Governor Calvert be given charge of her, Margaret. How sayest thou?"

"We shall endeavor to make a devout and pious Christian of her." She turned to the girl. "What's thy name, child?"

Mary knelt and murmured to the girl in her own language.

" 'Tis not a word that falls easily from an English tongue." Mary smiled up at them all. "Until she receives her baptismal name mayhap we could call her Kitt."

"Kitt it shall be then." Margaret held out a hand, but the child just stared at it. Margaret couldn't tell from her stoic expression if she was confused or frightened, curious or merely indifferent. "She may stay as long as she wishes," she said.

"Her wishes do not count in the matter." Father White put his palm on Kitt's back and pushed her gently toward Margaret. She veered, however, and took Mary's hand.

With the back of the ax Anicah knocked the frozen chunks of oak loose from the stack, and stamped her feet in an attempt to return sensation to them. With stiff fingers she piled the wood in her arms and waded through drifts halfway to her knees. She especially resented this snow because it had come so early. November had barely begun.

At the kitchen door she turned and looked at the white-shrouded bushes, the river sparkling below and the bare trees on the far shore. She wondered where Martin was in that measureless wilderness. Where had he slept last night as the lovely, cruel flakes drifted down? How had he lived for a year and a half?

She knew almost exactly how long ago he had run away. She had carved a slash in the big beech each new moon since he had left. She marked each month of her service to Goody Smythe and also her share of Henry Fleete's card winnings. She didn't trust either of them to keep a strict accounting.

She didn't expect Fleete to pay her, but the marks cheered her as they slowly multiplied. The other two sets didn't. The longer Martin was gone, the less she could hope to see him again. And even after she served her term with the Smythes, what use was freedom without him?

She entered the kitchen to find Robert Vaughan standing

in the fireplace with his back to her and his breeches around his knees.

"The goodwife would take her switch to yer hairy nates if she caught ye pissing in the ashes, Sergeant." She dropped the wood on the hearth. "Only she's allowed to wet them down."

"The goodwife is absent, my toothsome wench." He pulled up his breeches and tied the laces that fastened them to his old leather doublet. "Besides, I am a man of breeding. I piss at a goodly distance from Dina's kettle and skillet."

Vaughan corraled her in his long, thick arms and kissed her on the mouth. She inhaled the heady, masculine mix of wine and tobacco, smoke, sweat and the mellow odor of old cowhide. She missed the feel of a man more than she could say, and she was adept at expressing that sort of thing.

He kissed her again, harder this time, and she shivered at the bright pain of his teeth nipping her lip. A sensuous languor washed over her.

"Methinks the maid smells very sweet of musk." Vaughan licked her ear, sending tremors of pleasure to the cold soles of her feet.

"I have a case of the green sickness," she murmured, "for the want of Martin Kirk."

Vaughan ran his thick fingers into the wildness of her hair and stared down at her. She could see pity in his errant eyes, and desire. And disappointment of a deep and abiding sort.

"Ani, your great, comely ox of a yeoman won't come back to you."

"He will." Tears welled up and she wrenched away from him. "He's alive. Mistress Mary Brent told me so. An angel cares for him."

"Mistress Mary . . ." Vaughan paused. "Mistress Mary could be wrong. And even if Martin lives, he knows the law won't forget his offense. He would return to a hangman's necklace." He reached for her again. "I would buy your term and take you to wife, Ani."

"I must refuse yer kind offer, as I am already bespoke." She caught his hand as it slid around her waist. She guided it between his legs and pressed it firmly on his crotch. "Ye must mount a corporal and four, sir, and please yerself, for I shan't."

"Shitting in the kitchen ashes again, are you, Sergeant Vaughan?" When Dina closed the door behind her the wind whined on the other side of it like a dog wanting in. "If the dooryard is too far for you to travel, conduct your business in the common room fireplace like everyone else."

"I did not shit in the ashes, goodwife." Vaughan hiked up his breeches and his dignity and left the kitchen.

"Did he offer to take you to wife?" Dina asked.

"Aye."

"Then by my reckoning, every unmarried man to enter in the province has done so, and a few married ones too."

"I do not fancy any of them," Anicah said. "I do not fancy love either."

"All the world fancies love."

"Not I. 'Tis a fire that burns to the cellar the poor silly soul it should but warm." She turned suddenly. "Dina, ye can divine the future. When will Martin come back?"

"I don't know, but if you pay me I can make up the sort of pretty prophesies I sell to the fools who ask them of me."

Anicah sighed and returned to the common room, crowded now with burgesses just come from the first day of the autumn Assembly. They were a contentious lot, quite taken with themselves as the elected representatives of the planters of their districts.

Goodman Smythe was drunker than usual, probably in celebration of his wife's absence and the business the Assembly sessions always brought. He wandered from table to table, laughing at his own aged jests and halting the flow of conversations and setting them off on abruptly different courses.

"God keep ye all." Joan Parke grinned as she slammed the door behind her.

Anicah saw the dread appear in Smythe's ruddy face. Joan always caused trouble and he was generally powerless to stop her. Secretary Lewger would no doubt cite him again for keeping a disorderly house. And when his wife returned she would scold him and slap his ears till his brains rattled.

"Death and the devil, make way, ye bachelors' sons. I have news to impart." Joan hiked up her skirts and used a stool to climb onto the table.

Smythe headed prudently for the kitchen, the turnspit dog trotting behind him.

"The popish whore did lie with a salvage in the corn." Joan returned to the mischief at hand. "Her with her wren's legs about the heathen's waist and his dusky double jugs a-waggling." She undulated her broad hips forward and back.

"Which popish whore would that be?" Anicah asked.

"The lunatic whippet, Mistress Mary Brent."

"Ye saw her in the cornfield, ye say?" Anicah stood with arms crossed on her chest. Regulars recognized the stance. She adopted it when about to take issue with someone. They moved closer to watch.

"Aye."

" 'Tis bloody cold in the cornfield this time of year."

"He did occupy her this Michaelmas past."

"How passing strange ye would air it now."

"D'ye call me a liar, ye draggle-tail little bung-nipper?"

"Aye, Miss Parke, and a prater of much nonsense." Anicah looked up at her, her eyes wide and innocent. "And if ye've not fucked an Indian yerself, 'tis the only creature to escape yer attentions, as any mangy dog in the village can attest."

"A cluster of poxes on ye and no pesthouse to pity ye." Joan looked down menacingly from her great height. "Meddle with me and I shall fling ye in the fire."

The men who had crowded around for the view up Joan's petticoat tails moved prudently away from the table.

"Then ye shall want a poker to turn me till I'm done."

Anicah seized the iron rod from the hearth and with both hands swung it across the tabletop at ankle level. Joan hopped in an effort to avoid it, but her feet tangled with it and flew out from under her. She fell, one mighty buttock hitting the edge of the table with a thud. She rolled off and landed on her back on the floor with her legs in the air.

"God scald ye, ye reeking notch," Joan screamed.

Still brandishing the poker Anicah backed toward the street door. Outside she would have more room to maneuver and to run. She knew the poker wouldn't stop Joan, and that she would most likely get hurt. At least she had distracted her from her lies about Mistress Mary.

With head lowered and an arm up to fend off the poker, Joan charged. She butted Anicah in the chest, braced her feet and pushed. Anicah dropped the poker and grabbed fistfuls of Joan's snarled, ember-red hair. She yanked with all her strength, but Joan bowled her over as though she were no more obstacle than another head louse.

At that instant the door opened and the two women's momentum carried them through it. They hit Giles Brent who had been about to enter and sent him backward into the ankle-deep slush of melted snow, ice, mud and pig feces. To compound insult and injury, they landed on top of him. Everyone in the taproom squeezed out the door and into the yard to watch and wager.

"Damn me!" Giles struggled to extricate himself, but Joan and Anicah continued biting and scratching and flailing at each other. "Damn me, I say, do help me here."

Robert Vaughan waded in to separate the women. Harry Angell gave Giles an arm up. He solicitously tried to brush the mud off with his hat but only succeeded in smearing it around.

"Such a shame, squire. 'Twere yer new red velvet too." If there was irony in Harry's voice, Giles couldn't hear it over Joan's caterwauling. "They are women of quarrelsome measure, yer honor," Harry added, as though Giles couldn't figure it out.

" 'Sdeath!" Giles looked for something to beat them with. He had just decided on the flat of his sword when Dina appeared in the doorway.

"The tapster's dead." No one heard her above the hubbub. She shouted the news again. "The tapster's dead."

Chapter 38

A cold drizzle of a rain started about mid-morning. Goodman Smythe lay under the table with his feet sticking out from one end. His pudgy hands were clasped on his hillock of a stomach and a plate of salt was balanced on his chest. The turnspit dog lay at his side with his muzzle on his paws and stared sorrowfully out at the goings-on.

If Smythe had been in a condition to notice, almost 360 degrees of his view would have consisted of mud-caked shoes and hairy ankles or sagging, moth-chewed hose. The crowd was a noisy, exuberant one, but Anicah thought it lacked real mirth. The man who could have supplied it was the very one laid out.

Goody Smythe had set out bottles of her poorest beer and hard cider on the table over her late husband's corpse. Anicah stood in the middle of the shouting, jostling mob and maintained a small island of order while the goodwife sat by the fire and accepted condolences, toasts and drinks in equal measure. William Howkins doled out cheap clay pipes and pallid, second-growth tobacco. Howkins sported a proprietary air and the sanctimonious smirk of one who regularly picked pockets in church.

Dina was telling, again, the story of Smythe's death.

"He was heading for the cider barrel when the turnspit ran between his feet and tripped him. The tapster pitched forward like a felled tree and hit his head on the chimney corner. He fell facedown in the coals. I grabbed his feet and pulled him out, but his hair and clothes were afire."

"Broiled like griskins, he was," Anicah added. "His singed hair did stink up the kitchen for hours."

"I threw a blanket atop him to smother the flames, but he had already gone. The blow to the head kilt him."

Dina and Anicah had helped Widow Smythe wrap the tapster in one of the ordinary's canvas coverlets. Considering the damage the fire had done to his face, a shroud was a good idea. Anicah knew, though, that when he lay poised on the edge of the open grave, his widow would spin him out of it like a top from its winding of string. The canvas would cover some living soul that night. Anicah hoped that when Goodman Smythe toppled to his last rest, someone would make sure he lay on his back, facing up at the world he had just left.

Anicah had heard the usual extravagant eulogies. Smythe had been declared an ornament to his country and a prince among men. People who hardly knew him farded his faults and endowed him with virtues totally unfamiliar to him.

Anicah had expected an extraordinary attendance for the Sabbath wake of a tavern keeper. She was surprised, though, by the number of people who brought funeral doles—bundles of tobacco leaf or baskets of corn. They were the ferryman's fee to carry Goodman Smythe across to Elysium. Smythe had more friends than Anicah would have supposed, given the many jokes at his expense. Even now they laughed about putting Smythe to bed with a shovel. They were determined that there would be no slacking of cheer just because the host happened to be dead.

Original Brown thrust a penny in Anicah's face, distracting her from her duties. "We must unwrap him." He was more distraught than grief or cider would warrant.

"Nay, me ancient mate." With Dina's long wooden ladle Anicah rapped a set of knuckles reaching for a bottle. The man yelped and sucked on them as he tottered back to his game of hazard.

"St. Peter won't accept leaf," Brown said. "He must have

copper and it must be tucked under the deceased's tongue, else he shall not find it."

"To pass a Marylander through his turnpike St. Peter'll take leaf same as everyone else."

"Ani . . ." Brown clutched her sleeve. "Do promise that when I go to Rot-his-Bone ye shall put a penny under me tongue."

So that was what was bothering him. Anicah shook his hand away so she could work. "Yer sweethearts can do it." She knew he had none, but he boasted so often about them she couldn't resist teasing him.

"Nay." He shook his head sadly. "They be a fickle flock."

"Give way." Dina turned sideways to move through the press. Over her head she held a loaf of bread and a bowl carved from a maple burl. "Give way for the mazer bowl." She put them both on the table.

"A loaf for the sin eater." Everyone took up the cry.

Anicah poured beer into the bowl while Brown watched raptly. Goody Smythe handed the disk of corn bread to him. He crumbled off chunks of it and chewed them with his few good teeth. He washed them down with the beer.

Goody Smythe had hired him as sin eater. By eating the bread and drinking the beer he took upon himself all of the tapster's peccadillos. With a clear conscience Goodman Smythe's shade wasn't likely to hang about the ordinary where he would have caused his wife as much inconvenience in death as he had in life.

In the relative silence that accompanied Brown's solemn duties a distant boom sounded. The Catholics had dropped their pew seats. The monthly service had ended.

When the gentry reached the muddy stretch in front of the ordinary, Robert Vaughan was waiting for them. He had been celebrating Smythe's passing as the tapster would have wanted and was rather drunk. He held the door open while those inside complained loudly about the cold air rushing in.

Warm wine and a fire were too tempting to pass up. The Brents and several others entered. To make room for them Howkins carried a keg of cider outside. He ushered the common folk out to the dooryard where the rain had stopped for the time being.

As the Lewgers went by John Lewger muttered about the inconvenience of the tapster's dying intestate. His wife glared at Vaughan as she passed.

"And right you are to spurn this establishment," Vaughan called after them. " 'Tis a nest of Protestant vipers."

Mistress Lewger speeded her pace, struggling through the mud in her high pattens.

"When the Puritans take the country they'll burn Roman Catholics for sport," Vaughan shouted. "And faggots will be as dear as in Bloody Mary's day." He was still chuckling when he came back inside.

"Sergeant Vaughan . . ." Margaret shook her finger at him and tried not to smile. Whatever discomfited the Lewgers amused her. "Thou art an incorrigible rogue."

"Giles, my friend," Vaughan roared. "Where is your new red velvet?"

"Damn me, Vaughan." Giles turned as crimson as the suit before it accompanied him into the mud. "Damn me, it'll never come clean."

The gentry stood about drinking the Serez sack that the widow reluctantly broached. Their servants lined the walls and savored the cider and the time away from their labors. Anicah glanced up from the cider cask and saw that the Brents' Indian child was staring at her, solemn as an undertaker's dog.

Anicah winked and the girl drew closer. While Vaughan distracted everyone with one of his more vulgar songs, Anicah held her hand up. Kitt followed it with her eyes as Anicah dipped it quickly into the pocket of Giles's old brown wool suit and pulled out his snuff box. She cupped her other hand around it so only Kitt could see it. She winked again, then slipped it back into the pocket just as Giles legged off in search of Fleete and his cards.

Kitt smiled. Anicah didn't know it was the first time she'd done so in the two weeks since Father White delivered her.

"Here, here, what's she doing?" Widow Smythe flapped her apron at Mary Brent who had knelt beside the shrouded corpse. "I'll have no popish incantations here."

Howkins hurried to intercede. "Forgive her, m'lords and ladies. She be frantic with grief."

"And drink," Anicah murmured.

Margaret drew herself up inside her stays, increasing her height and dignity. "My sister was but praying for the repose of the deceased, Widow Smythe."

"We want none o' your prayers."

Anicah opened her mouth. She almost said, "Mistress Mary means no harm." And she would have meant, "They be better souls than you, Goody Howkins, papists or not." She closed her mouth without saying anything, but Margaret saw the small tussle on her face. She twitched the corners of her wide mouth in a smile of thanks.

Instead of beckoning to Kitt, Margaret came to get her. She leaned down to speak so only Anicah could hear her. "I thank thee for thy defense of my sister's honor yesterday."

Before Anicah could think of a reply, Margaret took Mary gently by the elbow. "Sister . . ." She helped her to her feet. "We are not welcome here."

As Anicah watched them go she contemplated the fact that not one of the goodwife's dour sect would likely offer prayers or good wishes for the soul of a papist.

A burst of laughter woke Anicah. She glanced at the fireplace. A few coals still winked there, but the hour was late. While she debated getting up to investigate she curled more tightly to avoid the cold puddles of air that seeped under the thin covers. Then she heard a murmuring and curiosity got the better of her. Wrapping her coverlet around her she tiptoed in her stockinged feet to the half-opened door and peered around it.

The taproom was dark but for the glow around the fireplace

and a stick of lighter pine burning in a bowl of sand on the table over Goodman Smythe's corpse. Patience Smythe and William Howkins sat at right angles to each other with the corner of the table between them. A large bottle of sack stood in front of them.

"We shall decide the matter with a wager," Widow Smythe said. She reached into the cape wrapped around her and drew a pack of cards from her chemise.

Howkins tried to put his hand in the place formerly occupied by the cards. Goody Smythe giggled and slapped it away.

"I propose a game of all-fours, with our bodies and worldy goods the stakes," she said.

"I would have the comfort of your body now." He half stood and tried to hug her to him, upsetting the bottle. They both laughed as they righted it, uncorked it and took another drink.

Anicah felt weighted with melancholy as she crept back into bed. The turnspit whimpered and curled against her chest. Anicah put her arm around the dog and resolved to find a purple thread somewhere tomorrow. She would throw it into the river to carry away any of Goodman Smythe's sins that Original Brown might have missed in his role as sin eater. Maybe Smythe's shade would see it and know that at least one person would truly miss him.

Chapter 39

Anicah shifted the two heavy sacks of cornmeal as she trudged along the path from Thomas Cornwaleys's mill. With most people living as servants or tenants on the scattered freeholds, St. Mary's was deserted as usual. Anicah set the bags down and untied one of them. Looking furtively around, she turned her back to the late December wind and scooped out a handful of meal. It was powdery and laced with tiny chips of rock from the grindstone, but she licked the last of it off her palm. Still her empty stomach pained her.

When she reached the rotting palisade she saw Harry Angell digging behind Joan Parke's house. Digging was not something she had ever seen Angell do. She slid through the opening left by a falling paling.

"Planting out of season, Harry?"

Angell whirled, shovel raised to strike her. She gave him an artless smile.

"Joan bade me bury her refuse. By order of the governor."

"Joan wouldn't bury refuse by order of God." Anicah looked into the pit.

"Begone, Spaniard, ere I become annoyed."

"Sophisticating the second crop of sot weed, are ye?" Anicah squatted and sniffed at the odor of urine rising from the sacks of inferior tobacco Harry was uncovering. "So this is where the alewife's beer ends when it passes through ye." She grinned up at him.

"Goody Smythe uses melted pig fat and the lees from wine to fortify her tobacco seconds. Piss should give it a bang-up taste, though."

Anicah remembered the wax mold of the governor's crest she had seen Angell pass to John Dandy the time they had smuggled spirits to St. Inigoes almost two years ago. Dandy must have cast a seal from it, and now Angell was using it to mark casks of inferior tobacco as though inspected and passed by the governor's men.

Harry stuck his shovel blade into the dirt and untied his breeches. He balanced his toes on the edge of the hole and urinated onto the sacks.

"Waste not, want not." He shook off the last drops.

"And Master Ingle will lade the weed aboard his ship, I suppose."

"Aye." He grinned cadaverously.

Once the sacks were out Harry filled in the hole. He put his shoulder against a ruined wood shed. Anicah leaned her back against it too and pushed with her feet. The two of them shoved it over the freshly turned dirt. The effort made her dizzy. She swayed and put a hand out to steady herself.

"Ye look peaked, Spaniard." Harry began piling the sacks inside the shed, filling it completely. "Does yer new master, Tapster Howkins, not feed ye well?"

"He starves me." She put her fists on her hips and looked boldly up at him. "Harry, make Captain Fleete pay his score with me so I can buy me term the sooner."

"I could easier wring wine from a rock."

"Fleete brags on his wealth."

"He brags about the extraordinary length of his prick too, yet it is a puny thing." Harry shouldered his old shovel and walked away without looking back.

Anicah heaved the sacks of cornmeal onto her shoulders and staggered under the weight of them. When she heard hoofbeats approaching fast behind her, she veered off the path. Mistress Margaret liked to gallop her mare now and then, when she thought no one was around.

"God keep thee." The voice wasn't Mistress Margaret's.

Kitt sat straddle-legged on the mare's bare back. Even in the cold her skirts were hiked up on her thin brown thighs and the mare was lathered. She reached down for the cornmeal.

"The ordinary is no farther than a pig can smell a turd." But Anicah was too tired to be polite and decline the aid.

She let Kitt help her tie the sacks together and heave them across the horse's shoulders. Then Kitt reached behind her and patted her mount's back.

"Nay." Anicah went into reverse, putting distance between her and the mare. To her, horses were as alarming and unpredictable as tornadoes and floods.

But Kitt reined the mare around to block the path. Too exhausted for such games, Anicah climbed on top of a broken keg, then scrambled onto the horse while Kitt hauled at the back of her bodice.

Before they'd reached the end of the palisade, Anicah was surveying the world from her perch and crowing, "I'm the queen of England, I am." But as soon as the ordinary came into view dread settled back over her.

Widows did not stay single long in Maryland, but Goody Smythe's mourning was the shortest on record. The night after the last clod of earth was tamped into place on the tapster's grave, Howkins was filling the sag in the bedstead left by his predecessor's wide backside. There was no Protestant clergyman to sanction the union, but Howkins applied for a license to run the ordinary and Leonard Calvert granted it. And Anicah's life became a bundle of misery.

Howkins lounged about in a cloud of tobacco smoke, wine fumes, and ambitious talk. He dispensed free beer to his friends and he suddenly acquired a lot of them. He was amiable to the customers, but when he had too much drink in him, or not enough, he turned vicious. Bruises covered Anicah's arms and legs and back.

When the mare reached the kitchen door Kitt and Anicah slid off. Chattering half in Piscataway and half in broken English Kitt helped Anicah haul down the sacks.

"What is thy name?" she asked.

"Anicah Sparrow."

Anicah already knew Kitt's name. Everyone did. That a red Indian had come to live with the Brent sisters was choice gossip. Some opined that Giles had sired her, although the arithmetic didn't substantiate the rumor.

"What means Anicah?"

Anicah started to say she didn't know, then she remembered what Father Poulton had told her. "It means 'graceful.' "

Kitt was telling her what she would name the cows her aunt was going to buy for her when that same aunt strode into view. Margaret's look was stormier than the iron-gray clouds gathering overhead. Kitt's smile vanished. She curtsied, then stood silent and expressionless.

"Mistress Kitt . . ." Margaret's voice was hard with fury. "How many times must I tell thee not to take the horse and gad about the countryside like a Gypsy?"

Anicah was amused by the look of incomprehension on Kitt's face. It was masterful.

"Hie thee home," Margaret said. "Thou shalt have no supper and thou shalt do a penance of fifty Ave Marias."

Kitt picked up her skirts and flew toward the path to Sisters' Freehold.

"And do not run like some vulgar hoyden." Margaret gave Anicah a hard look, as though she were to blame for the child's behavior. Then she led the mare away.

A bitter wind moaned in the ordinary's chimney. The turn-spit dog lay with his belly as close to the kitchen fire as he could get without singeing his fur. Anicah picked another ear of corn from the chest-high heap of them in the corner and began shelling it against the sharp edge of the skillet handle.

Henry Fleete slipped in the back door. "God keep you."

"How fare ye?" Dina asked.

Fleete sneezed onto the dirt floor. "Well enough. We sail for Virginia tomorrow, if God sends a fair wind."

He had a furtive, irritable look about him. He pressed a coin into Anicah's hand and closed her fingers over it. She rubbed her thumb across the flat, hard surface, warmed in Fleete's pocket. It felt like a shilling. She reached into the slit in her skirt and slipped it into the pouch underneath.

" 'Tis what I owe you."

She eyed him skeptically.

"Save your sour looks, wench. I always planned to pay you." He turned on his heel and left the way he had come in.

"Thank ye, Harry Angell," she murmured, for she was sure he had arranged this.

"Squared with you, did he?" Dina looked skeptical too, as though certain Fleete would find a way to get it back from Anicah.

"Aye." Anicah was still fingering the coin through the folds of her skirt when William Howkins wandered in and dipped out a ladle of hominy mush.

"I saw ye consorting with that filthy heathen, ye thieving baggage." He waved the ladle at her. "She does not enter here, no matter what gentleman spawned her."

"She was but helping me carry the meal from the mill."

"Until yer term is up in three years, ye haul the corn yerself."

"Me term ends St. Andrew's day, less than a year from now." Anicah clutched at her skirts and the small bag containing Fleete's shilling, the sprig of lavender and string of beads Martin had given her and the snuff box with her father's will and her paper of indenture.

"Ye insolent, duplicitous cunt. Ye've three years more to serve and ye'll not cheat yer mistress of a day of it."

Howkins hooked the toe of his boot under the dog's side and heaved him across the room. He threw the ladle after him. The dog yelped as he landed in the heap of corn. He scrambled out, sending cobs rolling across the floor. He tucked tail and skittered behind the water barrel.

"Useless vermin," Howkins roared after him. "Ye do no work. We've not even a haunch of venison to roast in this damned hovel."

Dina used her iron skillet to point the way to the door.

"I'm yer master now." Howkins had never succeeded at bullying her before, but he still tried.

"I served my term," Dina reminded him. "I work for wages, and damned paltry they be too. Toddle along or I shall not cook." A lingering, ominous smile riffled the smooth brown curves of her face. "Or perhaps I *shall* cook."

Dina had never exactly threatened to poison his food. She merely entertained him with stories of mysterious deaths on the island of Jamaica. People wasted away slowly there and never suspected that they'd been poisoned, she said. A common root served the purpose.

Anicah watched him leave the kitchen, cross the empty taproom and slam out into the street. "He's in a pet."

"He's been looking for the key again." Dina wasn't in a good mood herself, but her husband's crops had been meager and she could at least pilfer food from the ordinary's stores.

Whenever Goodwife Howkins left the house Howkins ransacked the place. He was searching for the key to the padlock that hung, big as a fist, on the barred gate behind which sat the barrels of spirits. Another fastened the trapdoor to the cider cellar.

"She scorned Goodman Smythe while he lived," Anicah said, "yet now I wager she would dig him from the dirt with her fingernails." Anicah's one consolation was that Howkins made the widow Smythe's life miserable.

The dog slunk out from behind the water barrel. He lay down across Anicah's feet and she stroked him absentmindedly. Dina pointed her tongs at him.

"He'll be gone soon."

"The alewife will never sell him. The gentry have all offered to buy him, yet none has his price."

"The governor will have him. He says that anything that has caused the death of a human must be offered to God or at least forfeited to the king."

"Think ye so?"

"Mistress Lewger said as much in Goodman DaSousa's hearing. The value of him shall be distributed as alms to the poor, though I ne'er saw the poor receive a penny the last time."

"When was that?"

"Six years ago a tree fell on a man. Crushed his head like an eggshell. The tree was forfeit to his lordship."

"I would not think a tree worth anything here, they being thicker than the hairs on my notch."

That night, after Anicah had hung the drawstring sack around her neck under her chemise, she crawled between her thin blankets in the ashes and draped her skirt and petticoat on top of them. She curled up and held the dog close.

Long after the last ember had winked out in the fireplace she heard a noise in the doorway. She wasn't surprised. She had been expecting Howkins to try her. She feigned sleep, on the chance that he only intended to piss in the fireplace or get a drink from the water barrel. The dog growled softly though and Anicah felt Howkins looming over her.

He drew the covers back and lay down heavily on top of her. He had breath like a bog.

"Fie, sir." She kept her voice low. Goody Howkins would never believe she was innocent in this tussle. "What mean ye?"

"I mean to punch ye well, wench," he whispered.

Pinning her with his body, he groped for the hem of her chemise with one hand while with the other he mauled her breasts. She squirmed and pitched, but couldn't dislodge him. She could feel his member shoving against her leg. She wriggled a hand free, slid her cutpurse's shiv from under her blanket and slashed his ear.

"Curse ye, ye foul trull!" He sat up, supporting himself with a heavy hand on her chest and holding his ear with the other.

"William?" Goody Howkins's voice echoed in the other room.

"I am but pissing." He wound a fistful of Anicah's hair around his hand, pulling it so tight she thought he would rip it from her scalp. The pain brought tears to her eyes. "Ye'll pay fer that little trick, ye punk." He heaved himself off her, straightened his long wool shirt, and left.

"Shitten-arsed gib," Anicah muttered.

She lay awake most of the night, waiting for him to take revenge. When she saw light at the cracks of the door she put on her shoes and cape and hurried out into a driving sleet. She walked to the beech and stared at it.

At first she thought the pale scar there must be a trick of the dim light or of her sleep-fogged eyes. She touched the wide swath where the bark had been hacked off. Someone had obliterated the marks she had cut. She reached under her cape and laid her palm against her chest. The bag, her indenture paper, the shilling, her father's will, her only tokens from Martin, they were all gone.

Chapter 40

S tray particles of sleet and the spiraling wind that raved down the parlor's chimney caused the flames to dance and sputter, but still they roared high into the wide funnel of the opening. From the kitchen came the laughter of the servants. Usually Margaret and Mary would have been there too, so they would only have to heat one room, but Margaret was figuring Giles's accounts for his town lands and Kent Fort Manor. The task required more than the usual concentration.

Mary Brent occupied a chair in the fireplace itself and Kitt sat on a stool at her feet. With winter-stiff fingers Mary mended clothes while she catechized Kitt, asking the questions and correcting the answers the child was memorizing word for word.

Margaret had draped a wool shawl over Mary's thin shoulders, but still she shivered. Margaret knew that she would shiver until Eastertide. Margaret also knew that she would have to endure her sister's icy feet in bed even after that.

She took off her spectacles and held her hands over the fire to warm them. She had had the tall desk moved here from its place against the wall because the ink kept freezing. Even this close to the flames she could feel the room's cold breath. It hit her back with each gust of wind blowing through the chinks around the door and in the warped window shutters.

Margaret was trying to make sense of Giles's accounts. He had not mastered the simple principle that expenditures should total less than income.

"Giles, Giles," she muttered.

"A mistake, Maggie?" Mary looked up from her sewing.

"I cannot say." She put the spectacles back on and the blurs of ink sharpened into lines. "His figures are in such disarray, like an army in full rout. Expenses, income, they mingle, then retreat onto another page or go missing altogether. They are casualties in the battle of his wits."

"Perhaps because he never expected to have an estate he did not apply himself to learning the necessary skills."

"Neither did we expect to have one, yet either of us could do better than he."

"Giles hath a generous nature."

" 'Tis true that he's more adept at scattering than amassing."

"Someone come." Kitt stared at the door.

" 'Comes,' Mistress Kitt," Mary said. " 'Someone comes.' "

Rather than call a servant from the kitchen and keep the visitor waiting, Margaret hurried into the entry hall herself. As soon as she left the hearth she felt the cold close in around her. She cracked the door and peered into the gray curtain of sleet.

"Come in. Don't dawdle." She opened it enough for a bundled figure to squeeze through.

The wind had blown Anicah's hood off her head and ice sparkled in her dark hair. She stood with her back against the closed door. She clutched the trembling dog and the mill sack with her belongings. The sack was mostly empty.

Her teeth chattered. Her ears and nose were red, her hands and lips the bluish-gray of a drowned corpse. Tiny icicles formed by the moisture of her breath hung from her eyebrows. The loud peal of laughter from another room sounded hollow and unreal to her.

"Warm thyself at the fire, Maid Anicah." Margaret followed her to the hearth and watched her closely. She more than half expected her, even with her hands full, to palm some trinket and slip it under her cape.

Kitt had on her solemn face, but glee sparked in her eyes at the sight of Anicah. Bess appeared in the inner doorway and the other servants craned to see around her. Anicah walked through the clean rushes on the floor as though in a dream. Her old shoes crushed the dried lavender and rue strewn among it and released their sweet piquancy. The aroma of the lavender made her long so for Martin she almost cried.

When she reached the fireplace she turned and faced out with a dignity that bordered on defiance. She held onto the dog and the sack as though someone might try to wrench them from her. As the ice melted her hair became wet and clung to her forehead.

Quaking convulsively, she looked around at the large, ornately carved chests and a small, heavy-legged table with a pot of dried marigolds on it. Turkey carpets hung on the north wall to block the wind and the bedstead was curtained in heavy red baize. The freshly limed walls glowed in the fire's light. Sprays of herbs and strings of dried pumpkin and apples hung from the rafters. Anicah noticed the wide-brimmed straw hats on pegs by the door, remnants of summer, of warmth and green growing things.

The long, scrubbed trestle table had been laid for breakfast, and from the number of settings there, Anicah could tell that everyone ate together. Baskets of turnips, nuts, apples and peas lined one wall. Anicah even noted the perforated knit cap dangling at the mantel and the virginal next to the flowers on the table. She had never known order or serenity in her life but she recognized them when she saw them.

"Hast thou a message to deliver?" Margaret asked. "Hath someone fallen ill?"

The details of the room so engrossed Anicah that she almost forgot why she had come. Errands had taken her to Cornwaleys's mansion and inside Leonard Calvert's and John Lewger's, but the first two lacked a gentlewoman's hand and the last might as well have. None had been so inviting as this. Then she realized that Mistress Margaret had asked her a question.

"Nay, mistress, no one is ill." Another silence hung in the cold room.

"May we help thee in some way?" Mary put in.

"Aye, mistress." Anicah turned to her with tears welling in her eyes. "If it should please ye."

She blurted out the story of her mistreatment, of William Howkins's claim that she owed three more years. "He pinched me paper and the bit of chink I earned over the years. I was saving it to make me way when me time was up. I wouldn't be no ward on the dole.

"And he would kill the turnspit here. He said he would rather feed him to the rats than have his lordship take possession of him." Anicah had made that last part up, but she figured Howkins would have said it if he had thought of it.

"Hast thou proof that he stole from thee?"

"Nay, but I know he did it." Anicah launched into a performance of terror and grief better than any she'd seen in Bristol's theater. The tears were real though. She knew what serious trouble she had brought down on her own head. "I pray ye, kind mistresses," she sobbed. "Send me back if ye must, to be scragged for running away. I was a wicked sinner in me youth and deserve to die, but spare this poor creature."

She held out the quaking dog. He whined like a windlass and stank like wet wool.

"Mim," Margaret called. "Carry the turnspit into the kitchen and dry it. Use straw, not a dishclout. And feed it some of yesterday's Indian bread."

The maid took the dog and dangled him well away from her, though his tail beat a grateful tattoo against her forearms. Bess hung up the bedraggled cape while Anicah stood as close to the fire as she could without igniting her skirts. Steam rose from her wet hair and clothes. She held her trembling hands over the flames and waited for Margaret and Mary to decide her fate.

She knew she could be hung for running away, so she had reasoned that she might as well take the dog with her. The Brents no doubt coveted him as much as everyone else did. Being noble and rich in the bargain, the old huddles could buy her term if they wanted. Anicah hoped that getting the dog too would sweeten the offer.

She also knew how desperate the gentry were for servants. They might not hang an able-bodied one. And if Mistress Brent took her in, she could hardly treat her worse than Howkins. Anicah knew she would have to step lively to avoid the attentions of their brother Giles, but she was used to that.

"Go into the kitchen," Margaret said. "Bess will give you something to eat whilst we discuss the affair."

"Aye, mistress." She bestowed on Margaret and Mary a complex masterpiece of a smile—wan and piteous, stalwart and resigned and guileless and charming. They had probably never seen its like except on the plaster statues of martyred saints.

Anicah followed the servants into the kitchen and sat on a stool by the fire. She answered everyone's questions, but her own voice sounded like someone else's. A high-pitched ringing vibrated in her ears. She knew her life would change radically today or it would stop abruptly at the end of a rope. Even so, all she could think of was being warm, of baking like a pudding inside her own skin.

Kitt beckoned to her from the doorway and Anicah returned to the parlor as though entering a courtroom. She stood by the fire, her hands at her sides, while Margaret stared at her from the depths of the second chair. The crackling of the flames intensified the sisters' silence. Anicah started to feel dizzy under Margaret's unwavering, gray-eyed scrutiny. She would sooner have stared into the gunmetal-gray barrels of two pistols. She listened for the hallooing of the hue and cry.

"We do not shelter thieves," Margaret finally said.

"For me past sins I am truly sorry, mistress. I ask God and yerself to forgive me. I would ne'er steal from ye."

"But thou didst steal from me and from my sister."

"Being much pinched by Dame Famine, I stole from strangers, but I would ne'er steal from ye now."

"What passed with the belongings you took in Bristol?"

"They bought me transport here, mistress, a thing I did not desire. Evil deeds beget evil consequences. The many kindnesses ye have done me since have caused me to repent my sins."

Margaret continued studying her through narrowed eyes. "We cannot feed a maid who will not work."

"If ye buy the remains o' me term, m'lady, I will work the hardest of any here."

"Mayhap God hath brought her to us for the salvation of her soul," Mary said.

"Aye." Margaret rubbed her chin thoughtfully. "And she's been through the seasoning."

"I'm sound as an ox, mistress."

And lickerish as a goat, Margaret thought. She didn't relish the prospect of chasing off the men who would come sniffing around after this wench. But behind Margaret's flinty look, she was pleased. Here stood an opportunity to gain a maid servant and a turnspit dog, and to inconvenience Goodwife Howkins besides.

Margaret disliked the alewife. The ordinary should have been a convivial place to spend an evening, sipping wine and conversing with friends, singing and dancing in a private chamber. Instead, Patience Howkins had made of it a haven for those who defamed their betters and conspired to overthrow Lord Baltimore's rightful rule.

Then there was Anicah's brawl with Joan Parke. By all reports, it had been livelier than a bear-baiting. Margaret wished she could have seen it. Anicah was solid, but small, and Margaret doubted she herself would have had as much courage had she been in the maid's place. Anicah had defended the Brents' family honor. For that Margaret owed her protection in return, grudging though it might be.

"I will endeavor to buy thy term from the tapster's widow . . ."

"Thank ye, mistress."

". . . on the condition that you serve here two years added to the months you already owe."

Anicah froze in mid-curtsy. "That makes nigh three years, mistress."

"To train thee in proper behavior will take that long. To keep thee less will not merit our effort. If thou likest it not, return to thy present mistress."

The choice was three years here or three years with Howkins. Circumstances had made abrupt turns and hops before in the dance of her life. Maybe they would again and her time would be shortened.

"I accept the conditions, mistress."

"Thou mayst sleep with the maids tonight." Margaret wasn't softened by the glisten of tears in Anicah's big brown eyes. Too many maids had used them before in attempts to fool her. "I will send word to Goodwife Howkins that I have need of thee until the morrow so she shall not raise the country with a great hulla-balloo. Mayhap we can come to an agreement and thou wilt not hang yet, though thou doth deserve it."

Chapter 41

Anicah felt at ease with the Brent maids. More than three years had passed since they had shared the accommodations of the ship's hold, but she had learned all about them on that voyage and they had heard various versions of her life.

She sat with her back against the chimney piece in the kitchen. She had hiked her skirts up so she could put her legs around the stone mortar. She poured a gourdful of corn into the mortar and pounded it with the heavy pestle. As she worked she entertained the maids.

"So the maiden rides the mare to market without a saddle. And when she gets back she says, 'Oh Mother, I'm quite undone, I'm all o'ergrown with hair.' 'You silly goose,' her mammy says. And she pulls up her own skirts to make the matter plain. 'Oh, Mother,' the maid exclaims, 'you're ten times worse. You must have ridden upon the horse's mane.' "

Mim and Lizzie laughed, but Bess hadn't time for stories. She rushed around the kitchen, chopping and basting, stirring and shouting orders. When Mary Lawne Courtney cooked for the Brents she made the complex task of assembling a meal look like a dance. For Bess it was more of a cudgel match.

When Anicah had ground the corn fine enough, the maid, Mim, scooped it into a basket and sifted it into a wooden bowl. Anicah added more corn to the mortar and Mim returned the coarse grains left in the sieve.

Anicah finished and let her arms dangle at her sides. Mistress Margaret had decided it was time to begin making soap. All morning Anicah had hauled buckets of water from the well to leach lye from the winter's ashes. Her fingers were sore and her shoulders bruised by the yoke. She could not think why the Brents needed so much soap. Goodwife Howkins certainly made do with much less.

The cheerful clutter of the kitchen seemed at first to have no plan, but Anicah had discovered after only two days that nothing in Margaret Brent's house was without plan. Utensils hung where they were most needed. The water barrel stood by the door near the stone sink to keep the servants from slopping water across the earthen floor. Baskets of peas and corn and parsnips sat under the worktable and out of the way.

On the long shelves, glazed ware and wooden and pewter plates stood on their rims against the oak-paneled wall. The dishes with their bright flowers and blue geometric designs were so lovely Anicah thought it shocking that people, even gentry, would eat off them. The plates had been scrubbed until no old food remained, and the pewter had been polished to a soft sheen.

The majolica bowls and pitchers were part of the goods Margaret imported for resale to other planters to supplement her income. Their rich claret glaze glowed in the fire's light as though it had an inner flame of its own. Tankards, posset cups, noggins and long-necked green bottles were arranged precisely. The bowls, pitchers and mugs were turned upside down so dust and soot couldn't settle in them. Spoons nested in lidded wooden boxes.

Anicah had never imagined she would rub against such opulence for longer than it took her to filch it, but still she was restive. There was too much order here. She felt as regimented as the plates lined up against the wall. Already she missed the excitement and haphazard anarchy of the ordinary. There had been no fistfights or even an exchange of shouted insults since she'd arrived, and she doubted there would be.

"I reckon this be like soldierin'." She lifted her chin and let her head fall back against the wall.

"Why say you so?" Bess's round, pink face was shiny with sweat and grease and streaked with soot. Her eyes were red from the smoke. She had burns on her hands.

"Lectures before first light, then work ever after and a sergeant to deliver stripes if ye flag. Yet I misdoubt soldiers have such sore knees." Anicah rubbed her own. They were bruised from the hours spent in morning and evening prayer.

"You're an impudent and ungrateful wretch."

"Think me not so." Anicah was repentant. "Were it not for the mistresses, 'twould be wry mouth and pissin' breeches fer me." She twisted a towel into a noose and pretended to hang herself with it, pupils rolled up under her lids and tongue lolling. Mim laughed.

Bess looked up from tending the fires. "Rather than play the fool, do sweep the place." Drops flew off her ladle when she waved it at the parsnip peelings and eggshells, duck feet, feathers, fish scales and bones on the floor.

The turnspit dog had been nosing out the duck guts and the curled strips of fish skin. Anicah could hear him gagging on a sturgeon bone.

"Mistress Margaret shot some blue wing on the river," Mim said, "and ordered their breasts poached in a wine broth."

"But it's fish chowder for those below the salt." Bess stirred water into the cornmeal and added reconstituted pumpkin.

"When Eastertide comes, then you'll see a feast," Mim said.

"Better than yesterday's?" Anicah had been amazed at the platters and bowls of food covering the table boards the day before. She had been more amazed at how offhand the household seemed, as though such abundance were an everyday occurrence.

"At Easter 'tis ginger bread and marmalades and a pudding as big as your head."

As she swept Anicah decided that should Mistress Brent buy her term maybe she'd stay until Easter before she ran away.

"Last winter we had naught but samp and corn bread and turkey, and praised God we could get it," Mim said.

" 'Tis a strange circumstance that finds the likes of you in the service of nobility such as the Mistresses Brent." Bess shook her head. First a salvage hoyden moved in and now a pick-purse and tavern wench. Life kept becoming more interesting.

"Aye, it's a bloody strange circumstance, that I'll trow." Anicah took no offense. "But nobility or not, we all shite from the same end."

"Enough of idle chatter." From the corner of her eye Bess had caught a glimpse of wool skirts.

"Good day, mistress." The maids curtsied to Margaret.

Margaret pointed her willow withe at the offal behind the corn barrel. "We shall have no slut's corners, Anicah."

"Beggin' yer pardon, mistress." Anicah gave the withe a wide berth as she hurried to sweep the debris out the back door.

"I'll be inspecting the fencing in the west field," Margaret announced. "And Squire Cornwaleys will advise on the suitability of the soil there for flax. My brothers and Captain Vaughan are arriving from Kent Fort Manor with three servants. Still, we'll be but seventeen for supper and so will keep to the parlor."

"Aye, mistress." Betsy curtsied, with an anxious eye on the fire under the chowder which threatened to boil over.

She was calculating the time her mistress would take for her daily inspection of the fields and outbuildings, factoring in the consultation with Squire Cornwaleys and assessing how much she still had to do in the kitchen.

"Be sure to scum the pot, Bess, and have Mim and Lizzie dress the table boards with the holland rather than the damask." Margaret turned to Anicah. "Why dost thou loll about here? Thou hast neither shut up the fowl nor served the swine."

"Beggin' your pardon, Mistress Brent, but am I to stay?"

"I spoke to Goodwife Howkins this forenoon. She put up a howl and threatens to throttle thee before the hangman has his day." Margaret paused. "She says thou art a thief, a liar and a wanton and will bring but shame and loss to any who shelter thee."

"Then she will not be wanting me back, will she?" Anicah grinned at Margaret who almost smiled despite herself.

Margaret knew she should be furious, but she felt again the undefinable kinship. She thought that had she been born into poverty and ignorance instead of privilege, she might have turned out much the same as Anicah Sparrow.

"The upshot is that after much huffing she agreed to bring no charges against thee, or against me for sheltering thee. In return I shall recompense her for three years' term of indenture."

"But I owe less. . . ."

"I told her so, but thou hast no proof, and she holds with her story. We higgled and haggled until finally we settled that I should pay for two years and thou wilt serve me for three. Governor Calvert will take the dog as deodand and I will buy him back, the price to go to the poor. If the arrangement likes thee not, take thy belongings and return to the alehouse."

Anicah paused long enough to give herself the illusion she had a choice. "I'll stay, and it please ye, mistress."

"Mr. Packer will draw up the paper." Margaret started to leave, then turned back. "There is no necessity to sneak food from the table, Anicah. You may partake of the back of whatever lies in the kitchen after the meal."

Anicah blushed. The bits of bread and cheese and pasty in her pockets seemed suddenly heavy and bulging. "Aye, mistress."

Margaret left the kitchen and Anicah was heading for the back door and the bucket of swill there when she glimpsed Kitt's head in the doorway. Kitt held her hand up, palm outward and fingers and thumb curled, then she disappeared again.

Bess squealed and clapped the side of her head. "Heathen spawn of Satan!" Rubbing her ear under her lawn cap she leaned down and picked up a long, triangular piece of flexible whale ivory, a stay from a woman's corset. Kitt had made a missile of it and delivered it with great accuracy. Bess held it up for the others to see. "She's the very devil come to torment us."

Anicah left her grumbling and walked outside with the swill and the pig stave. As she crossed the trampled yard she contemplated the fetid knee-deep stew of the sty and the rude mauling the three-hundred-pound sows would give her in spite of the cudgel. She wondered why the Brents didn't let their swine run loose in the forest as sensible folks did.

Anicah's second supper was as wondrous as the first. When the servants had fed the livestock, cleaned the tools and tidied and locked the outbuildings, Mim lit the splinters of candle pine in their iron holders and everyone gathered in the parlor. They sat according to rank at the long table boards with an extra place set next to Mary Brent.

Anicah didn't think it odd. The maids said that Mary's angel didn't eat as humans did, but enjoyed being included anyway. Just as Bess, Mim, and Anicah carried in the food, Edward appeared and sat at the empty place. When he saw Anicah in the Brents' parlor, the look of surprise was too swift and nebulous for anyone to detect, except possibly Mary Brent.

"Thou hast an uncanny knack for knowing when food's to be served, Edward," Margaret said.

He relinquished a tic of a smile and Kitt brightened at the sight of him. Giles's three servants muttered among themselves, though, and stared at him from the corners of their eyes.

"I expect they think your heathen friend shall slay them in their sleep," Giles said cheerfully. "Can't blame them really. The Susquehannocks threaten day and night on Kent."

"I should like to visit the manor there, brother."

"I shouldn't recommend it. Affairs are in a precarious state."

After the maids served the gentry, they heaped baked beans and pumpkin bread onto the wooden trenchers and chowder into the bowls the servants shared, two or three together. Giles's dogs and the turnspit prowled underfoot, snapping up what dropped from the boards. For a while the only sounds were the clatter of pewter and wooden spoons and the loud slurping of broth and gravy.

"Maid Anicah . . ." Robert Vaughan leaned forward to sight down the table at her. "What say you of the squabbles in England?"

"Me, Cap'n?"

"Aye. What have you heard lately of the Royalists and the Parliamentarians? I have languished on the far Isle of Kent these past weeks, which is like dwelling at the bottom of a well."

Robert suspected that though Margaret was a shrewd woman, she had yet to discover the source of information that had taken refuge with her. News always stopped first at a tavern.

Everyone turned to look at Anicah.

"The last I heard was that the Puritans have forbidden all entertainments there," she said. "No wrestling or cudgel matches or bowls, no ringing of bells nor plays, nor dancing nor masques." This was the one aspect of England's political turmoil she had noted and remembered. She could hardly imagine how dreary life must be in Bristol these days. "Football," she added, "puts them in a particular pet."

"I knew it would come to this," Giles said. "We're well out of it, I tell you."

"How knowest thou this?" Margaret asked.

"A mate of Mariner Howkins, newly arrived from Virginia, did hear it of a seaman come from Barbados." Anicah broke off a piece of ash cake and remembered to put the remainder back on the plate rather than passing it in her bare hands. "I hear that the Puritans further propose to set the brisket-beaters . . ." She corrected herself. ". . . the papists and Anglicans by the ears." She reached for the butter.

"Trowl not the butter upon thy bread with thy thumb," Margaret reminded her. "And Mistress Kitt, snot thy nose or thou shalt not sup at table with us."

Kitt wiped her nose politely on the hem of the board cloth, and Giles muttered about the inconvenience of raising someone else's brat. Giles much preferred hounds to children.

In celebration of the new year, the evening's entertainment lasted well after supper, with hard cider for the servants and wine for the gentry. While the maids cleared the dishes and washed them and set the table for the morning meal, Margaret played the virginal, accompanying Mary's high, sweet voice. To Anicah's astonishment, the austere Margaret Brent danced a gigue-à-deux with Mary to the rhythm of Giles's hand drum.

The gentlemen and even the servants sang, and some of the ditties were bawdy. When Anicah and the maids had finished their kitchen chores, they danced while the others clapped time. Edward couldn't move without tripping over Kitt. He finally yielded to her persistence and danced with her, though the top of her head only reached the middle of his chest.

It wasn't the alehouse fun Anicah was used to, the sort that could turn mean in a moment. The gathering in the parlor was amiable and spontaneous but with an air of ritual, as though it happened every night in just this way.

When they weren't dancing the maids mended clothes or carded wool. The men servants shelled corn and repaired tools and plaited rope as they shared news and jests they'd heard that day. They were all interested in Anicah's stories, her tales being fresh.

As Anicah listened to the banter and bickering of people who knew everything there was to know about each other, she realized that this must be what a family was. She was to be part of a family. The thought struck her with such force that tears welled up and one escaped down her cheek before she could wipe it away.

"Art thou ill, Ani?" Kitt whispered.

"Nay." When she smiled, her eyes glittered with the fire's light. "I be very well indeed."

About eight o'clock the logs that had been set on the fire at suppertime had almost burned to embers and Margaret gave instructions for the next day which would begin before sunrise. Besides their usual duties, the women would bake wheat bread from the flour Thomas Cornwaleys had presented as a gift. They would clean the wool Giles had brought from Kent Fort Manor. They would make soap of the lye they had just leached and the lard they'd saved from the autumn slaughter. The men would finish the fence at the south field, cut wood and clear a new field. Anicah didn't see how so few people could possibly get so much done.

"The wild Irish, Baltasar Codd!" Anicah shook her head. "I have it on good account that he o'erset Squire Cornwaleys's dairy wench."

Bess looked up from the dough she was kneading. "You lie, Anicah Sparrow."

"I swear on these ten bones." Anicah spit on her fingers, then made an **X** over her heart.

Bess pondered the information as she worked. She had added water and a little flour to the barm, the bubbling foam collected from Margaret's home-brewed beer. It had fermented and risen to the point where she could add the rest of the ingredients.

Normally Bess would have been nervous about it. Setting the sponge for wheaten bread was a delicate process and one she hadn't much occasion to practice. But she had poured off small portions of hard cider from each bowl served this evening and hidden the bottle of it under her skirts. By now she and Anicah were both tipsy. From the parlor they could hear the muffled voices of the gentry discussing the next tobacco planting and the evil deeds of the Puritan-controlled Parliament.

"I shall make Baltasar Codd love me." Bess laid her finger to her lips and giggled. Singing softly, she climbed ponderously onto the table.

> *"Stroke me smooth and comb my head,*
> *And thou shalt have some cocklebread."*

She positioned her feet on either side of the white mound, gathered up her petticoats and squatted so that her breech brushed the dough. She swung her broad bottom to and fro as though kneading it and sang.

"My dame is sick and gone to bed
  and I'll go mold my cocklebread,
  Up with my heels and down with my head,
  This is the way to mold cocklebread."

"What mean ye by such foolery?" Anicah wasn't familiar with the lore of the kitchen.

"I shall bake the bread and give him a bit of it to eat. Then he shall love me."

"How shall ye deliver it?" Anicah helped her down.

"When I carry the corn to the water mill in the morning." Bess crossed herself, bowed over the dough and murmured the old prayer of the kitchen alchemists who baked bread. "Dear God and St. Stephen, send me a good batch and an even."

Chapter 42

Snow smothered the earth and muffled the sighs and whispers of the forest. Now and then a branch broke under the weight with a crack loud as musket fire. The thickets of laurel stooped under the covering like silent crowds in hooded white dominoes on their way to a ghostly masque.

For two nights and a day the wind had slung snow against the domed shelters of Edward's uncle's hunting camp. It shoved up drifts as high as waves at mid-ocean. Now the sun hung like a tarnished brass medallion low on the pale breast of the western sky. It radiated no warmth into the crystalline cold.

A single mound of dark fur stirred in the glittering white expanse. Under his wolf-pelt mantle Martin crouched in the narrow trough made by animals and deepened by the moccasined feet of the Piscataway. He pulled his new matchcoat of blue blanketing tighter around him. The English had awarded the coat to Kittamaquund for returning a runaway servant, a tricky-eyed individual who had been bartering beaver skins for barrels of hogwash, soured beer that smelled like bile. Kittamaquund, who appreciated irony, had given the coat to Martin.

Neither the pelts nor the matchcoat kept Martin's bones from turning to ice. He thought he could feel them, slick and cold, chilling him from the inside out. He blew on his numbed fingers and dipped them into the pouch of rabbit musk.

Shivering, he tried again to tie the slipknot in the cord. He coaxed the end through the quivering loops and used both hands and his teeth to tighten the knot. He fumbled the wooden trigger into the notch of the stake driven into the ground. He draped the other side of the noose on a snow-laden twig and arranged it across the narrow animal track. If he had made the noose the right width, a fox or rabbit running into it would release the trigger. The bent sapling fastened to it would snap upward, tightening the cord around the animal's neck.

Martin was still only a middling shot with a bow and arrow, but he knew how to construct any kind of snare. The belief was spreading among the Piscataway that he possessed a special magic, that animals came to his traps more often than to others. Martin shrugged off the rumors or laid his success to luck, which only added to his reputation as a hunter of unusual power for an Englishman.

Martin had poached game in the wastes of Dorset since he was five. His father had begun teaching him the tricks of it then, mostly by example, since he rarely spoke. Martin always thought the wealthy speculators in grain were to blame for his father's silences, they and the country squires who enclosed the common fields for their sheep.

Given the grand thievery perpetrated by his betters, Martin had never considered poaching a sin, much less a crime. The parish constabulary thought differently, though, and he had learned to move stealthily and to cover his tracks. At least he had thought he knew how. Since living with the Piscataway he had discovered how ignorant he was of the forest and its creatures.

He backed cautiously away so as not to trigger the snare. This was the last in his line of traps. At first light tomorrow he would return to see if they held anything. He made the sign of the cross and murmured a small prayer that they would. This fall more than ever before they had heard the guns of English hunters in the forests and the game had scattered. Martin wondered if the corn supplies would last until the summer harvest and if the English traders would find a way to take what little was left.

He tucked his hands under his arms and set off, shuffling across the snow on his bear-paw snowshoes. He fell into drifts and climbed doggedly out. His feet had turned to stone in his moccasins, in spite of the grass stuffed inside them. His breath scraped his nostrils and lungs on the way in and formed icicles on his eyebrows when it left.

The sun was resting in the trees when he neared the clearing where the bark shelters hunched in the snow like big tortoises. Martin thought of the gruel of parched corn in the pot at First Wife's hut and the pile of bearskins on the sleeping bench. He was imagining curling up into a tight ball under them when he saw something dark and angular, at odds with the undulating white contours of the world.

He took his cudgel from the loop at his belt and approached the edge of the hill that had been a gully a few days ago. At first he thought the object in the center of it was a forked branch, broken off under the weight of the snow. He wiped the ice from his eyelashes and blinked. Two moccasins and the bottom half of a pair of leggings stuck up out of the drift. They were Uncle's.

Martin tried to clamber out to them, but the slope had frozen smooth as glass. He tried hacking holes for his feet with his hatchet, and gave it up when he could see it would take too long. The camp was just around the bend but he didn't dare shout for help. Shouting drove away game and attracted two-legged predators.

He set off at a floundering run, pushing his leaden feet forward. The vision of Uncle's corpse haunted him. He had never seen the inside of the big burial house outside Kittamaquund's town, but he had smelled its contents.

The holy men cut the skin from the bodies of the Piscataway leaders and removed the organs. They flensed the flesh from the bones and dried it. Then they laid the skeleton with the others on a scaffold. They draped the tanned skin over it and rolled the dried flesh into a mat to set at its feet. Priests kept guard for years, until the remains and those of people of lesser importance were buried together with great ceremony.

In England, Martin had seen death carts heaped with rigid

corpses, victims of the pestilences that swept his parish. He had smelled the stench of mass burial pits. But the dead had never been flayed and butchered like deer.

He reached First Wife's shelter and called softly. Snow sprayed from the hide door as Edward threw it aside.

"Uncle is buried in the drift." Martin beckoned to him. "We need axes to dig him out."

Edward passed along the news to the rest as he trotted along behind Martin, raising a muted hubbub in their wake.

"He may be alive, brother." As Martin ran he tried to reassure Edward. "I have heard of men freezing, yet miraculously recovering when thawed. In the village where I was born they tell of children drowned in ice-covered water awaking at their own funerals."

"I pray to God such stories be true," Edward said.

When they reached the drift Martin attacked it like a man possessed. He hacked and clawed at the ice with his hatchet until blood dripped from his knuckles. His breath burned in his chest and his arms ached.

He had made some progress when a laugh stopped him. Angry and bewildered by such cruel indifference, he rounded on the others. Only then did he realize that no one was helping him, not even Edward.

He stared at them, young and old, shaggy as a herd of bison in their animal skins. They were all smiling, except one toothless old man who never smiled, but who was the wittiest of the lot. Martin studied the legs and moccasins. The laughter spread, infectious as a cough during divine service. Martin could feel the heat of a blush under the cold skin of his cheeks.

"*Asotu.*" He referred to himself diffidently in the third person. "He is foolish."

Everyone laughed harder and Martin shook his head. He should have known. They constantly played tricks on him. They occasionally played them on each other too, but that wasn't much consolation.

He remembered the morning his bare toes encountered rabbit entrails in his moccasins. Many times he had had to search for his breechclout and leggings, and found them flung on top of a house or dangling from a tree. He remembered the live fish the *tayac*'s daughter had dropped down the back of his breechclout during a solemn interview between himself and her father.

When Kittamaquund sent the imp to meet her match in the formidable Brent sisters last fall, the number of pranks diminished. Martin no longer had to drape his old shirt around his waist to hunt through the town for his other clothes. He had hoped his new people had lost interest in tormenting him. Apparently they hadn't.

He watched Edward step from Wolf's bent knee onto his back and from there into the crotch of the ash. He walked out onto the branch that arched over the snowdrift and shinnied down a rope, holding it with one hand to keep from slipping on the ice. He retrieved the moccasins from the sticks poked into the leggings to support them. Then he pulled the stiff leggings out of the holes hacked in the snow and slid down the slope with them. Still laughing, the rest of the folk wound single file back to camp in the gathering darkness.

Martin entered the smoky hut and found Uncle sitting under a woolly bison robe by the fire. His breath escaped in moist clouds. He took his white clay pipe from his mouth and said gravely, "*Tahkees*, a little cold."

"*Ha ho, Nosusses.*" That is so, Uncle. With a clamshell, Martin scooped samp from the pot.

Uncle liked Mah-teen. The boy didn't lose his temper, or threaten or complain or lie like others of his species. He faced adversity and favor and mischief with the same stoicism.

"Is it cold in your country, Toweu?" Uncle used the children's name for him. Flyer.

"The year I was born . . ." Martin also patiently answered Uncle's questions. ". . . the cold shattered the mirrors on the walls of the houses and froze the milk in the cows' dugs. The snow fell for a week until it covered houses and walls and churches. The vanes of the windmills, tall as pine trees, could not turn for being blocked by it. Men had to walk onto the roofs and dig away the snow from the upper windows to enter their houses. They had to dig tunnels to the barns to feed the animals."

Uncle looked skeptical. "Yet you did not see it?"

"I was only a babe, but so the old people tell it in my country."

"Then it probably isn't true." Uncle relit his pipe. "Not only are the English liars, but they make liars out of everyone who consorts with them, as a carver creates a grotesque mask from a handsome piece of wood." Uncle had no word for liar at his disposal. He had to make do with one derived from *panne nowau*, "he speaks wrongly."

"When I was young," he went on, "I heard a Powatan speak. He had ridden one of the English's great canoes. He said he'd been to where the sun rises, a voyage of two months. Those who knew him said when he left he was an honest and sensible man, but he returned with stories no one could believe."

"I visit the English, Uncle," Edward said. "Am I a liar? Is Mah-teen?"

Uncle waved his hand as though to shoo away the objection. "Two white deer don't mean the rest aren't brown."

Martin understood most of the talk that went on around him these days. Maybe that made him bold, or maybe the pain in his hands, torn trying to rescue an empty pair of leggings, had finally eroded his extraordinary patience.

"The English do not torture men captured in war." He ventured into the unfamiliar territory of debate. "They do not roast and eat collops of their captives' flesh while they yet live."

"*Ha ho*, that's true." Uncle paused long enough to let Martin think he had won a point. "They torture their own children and servants instead, as your master tortured you." He turned to the others, including the women sitting under fur robes and blankets on their sleeping benches. "Imagine beating one's own children."

The women raised a hum of comment. Not one of them could imagine it.

"I came to your town with Kittamaquund to see the cord put around the Potomack's neck for killing a man," Uncle said. "They strangled him like a dog instead of demanding compensation for the dead man's wife and children. What is the use of a dead body? The victim's widow and orphans cannot eat it. The English have a very strange sort of justice."

Uncle wasn't through.

"And my nephew tells me the English throw men and women and even children in cages and starve them like beasts because they have no . . ." Uncle paused to remember another word he'd had to take from the pale newcomers. *". . . mone' ash."* Money.

Everyone muttered their disbelief in the notion of prisons.

Edward took pity on Martin. He yawned loudly and stood up, signaling that he, at least, was through with the discussion. He wrapped his bearskin robe around him and picked his way through the clutter of the crowded shelter. He knelt on the pile of mats below the cross he had carved and hung on the bark wall. Martin joined him. While the two of them murmured the Lord's Prayer, the others continued their conversations, volleying them across the hut from bench to bench until they dropped off to sleep.

Martin heard Edward chuckle softly to himself about the leggings. Now that Martin was warm and fed he smiled into the darkness too.

"So, brother," he said. "You are taking over Kittamaquund's daughter's office as my tormenter."

"Life is less interesting now that she's gone." It was a startling admission, given Edward's complaints about her.

Martin lay awake next to Edward long after the last drowsy comment had been made and he could hear only breathing and occasional snores. He could see the reasoning behind most of Uncle's criticisms of the English, but there was one with which he couldn't agree. Uncle said that ownership of the earth was impossible, and to try to buy and sell it was a fool's enterprise.

As he lay under the heavy robes Martin imagined plowing his own parcel of cleared ground. He pictured the tall stalks of Indian corn, cool and green and chuckling with him in the breeze. He and Anicah would build a stout cottage and sit together by the hearth. They would have a wood lot and a cow with calves gamboling in the pasture. And they would have children.

Tears filled Martin's eyes when he thought of Anicah nursing a baby at her breast. The image was as beautiful as any of the blessed Madonna and Child. The desire for her was more pervasive than the cold.

He longed to lie with her in his arms, to feel her spine and haunches curved against his chest and groin. To cup her small breast in his big hand, taking pleasure in the way it fit there so perfectly.

Edward had brought the news that Anicah was serving with the Brents. Martin was grateful that she would be better fed there, but communicating would be even more difficult. He dared not send word of his whereabouts. Prudence was not in the inventory of Anicah's small store of virtues, and the authorities would be watching her. If they thought she knew anything about him they would arrest her for complicity.

He fell asleep thinking of her and woke when an icy draft chilled his left side. He pulled the robe closer around him and realized that Edward had gone. He had probably sneaked off to plead the favors of his latest sweetheart, a plump beauty with restless eyes and a laugh like a fox's.

Martin glanced at the fireplace in the center of the dark hut. Only a few embers glowed. Dawn must not be far off. He was about to drift back into sleep when Edward threw back the hide door and let in a gust of freezing wind.

"Enemies." He groped for his bow and quiver, his ax and the two-foot-long tomahawk. "I warned Wolf and Sowacha and Kesuk."

The shelter suddenly boiled with activity. Uncle and Martin pulled on their moccasins and collected their weapons hanging over their sleeping benches. Edward left his matchlock. He wouldn't have time to build up the fire to light the slow match, a smoldering cord soaked in saltpeter to ignite the powder charge.

Edward's young cousins raced into the darkness to tell the others. A shot cracked the silence, then a volley of them. The camp's dogs began barking. The raiders screamed their war cries from the surrounding trees.

"Susquehannocks!" Uncle had just cleared the door when a ball ripped through the side of the hut and the bison robe that had covered him and bored into the bench.

Martin gasped with the cold as he emerged into the frigid grasp of predawn. In the hut behind him he heard First Wife rattling out orders to the women. A full moon hovered low in the west. It lit the clearing and illuminated the running forms of the Piscataway men.

Most of the attackers were reloading after their first volley, but Martin saw one last gout of flame. With trembling hands he drew his bow, set an arrow and fired at it. He didn't have time to wonder if he hit anyone. He didn't have time to think about what barbarities the Susquehannocks committed on captives.

The raiders charged out of the blackness of the forest and into the moonlit clearing. Using the hut for cover Martin waited as two of them ran toward him. Then he stepped into their path, his cudgel ready.

Chapter 43

The first ship of the fall season arrived in mid-September of 1642, the earliest anyone could remember. It seemed even earlier because the heat felt like July. Margaret sat on her mare at the top of the bluff and looked down onto the ship. She wiped her glistening face with her handkerchief and imagined what the temperature must be belowdecks. Her new servants and the other transportees still huddled there waiting for the doctor to pronounce them fit to land.

Margaret suffered equally from elation and dread. The five men whose passage she had paid would earn her a patent for a two-thousand-acre manor from Lord Baltimore. The prospect of it had her giddy. But she also wondered what sorts of pestilence had shipped in the hold with the newcomers. What deadly horrors would they bring into her household? Fever, bloody stools, bile-green vomitus?

She shook her head to dispel the fear, murmured a prayer for everyone's survival and wheeled the mare. She rode her across the hog-harrowed, weed-grown common and along the path to the governor's house where the upper and lower houses of the Assembly were meeting. Women weren't allowed to watch the legislative proceedings, much less vote. Secretary Lewger said the men's rough discourse was not fit for a woman's ears, but Margaret heard all the issues debated in her parlor, often before they ever reached the official sessions.

The sun would set soon. Leonard Calvert should already have adjourned today's sitting, but Margaret could hear the shouting from the great hall long before she passed through the gate and into the yard. Robert Vaughan's voice was unmistakable above the noise.

"If your lordship will not allow us burgesses to meet by ourselves," he roared, "nor give us the right to veto your proposed laws, we will oppose a march against the Susquehannocks."

"Hear, hear!" The other burgesses noisily encouraged his rebellion.

Margaret shook her head at Vaughan's ox-headed audacity. The planters on the Isle of Kent had elected Vaughan burgess. Now he was trying to wrest autonomy for the lower house from Governor Calvert and his council of six gentlemen. Margaret sympathized with Vaughan's frustration, but she agreed with the governor. Vaughan was sensible enough when sober, and literate too, but allowing the rest of the unlettered rabble to make laws was as dangerous a notion as it was ludicrous.

"You have not the right to dissolve these sessions!" Calvert's voice ascended to something very like a shriek. "Furthermore, I will not advise with you whether there should be an expedition against the Susquehannocks or not. Your part is to contribute your assistance should I think fit to send men."

"Then I hereby declare this sitting of the burgesses adjourned," Vaughan bellowed. He must have grabbed the gavel because the blow resounded with more force than Calvert could give it.

"I disallow your motion of adjournment," Calvert shouted.

Before Margaret dismounted she glanced in at the window, curious to know if the two of them were tussling for possession of the gavel. Instead she saw Secretary Lewger bustle over and drop the heavy baize curtain in her face, as though she were a serving wench spying on her betters. Margaret's cheeks grew hot.

She left the mare with one of Leonard's servants, handed her cloak to the maid in the entry hall, and went into the parlor. She settled into Calvert's good chair and accepted a cup of Canary wine from the kitchen maid. She was sipping it when she heard the great hall's door open on its squeaky iron hinges across the entryway. It had the effect of broaching a beehive to expose the uproar of the swarm inside. At least that would have been the effect if bees shouted "Damn me!" a lot.

Still arguing, the men spilled out into the yard and dispersed, their outrage fragmenting and diminishing in volume but not in passion. When Leonard entered the parlor his narrow shoulders drooped in his welted velvet doublet. His hair, usually immaculately dressed, looked like the frayed end of a hempen hawser. He didn't seem happy to see his guest.

"I pray all is well at your house, Margaret."

"A few suffer from the usual malaises, but we're well enough, thanks be to God. How fare you here?"

"God has seen fit to grant us good health." Calvert expelled a little sigh and shuffled through the scramble of papers that covered his high desk. Margaret looked at them avidly, wondering which was Lord Baltimore's patent for her manor.

"I'm considering the importation of slaves from Africa," Calvert said. "I've heard that strong, healthy ones can be obtained on the Guinea coast at little expense. They are inured to heat and fevers. I tell you, Margaret, they will be the solution to our shortage of laborers."

"I shall be interested to learn how the venture fares."

"God grant you health, Mistress Margaret." John Lewger bustled in, blank sheets of velum in hand and a quill pen stuck behind each ear.

"John," Calvert said. "Mistress Margaret and I have business to discuss. Be so kind as to draft Brent's commission in the great hall."

Calvert sounded as weary as he looked. Margaret thought it odd. Tiffs with the burgesses usually set him to pacing and grumbling for hours at a time, often in her own parlor. She had chided him on occasion for wearing out the floorboards there.

"A commission for my brother?" she asked.

"Aye. The council and burgesses voted to authorize Giles to

recruit men on the Isle of Kent and lead them against the Susque-hannock war party."

Lewger cleared his throat. "If I may be blunt, Mistress Margaret—"

"If thou wert not blunt, Secretary Lewger, thou wouldst speak not at all."

"I wonder if thy brother hath enough influence with the Kentishmen to raise a force amongst them. He cannot even pre-vent them from stealing his sheep and cattle."

"You shall have to ask him when he returns from Kent, Mr. Lewger. I'm but a weak-minded female and know little of such complicated matters." Margaret threw Lewger's own words back at him whenever she had the opportunity.

"I mean no personal offense, Mistress Margaret, but history hath proved women to be no fit participants in affairs of state."

"As our virgin queen, for example." Margaret never thought she would be defending Queen Elizabeth, but Lewger did gall her.

"Just so. Her heretical policies caused the pope to excommu-nicate her. Utter ruin will come when women seek to rule." He bowed. "I'll bring the draft when it's finished, Leonard."

"Thank you, John."

When he had gone, Calvert searched through the disorder on his desk until he found a folded parchment sheet just delivered from the ship. It had Lord Baltimore's crest impressed into the disk of red wax that had sealed it closed. Margaret felt light-headed in anticipation.

Calvert handed her the letter. "Margaret, my brother hath al-tered the requirements."

Margaret's hands trembled as she read. To receive a patent of only one thousand acres, she would have to pay transport for twenty people within one year. Baltimore had also furnished a list of arms and ammunition that she would have to supply.

"He raised the quitrent to forty shillings sterling payable in the commodities of the country." Calvert spoke into the bitter si-lence, as though unable to bear it any longer.

Margaret hardly heard him. Disappointment and rage tolled in her ears. She had worked for four years to keep her own enterprises running and Giles's and Fulke's and to raise money for five men plus a few extra. She could not scrape together enough to total twenty before year's end. Lord Baltimore may not have intended his new conditions as a personal affront, but she took them as such. Resentment lay hard and heavy as a sharp stone in her chest.

"Thou wilt receive fifty acres of town lands for each of the five men thou didst transport, with a quitrent of twelve pence per acre."

"Two hundred and fifty acres." Margaret glared at Leonard, though she knew none of this was his fault.

"If my brother cannot picture our difficulties here, Margaret, neither can we imagine what he must endure. His position is precarious in the extreme. King Charles has at least tolerated this enterprise as well as our Holy Church. Now Parliament is trying to depose him."

"Be that as it may, Baltimore gives great offense to myself and my family. My sister and I ventured our portions, our lives, our futures, to further his cause. Are we to receive nothing in return but a paltry piece of ground? I cannot collect rents enough on two hundred and fifty acres, nor raise crops sufficient to prosper."

"I can only say how sorry I am, Margaret. Thou mayest remonstrate with him thyself. He writes that he plans to take ship this month." The prospect of Lord Baltimore arriving to interfere in Leonard's administration made him even more morose.

"Remonstrate with him I shall."

Margaret didn't wait for the maid to fetch her cloak. She snatched it from the hook in the entry hall and marched out of the house at such speed it floated behind her like a battle ensign.

She trotted the mare through the corn and tobacco stubble and the festering refuse that filled the areas between the tumbledown houses. The squealing of a hog came from the wrack of the palisade, so overgrown with vines it looked like some fort-shaped topiary.

As Margaret approached, she wasn't surprised to see Joan

Parke Hardige threatening three men with the knife she used for castrating her boars.

"By God's codpiece, I shall cut off yer hands and feed 'em to that porker if ye do not loose him," Joan said.

The two men who were trying to stuff the struggling animal into a sack wiped the sweat from their eyes and looked at Sergeant John Price for instructions. He signaled them to continue their work.

"Goodman Brown cried the news of the levy," Price said.

Margaret marveled that he bothered to reason with the woman at all.

"What levy?" Joan asked.

"To supply the expedition against the Susquehannocks for their recent outrages in Virginia and the Isle of Kent."

"Virginia! A French itch on Virginia! I care not a turd for Virginia, nor Kent either."

Price took his commission from his doublet, unfolded it and read aloud.

" 'In order to supply an expedition against the Indians for the honor of our nation and also to deter the like outrages for the future, his lordship, the governor, has ordered a levy of twenty pounds of tobacco per head, and corn, pork, beef or mutton of planters, tenants and freeholders, each according to his capacity.' "

"The governor may kiss my capacity." Joan bent over, pulled up her tattered skirts and presented the plump twins, pale and rumpled as clabbered cream.

This, Margaret thought, is the sort of rogue that Calvert and Lewger expect to supply Giles's soldiers. Rage suddenly swept over her. She was furious with Joan, first for defaming Mary and now for putting her brother's expedition at risk. She was furious at Lord Baltimore for stealing her manor and her hopes, and at St. Mary's itself for being such a sorry show of a town.

She leaned down and with all her strength lashed Joan's bare buttocks with her leather riding crop. Joan shrieked, straightened up, and backed away.

"Surrender that pig, thou worthless drab." Margaret pointed the crop at her. "And if thou barest thy ill-favored meat in my sight again, thou shalt rue it till the devil calls thee to thy reward."

Sergeant Price touched the slumping brim of his tall sugarloaf hat in salute to Margaret. His men finished their task and the three of them hustled away before Joan recovered her voice and ire.

Margaret transfixed Joan with the look that for the members of her household was somewhere between censure and sorcery. Then she reined the mare toward the path to Sisters' Freehold. When she reached the big maple tree at the first curve, she dismounted and leaned her head against it. Disappointment and loss filled her to overflowing. She sobbed like a broken-hearted child while the hungry mare butted her between the shoulder blades and whickered.

Chapter 44

ight from fat pine torches sent the huskers' shadows shin-
ning up the rough clapboard walls and into the darkness
pooled among the rafters of the barn. The Brents' servants
and a score or more from neighboring freeholds had reduced the
mountain of corn to a chest-high foothill. They had also reduced
a barrel of Margaret's cider to the dregs. The revelry could be
heard all the way to the house.

But revelry was expected at a husking, and besides, Margaret
Brent wasn't in the house. Court was in session, and bitter discord
in England, and Indian raids on the Isle of Kent, could not im-
pede the collection of debts. Margaret had docketed several suits
and was prosecuting them herself. She planned to stay at Leonard
Calvert's tonight.

Mary Brent had spent most of the previous night nursing one of
the new servants in the last throes of typhus. She had fallen asleep in
her chair while catechizing ten-year-old Kitt. And Kitt, dragging
Edward with her, had sneaked away to the festivities in the barn.
All afternoon she had thrown shucks at Edward and chased him
with a broom and tried to stuff corn down his breeches. He ignored
her when he could and pushed her away when he couldn't.

Watching Kitt's childish courtship made Anicah feel old and
staid, though she didn't look it. Bits of husks lodged in the dusty
mass of hair radiating out around her face. Straw covered the
back of her doublet and skirt from her tussle on the floor with the

Greenes' gangly cowherd. She had given him a bloody nose for a keepsake.

The chaff that he had stuffed down the front of her chemise itched her until she had to unlace her doublet, lean over and shake it out while the men cheered. Anicah sneezed and scratched her arms and chest and wriggled inside her clothes. Like the rest of the young folk in the barn, she was tormented by an itch of another sort.

She didn't care for any of the swains present. Except for Edward, they were a sallow, pimply, awkward lot. Not a one could compare with Martin, though their thick west-country accents reminded her of him. But the weather was warm for early October, and the sight of so many of them naked to the waist tantalized her. Their clumsy, eager caresses fired a heat in her. She would have traded ten years of her life to hold Martin again.

Anicah and Kitt had pinned their petticoats up so they fell in swags around their thighs as they stood knee-deep in the corn. They stripped back the husks, broke off the stems and threw the ears over their shoulders. They sang a round that Anicah had taught Kitt. Anicah started and Kitt followed, their two parts making a harmony.

> "My lady and her maid, in a very merry spin,
>   They made a match at farting to see which one
>   would win.
> Joan lights three candles tall and sets them bolt
>   upright.
> The first fart blew them all three out, the
>   second gave them light.
> Next comes my lady then, with all her might and
>   main,
> And blew them out and in and out and in and
>   out again."

Everyone chorused, ". . . and in and out and in and out again."

"A red ear!" The cowherd held up the same ear of corn that had been appearing all evening, hastily rewrapped in its shucks.

Shrieking with laughter and making loud kissing noises, the women shoved him onto the heap of husks. They fell on him in a flourish of legs and petticoat tails. After they had covered him with kisses and untangled themselves and gone back to work, Kitt slipped the red ear onto the pile in front of Edward.

"Edward has a red corn," she cried.

No one demanded a kiss, though, and the sudden silence lengthened. The women hadn't turned shy because Edward was ugly. Far from it.

At seventeen, the chiseled planes of his jaw and cheekbones had sharpened. They formed a perfect setting for eyes dark as a deer's and always faintly amused, even now with their owner the center of so much animosity and embarrassment. He was tall and lithe and his skin was the color of new-cut cedar. He had a fine, arched nose that flared into bold nostrils. He had let the hair on the shaved side of his head grow until it fell in black waves to his shoulders, but he still wore a hawk feather in it. Even in his tow-linen shirt and wool knee breeches he could never be mistaken for an Englishman.

"A buss on the neb, Edward." Anicah gave him a quick peck on the cheek, then shoved him playfully. "They fear yer savage ways will rub off on them, mate, they being such cultured folk."

She winked at him and he grinned. Kitt stood on tiptoe and grabbed the front of his shirt. She pulled him forward and down and planted a determined sort of kiss square on his mouth. He jerked back as though a bee had stung him.

"What's all this?" Margaret stood in the doorway. Her voice sent everyone into a scurry. Husks flew as if a whirlwind had blown in with her.

"We were but having a bit of a frolic, mistress," Anicah said. "To make the work go faster."

Margaret stood staring at them awhile longer before she withdrew. She had expected foolishness, but she couldn't allow it to keep the work from being completed.

When she went outside, Robert Vaughan was waiting for her

in the moon shadows. He put a finger to his lips and a hand on her elbow and led her toward the house.

She spoke in a low voice, though the noise in the barn rose as soon as she left, and no one there could hear her. "Why didst thou send thy man for me with such secrecy, Robert? And why didst thou abandon the expedition on the Isle of Kent?"

"I came by canoe to tell you your brother has abandoned the expedition."

"Giles?"

"Aye, Maggie."

They reached the house and Vaughan peered into the parlor where Mary still sat, snoring lightly. He carried two stools to a far corner of the great hall and beckoned for Margaret to sit on one of them. He sat on the other, his knees almost touching hers. Even though the house was empty of servants, he spoke in a whisper.

"The Kentish planters convinced Giles that they could not leave their farms unguarded to pursue the Susquehannocks."

Margaret stared at him, incredulous. "He didn't carry out the governor's commission?"

"Nay. His army has dispersed to continue whatever mischief they usually indulge in, and he drinks and games and pursues what few women reside there. He sends me to ask you to loan him more money. He says he may be able to bribe the men to cooperate, but I think he'll end in wagering it at cards and losing it."

Margaret put her face in her hands and sighed. "Secretary Lewger will accuse him of dereliction at best and treason at worst."

"Aye," Vaughan said dryly. "He'll fly into a passion, huffing and snorting and sucking in quantities of snuff. But this is the excuse he's wanted to deprive Giles of Kent Fort Manor. He'll put the worst possible face on it when he writes Baltimore."

Vaughan sat patiently while Margaret thought. He had seen her operate. He trusted her to find a way to salvage Giles's foolishness.

She smiled grimly at him. "I have an idea, but you must paddle that hog trough back to Kent as fast as ever you can."

When Giles returned from Kent, he left his sloop anchored in St. Mary's harbor and headed for Governor Calvert's mansion. His feet turned right instead of left, however, and were carrying him toward Howkins's ordinary for a drink when John Price hailed him.

"Squire Brent, as high sheriff of St. Mary's County I must deliver this writ." He held out the paper, folded and sealed with the Calvert crest.

"Damn me, what's this?" Giles made no move to take it.

"It requires you to give bond to answer to charges of dereliction and to be of good behavior until the next sitting of the court."

"Damn me!" Giles turned abruptly and stalked off toward Governor Calvert's house. He found Calvert there with Lewger. He wasted no time with pleasantries. " 'Tis reprehensible, to serve a gentleman with a writ."

"A gentleman must be held more accountable for his actions, or inaction . . ." Lewger paused for effect. ". . . than the lower orders."

Calvert cleared his throat. "Thy raising of a force on Kent and thy failure to pursue thy commission indicates an intent to disaffect that island and withdraw it into sedition."

"Thou knowest me better than that, Leonard. Thou hast heeded that prattling magpie . . ." He pointed at Lewger. ". . . instead of thine own sweet reason."

"Nevertheless, I must ask sureties for thy good behavior."

"Thou shalt not have them."

"Then thou must not leave the county until the court sits in December, or thou shalt lose all rights and privileges."

"I intend to pass the Nativity here in any case." Giles started to go then turned back, as though on an afterthought. He pulled a folded paper from the pocket in the lining of his wide boot cuff. "I would that the secretary enter this into the record. It has been duly witnessed and signed." He left without bidding either of them good-bye.

The document was written with Giles's usual disregard for punctuation.

These presents witness that I Giles Brent of Kent fort manor in the Isle of Kent do hereby convey and sell unto my sister Mrs. Margaret Brent of St. Maries in Maryland all my lands goods debts due to me in the Province aforesaid, all my cattle chattles and servants to her heires and assignes for ever irrevocably. All this for the consideration hereafter expresst, viz, for satisfaction and payment of 73 pounds English money which I doe owe to herself.

Calvert read it aloud and glanced at Lewger. "Thomas Cornwaleys set his hand and seal as witness."

"Cornwaleys is in league with Brent." Lewger's face turned bright red. "When was this document drawn up?"

"October tenth, three days ago." Calvert heard Lewger snap his clay pipe in half and he smiled to himself.

Dux femina facti, Calvert thought. "A woman was the leader in the deed." Margaret Brent had made sure Kent Fort Manor stayed in the family, no matter what actions might be taken against her brother. And in the bargain she had gotten twice the thousand acres she had requested from Lord Baltimore.

Secretary Lewger would never reconcile himself to being bested by a woman, and that was what had happened here, Calvert had no doubt of it. After four years he had learned to recognize Mistress Maggie Brent's hand. And though he wasn't sure about Giles's loyalty, he was certain of Margaret's. He wished, as he often had in the past, that she were a member of his council instead of a few men he could name.

Giles held Kitt by the back of her doublet and yanked the ashwood bow from her grasp. Her grasp was a lot stronger than he expected, and so was the bow. It looked like a toy, but its arrow had killed one of Squire Greene's pigs. She lay on her side, her hooves curled back as though frozen horizontally in the act of running. She was a slender, long-legged, bristly beast with great spots of white on her brown hide and a mud-crusted snout as big and tough and cylindrical as a tarred leather tankard.

Kitt bit into the fleshy base of Giles's thumb. He tried to shake her off but she held on as firmly as his mastiff with his teeth in a bear.

"Damn me, thou bloody little heathen." When he finally pried her jaws loose his thumb bled and throbbed.

Holding her by the nape of the neck he lashed her back and shoulders with the bow. She flinched but she didn't cry or plead for mercy or feign terror and pain as his servants did. When he stopped, she stared at him sullenly from behind the glossy black fringe of hair that always hung in her eyes, no matter how Margaret and Mary might try to crimp and knot and pin it into obedience.

"Why didst thou kill Squire Greene's pig?"

She continued to stare at him, as though she couldn't understand what he was saying. Ever since Giles had ceased being a child himself he had thought children an alien race. This one was more unfathomable than any he had had the misfortune of meeting.

Holding her at arm's length by the back of the neck like a poisonous snake, he marched her home. He found Margaret watching her man scrape mud off the mare with a flexed length of split oak from the cooper's shed.

He held up the bow and arrows. "See here, Margaret, the little hoyden has slain Greene's speckled gilt. I whipped her soundly for it, but she seems to harbor no remorse, nor fathom a word of remonstrance. I think she's wanting in intellect."

Margaret took the handful of arrows. Edward had made them and the bow for Kitt. "Greene's yearling?"

"Aye."

"She killed it with one of these?" She tested the chipped flint points with the tip of her fingers.

"Shot it through the eye."

Margaret knew she should be outraged at this crime against property, but she wasn't. "Well done, wouldn't you say?"

"I would not say!"

"Well aimed and strongly launched, I mean." Margaret cocked

one eyebrow at Kitt. She would have to teach the child to shoot the pistol. "I'll send Mr. Packer to make amends, lest Squire Greene raise the country with alarums of an attack by salvages. Mayhap he will invite us to a meal of roast pork."

"This is no matter for jesting, Margaret."

"All summer that gilt found a way through the fences and made free with the Indian corn and ate the whey in the dairy and laid waste the garden. I shan't be sorry to see her dead."

Giles glared down at Kitt who stared back with poorly concealed insolence. "I would there were a better way to propagate the species than by getting children." He stomped away, slashing at the bushes with his sword as he went.

Margaret sighed. He had been in a foul humor ever since he discovered that she took the sale of his manor seriously. She intended to be the owner of Kent Fort Manor in fact as well as in name.

When he was out of hearing, Kitt spoke. "English pigs eat our corn. We're very hungry and sometimes we almost die."

"The pigs belonging to the planters on Piscataway Creek?"

"Everywhere. Everywhere English pigs eat our corn. If we kill them the English say we are wicked. They say they will hang us. Like they hang the dead pigs in the chimney."

"The king's justice will serve your people as well as mine."

Kitt looked dubious about that.

"You must behave at all times with dignity, Mistress Kitt. One day you will be queen of your people and will lead them into the true faith."

"Like Queen Henrietta Maria?"

"Yes, exactly like her majesty."

"Does Queen Henrietta Maria gather kindling and carry water and pound corn?"

Margaret was wondering how to answer that when Governor Calvert's man found her. He bowed and handed her a letter. "He says I am not to wait for a reply but to tell you he will be at home, should you wish to speak with him."

She nodded and he hurried away.

"Mayhap it's news from the ship that arrived last night, Aunt Margaret," Kitt said.

"Mayhap." Margaret felt a flutter around her heart.

Had one of her siblings died in England? Had the constables and their roving bands found a crucifix in the Brents' manor? Had pursuivants smoked out some unfortunate priest hiding in the false masonry of the chimney? Was her family languishing in prison? Had the Puritan heretics decided to impose their religion by *ferro et flammis*, iron and flame?

Margaret walked with Kitt toward the house. She wanted to open the letter before she showed it to Mary, but she couldn't. She and Mary had shared the good and the bad, they would share this too.

She found Mary murmuring the Angelus Domini while she plucked a chicken. Downy feathers fluttered in her hair. "Thou hast news, Maggie?"

"Aye. From Leonard." She held up the letter. "Methinks it concerns England." Margaret slid her thumbnail under the wax disk, unfolded the paper and held it so Mary could read it too. The message was hastily scrawled in Calvert's careless hand. It contained one word. "War."

Margaret stared at it, trying to connect the three letters with the horror they named. "We're to go to St. Mary's for details."

Englishmen hadn't set out to kill each other in great numbers in generations. But England still bore the scars of thirty years of fighting between the Houses of Lancaster and York. It was the worst sort of carnage, with folk of different villages, neighbors, even families, killing each other. Armies swarming like black ants over the green hills of the lush Vale of the Severn. The smoke from burning manors and cottages alike rising. Men maimed. Women violated. Children orphaned. No refuge anywhere.

On the one hand, Margaret didn't want to wait for the mare to be saddled. If running hadn't been such an affront to dignity, she would have set off at a trot to find out what Leonard knew. On the other hand, she so dreaded what she would hear that she was tempted to go about her day's chores as though nothing had happened.

"There is naught we can do about it, sister," Mary said gently.

Margaret nodded. If armed conflict had finally broken out between the forces of the heretics in Parliament and those loyal to King Charles, it had been going on since the ship left England six weeks ago or more, even as she went about her daily chores. Why should she alter her routine now?

Mary began murmuring the prayer of intercession. Margaret prayed with her. The familiar words calmed her. She felt removed from whatever madness was happening elsewhere, and safe. Not just an ocean separated her and Mary from England, but a lifetime. Let them do what they would there. God had provided a haven here.

Mary began reciting from the writings of St. Teresa of Avila.

> *"Let nothing disturb thee, let nothing*
>   *affright thee;*
> *The trials of life pass away, but God*
>   *never changes.*
> *Patience endures all things;*
> *Those possessed of God want for nothing.*
> *God alone suffices."*

Chapter 45

An icy wind knifed through the warped boards of the barn's north wall. In spite of the two cows' warmth, Martin wrapped his matchcoat tighter around him. Laughter arrived on the next gust, and the sound of singing. The mistresses Brent and their servants and guests had left the house. The song grew louder, until Martin recognized it as "I Saw Three Ships Come Sailing in," one he had sung while wassailing with his friends in another lifetime.

The sows grunted and the mare whickered, as though anticipating more company on Christmas Eve. Martin ducked behind a barrel and crouched, shivering. His leggings and breechclout let in a lot of cold air, and having half his skull shaved wasn't practical in winter.

Martin feared that the sheriff had found out he was here and a jolly hue and cry was coming to take him. He imagined them all singing and drinking healths around the gallows while he dangled.

The song ended and people laughed and talked as the bolt slid back and the door creaked open. Martin shrank back farther into the shadows, but the pigs rushed to the rail of their pen and squealed for food. The revellers crowded inside, rustling the straw underfoot. An occasional rill of laughter sounded over the murmur of their voices. The barn seemed warmer in the glow of torchlight and goodwill.

They grew quiet except for the usual snuffling and coughing, and Martin heard Father White intone a blessing in Latin. When he finished everyone gave a shout and launched into a Gloucestershire wassail that toasted each animal, wished for a good crop and a happy new year, and praised the bowl of strong ale they'd brought.

"The mistletoe," someone shouted. "The mistletoe."

The maids insisted on kissing whomever hung the sprigs over the animals' pens. Martin wondered if Anicah was kissing him too. He pulled his arms and legs in tightly and burrowed under a pile of straw, hoping it wouldn't make him sneeze. The men spread clean bedding, and though their pitchforks came close to his leg, they didn't notice him in the shadows.

"An air from Maid Anicah," Margaret Brent said.

At the sound of Anicah's name Martin's heart thumped so loud he thought someone would hear it. Even if he were caught and hung for it, he had to see her. He peeked around the barrel and watched her step in front of the group.

When she threw her hood back the tangled tips of her hair shone like dark spun cooper in the torchlight. She faced the animals, and Martin stared at her lovely profile. The longing for her clenched around his heart.

Anicah's voice was high and sweet, strong and clear and confident, but Martin heard the sorrow in it.

> *"Joseph was an old man, an old man was he,*
> *When he wedded virgin Mary, in the land of Galilee,*
> *When he wedded pretty Mary, in the land of Galilee."*

Even the animals grew quiet and the notes hung shimmery as bubbles in the cold air. It was a long carol, slowly sung, and when Anicah finished no one spoke. Then Kitt's new cow, Fillpail, lowed and everyone laughed and started chattering again. Anicah came over to scratch the cow's ears, and Martin could almost touch her.

The wassailers passed the bowl among them, each taking a sip.

Then they jostled their way back into the night and slid the bolt
home behind them. The sound of it echoed with a cold finality in
the barn. Their going plunged Martin back into darkness and silence and despair. He sat in the fragrant new straw, buried his
head in his arms and wept.

The inside of Margaret and Mary's house looked like a forest
glen, so green was it with bay and holly, glossy magnolia and
mistletoe. Pine torches burnished the rooms with golden light.
The logs burning in the fireplaces took up the entire ten feet of
their width. Anicah had never seen such a Christmas. She had
never smelled bay laurel and roast beef, pork, cinnamon, ginger,
mace, and freshly grated nutmeg, wood smoke, strong ale and
plum pudding all mingled together.

So many guests and their servants had trooped to Sisters' Freehold that Margaret's people had set up extra table boards and covered them with linen cloths. They filled both front rooms, and
Margaret ordered the doors left open so people could shout back
and forth across the entryway. The gentry sat in the parlor and the
servants in the great hall. The maids scurried out of the smoky
kitchen with platters and bowls and pitchers. They circulated
through the maze of tables and hurried back into the clamor and
heat of the kitchen.

This was not the twelve days of merrymaking the Brents had
known in England, but they had combined their resources to produce for one night the grandest celebration since their arrival. It
was also a defiant one. They were doing it in the teeth of Puritan
censure that may have been distant, but ominous nonetheless.

They were also celebrating Giles's acquittal of charges of allowing the Susquehannock expedition to fail. Whatever his abilities as a
commander, Giles was skilled with words. He had pointed out that
had the men of Kent left the island unprotected, they would have
returned to find their houses and crops burned, their families and
livestock slaughtered. It was a defense the jury could understand.

When the first panel found him innocent in a civil suit, John Lewger filed a criminal case. That had come to naught too.

Leonard Calvert had not only forgiven Giles, he had appointed him commander of the newly formed Kent County, with Robert Vaughan as commissioner. Now Calvert was feasting and laughing between Giles and Fulke. Edward occupied the angel's place between Margaret and Mary.

The mulled wine and the cold walk back from wassailing the animals had turned Robert Vaughan's nose bright red. A wreath of bay leaves encircled his head and his hair stood out around it. His wild green eyes seemed to be trying to peer into every corner at once.

Margaret leaned over so he could hear her. "Thou look'st like an owl in an ivy bush, Captain Vaughan."

He regarded her very seriously and warbled the call of the woods owl. It sounded like "Who cooks for you? Who cooks for you all-l-l-l-l?" Margaret laughed.

She had appointed Vaughan Lord of Misrule and yielded her seat at the head of the table. He visited so often she had come to think of him as a member of the household anyway, and he was by far the best man for the part. Margaret flinched, though, when he rapped his pewter spoon on her Murano goblet for attention. He held up his willow wand and adopted Margaret's stern look.

"As Lord of Misrule, I would assign your duties for the morrow, good people." He began giving instructions as she did each evening for the next day's work. "I would that thou, Bess, set bread enough to feed all the children of Israel. Jack, thou must part the river's waters so that I may pass to the other side without wetting my dainty feet." Robert raised one of his big boots for the company to see.

As he named each servant the tasks became more and more absurd. Finally, he ordered Anicah to sing down the moon and dance up the sun, since singing and dancing were the only work at which she excelled. His mimicry was so cunning Margaret's people whooped and shrieked and fell on each other's necks. Vaughan pounded for order.

"I also forbid disputes of a religious or political nature."

"Disputandi pruritus ecclesiarum scabies," Father Copley said.

" 'The theologian's urge to debate is an incurable disease.' " Giles showed off his knowledge of Latin whenever he could.

"Actually," Copley corrected him, "It means, 'An itch for disputation is the mange of the church,' but I for one shall refrain from scratching this night." He held high the wineglass he and Father White shared. "A toast to Mother Church and to the sanctity of friendship."

An Anicah passed Vaughan she murmured in his ear.

"Quiet!" Vaughan shouted. "Our nimble-fingered gallows lark would speak."

"I mean no disrespect, kind lords and ladies, to make bold with a humble wish in such genteel company." Anicah curtsied. "I have no kin in England nor had I a house, not even a cote such as a sheep might shelter in. But I pray God keeps safe there the families of all of you in these perilous times. For ye have treated me kindly and I do sorely hate that which grieves ye."

She picked up Vaughan's glass, using the general uproar as an excuse for overreaching her station. "I offer a health to those whom God hath blessed and who share their blessings with the lowest of us." Firelight hit the crystal and shattered into brilliant colors when she held it up in toast to the Brents. "And a health to Mistresses Margaret and Mary, with me gratitude everlasting, base and worthless coin though it may be."

"Bis vivit qui bene vivit." Margaret raised her own glass. " 'He lives twice who lives well.' A health to Christmas and to our loved ones at home. May the Blessed Virgin and her angelic host carry them safely through the storm." She paused. "And may God watch over us here."

With the first of the toasts taken care of, everyone fell to eating. The rooms echoed with the clatter of the spoons and knives. When they all had eaten their fill and the table boards had been cleared away, two servants carried in the huge wassail bowl with ribbons trailing after it. Everyone had a taste before it disappeared back into the kitchen to be refilled. Original Brown and his flute were shouted out from the far end of the commons' table. One of Calvert's men took up the tabor.

The boards and trestles were stacked against the wall. A double line of dancers, servants and gentry together, snaked around the great hall, through the entryway and into the parlor. In the kitchen Bess tapped her foot to the music. Her apron rode considerably higher on her stomach than before. When Baltasar Codd had fled the country three months before, he left more than debts behind him.

Robert Vaughan held out his arm. "Mistress Margaret, shall we fetch a frisk?" His large blunt features looked even homelier above the big lace collar of his shirt. The brown kersey of his doublet had been unpicked and refashioned from an earlier style, and the darker lines of old seams were visible. But at least his stockings matched tonight.

"Thou art lord and I am thy servant, sir." She realized that the skips and capers of the trenchmore would take her under the mistletoe, but she accepted his arm anyway. He was, after all, an uncommonly fine dancer and for that she could forgive him a great deal.

When the company had danced up midnight, Vaughan raised his arms and shouted for attention.

"All for the bonfire. Its flames will reduce to ashes any bones of contention among us."

Everyone surged for the cloaks covering the wall by the door. With their torches trailing light and smoke behind them, they poured out into the snowy night toward the fifteen-foot-high stack of wood and bones.

Anicah trailed behind the crowd. The ale had made her melancholy. In the midst of the laughter she felt alone. Without Martin to share the feast, it seemed empty and garish. It was a sensation she had never had the opportunity to experience before, guilt at her own good fortune.

She started when Edward caught her by the elbow.

"Come." He tugged her toward the barn.

She waited while he slid back the bolt on the barn door. He opened it, handed her the splinter of fat pine he carried and pushed her inside. When she turned to look for him the night had devoured him without a trace of a feather or a button.

"Anicah."

"Martin?" She held up the torch and peered into the darkness.

Martin rose stiffly from the shadows. Anicah hardly noticed his ferocious appearance. She put the torch in the cresset on a post and ran to him. She threw her arms around him and pressed against him. The wool of his coat was rough and cold against her cheek. His arms encircled her so tightly they almost squeezed the breath from her, but she didn't care. This was how she wanted to die anyway.

"Martin." It was all she could find voice to say.

She stood on her toes to kiss him. His lips were chill, but she warmed them. He held her face in his icy hands and kissed her brows, her eyes, her cheeks and neck and chin, then her mouth again.

He trembled in her arms, but it was no longer from the cold that had soaked through him while he waited here so many long hours for her. His touch was stronger, surer, than she remembered. It was a man's touch.

"Martin, me love, me heart, me sweet marrow, leave me not again."

"Would that I could stay." He laid his cheek against her head and closed his eyes. "If they find me they shall hang me," he murmured. "Or at best send me back to the gunsmith."

"Mistress Margaret will save thee, I'm sure of it."

"Nay, Ani. John Dandy would kill me or I him. 'Tis a certainty."

"Then I shall go with thee."

"You cannot."

"I care not where circumstance takes us." Anicah clung to his coat with both hands and looked up at him, her eyes wide and pleading in the flickering light. "I shall sleep in a salvage's hut with thee or on the ground. I shall eat roots of the forest." Tears ran down her cheeks. "Only do not leave me here."

"I will be happy knowing you're safe and well." He held her in his arms and rocked gently with her from side to side, as though soothing a child, but tears glistened in his own eyes. "I shall come for you when I can. And Edward will watch over you when I cannot."

"Ye're abiding with the salvages, then?"

"Aye."

"Anicah." Robert Vaughan's voice drifted from somewhere very far away.

"Anicah." Others took up the call.

"They think the salvages have carried me off."

"One of them wishes he could." The tickle of her hair on Martin's lips sent a shudder of grief and pleasure through him. "You must go."

He glanced over her head at the pine splinter, almost burned to a nub now, but still giving off a feeble light. If the Brents and their people saw it through the cracks in the barn's weatherboards, they would come to investigate.

Finally Anicah pushed gently away until she held him at arm's length. Even that close, she could not make out the details of his face and form in the dark shadows. She reached up to kiss him again. "I shall think on thee every day. Do not forget me."

"Anicah." The calls were sounding more alarmed.

Anicah blew out the torch. With their arms around each other they made their way to the door, opened it and slipped outside. When Anicah finished sliding the bolt home she turned for one last kiss, but Martin was gone.

Chapter 46

Margaret and Mary stood on the half-deck of Master Richard Ingle's ship and watched the low, brown tip of Kent Island spread outward as the ship approached it. Ingle was below, much to Margaret's relief. He was polite to her, gallant even, but he wasted his weasel-eyed charm on her. He supported Parliament against King Charles, and Margaret wouldn't forgive him that.

This was Margaret's first trip to Kent Fort Manor since she had bought it from Giles over a year ago. The three-day voyage up the Chesapeake had been untroubled by the storms that could pounce in late autumn. The surface of the bay was rumpled but calm. Ragged wedges of geese honked overhead like warring oboes.

"It looks so tranquil and untouched by strife," Mary said.

"Strife hath not touched the Isle of Kent, dear sister, so much as boxed it about the ears." Margaret spoke in a low voice.

The man at the ship's wheel was one of the planters still loyal to Kent's original settler, the hard-headed William Claiborne. Margaret had no doubt that the helmsman and many others here would side with Claiborne were he to make good his threat to return from Virginia and try to take the island back.

The sorts of people willing to come to Maryland were a recalcitrant and independent lot. The inhabitants of this island were the most recalcitrant of all. The helmsman, Peter Knight, could be counted with the most insolent of Kent's riffraff.

The crew fired the thirty-two pounder to let Kent's planters and traders know the ship was coming. Its roar echoed across the open water and into the wind-bent pines lining the shore. Thousands of ducks and geese and swans rose with the noise of a cannon volley. Feathers drifted down like snow. The ship nosed through a blanket of them as it followed the thread of a channel, sliding over the encroaching grass. The planters' canoes, pinks and shallops appeared, their rakish triangular lateen rigs skimming the water like gray-brown moths.

Robert Vaughan and his two spaniels were waiting at the landing. Behind Vaughan rose the only elevations in the area, a line of low mounds. They were the eroded remnants of an earthwork William Claiborne and his men had thrown up against Leonard Calvert's attack almost six years ago. In the distance loomed the palisade known as Kent Fort. Its cannons formed a sparse bristle from the diamond-shaped bastions at the corners.

Under the lead-colored sky the place looked desolate and wind-stripped and possessed of the intransigence of Billy Claiborne himself. It also exuded a wild and heady freedom. Margaret liked it.

"Mistress Margaret, Mistress Mary." Vaughan smiled broadly, as though anticipating an improvement in his diet with the arrival of Bess. "Welcome to Kent Fort Manor."

"Good morrow, Sergeant Vaughan." Margaret leaned forward to receive his brotherly kiss. "How farest thou?"

"I am well, and all here likewise, God be praised." He glanced at Ingle. "I trust you had a good voyage, Master Ingle."

"Aye, thanks be to God." Ingle turned to Margaret. "I shall be along directly I settle things aboard ship, Mistress Margaret. We can begin lading the sot weed tomorrow." Ingle made a courtly sweep with his hat brim. "Sergeant Vaughan, I have some items you may find of interest—a pair of bottles of Faial wine I set aside for you and two books but lately printed."

Vaughan smiled and bowed.

"Master Ingle." Harry Angell came striding over the mounds,

his baggy new boots kicking up sand. "I would have a word with you about a shipment of weed." Harry bowed to Margaret and Mary. "Mistresses Brent, what a pleasure."

Margaret nodded curtly. Harry's hemp scar had faded to a blur and he dressed well, but he still had a ferret's eyes.

Ingle ushered Harry into the lighter, then climbed in after him. Margaret watched the mariners shove the prow into the water, vault in and man the oars.

"What business brings Angell here, Robert?"

"He is buying respectability by the bolt and the hogshead. Soon he shall have his arms entered in the book of heralds."

"Then he shall have like imposters for company." Margaret watched the lighter diminish. "Such as he are cropping up thick as toadstools in England."

"Last March he transported seven men," Vaughan said. "He demanded a patent for three hundred and fifty acres here on Kent. It was posted on the tree near the chapel in St. Mary's and no one objected."

"I would have objected."

"You were in Virginia, Margaret, cajoling more servants from your friend, the governor."

"Angell is a felon, a scape-gallows. Where would he get money enough for a headright?"

"Perhaps a legacy." Vaughan laughed. "Dig too deeply in people's pasts here and one uncovers what's best left buried."

"Giles will be staying at St. Mary's." Margaret changed the subject. "Governor Calvert took ship for England and named Giles lieutenant governor in his absence."

Vaughan raised one furry eyebrow. He knew that Squire Cornwaleys would be irritated and Secretary Lewger outraged by the appointment. The other gentlemen would at the very least be envious.

Margaret picked up her skirts with one hand and took Mary's arm with the other. "Lead on, Sergeant Vaughan."

"Perhaps you would rather your maids swept out the place

before you enter. We could inspect the tobacco houses and orchards and mill first."

Margaret tilted an eyebrow at him. "I know how my brother keeps house, Rob. I'm prepared for the worst."

She and Mary followed Vaughan along a path sunken below the surrounding area and exactly a tobacco hogshead's width.

"Tell me the news," Vaughan said.

"King Charles's forces under Prince Rupert are prevailing against Cromwell and his murderous heretics. Thanks be to God."

"And how found the jury in the murder of the Yoacomico's king?"

"They refused to indict the assassin." Margaret still felt bitter about it. "Howkins was on the jury. He upbraided the court, saying that if an Englishman had been killed by the Indians there would have not been so much made of it."

"But for the Yoacomico king and his people we would have slept that first winter like Diogenes, each in his hogshead, and frozen there belike." Vaughan shook his head as he followed Margaret and Mary through the palisade's front gate. "Now a bit of English flotsam has killed him for his coat and gone unpunished."

Inside, Giles's new manor house was almost finished. Billy Claiborne's old cabin stood nearby, looking small and shabby by comparison. Margaret noticed the loopholes cut into the sides and gable ends of the new place. They were an admission that everyone expected the troubles here to continue, in one form or another.

"What a lovely house Giles has built." Mary turned and smiled brightly to one side. "Think'st thou not so, Raphael?"

Margaret and Vaughan exchanged glances while they maneuvered around the stacks of barrel staves and wood and broken hogsheads in the yard. Vaughan opened the door and stood aside so Margaret could enter the great hall. It contained a single chair, a few stools, a bench, and a trestle table.

The disarray exceeded her expectations. The rotting rushes on the floor were laced with ordure and dog-gnawed marrow bones.

Badly cured pelts hung from the walls on wood-splint frames. A cat had littered in the chair and her kittens mewled around her. Margaret could smell the evidence of their presence. The corners of the room and the hearth had been used as a privy.

"Giles hath always said he preferred a house not so neatly kept as to shame his dirty boots," Margaret said. "He hath no reason to fear that here."

Bess screamed in the kitchen. Margaret found her standing on the table that sagged under her weight. Bess had widened while carrying her child and had stayed that way after the birth. Kitt held up a terrapin as long as her forearm. Its legs churned furiously as she thrust it at Bess. Kitt sometimes forgot that she was the future queen of the Piscataways and the ward and adopted niece of English nobility. Anicah hopped about, gingerly trying to recapture three other turtles that had escaped from their basket and were scuttling across the dirt floor toward cover.

Vaughan beamed in the doorway. "The Kentishmen are heartily weary of turtle soup, but I wager you'll declare it the best chowder you have ever tasted, Margaret."

The mastiff growled and Anicah stopped and listened. The distant rumble sounded familiar. Someone was rolling a hogshead.

The mastiff growled again and Anicah ducked into a thicket of alders. She put a hand on the dog's back to quiet him and watched two men roll a hogshead out of the drying house and two more replace it with another. Anicah wasn't surprised to see that the fifth man was Harry Angell.

She waited for a long time after the man had left before she walked to the barn. Everything seemed to be in order. Each of the hogsheads was stamped with the governor's seal. Anicah ran her fingers over the quartered diagonal checks and the ornate crosses of the design.

She started to smile at Harry's audacity, then frowned. He was stealing from the people who had taken her in and treated her kindly.

"Good morrow, me fair scapegrace."

Anicah whirled to face Harry. Besides his firelock he carried a cudgel. A dirk projected from his belt. In spite of his smile, or maybe because of it, Anicah knew he would kill her with only the least of regrets. Her body would never be found in this God-abandoned wilderness.

"G'day to ye, Harry." She smiled ingenuously. "I was just lookin' fer one o' Mistress Brent's ewes."

"One frequently encounters sheep in drying houses."

"I shall be going now, afore they miss me at the gentry house." Anicah backed away. "Nothing here to report."

Harry moved forward and the mastiff growled, a low roll of murderous intent from deep in his throat. He bared yellow teeth sharp as adzes. Harry stopped abruptly.

"A pity ye've nothing to report." He looked hard at Anicah.

"Nothing at all."

"Good day to ye, then."

"God keep ye." Anicah turned and walked away so fast the mastiff had to trot to keep up.

Anicah decided she would say nothing of this. Most likely the substitute weed would be trundled aboard Ingle's tubby pinnace and stowed in the hold with the other identical barrels. It would slide down over the edge of the horizon with the ship, and none the wiser.

Chapter 47

T he bow of the canoe burrowed into the sand of the planters' landing. Robert Vaughan helped Margaret out while her servant waited in the stern with the paddle across his knees. Margaret had come to barter for barrel staves. As she neared the end of the path through the twenty-foot-high growth of bushes and vines, she sniffed the odor of roast meat.

"Methinks they've been barbecuing, Robert. Most likely we'll find one of my pigs on the spit."

Vaughan unshouldered his crossbow, set a quarrel and took the goat's foot from his belt. Margaret watched him hook it to the string and the stock and crank its articulated levers to draw the bow.

"Think you they'll resist when we reclaim the pig, Robert?"

"The amount of smoke bespeaks a very large fire, Margaret."

Margaret crossed herself and loaded her fowling piece. She took the smoldering match from its perforated tin box and clamped it into the serpentine. Cupping her hand around it she followed Vaughan up the path.

When she came to the clearing she saw that the roofs of the clapboard shack and tobacco barn had burned away. The walls still smoldered. An arrow protruded from the lintel.

Vaughan pulled it out and studied it. "Susquehannock."

Margaret pushed open the door with the muzzle of her piece and peered inside. Two charred corpses lay sprawled on the earthen floor. The fire had burned off their clothes and melted their features.

It had rendered the fat in their bodies, leaving a dark circle of greasy dirt around them.

Margaret backed away and put a hand to her mouth to stifle the gagging. Vaughan grabbed her arm and hauled her at a run to the landing. The panicked servant pushed off when he saw them coming. Cursing him, Vaughan scooped Margaret up, fowling piece and all, and splashed into the water. He dumped her into the bilge and leaped in after her. Both men dug their paddles deep and pulled hard.

Margaret stared at the wall of black willows moving past them with terrifying slowness. She gripped the gunwales to keep her hands from shaking. "We should give them a proper burial."

"We'll bury them later," Vaughan said. "Or at least what the wolves leave."

The two men were perspiring in the December chill by the time they reached open water and the tall canvas vanes of Kent Fort's mill came into view. Canoes and small sailing vessels lined the landing. Scores of people milled about the palisade. Some of them were already chopping at what few trees remained.

"Good Lord." Margaret bolted out of the canoe, hardly waiting for the servant to drag it ashore.

Inside the palings the refugees had already set up makeshift tents and lean-tos and built cooking fires. Pigs, chickens, and children swarmed about the place. Margaret whirled on Vaughan.

"Robert, clear them out of here. All of them." She waved her arm in their direction.

"This is the only fortification, Margaret."

"I won't invite the foxes into the henhouse. They'll steal everything."

He gave her a chiding look and she relented. "They can stay outside the walls and come in only if the salvages attack."

Then she saw Mary wandering through the crowd with a basket of herbs and simples. Bess followed with a hamper of bread and a pail of pease porridge.

"Dear God, give me patience," Margaret muttered.

It was bad enough that she must shelter the very Protestants who maligned her family, blasphemed her religion and stole her livestock. But Mary would deplete the manor's stores for them. She would give her last morsel to an enemy, which was all very well for her, but Margaret knew from experience that living with a saint could be a trial to those around her.

"Aunt Margaret." Kitt dodged through the milling crowd.

She wore Margaret's big pistol at her waist. She had grown tall and long-legged in the last six months, but the weight of the gun pulled the belt down on her slender hip. The broad leather bandolier with the dangling cartridges, powder flashes and flint box obscured her narrow chest. She swung a short cudgel at the pigs, dogs, and small children in her path.

"Peter Knight chopped a hole in the back wall of the barn and stole the black ewe," she said. "I fired on him, but I missed." Kitt looked disappointed. She had hoped to hang another ventilated cap over the mantelpiece. The bullet holes and the moth holes in Baltasar Codd's relic had finally joined and the cap had moldered to a fine dust. "I ordered Jack to cover the hole with deal boards and stand watch."

"James . . ." Margaret beckoned to the servant. "Get into the canoe. We're going to Knight's den."

"I'll see to it, Margaret." Vaughan looked sternly at her. She always wanted to confront those who wronged her, but he was the magistrate here. "I'll bring a report, and some mutton for the kettle."

The whippet, long and elegant and angular, slept with her muzzle on her paws in the clean, herb-scented reeds on the floor of the great hall. The rest of the dogs sprawled in a heap around Robert Vaughan's feet. The two spaniels chased ducks in their dreams. The turnspit lay nestled against the mastiff who had draped a massive foreleg over his taut little sausage of a back.

Urine-soaked linen cloths for Bess's baby hung on a rack in front of the fire. Their smell permeated the house. When they dried Bess would fold them and use them again. The rags soiled with feces were more of a problem. Bess spent a great deal of time rinsing them.

Vaughan could hear Margaret in the kitchen giving instructions for the next days' work. Mary Brent and Kitt were reciting the Little Office of the Blessed Virgin in the closet that served as a chapel. The sun was setting, but outside the palisade dogs still barked, children cried, mothers scolded.

Vaughan stared glumly into the fire. One of the reasons he preferred the eastern shore was that its people usually kept to themselves. The theft of solitude was one more grudge he held against the Susquehannocks. Vaughan also brooded about his encounter with Peter Knight. He'd found the bloody remains of the ewe in the rat-infested cockloft of Knight's house. He had had to seize the evidence, and his supper, by force of arms. He suspected Knight hadn't shot him in the back only because he needed his scant supplies of lead and powder to kill Indians and his neighbors' hogs.

The devil take the entire misbegotten, mossy-toothed rabble, he thought.

Vaughan sighed and consoled himself with St. Matthew's words:

Take therefore no thought for the morrow: for the morrow shall take thought for the things of itself. Sufficient unto the day is the evil thereof.

He decided that if his name were ever listed in the Book of Heralds, he would choose the last line of that verse as his motto.

He was roused from his mope by Giles shouting at the people outside. Margaret came into the parlor and exchanged a quizzical look with Vaughan. This was an unexpected visit. It wasn't likely that good news had shaken Giles loose from St. Mary's and his duties as deputy governor. From the sound of him, he had passed the time on the voyage drinking. Giles slammed open the door. He didn't seem to notice that the place was a great deal neater than he had left it.

"Damn me, Vaughan, thou foresworn rogue." As he clomped across the room his boots left a trail of feces-laced mud. "Thou hast cheated me and stolen from me and broken the sacred trust bestowed upon thee as my attorney."

"God keep you also, Giles." Vaughan looked up with an amused hitch at one corner of his supple mouth and a glint in his drifting green eyes. "Sit you down and take a pipe."

"I think that a surfeit of spirits hath addled what little sense God gave thee, brother." Margaret, hands on hips, glared at him. The chatter in the kitchen hushed as the servants listened.

"Of what treachery stand I accused?" Vaughan asked.

"Calvert's inspector says the eight hogsheads of tobacco sent on board Ingle's vessel from my landing here are unmerchantable."

"*My* landing," Margaret said.

"The leaf was sound," Vaughan said.

" 'Twas tainted, turned, burned, wormed and farced with stones the size of bread loaves." Giles inhaled a pinch of snuff from his silver box. In his excitement he sneezed, blowing the box's contents across the room, which put him in an even worse temper.

Vaughan frowned. Lewger had filed a similar complaint for tobacco taken from his landing at nearby Broad Creek.

"I saw the tobacco laded," Margaret said. "All the barrels were stamped with Baltimore's seal and in good order."

Anicah appeared with a salver of mutton stew and venison hash and an ewer of brandy. She set everything out on the table with deft, sure grace. Margaret's relentless instruction was showing. When she finished she curtsied prettily to Giles. Giles reached reflexively to squeeze her lovely buttock, remembered his sister's presence, and stopped in mid-letch.

"Where's the brat?" he said. "I have tidings for her."

Kitt appeared at his elbow and he kept her waiting while he inhaled more snuff. "Mistress Kitt, your father has died."

"Giles!" Margaret was horrified at his delivery of the sad news.

"Damn me, he did. A fever or something. Typhus perhaps,

from some pestilential trader." He waved a languid hand. "I thought she should know. Her mother went too, I'm told."

"Niece," Margaret sat down so her eyes were on a level with Kitt's. "Your father's with God now."

But even before Margaret spoke a transformation came over Kitt. She pulled herself up taller inside the chemise, doublet and skirts she had sewn under Mary's instruction. She tossed her head to throw her hair out of her eyes and lifted her chin.

"Thou art most kind, Aunt." She made a perfect curtsy. "I must be queen now. Therefore I ask to be baptized in the true faith. I would take as my new name that of the Blessed Mother Mary."

"We'll talk about it in the morning." Margaret tucked a stray lock behind Kitt's ear. "Say thy prayers and go to bed."

Giles waited until she had had climbed the stairs before he spoke again. "I have decided to wive." He giggled at Margaret's open-mouthed stare.

"Whom dost thou intend to marry?"

"Your ward." He swirled the brandy in his glass, enjoying the stunned silence he had created.

"She's only eleven years old at most."

"Pocahontas was but twelve when she granted Captain John Smith her favors."

Vaughan snorted. "Smith, the great prevaricator, made that story up from the whole cloth. And it is just the sort of nonsense posterity belike will remember of him."

"How sayeth Father Copley of this plan?" Margaret asked.

"He hath agreed to perform the ceremony as soon as I wish."

"Before Leonard Calvert returns from England, I would imagine." Vaughan realized where this scheme was going.

"And Father White?"

"He's at Portobacco, converting the queen of the tribe there. That's what gave me the idea." Giles seemed surprised that Margaret didn't share his enthusiasm. "As you know, inheritance and right of rule pass through the female line among the Piscataway.

Kittamaquund had no sister, therefore Kitt is the rightful heir. Kitt's father's holdings encompass more than the combined estates of a leash of earls and a knight of the realm."

"And when married by English law," Vaughan added, "her property reverts to Giles." He was admiring and envious. No wonder Copley was agreeable. It would put a great tract of land into the hands of a loyal Catholic and a supporter of the Jesuits. It was a brilliant plan if it worked. If it didn't, it would bring ridicule and ruin down on Giles's head.

"Leonard will not stand for it," Margaret said.

"He's not here. And besides, such a case is not covered in Baltimore's Conditions of Plantation concerning gifts of land from the Indians." Giles had obviously given this more than his usual cursory thought. "Baltimore's powers are extensive, but he cannot tell his subjects whom to wed or bed."

"Giles!"

"Fret not, dear sister. I shall not roger the brat until she has had her first course of the moon."

Or until she's twelve and lawfully available, Vaughan thought. He decided it was time to divert the conversation before it became rancorous. He drew his pack of cards from his doublet. "Shall we play a game of put, Margaret?"

Giles continued to drink until he fell into a stupor in front of the fire, muttering and jerking in his dreams like the spaniels.

Vaughan and Margaret played cards by the light of pine splinters attached to the backs of their chairs. They cheated wildly, of course, and Vaughan was impressed at how much brandy Margaret drank and how steady her hand remained in spite of it.

He suspected that Giles's announcement had unnerved her. Margaret was a shrewd judge of character, but she couldn't read her own brother's heart. Vaughan, on the other hand, knew the Brents better than anyone, maybe better than they knew themselves, and he understood what had motivated Giles's decision.

In spite of the offices and favors and land Lord Baltimore had bestowed on Giles, Leonard Calvert sought Margaret's counsel more frequently than his. No matter what honors Giles attained, Margaret continued to treat him as a slightly addled and inept younger brother. And though most people still considered Kent Fort Manor his, he knew he had lost it to Margaret through his own incompetence and her resourcefulness.

No wonder he was so pleased with his plan to outwit them all and obtain a vast estate in the bargain. Vaughan felt sure Giles himself hadn't thought of the added nicety that he was wounding Margaret by taking her niece, and tupping her too.

As Vaughan contemplated his cards he sang to himself.

> *"This single life is wearisome,*
> *Fain would I marry,*
> *But fear of ill choosing*
> *Makes me to tarry."*

"They say that a woman who does not consent to be the property of one man is content to be the property of the entire species." Margaret looked up at him. "In other words, a whore."

"Religious women like yourself being the exception, of course."

"I would not marry even had I not taken a vow of chastity."

Vaughan raised an eyebrow at such a preposterous notion.

"If I married, my legal rights would be usurped by my husband. My title to my lands would be annihilated."

"Um." Vaughan knew he was about to hear more than he wanted of Margaret's thoughts on an intimate subject. Probably more than any living being had heard. Brandy affected people that way.

"I had a few proposals in my youth," she said.

"I shouldn't doubt it, Maggie. I myself proposed to you once, though you've belike forgotten such an insignificant event."

She smiled fondly at him to show she hadn't. "When I was but thirteen and a rawboned rack of a girl, one elderly squire . . ." She shook her head. "Well, Rob, he seemed elderly, but he was only forty. Giles's age, actually. He said that he liked me well enough, but would have my father settle a thousand pounds sterling more on me. I thought so ill of the silly old fart that a thousand pounds less would have seemed far too much."

Vaughan giggled over the "silly old fart" reference.

"Imagine being bought and sold, Rob."

"I cannot imagine it, Maggie. Yet the system seems to work well enough."

"People who ought to know better say that kindness will grow after marriage, though it be absent at the start. Yet I do not think marriage a sort of sorcery that can conjure love out of indifference, yea, even out of mislike."

"Plato relates the myth that each creature at the beginning was cloven in two," Vaughan said, "then must spend the rest of its life searching for its other half."

Margaret dealt another hand into the silence that followed. "I would not be a toad eater in my eldest brother's house," she said suddenly.

Margaret Brent would never sink to that level, but Vaughan knew what she meant. Gentlewomen often lived in their richer relatives' households where they served as objects of scorn. They were named after the mountebank's assistant, ordered to perform unpleasant tasks, including eating supposedly poisonous toads to prove the efficacy of his master's elixirs.

"Nay, I would not be a toad eater." Margaret said it with a sadness that tugged at Vaughan's heart.

He leaned across the table and kissed her lightly on the lips. "You and your sister are the finest women I know, Maggie."

A baby wailed upstairs and they heard Bess trying to soothe her daughter. No one had gotten a complete night's sleep in months. The servants were irritable and exhausted. Margaret was irritable and exhausted.

A child is a gift from God, Margaret thought. She should be loved and prized, not cursed and resented.

Margaret had talked Secretary Lewger out of having Bess stripped to the waist and given twenty lashes for fornication. He had settled for a fine of five hundred pounds of tobacco. Bess had agreed to serve another two years to repay Margaret. Margaret dreaded the scene when the baby was weaned. The court would most likely bind the child out to someone else, because her mother couldn't do her work and care for her too.

Finally the crying stopped and Margaret excused herself. As she lay next to Mary in the bed in the parlor, her thoughts whirled from the brandy and she felt the ghostly touch of Robert Vaughan's kiss. She rubbed her mouth to erase it.

She hadn't anticipated worrying about Kitt's future for another two or three years, but Giles had changed that. The more Margaret thought about it, though, the more reconciled she became to the plan. People of her rank were often betrothed at twelve, and for the same economic reason Giles had given.

Margaret knew she might die of any one or a combination of diseases and calamities. People all around her did. At the very least, Kitt would remain in the family, her future and her fortunes assured. And Giles wasn't a bad man, as men went. Margaret could think of no one of rank in the colony for Kitt to marry except Leonard Calvert. She had planned to broach the subject of a liaison with Calvert in a few years, but it was too late now. Giles had outmaneuvered her, for the first time in his life.

In spite of the icy air upstairs, Anicah and Kitt lay half off the pallet they shared. With their faces turned toward each other and their ears pressed to the crack between two of the floorboards, they listened to Giles announce his plan to marry Kitt. Then they eavesdropped on Margaret and Vaughan's conversation until the baby's cries cut it short.

They crawled back into bed and pulled the covers over their heads to muffle their voices. Shivering with the cold they lay close together and whispered in the blackness.

"I'm sorry about yer mum and dad passing, Kitt."

"I envy them. They're in heaven."

"Will ye run away to your people rather than wed the squire?"

"No." Kitt lay silent until Anicah thought she had fallen asleep. When she spoke again she sounded much older than her eleven years. "Aunt Margaret and Aunt Mary are my people now. I would not offend them or God by shirking my duty."

" 'Tisn't your duty to marry a posturing old man." Anicah couldn't believe that Kitt had actually taken to heart Mistress Margaret's ceaseless sermons about duty and honor.

"For people of our station marriage has nothing to do with happiness. The English are like the Piscataway in that respect. We of the aristocracy must form alliances to benefit the family, the nation even."

"'Tis a bloody lot of foolishness," Anicah said fiercely. "I agree with Squire Plate."

"Squire Plate?"

"Aye. The wight who said that people get split before birth and must find their other halves and marry them."

"You mean Plato."

"Aye, him. Martin is my other half and Edward is yours. Ye cannot live your life with half of yer heart and yer soul missing."

When Kitt didn't answer Anicah put out her fingers and touched her cheek. It was wet with tears.

"I did not mean to make ye weep, Kitt."

Kitt sighed and kissed Anicah on the forehead. " 'Tis nothing you said, Ani."

The two lay quietly, each absorbed by her own thoughts.

Now that she had the leisure, Anicah remembered the tainted tobacco that hadn't made it to England in Ingle's ship before it was discovered. She felt a bit guilty for not telling Mistress Margaret that Harry Angell was responsible; but after all, Giles insisted it was his tobacco, and what did she care about him? In any case, the gentry had money enough. Let them sort it out.

"Kitt," she said, "with your father gone and all, are you queen of his realm now?"

"I suppose so."

"Then I've been sleeping these past two years with a princess and now I'm bedding with a queen. Fancy that."

Kitt gave a small laugh.

"Your majesty . . ." Anicah shoved her. "Take your royal, bloody icy foot off me leg."

Chapter 48

M ary Brent walked through the corn and tobacco stubble that carpeted St. Mary's. Anicah and Bess, her eight-month-old daughter whimpering in a sling on her back, trailed after her. Mary had started from Sisters' Freehold with a hamper of mirrors, wooden combs and clay pipes. Margaret would be furious when she discovered that her sister had redirected the goods she had imported for the Indian trade, but Margaret's displeasure had never stopped Mary before.

The sixth of January and Epiphany, marking the arrival of the three magi, had happened a week ago, but Mary was delivering gifts to the poorest of St. Mary's citizens anyway. She said they needed the cheer, and she was right. Few who survived their indentures were able to acquire the hundred fifty pounds of tobacco necessary to register for their fifty-acre freeholds. Even fewer managed to pay the clerk's and surveyor's fees and build a house. Most became tenants on a gentleman's lands and worked for a share of his crop. Those who were ill or unable or unwilling to farm moved into the hovels hastily lashed together by the first settlers. They shivered and froze through the winter.

Mary was also offering them remedies from her garden—horseradish mixed with grease for sores and bruises, coltsfoot and honey for catarrh, and honey-leaf balm steeped with borage to cure melancholy. Anicah and Bess carried baskets of the most effective palliatives, succotash and cider.

The hamlet huddled against a frigid draft that scoured away all that was green and pleasant to the eye and blew trash in drifts against the few houses and fences. St. Mary's suffered ill will as well as an ill wind. England's parliamentarians and royalists were fighting their war across the ocean, but its detritus of animosity and discord had washed ashore here. Shouting bouts, cudgel matches and fistfights over religion occurred daily. The January court session was the most contentious ever.

For all the misery here, Anicah was glad to be back. Richard Ingle's ship had returned from the eastern shore, and Anicah could hear the seamen roaring in the ordinary. Through Leonard Calvert's open gate she could see a small crowd peering in the window of the courtroom where Mary Lawne Courtney was suing for the loss of a good name she had never owned. Compared with the Isle of Kent, St. Mary's was a metropolis.

Anicah hefted her basket, light now that almost everything had been distributed. "Mistress Mary, might we take some cheer to old Original? He complains of pains in his belly."

"Goodman Brown? Of course."

Scraps of canvas, broken barrel staves and torn sacking replaced the bark sheathing that had rotted away from Brown's Yoacomico house. His bird net dangled around it like a tattered garland flapping in the wind. Bess waited outside, trying to soothe her fitful babe while Mary pulled aside the canvas door, letting in a pallid pool of sunlight. Brown may have been searching for a red bird, but a magpie best suited his habits. He had filled his domed house with broken and useless things.

"May God keep thee well, Goodman Brown," Mary said.

Brown squinted from the pungent deeps of his bear hide. He held its stiff edges closed with fingers as gnarled as mandrake roots.

"We have brought thee a distillation of mint and purslain for thy stomach, and sassafras tea for thy joints," Mary said.

"And corn mush fer the wolf in yer maw." Anicah held up a gourd of hominy.

Hunger and suspicion quarreled around Brown's hollow eyes

and sunken mouth as he stared at the gourd. "Nay," he croaked. "Ye'll not trick me with stolen viands."

" 'Tis not stolen," Mary said patiently, "but freely given."

"They thrust a bodkin through Will's tongue and chained him to a tree till he starved." Brown pulled farther back into the bear hide. "He's speaking of his brother," Anicah said. "In Virginia in the starving time he stole a fist of breath." She shoved the gourd within Brown's reach. "No one will punish ye fer the takin' of this grub."

"Think not to bribe yer way into me breeches, wench." He glowered at Anicah as she and Mary backed out of the hut, but he grabbed the gourd. "A man must have a care about women," he shouted after them. "They're more hot and wily than goats and foxes."

Bess's child was screaming again, her tiny face puckered with the pain in her bowels. Bess was trying to nurse her, her breast blue with the cold.

"We'll carry the babe home." Mary laid a gloved hand on the child's forehead and she quieted briefly. "Anicah, deliver this simple to Master Ingle. He hath complained of a constriction of the bowel. He said he would be at the ordinary this afternoon."

"But he's against the king, mistress."

"God will judge him."

Mary picked up Bess's empty basket and put an arm around her and the baby. As soon as she had gotten out of hearing, a lanky individual in greasy leather knee breeches, a moth-eaten wool doublet and short cape sidled from behind a drying shed. He touched the brim of his hat and smiled at Anicah, exposing black stumps of teeth in a wide, forward-slung jaw.

Anicah didn't wait for him to speak. "The answer is no, as always, Goodman Harwood. I will not have ye."

"I shall buy yer term from the old papist tabby, and then ye shall have me."

"Mistress Margaret has refused yer offer a dozen times. So cease yer panting after me like a lickerish hound." Anicah picked up a cudgel-sized limb lying by the path. She pointed it at three other chronic suitors easing toward her as though they happened to be headed her way. "The same for all of ye. I'm bespoke. Pester me and I'll rattle yer brains."

She stalked past them to the ordinary. Ingle would most likely be in the new room tacked onto the side of it. Before William Howkins absconded to avoid prosecution for debt, he had named the addition the Star Chamber. It stood now as a leaky, misaligned monument to his bootless ambition.

Anicah leaned her right shoulder against the wall under the shutters. She pretended to relace her bodice and pull up her stockings while she listened to the conversation inside.

". . . Charles is no king unless he joins with Parliament. If I had him on board, I would whip him at the capstan."

Anicah recognized Richard Ingle's treasonous opinions. She'd heard him say much the same when she worked in the taproom.

"'Tis most fortunate we took this from the traitorous dog." The sound of Ingle's boots rose and fell as he paced. "God hath lent His hand to our cause."

"How reads the paper?" The second voice was unfamiliar.

An arm wrapped around Anicah's chest from behind. Another encircled her waist and lifted her off the ground. The seaman carried her kicking and flailing through the taproom and the cheers of those assembled there and into the private chamber.

"I found her spying under the eaves, Master Ingle."

" 'Tis the papists' wench, the former tavern maid." Ingle stood in front of the fire with his first mate. "Let her go."

Anicah whirled to kick the shins of the man who held her. She threw a tankard at him as he limped out the door. She felt the exhilaration of being an ale wench again, if only for a few moments.

"May I never piss again if I do not see that little pustule scalded, scraped, and quartered for laying hands on me." Brimming with injured dignity, she pulled the tatters of her cape regally around her.

"Tell thy business here."

"Me mistress sends this simple fer yer bowels. Rosin of jalep and byrony root in honey." Under her cloak Anicah worked loose the cork in the earthern medicine jar. Holding the cork in place, she tilted the jar so the contents flowed to the top of it. When she handed it to Ingle she stumbled and thumbed the cork out, spilling the contents down the front of his new velvet doublet.

"Fergive me, squire. I'm such a walloping great oaf." She smeared the mess around with the hem of her apron.

"Get off." He was too angry about the doublet to propose the flourish he had intended to take with her.

"I'll scour off home and ask the mistress to mix ye up another batch."

"Begone, then." Ingle waved a hand in dismissal.

Anicah curtsied and fled. As she hurried down the path toward home she put her hand to her bodice and felt the folded document she had foisted from the front of Ingle's doublet. It was sticky with honey, but Mistress Margaret would probably find it interesting anyway. Best of all, Master Ingle's bowels would stay constricted a while longer unless he sucked the medicine from the velvet pile of his doublet. Anicah smiled and hummed a cheerful ditty.

The sun was setting when Anicah found Bess in the yard watching lye boil down to the right viscosity for soap. She had swaddled her daughter in a piece of blanketing and laid her in a basket.

"Bess, ye're needed in the kitchen. The new girl will finish this."

"The silly wench doesn't know when 'tis thick enow."

Anicah knew Bess chose outside chores even in icy weather so the family would have a respite from her daughter's crying. The fact that neither Margaret or Mary had been able to cure the child of her maladies made her a constant and not-so-silent reproach.

"Shall I add another bucket of ash?" Anicah stared into the seething gray liquid.

When she got no answer she looked up to see Bess, chin up, listening intently. But there was only silence. Bess dropped the sassafras paddle into the lye and ran to the basket. She picked up the child, tore away the swaddling and laid an ear to the little chest. She was trying to shake life back into the baby when Anicah took the child from her.

Anicah carried the little corpse to the house while Bess followed, wailing.

Bess was still shrieking upstairs and the other maids were crying with her when Anicah served Margaret and Kitt their supper of ash cake, cold venison and succotash sweetened with bear fat. Mary was praying for the soul of Bess's child at her altar in the chimney corner when Giles tromped into the parlor.

"Good evening, fair damsels." He wore his soldier's knee-length leather buffcoat and he looked about to burst it with self-satisfaction. He swung his sword out of the way, kicked a stool from under the table and settled his lank hams onto it. He glanced up at the ceiling. "I say, what's the row upstairs?"

"Bess's babe has died."

"Damn me, fancy that." Giles let pass a moment of silence he judged was long enough to be respectful before he spoke again. "I have just arrested Ingle and his heretical crew and confiscated his pinnace and everything aboard it. Sergeant Price and his men are standing guard aboard the ship now."

"You arrested Richard Ingle?" Margaret had trouble believing even Giles could be that impulsive.

"Acting under King Charles's orders I have struck a blow for him, our religion and our country."

Giles waved the letter that Anicah had stolen from Ingle who had earlier taken it from a loyalist ship's master in Virginia. Margaret regretted ever giving it to Giles. The crimson wax of the king's seal crusted the two edges of the original fold.

Giles read aloud from it. " 'We command those that do love us to seize all goods, vessels and crewmen of ships' masters holding with Parliament.' " He beamed at Margaret. "Secretary Lewger wrote out the arrest warrant."

"Ah, Lewger. Well, there's a cool hand."

Giles didn't notice Margaret's caustic tone. "Damn me, but it was bloody brilliant, Maggie. You should have been there."

"I dare say I should have."

Margaret thought of the bear her servants had trapped in the dairy house last spring. Once it was locked inside, they didn't know what to do with it. It had destroyed the dairy, killed a pig, mauled the mastiff and raked the skin off a man's back before they had gotten it out of the yard. This could turn out far, far worse.

"And what dost thou intend to do with him, Giles?"

"Why, try him and hang him, of course."

"Goodman DaSousa would have a word with ye, mistress." Anicah stood aside so Mathias DaSousa could enter and warm himself at the fire.

Margaret turned to motion Anicah to bring him a noggin of hot cider, but she was already on her way to the kitchen for it.

"I thought you would want to know of the murder. . . ." DaSousa looked up to the beams, beyond which Bess's shrieks had subsided into great, rolling sobs. "But mayhap you have already heard."

"We have no news of murder," Margaret said, "though every other calamity has befallen us this day."

"A body was found in the river near John Dandy's smithy. Dandy has confessed to shooting the lad, an Indian whose name he says is Edward."

Kitt gave a strangled gasp and her brown cheeks turned ashy. In the doorway Anicah stared open-mouthed while the cup tilted in her hand, splashing cider onto the floor. Even Mary rose and watched intently from the shadows beyond the fireplace.

"We shall identify the body tomorrow and give it a proper burial." Margaret kept her voice calm. "Didst thou see it?"

"Nay, mistress. The sheriff says the face was too damaged to recognize and buried it immediately."

Kitt knelt and bowed her head. "With thy kind blessing and permission, Aunt Margaret, may I be excused from table?"

"May the Lord God bless thee, child." Margaret signed the cross. "Rejoice for Edward, Kitt." But Margaret's eyes glistened and her voice faltered. "He hath received baptism and is with God."

"Yes, Aunt." Kitt put out a hand to steady herself as she climbed the steps to the second floor.

"With permission, mistress." Anicah dropped in a hasty cursty and hurried after her.

She caught Kitt at the head of the stairs and put an arm around her. Her touch loosed the tears. Kitt was sobbing when Anicah helped her to the pallet and the two of them knelt on it.

Anicah thought of Edward's smile and the way Kitt lit up when she saw him. She thought of Martin, alone now and friendless in the wild. She held Kitt tight while hot tears ran down her cheeks. The maids and Bess knelt with them, and Kitt, her voice strained and unrecognizable, recited the Ave Maria. "Holy Mary, Mother of God, pray for us now and at the hour of our death . . ."

In the parlor the lamentation above made talk impossible. Giles gave up trying to tell Margaret the details of his triumph over Ingle.

"I wonder, sister, that thou wouldst allow such caterwauling." He had to shout to be heard.

"Mayhap thou wouldst be more comfortable at thine own hearth," Margaret said coldly.

"Damn me, but I think I would." Giles gathered his cloak and his dignity and stalked out.

Margaret knelt with Mary at the altar. They prayed for the dead and asked the Holy Mother's protection of the living. The two sets of recitations joined and the Virgin Mary's psalms filled the house.

As Thomas Cornwaleys's shallop pulled away from the ship he heard the squeal of rope through pulleys and the complaints of the capstan. The ship's pale expanse of canvas bloomed and rippled in the moonlight.

Cornwaleys didn't regret ordering the guard to let Ingle go. Holding the man would have brought retribution from Cromwell's people as fresh dung drew flies. It would have meant disaster for the entire colony. Calvert should never have put that ninny Brent in charge.

In less time than Cornwaleys would have thought possible, the ship was gliding downriver. From the darkness Cornwaleys heard Ingle swearing resourcefully at his crew.

Chapter 49

Anicah paused in the ordinary's back dooryard to enjoy the imminence of April. Even this late in the evening she could feel a fugitive warmth, like Martin's breath under the covers when they had shared a pallet so long ago on the ship. When she went inside, the new maidservant stared slack-mouthed at her from the smoke billowing out of the fireplace.

A country pullet, Anicah thought, still smelling of green hay and manure.

The young woman wiped her glistening face on her plump arm, and thin hominy gruel dripped off the ladle she was holding. She jumped when Goody Howkins burst through the door, shouting orders as she came.

"God keep ye, goodwife." Anicah curtsied perfunctorily.

"What brings the papists' dishclout here, all pranked up in gaudy attire to tempt the devil?"

Anicah glanced down at her threadbare chemise and bodice and skirt of rough butternut wool. "Me mistress sent me to fetch someone."

"Her wastrel muckworm of a brother, no doubt." Even though the goodwife's livelihood depended on wastrels, she had never developed an affection for them. She liked Giles least of all.

As always, upheaval ruled in her kitchen. It had once seemed a prosperous place to Anicah, the best she had ever known. Now it looked as squalid as the Brents' pig sty, and worse, inefficient.

Offal floated in the permanent swamp around the water butt. Pots and utensils lay wherever they were last used. Greasy soot covered everything. Baskets sat heaped on top of each other, making it laborious to retrieve whatever was in the bottom ones. Anicah could imagine Margaret Brent whirling in here like a hard March wind and clearing out the clutter.

Anicah looked around in the stubborn hope that she would see the small drawstring bag with her treasures, the one William Howkins had stolen. But he had fled Maryland and belike had taken it with him. She lifted her skirts and picked her way through the jumble toward the common room.

"See her prance and smirk like an old bawd at a christening."

"And do ye pine fer yer dear husband, goodwife?" Anicah called over her shoulder. "Run off to escape the bum-bailiff?"

"I have managed a public house with two husbands and none," Goody Howkins said bitterly.

Anicah's reception in the common room was more cordial.

"The Spaniard!" several shouted. "Bring us thy pert boobies that we may fondle them!"

"The very subject of our discourse," Robert Vaughan added. "A young lady."

"Young ladies are the most useless of God's creatures," grumbled John Lewger.

Giles pounded his empty pot on the table and the ale wench arrived looking harried and out of sorts.

"Tomorrow Captain Brent receives his life's fair fetter," Vaughan roared.

He tossed a large boiled egg to Giles who made a show of swallowing it whole. It was a heron's egg, a powerful aphrodisiac.

"Give us a song for the condemned man, Ani," Vaughan said.

Anicah was tempted. Most of St. Mary's elite was here—the chirurgeon, Squire Gerard; the Brents' neighbor, Squire Greene; Secretary Lewger, looking as though his breeches chafed him; and Cornwaleys's steward, Cuthbert Fenwick. The only one missing was Thomas Cornwaleys himself. Rather than face charges for releasing

Richard Ingle he had sailed for England on Ingle's ship. Fenwick and a few weeping household servants had bid him good-bye.

Anicah glanced around at the familiar room. Original Brown and his long-handled bird net occupied their place on the ale bench, Brown sitting erect and solemn. The wall behind his shoulder blades was shiny with the years of rubbing from his greasy leather jerkin.

"Just a short ditty, then." Anicah winked and jigged a few steps as she sang.

> *"When I was a young maid and wash'd me*
> *mother's dishes,*
> *I put me finger in me cunt and pulled*
> *out little fishes."*

They shouted for more, but she shook her head.

"I've come to fetch the squire." She took Giles by the arm.

"Arrested by the petticoat sergeant, Brent," Vaughan roared.

Vaughan helped Anicah heave Giles to his feet. She watched Giles warily. He had spewed on her before in this condition.

"One last health." Vaughan held high his pot of wine in Anicah's direction. "To the best cunt in Christendom."

Giles pulled himself erect, though he swayed some, and raised his own cup. "To *all* the cunts in Christendom!"

The Catholics had built their new church in the shape of a cross, gazing up at God from the mud and manure of the chapel field. It boasted casement windows of leaded quarrels and six massive box pews for the lords of manors. The pews' ends were lumpy with carvings of angels and Adam and Eve amid flowering vines, St. George and the dragon and a host of apes scampering into hell.

The Catholics were inordinately proud of it. And though Anicah appreciated the rest from labor that the popish ceremonies provided, it served no other purpose that she could see. Mistress Mary's explanation made the most sense to her. "We build houses for ourselves to live in," she said. "Ought not God's to be the finest of all?" Maybe, but Anicah would have provided God's house with a hearth to warm a body in winter and boil up a kettle of hominy at any time of year.

Today at cock's crow Margaret and Mary had supervised the decoration of the chapel with fragrant greens and early spring flowers. Even for a heretic such as Anicah the place was lovely. Father Copley, however, looked more like Death-in-a-cassock every day. His sallow skin draped loosely over the heights and sinks of his cheeks and jaw and nose, to give him a cadaverous aspect.

His funereal intonement of the wedding ceremony seemed fitting to Anicah. She sat on the bench with the rest of the Brents' maids, folded her arms across her chest and scowled. She may have mocked the foibles of her betters now and then for a laugh in the kitchen, but she didn't often presume to disapprove of them.

She disapproved of this wedding, though. Giles was so advanced in years he had begun instructing the barber to arrange his thin flaxen locks over the bare expanse where his hairline was creeping up on the crown of his head. To Anicah it was a certain sign that a man had lost not only his youth, but his good sense as well.

Only the closest family friends and their households had been invited to the ceremony—the Greenes, the Gerards, Edward Packer, and a few others. Even Robert Vaughan, looking uneasy amidst so much popery, fidgeted at the rear of the room.

Anicah glanced at the empty place on the bench next to Margaret Brent's reeve. She still expected to see Edward there, dressed in the breeches and linen shirt Mary had sewn for him, the worn velvet doublet that would no longer lace across Giles's taut little paunch, and the matchcoat of blue blanketing.

Mary Brent only smiled when people offered their condolences. "The death of the lad is a sorrowful thing," she explained patiently. "But he is not our Edward. One simply cannot kill an angel."

The loss of Edward wasn't why the Brents' wedding guests looked grim. Marrying a member of one's household was considered an appalling social misdemeanor. To marry an Indian was unheard of. The gentlefolk discussed Giles's petticoat-hold and his aspirations of acquiring a goodly amount of Piscataway soil. A main subject of speculation among the lower sort was whether Indians did the deed riding-St.-George, with the woman on top like the dragon on the intrepid hero.

Kitt looked dazed. Dressed in the bodice and petticoats Mary had sewn for her baptism, she faced Father Copley. When Giles moved to stand next to her, the top of her head barely cleared his elbow. Anicah found some satisfaction in the fact that Giles looked as though he were regretting his celebration of the night before.

Copley finished the rite and Giles gave his bride an avuncular peck on the forehead. When she turned around, Anicah saw the glitter of tears in her eyes. She saw the look Kitt sent toward the bench where Edward usually sat.

Next to Anicah, Bess snuffled loudly and wiped her nose on her sleeve. Bess cried with very little encouragement these days. She had also taken a vow of chastity. She swore she would serve the Brents until she joined her babe in heaven, if God vouchsafed to admit her, sinner that she was.

Anicah turned away from Bess and stared through the frozen ripples of the glass window. Beyond it the ruins of the old building where the Catholics had worshiped seemed to undulate, as though underwater. Planters had scavenged timbers, siding and shingles from it. Vines grew over the roofless remains. Had she and Martin really held each other there, under the governor's pew, so long ago?

Tears ran down Anicah's cheeks. She ached to have Martin by her side in sickness and in health, never to be parted from him. Her youth, her bright, giddy years of dancing on the green were falling away behind her. She was nineteen, almost middle-aged. When Martin did return, and she believed he would, they'd have little time left.

She filed out with the others into the shimmering spring air. She was so preoccupied she hardly heard the jests.

" 'Twere fitting you married on April Fools' Day, Giles."

Robert Vaughan clapped him on the back. "I would advise you to cut off your stones now, and so avoid the siring of any ninnies."

"At least I have wived, unlike some whom none will have." Giles grinned at him. Then he shouted to the crowd, much merrier now that the churching was done and the eating and dancing could begin. "All for the bride ale."

Margaret had delayed this wedding, insisting that she had to order special food and cloth and trimmings from Virginia. Anicah suspected she was stalling, hoping Leonard Calvert would arrive and put a stop to it. But if Margaret had misgivings about the marriage, they weren't evident in the feast she assembled.

All afternoon she patrolled, making sure the stews and pies, the porridges, puddings and breads arrived in the proper sequence and at the proper temperature, each correctly dressed, seasoned, cooked and served. In the side yard under the oak, a dozen table boards on trestles sagged under the weight of the meal. It looked as though all of the seven hundred or more souls in the province had showed up for the celebration.

Two servants wound the jacks of the spit while half a steer revolved between them. Grease splattered into the fire and clouds of smoke billowed up to thicken and extend the pungent blue twilight. The flames had turned the meat and the men at the spit as brown as caramelized sugar. Both were shiny with oil and blackened with soot.

Fires burned in shallow pits. Kettles dangled from tripods over some of them, and the carcasses of pigs and deer spanned others. Big skillets squatted on trivets among the coals. Widow Courtney, her sleeves rolled above her elbows and her skirts pinned up, basted the ducks and pigeons spitted together like lumpy brown beads.

Music and laughter drifted around the house from the front yard, but the common sort milled among the roasting corpses. Twilight had fallen by the time the revelers were adjusting the drawstrings on their petticoats and breeches to accommodate the meal. The dancing began in earnest. Giles's men careened another hogshead of beer from the brew house. People crowded around as though lowering the level inside were their duty and they were determined to do it with efficiency and dispatch.

Anicah skirted the festivities, avoiding the men who cajoled her to dance. She approached a small, solitary figure and stood next to her.

"The gentry has life firm by the baubles," Anicah said, "but I envy them not their marriage beds."

She saw the apprehension skim across Kitt's face. She knew what the thought was. No matter what Mistress Margaret said about this being a marriage in name only, what would Giles do after the door closed behind the last well-wisher?

"Stay here," Anicah said. "I'll be back in a pissing while with a present to cheer ye."

She ran to the buttery where she had hidden several bright glass beads she'd found while spading the corn hills. She pushed the door open, but a faint, rhythmic pealing like tiny glass bells stopped her. With her hand on the door frame she peered into the gloom. Everything seemed in order except the huge cupboard against the side wall. It vibrated, setting Margaret's good crystal goblets inside to jigging and clinking.

Anicah leaned out to look around it. She saw a pair of boots and two spindly calves slanted inward, toward the wall. Above them an angular pink arse appeared beyond the edge of the cupboard, then disappeared with a rhythm that grew faster and more energetic as Anicah watched. The heels were obscured by the collapsed velvet folds of Giles's new breeches.

His unseen partner, one of Squire Greene's hussies, no doubt, gave several small squeaks and a giggle. Anicah backed outside and filled the pail sitting next to the water butt by the door. She returned to the cupboard and swiveled sideways to give the water a wide trajectory. Then she let fly.

She was already outside and headed at a run for the anonymity of the crowd when she heard Giles's outraged shout.

Chapter 50

argaret's stubby little pinnace, its flanks shaggy with algae and eel grass, lay on its starboard side like a fallen bison. The curved oak keel formed the ridge of its backbone. The scabrous port hull bulged outward, then sloped away over Margaret's head. Smoke wreathed it, as though it were being roasted whole.

In a sense, the workers were roasting the pinnace, scorching its timbers and stakes to kill the teredo worms that infested it. The air was dense with the stench of hot pitch and the hempen oakum used to caulk the seams. From the other side of the boat came the steady rasp of iron across wood as four men scraped at the crust of barnacles. On the alert for treason, Margaret strained to hear their muffled conversation.

Leonard Calvert had returned two months ago, in September, with news of disaster at Marston Moor. Parliament's iron-clad troops under the sturdy Puritan, Oliver Cromwell, had won their first big victory over the royal forces there. Since hearing about it, Maryland's Protestants had become even bolder in their criticisms of King Charles and Lord Baltimore. The men of Kent were the boldest of all.

Margaret jabbed the iron poker into a plank and bared the honeycombed tunneling of worms. She tapped the damage with the rod and glared at Peter Knight who glumly followed her.

"It should have been heaved down in August, immediately

after worm season," she said, "Not in November when so many other chores require tending."

"Cap'n Brent ne'er gave the order." Knight obviously didn't care if the boat sank and carried a cargo of papists with it.

Margaret tried to detect the insolence in Knight's eyes, turbid as a pair of muddy puddles. Years of accumulated grime had turned his thick features as dark and leathery as one of the hog carcasses hanging in the smoke of the chimney place. Margaret thought, wryly, that such a coating could hide a lot of treachery.

She had not forgiven him for stealing her sheep, of course, but if she refused to hire everyone who pilfered from her, she would accomplish almost nothing at all here. The eastern shore sheltered honest men, but like Diogenes, she thought she would need a lamp and a lifetime to find them.

Margaret's own servants were stripping tobacco leaves and ramming them into casks. They were slaughtering hogs and mending fences, splitting firewood and pressing apples. And the pinnace had to be kept seaworthy. It was the link with St. Mary's.

"Mistress Margaret." Anicah curtsied and held up a basket containing breakfast.

Margaret crossed the hard-packed sand, black with pitch and bilge filth. Barnacles crunched underfoot as Anicah followed her to where Knight's men had carelessly stacked the pinnace's chests, bales, canvas buckets and ropes. Margaret upended a keg and sat down. Anicah wrestled a chest into position in front of her, draped a cloth over it and set the basket on it. Margaret laid her pistols next to the basket.

"Did'st thou break thy fast, Ani?"

"Nay, mistress. Bess only just slid the bread from the oven, and I hastened to fetch it to ye ere it grew cold."

Margaret split the bread, cheese and bacon and set half out for her. While Margaret ate she kept an eye on the workers. Things had gone missing after previous careenings.

"Did'st thou not spend time in Bridewell, Anicah?" Margaret had wondered, now and then, about Anicah's past.

"Aye, though't weren't for any crime but starving. Me aunt and me was put there after the grain riots."

"What was it like?"

"The smell of rope puts me in mind of it," Anicah said. "We beat hemp till our arms liked to've dropped from their sockets and our throats were furry as ferrets with the dust. To make oakum." She nodded toward the hairy pile of it by the boat.

"Bridewell is a dark and dampish place wi' the stone floor fer a pallet and the ashes of the cooking fires fer a coverlet. We slept nose to arse like hogs on a dung heap. Such quarreling and hubbub you can't imagine, mistress."

"No." Margaret loosed a small smile. "I cannot."

"We young ones begged from the upper windows, else we'd starve, though the turnkey took most o' what we mumped. We'd lower baskets and call to those below." Anicah cried out in such a piteous tone that the men looked up from their work. " 'Sweet ladies, kind sirs, bread and meat for the poor prisoners. For Christ Jesus's sake, bread and meat.' " She glanced up from the meal she would have considered sumptuous in those days. "Did ye ne'er pass one o' the king's inns and hear them, mistress?"

"No, I did not."

Fair lass, bonny and brown. Strains from an old song ran through Margaret's head when she looked at Anicah. *Eyes black and great as an ox's.* But an ox's eyes were docile and trusting, and Anicah's were none of that. The hoyden had grown into a lovely maiden, almost twenty now, calculated from the plague year in which she said her mother gave her life.

An unruly tumble of auburn locks framed her delicate face. She had a fierce, straight nose above full dark lips. Her breasts strained the laces of her bodice. She still possessed the wit and impudence of the urchin and pickpocket, despite Margaret's dogged instruction in etiquette, religion and decorum. But behind it hovered a melancholy that gave her dignity.

Margaret thought she would go mad with irritation at the men who importuned her to buy Anicah's term. Here and in St.

Mary's they skulked about the house like lust-struck hounds. They begged, they bargained, they fought with each other for love of her. Anicah referred to them as "those great lumping loobies." And she clung to the belief that her sturdy runaway yeoman would return to her.

"America is England's farthest prison," Margaret said. "Where the worst of the nation are sent to wear out our patience and our ropes."

"I shall not mind seeing John Dandy wear out a rope."

"The governor hath pardoned him," Margaret reminded her.

She was as angry as Anicah that the gunsmith would not hang for murdering Edward, but Leonard Calvert had reversed several of Giles's orders. The governor had arrived in a bad mood anyway, furious about Giles's embroilment with Ingle. Before Calvert sailed from Bristol, Ingle had started proceedings in London against the colonial government.

"But Dandy must serve the governor seven years as bondsman and so cannot sue in court," Anicah reasoned. "If Martin returns, Dandy could not prosecute him."

"Knowest thou where Martin is?" Margaret expected the wariness in Anicah's eyes. She was surprised when sadness replaced it.

"The one who could carry the message to him is dead."

"Edward?"

"Aye." Anicah sighed. "Martin's abided wi' the salvages these many years."

"And thinkest thou he lives there still?"

"I pray God he does. Goodman DaSousa would bring me word of him, till penury drove him into indenture with Mistress Lewger." She brightened. "Mayhap Father White could ask the Indians to tell Martin 'tis safe to return."

"I would not say it's safe. Stealth of self is a felony."

The irony was that besides having to bind himself to Leonard Calvert, Dandy had also been sentenced to serve as executioner. If Martin were to return and be found guilty, Dandy would tie the noose around his neck. The job was supposed to give Dandy an idea of what he could suffer for such crimes, but many thought he would enjoy it. Others speculated that the next man to commit a crime that merited hanging might well be the hangman himself.

Margaret saw Anicah staring and turned to look. Harry Angell had arrived in a canoe. He jumped ashore and conferred with Peter Knight. The other men dropped their tools and joined them.

"Something is afoot." Margaret stood up. "They've put their heads together like so many vultures after the same bit of carrion."

Harry climbed back in the canoe and Knight sauntered over to Margaret. He made an indifferent pass at his greasy forelock by way of salute. "Me and the lads must be going."

"What takes you away in such haste?"

"Angell sighted salvages. We must see to our families and stock."

"Knowest thou which Indians?"

"Salvages be all of the same." He turned on his heel and strode away. His men picked up their muskets, gun rests, powder horns and shot pouches and trailed after him.

Anicah had begun packing the basket as soon as she heard the word "salvages."

In April, members of the Powhatan tribe in Virginia had watched from shore while two ships loyal to Parliament attacked a Bristol flyboat. The Indians slaughtered five hundred Virginians three days later. Their eighty-year-old leader had noted the fact that the Englishmen were fighting each other. He took advantage of the turmoil to make another try at ridding his country of them all. He almost succeeded before he was shot by a soldier.

Margaret found Kent Fort Manor in an uproar. The maids knelt in the kitchen praying loudly. Mary methodically measured powder into the cylindrical wooden canisters that would hang on the bandoliers.

"Where's Captain Vaughan?" Margaret asked.

Mary smiled as though she were pouring one of her powdered simples into the paper funnel instead of a remedy for the affliction that was life. "He's inspecting the rear of the palisade for rotted palings."

Margaret charged out the back door. Vaughan had already ordered a fire built outside, and a kettle of lead hung over it. As he walked the palisade, thumping each post high and low with the side of an ax, he shouted instructions at the servants he had assigned to mold bullets.

"Rob, what sort of Indians are they?"

Vaughan threw her a puzzled look over his shoulder. "No sort of Indians, Margaret."

"Peter Knight said Angell saw Indians."

"Maggie, you should know that no matter how hot the fire, one cannot render the truth from two liars."

"Then wherefore all this?" Margaret waved her hand at the preparations.

"Billy Claiborne is on his way to take the Isle of Kent as he promised he would back in 'thirty-eight." He sent her his wild-eyed smile and nodded toward the tumbledown house, a storage shed now, that Claiborne had built in 1631. "I would imagine he has felt the lack of his roof and wishes to sleep under it again."

Crickets shrilled outside the palisade. By the light of a three-quarter moon Anicah could see the shadowy figures of Margaret's men standing watch at the holes cut in the palings. In the center of the compound the maids had gathered with the extra muskets and ammunition.

Anicah shivered with cold as she and Kitt stood with their heads together and stared through the loophole. In the distance the bare trees were black against a sky lit by the moon and a brilliant spangling of stars. Anicah had slung the pouches of balls and powder across her chest. Their weight and the clink of the lead made her feel capable and dangerous.

She fingered the squares of silk in her pocket. If she had needed proof that the situation was precarious, watching Margaret rip apart her best petticoat for gun patches provided it. With the pinnace bottom-up they were trapped here. They had no way to send for help, and the island's inhabitants were set to rise against them. Anicah was delighted at the whole prospect.

She propped the barrel of the spare pistol on the rim of the hole and pretended to aim it. "In me youth I dreamed of turning highwayman."

"You must load it for me, Ani, not fire it," Kitt said. "Do you remember how?"

"Aye, Kitt. Ye showed me less than an hour past."

Anicah knew she should have called Kitt Mistress Brent, but the child didn't behave like a squire's wife, and Anicah chose to ignore the fact that she was. Kitt and Giles had hardly shared a roof and certainly hadn't shared a bed since the wedding eight months ago. Margaret had made sure of that.

Margaret and Robert Vaughan approached on their rounds.

"Thinkst thou the murtherers will fire?" Margaret asked.

"If they do, they'll shower the enemy with rust." Vaughan chuckled. "The last time they were discharged, Claiborne's men were shooting them at me. More than six years ago. How time passes."

"Cap'n Vaughan," Kitt said, "how many men thinkst thou Claiborne brings with him?"

"Some say he plans to storm the island alone. Others claim he commands hundreds of recruits from Virginia."

"Bess says he's a monster," Anicah added. "With great slavering jaws and hands like hams that dangle to his knees."

"Nay." Vaughan laughed again. "He's a cultured man and a wit. You would like him, Margaret." Vaughan gestured to the vast landscape lying beyond the walls. "After all, those rogues out there have remained loyal to him all these years."

"They would follow any man who promised them ill-gotten gain." Margaret snorted. "And why would he choose now to attack?"

"A time of war is the best occasion for settling old scores."

"Aunt Margaret, hark ye, the crickets have ceased their singing," Kitt said.

Margaret and Vaughan looked through the hole. The wavery

light of a pine torch emerged from the trees. It was accompanied by the clink of metal and the harsh whispering that children and drunks make when trying to avoid getting caught at some trespass.

Margaret started loading her fowling piece with shot and Vaughan hurried to his own post.

"If you value your lives, come no farther." Vaughan picked up his crossbow. "Where's Claiborne?" he shouted.

"He's not landed yet. We would parley with ye, Vaughan."

"Parley till you wear the moss from your teeth, Knight."

By the light of the full moon Peter Knight stood just beyond the range of the muskets. "Ye must relish the stink of papisher cunt, Vaughan, since ye hide 'neath the pope's whores' petticoats."

Kitt stared open-mouthed as Margaret loaded her fowling piece with more than a prudent amount of powder. Anicah quickly handed her one of the silk patches in her pocket.

Margaret held it up, as though instructing them in sewing. "Less drag in the barrel." Then she rammed it home. "Silk is an advantage Knight and his hounds will not likely have," she muttered.

She blew on the match and pulled the trigger. The blast of the added powder knocked her back a step, but it was worth it. Knight's tall, narrow-brimmed hat flew off and he became a blur in the wan moonlight. He fell on his rump and scuttled belly up for cover, using elbows and heels for locomotion.

Margaret hurried to her own loophole, while Bess hustled after her, trying to load as she ran. Kitt took aim, shot and handed the empty pistol to Anicah for reloading.

Tongues of flame erupted from the alder thicket at the forest's border, and the Brents' people shot back. After the first volley the reports popped at random as Knight's men fumbled with powder and balls, picks, and matches in the dark. An acrid blue haze, dusted with moon gilt, settled over the combatants.

Kitt picked up her skirts and took off running for the back gate.

"Are ye mad?" Anicah called softly.

But Kitt had already slid back the bolt and dodged through the gate. Anicah watched through the loophole as she sprinted across the field. She had grown tall and gangly over the summer and her long brown legs devoured the distance. She snatched up Knight's hat and raced back with it.

A sudden clatter of musketry from the pines near the shore startled everyone. The high, warbling cry that accompanied it terrified them. It rose from the grove and flapped toward them, mutilation and death transmuted into a witching song that ruffled the hair on the back of Anicah's neck.

Peter Knight and his crew retreated in disorder. When the crack of broken branches and the last cry of "Wait fer me, ye poxy curs" faded, stillness descended.

Everyone rushed to the southeast wall and stared through the firing holes and between the warped palings. Two figures walked toward the fort. The taller one held high a staff with a white cloth fluttering from the end of it. Even in the ghostly light of moon and stars Anicah could see they wore leggings. Feathers formed a shadow fringe to one side of their heads.

"I would speak with Mistress Margaret." The taller one spoke in a west-country burr.

"Martin!" Anicah raced across the yard. "Martin!"

She put her shoulder under the end of the squared log that barred the front gate. She heaved the timber up and out of the iron cradle. It bumped across her back to hit the ground and bounce with a clatter. She hauled the massive double-planked door open a crack and squeezed through.

Martin dropped the tattered shirt he'd used for a flag. He swooped her up and hugged her to him. She twined her arms about his neck and kissed him hard on the mouth as he whirled her around.

"Martin." Tears streamed down her face. "Martin."

She sobbed and said his name and sobbed some more. Her tears smeared the red and ocher stripes on his cheeks. She stamped staccato kisses on his nose and eyes and chin, his forehead and brows and ears, as though her lips were her seal making him legally and officially and forever hers. He laughed and tried to catch her mouth with his own.

Holding her up easily with one arm, he gripped the back of her head so he could kiss her again where she ought to be kissed. The force of her longing made her dizzy, weightless. She felt as though she were spiraling into him head first, as though she were falling from a great height. His lips, his tongue, his teeth became indistinguishable from her own. She could not imagine being without the touch of him. A steady roaring sounded in her ears. The voices prating around her made no more sense than cattle lowing on the other side of a rushing river.

Martin gently untangled her and set her down, but she put her arms around his narrow waist and locked her fingers at the small of his back so no one could wrest him from her.

"If ye hang, Martin, I shall twist wi' ye."

"Edward," Margaret said, "we feared thou wert killed. We thank God that He hath spared thee."

Anicah looked sideways at Martin's companion. "Be ye a ghost, Edward?"

"Only if ghosts must piss." He gave her his usual look, so solemn it had to be a mask for laughter. He bowed to Kitt who was struck mute by joy. "Mistress Brent," he said to her. "I congratulate you on your marriage." He moved off into the darkness and soon they heard the splatter of a stream hitting the ground.

Martin put his left arm across Anicah's shoulder and touched the brim of his nonexistent cap with the other hand. "Mistress Margaret, our companions are waiting. We have canoes enough to carry you all to St. Mary's."

Robert Vaughan turned to the servants. "Each of you pack a small sack of belongings to take with you. And no more than that."

"We shall not abandon all to that rout of ruffians," Margaret said. "Half the tobacco is in cask and the other half in the sheds."

Vaughan led her out of hearing of the others. "Margaret, do you think me a wight of some common sense?"

"Of course, Robert."

"Then listen to me." He held her arm tightly, as though to hold her by force until he could convince her with reason. Her

arm stiffened under his fingers and the muscles of her jaw taut-
ened. She did not relish being handled like a recalcitrant servant.

"We cannot defend Kent Fort against a populace set on taking
it. If they wished, they could starve us out."

He stared into her gray eyes. They glinted like chips of flint in
the moon's light. Running away wasn't in her nature. Without a
word she wheeled and began giving her people instructions.

"What chance of Susquehannock or Powhatan raiders?" Robert
asked Edward and Martin.

Edward shrugged and his mouth twitched in his version of a
smile. "We'll go where they aren't."

"Are there many hostile Indians about?" Margaret appeared at
Robert's elbow.

"So many that should they eat us all, they would still be hungry," Edward said.

"If we men take turns paddling we can make the journey
without stopping," Martin added. "It will be safer, but the women
will have to sleep in the canoes as we travel."

Anicah opened her mouth to protest, then closed it. She had
anticipated other sleeping arrangements.

"Raphael, how good to see you." Mary Brent arrived and
smiled expectantly at Edward. He knew from experience what she
was waiting for, and he could not tease her as he did everyone else.

"I bring no message from God, mistress."

"Yourself is message enough." She ran her fingers over her
small Bible, as though she could read the verse from Exodus
through the cover and the intervening pages.

"Behold I will send my angel who shall go before thee and
keep thee in thy journey, and bring thee into the place that I
have prepared."

Her smile broadened, as though she were suggesting an out-
ing. "Shall we start then?"

Chapter 51

As Margaret watched Anicah and Bess clear the dishes after the meager breakfast, she tried not to dwell on the fact that the Nativity season of 1644 was the gloomiest she had ever experienced. Even the sun was off sulking somewhere, leaving a cold, gray world to regret its absence.

With the fate of Kent Fort Manor and its crops and livestock uncertain, Margaret had to scrimp on everything. Bleak despond hung over the household, with the exception of Anicah who was so happy to have her swain back she sang the day long.

Margaret was glad to have him too. One of her own men had stayed on Kent with Peter Knight's rabble. She intended to prosecute him at the next court session, though he was shiftless and duplicitous, and a small loss. Martin on the other hand, was honest, hardworking and as strong as two men. Margaret had pleaded with the governor for leniency, considering that Martin may have saved the lives of everyone in her household. Calvert had decided he should serve out his original term with Margaret, since John Dandy was now indentured himself.

Giles had spent December trying to press men to storm Kent Island. He was defeated in the effort by the rumors that had settled onto the town like a flock of noisy crows. Most concerned William Claiborne, and they had people alarmed and bearish. The gossips said Claiborne was inflaming the Indians to kill every Englishman who opposed him. They said he was recruiting more men on the eastern shore to raid St. Mary's and take the province.

"A mahn's coom." The newest maid wobbled in a curtsy and snuffled loudly. She was a whey-faced child from the lawless Scottish border. She was unburdened by any notions of proper behavior.

"Snot thy nose, Anna, but do it not on thy sleeve."

The maid used the hem of her petticoat, exposing her newly sprouted copper-colored muff in the process. Margaret thought of the hours she would have to spend teaching her. At times like these she resented training young women for the men who would marry them.

"Pray tell me if this man hath a name."

"Cap'n Varn, miztress."

"Where is he?"

"Outzide, miztress."

"Do not leave guests to shiver on the doorstep."

Blessed Mother, grant me patience, she thought.

Robert Vaughan swept his hat off in a deep bow and hung it and his cape on a peg. He stamped in front of the fire to shake the feeling back into his cold-numbed feet. "I pray God hath kept thee well, Margaret."

"Very well, considering the plague of controversy all around us." She gave him a look of suspicion. " 'Tis early for thee to be about, Robert."

"I have come to collect a debt."

"Which debt?"

"One incurred many years ago. I would ask the loan of your crystal goblets, a large pitcher of water and a pair of bowls."

"Now?"

"Aye. I will use them in the parlor and so avoid being tread upon by the inordinate bustle and stir of your establishment."

Margaret caught her lower lip between her teeth. She was fond of Robert. She admired his intellect, his wit, his vibrant baritone and his dancing, but he was not a delicate man.

"I shall handle them with far greater affection than Bess does eggshells." As usual, he knew what she was thinking.

Margaret smiled ruefully. Bess crushed the shell of every egg before discarding it so no witch could prick it with a needle to bring her mischief.

Margaret ordered the glasses brought, and Robert lined them up on the table set in the parlor fireplace. At noon she had corn pone and cheese, succotash and a venison collop sent in to him. He chased the maids away and fed the fire himself. Margaret spent the morning mixing salves and rolling out pills in the stillroom. In the afternoon she walked the fields with her steward, deciding what to plant and when and how.

When she was in the house she listened for the shatter of glass. She heard only the faintest of chimes, as though he were tapping the goblets with something metal. She wanted to stalk into the parlor and snatch them away from him. But a bargain was a bargain. She was annoyed that he took six years to collect on this one, though, and that he had chosen her crystalware as his traveling companions when he took leave of his senses.

"Lord, how I wished for thee those longsome years," Martin murmured. "I thought to have perished a thousand times over for want of thee."

He and Anicah had sneaked into the wart, the small storage shed built into the angle of the chimney and the house wall. They stood at the rear where the sloped roof was the highest, but if Martin had tried to stand up straight he would have brushed his head on the beams. He leaned over Anicah and pressed her against the warm plaster. Usually it was cold because the parlor was rarely used in the daytime, but today a fire snapped and roared just behind the rough surface.

Martin rubbed his cheek in Anicah's hair. "Thy tresses are fine as mink and a trap to ensnare my heart."

Anicah laid her head back to expose her throat. She arched her spine to press against him. Even though the muddy puddles on the floor had frozen she had raised her skirts above her waist.

She held his hand against the ridge that tilted into the valley between her thighs. Each rub and stir and pinch of his fingers sent
tremors of pleasure surging through her. He nipped the rim of her
ear and nuzzled her neck and shoulders.

With his other hand he unlaced her bodice and untied the
drawstring at the neckline of her chemise. He pulled the chemise
off her shoulders and kissed her breasts. He took one brown nub-
bin in his teeth and worried it. His beard tickled her, but she stifled a giggle and tried not to knock over the rakes and mattocks
leaning against the wall next to her elbow.

She reached through the slit in his breeches and caressed him.
She stroked him until his breath came in small quick pants and she
felt the spasms that released the warm flood. He groaned and collapsed against her. She smiled with the joy of his weight.

Their ardor had stirred up a great deal of dust, but they dared
not sneeze and be discovered by Vaughan in the parlor on the other
side of the wall. As they kissed in the darkness of the tiny shed, the
faint chime of crystal sounded every so often, like fairy bells.

Margaret had reminded them of the evils of bastardy, as
though Anicah hadn't seen them well enough in Bess. Margaret
said that lecturing Anicah about japery was as effective as pelting a
rock with peppercorns, but she was wrong.

Anicah and Martin stole moments wherever they could. They
lay in the hay rick with their arms hooped about each other. No
matter how cold the wind blew, they stoked passion into a wondrous heat under the stairs, in the stillroom, among the barrels in
the cider cellar and the skimming pans in the dairy shed. With
gentle, insistent caresses they learned to fold pleasure over on itself, doubling and redoubling it until it grew thick and intense.
But for all that, Martin was careful not to loose his mettle where it
would start a new life.

"AAAnicah!" Margaret's voice penetrated the walls.

Anicah wiped her hand on her petticoat and smoothed her
skirt over it. She kissed Martin quickly, cracked the door and
peeked out, then hurried off around the back of the house.

Margaret was standing in the yard, her hands on her hips.

"Ye called, mistress?" Anicah lifted her skirts deftly out of the mud as she dropped into a graceful and repentant curtsy.

"Fetch two dozen eggs from Mary Courtney Clocker."

"For a wassail bowl, mistress?"

"Aye." A smile softened the fine webbing of lines around Margaret's eyes and mouth. "To let the Nativity season slip by unmarked is to deliver a victory to the Puritan heretics."

Anicah took the basket and hurried down the path. St. Mary's was as quiet as if the inhabitants had been spirited away. The houses, the fences, the stumps, stubbled fields and skeletal trees were all clothed in grays and browns as dull as homespun.

She passed one of the first English huts. The eaves were at knee level because the single room had been dug into the ground, then roofed over. The dooryard was a rectangular hole, with logs laid into the slope to form stairs leading down. Shreds of canvas flapped from the rotted lintel. When a high wind blew away Original Brown's Yoacomico house, he had moved up in the world by moving down into it. He had carried his belongings here.

Anicah rounded the corner and saw Original sitting on a broken shingle beside his new manse. He had on the same wool breeches and shirt and leather jerkin he had worn, summer and winter, since she'd met him. He had wrapped his ancient bear hide around him, but moths and rats had long ago passed most of the fur through their digestive tracts.

"God keep ye, Sir Decrepit. Wherefore sit ye in the damps?"

Original gazed up at her with watery, red-rimmed eyes. He quaked too violently to speak. Anicah walked down the steps to peer into the black rectangle of the doorway. When she looked up she could see gray sky through the roof. The recent rains had made a pond of the place. Now it had frozen. She found the wooden flute among the cast-offs he had gleaned from midden heaps and called his estate.

"Come with me, then. Mistress Mary'll see to ye."

She put the flute in with the eggs and helped him to his feet. He hardly weighed as much as the basket. She imagined his bones had shrunk to mere withes now, with but a membrane of skin drawn over them, thin as one of Joan Parke's sheep-gut penis sheathes.

She sang and chattered to him all the way to Sisters' Freehold. She escorted him through the back door and sat him, bearskin and all, on a stool in front of the fire.

"He cannot stop in my kitchen." Bess regarded him balefully. "That pelt harbors more vermin than the rest of us put together."

"He can play fer the dancing." Anicah ladled hominy into a bowl and gave it to him. "Mistress Mary says we must be kind to everyone, else we turn away an angel in disguise."

While he scooped the samp onto his fingers, she went to confess to Mistress Mary that she had brought home more than eggs. She knew Mary would intercede with Margaret.

She found the gentry with Father White and Father Copley who were warming themselves by the fire in the great hall. Kitt stood staring into the flames. Her face was set in a neutral expression that meant she was displeased about something.

Giles paced angrily. "Kittamaquund himself told me he would follow the English precedents and name his daughter to succeed him."

Father White tried again to explain. "According to Piscataway custom, a daughter is no more entitled to the throne than a son. The line must follow the mother's or the sister's offspring. Only the *tayac*'s nephew or niece may inherit the title."

"It's barbarous." Giles stopped pacing to light his pipe and expel a great agitation of smoke. "Whoever heard of women determining succession?"

White shrugged. "The Piscataway are a sovereign people and may choose whomever pleases them."

"Only if their choice suits Governor Calvert." Giles hated being thwarted. He wanted to ask Leonard to pressure the Indians to accept his wife as their queen, but Leonard was furious about the marriage. It had taken all of Margaret's skill at diplomacy to smooth his feathers.

Anicah could see how inheriting a huge tract of land would

be useful, even if it were a dismal wilderness of stealthy beasts and massive trees too numerous to be anything but a hindrance. But she wondered what Kitt would do with the throne of the Piscataway. Kitt had made it clear that she would never again wear animal skins or live in a domed hut or till fields with a sharpened stick.

"Anicah," Margaret said. "Carry another pot of sack to Captain Vaughan in the parlor."

Anicah was crossing the narrow entry hall with the wine when she heard the music. She pushed open the door and looked in.

Robert Vaughan still sat in the fireplace. Margaret's goblets were arrayed in front of him, each filled with a different amount of water to sound a note of the scale. He moistened his blunt fingertips in the two bowls of water and circled them delicately over the goblets' rims. He teased music from them as Martin drew ecstasy from Anicah with his caresses. The soft, plangent notes with their faintly harsh overtones sent shivers down her back and arms.

Anicah set the wine jar on the sideboard and hurried back to the great hall. She put a finger to her lips and beckoned. Margaret looked annoyed. Matters of great moment were being discussed, but she came anyway, and Mary followed.

The three of them stood silent, stunned by the song. The melody skipped from glass to glass, as though released by some magic emanating from the ends of Vaughan's fingers. The notes rose to meet and mingle in a sonorous pulsing air. They created an ache of undefinable longing—for beauty, for love, for peace, for the unknowable and unattainable. The melody was a bruise on the soul, delicate crimson and lavender and blue, and sore to the touch.

The rest of the household formed a semicircle at Vaughan's back. "Barbara Allen" was a beautiful ballad and everyone knew dozens of verses, but no one sang. They breathed quietly rather than shatter the crystalline sphere of music surrounding them.

Martin put an arm around Anicah's waist, and she laid her head on his chest. She closed her eyes, so that sight would not interfere with the melting of the music into her pores and the feel of Martin and the beat of his heart against her temples.

No one spoke until the last ripple of the last note died away. Then Margaret applauded and the rest joined in. Margaret and Mary each kissed Vaughan on the cheek.

"Second only to peace," Margaret said, "this is the greatest Nativity gift I could have asked for."

"I would have the return of Kent Fort Manor," Giles grumbled. "And a good price for sot weed in London."

"Play another tune," Kitt cried.

But Vaughan had already begun pouring the water from the goblets back into the pitcher. "Nay, child," he said. "Fleeting memories are often the most indelible."

He raised his arms over his head and grinned. He was the Lord of Misrule, from the disheveled nest of his cinnamon-colored hair to his mismatched hose. "And now for the dance!"

Bess's feet jigged under her wide skirts as she mixed the cider, spices and eggs for the wassail. In the great hall Mary thumped the tabor. Margaret played the virginal, though she had had to evict the mice from the nest of down and moss they had made in it. The rest of the household formed double lines encircling the room.

Anicah had not succeeded in coaxing Original Brown to play. At first he said his mouth was too dry to blow the music out the far end of his flute, but even after several bowls of cider his hands still trembled too badly to hold the instrument. Instead he sat smoking a pipe on a stool in the chimney corner, his back against the hot plaster. Mary had draped her best wool shawl over the finials of his shoulders. Original held his bony knees to the flames as though trying to ignite them. Translucent shards of a smile flickered about the corners of his mouth.

Everyone was merry on cider and sack and the good wishes of the season, but Anicah was the merriest. Robert Vaughan watched her whirl down the alley formed by the dancers. Her wild curls flew out around her, a dark cloud that flowed and bounced with the rhythm of her feet. Vaughan wished he had bought her term and married her. She had turned out to be more amenable to domestication than he would have guessed. But, of course, there was her very large, very strong swain.

Kitt, long and awkward and bony, danced with Edward. She was smiling for the first time Vaughan could remember.

Vaughan turned to Giles. "Think you of separating from your bride, Giles, now that you know how she stands with her people?"

Giles looked doleful. "Divorce is out of the question."

"Surely the pope would grant you an annulment." Vaughan gave a vague wave of the hand, spilling pipe embers onto his old doublet. "Or however it's done."

Giles shook his head and Vaughan knew why he rejected the idea. To separate from Kitt would prove what everyone already knew, that he had married her for purely venal reasons.

"I must admit that the pope's ban on divorce has a certain shrewdness," Vaughan said. "It holds a husband and wife's noses together like two spaniels on a single chain. In time they will cease their contention and learn to go together because they may not go apart."

"A song," Margaret called when the dancing ended. "Serve us a song, Captain Vaughan."

Vaughan thought a moment. "This one was composed by the Virgin Queen's favorite, in honor of all those so foolish as to love." He cleared his throat.

> *"Now what is love, I pray thee tell?*
> *It is that fountain and that well*
> *Where pleasure and repentance dwell.*
> *It is perhaps that sanctus bell*
> *That tolls us into heav'n or hell."*

While he sang, Anicah took Original another bowl of cider. He moved his lips, and she bent down to hear what he was saying.

"Come spring . . ." he murmured, "I'll catch the red bird."

Then he eased back against the wall. Anicah shook his arm

gently, but he was as limp as a stocking mop. She glanced around for help and Mary appeared at her side.

The two of them looked at each other and, without saying a word, they decided to let his shade enjoy the rest of the evening. Anicah laid a penny, her only one, under his tongue to pay the ferryman. Mary kissed him on the forehead, then slipped into the tiny room recently built for her altar. Anicah was comforted to know that she and her angel were praying for his soul there.

She also knew that as Brown's body cooled his herd of six-legged livestock would seek warmer quarters, so she sauntered to the other side of the room. No one else had noticed Original's departure, and Vaughan finished Sir Walter Raleigh's song with a flourish that showered the unwary with sack and tobacco ashes.

> *"Yet what is love, I pray thee sain?*
> *It is a sunshine mixed with rain.*
> *It is a toothache or like pain.*
> *It is a game where none doth gain,*
> *And this is love, as I hear sain."*

Chapter 52

Dressed in a wool nightgown, Giles crouched between the hogshead of shoddy wool jerkins and the one containing iron frying pans, scabbed with rust after their long voyage. The dampness of the 'tweendecks planks, chilled by the ice on the river outside, seeped into his bare soles and traveled up his knotted calves and bowed thighs. Above him axes battered at the door of the master's great cabin. He congratulated himself that when Ingle's hail and cannon shots had awakened them at dawn, he had had the wit to hide somewhere less obvious than the master's cabin.

The Dutch merchant ship, *Speagle*, had arrived yesterday at the mouth of St. Inigoes Creek. Giles had gone aboard to see what was for sale and to arrange for the shipment of the tobacco crop from his town lands at St. Mary's. Ever the cordial guest, he had drunk sack and proposed toasts to the king until the morning hours with the Dutch master and the loyal English merchant who had chartered the ship.

He rued it now. His stomach was in rebellion, but he knew that the noise of his spewing would carry a considerable distance. He concentrated on calming it and on dislodging the bolts of pain screwed into his temples.

The pounding of the axes stopped and Giles heard muted shouting. Richard Ingle's rout must have found the unfortunate merchant. Boots thudded overhead and clattered down the ladder to the 'tweendecks.

Someone cut the ropes holding the cargo. Stacks of crates toppled with a series of crashes that sent more agony stabbing into Giles's skull. A hogshead trundled the length of the hold, narrowly missing him and fetching up with a crash at the end of the compartment. Giles heard the shriek of iron bars on wet wood, and barrel lids rattling onto the floor.

" 'Od's knuckle bones." The man's Derby accent was hardly intelligible to Giles. " 'ats and 'osiery as wunna do us owermuch good, nay, naught a'tall."

"Ter biter said as we'd 'ave wine."

The squeals of water-swollen cask lids being prized off grew louder. Giles could not bear to think of being discovered crouched and quivering like a hare in a hole. He drew in a deep breath, gagged on the hold's aroma, and stood as best he could under the low ceiling. He tried to look imperious, but the effect was hampered by the nightgown and the obsequious stoop.

Ingle's men swarmed around him, committing outrage on their native tongue with every sentence. They were scarred and greasy and bearded, an abandoned lot if ever Giles had seen one. They did not know him personally, but his long, curly hair identified his political loyalties immediately.

" 'Tis a cavalier haunt," one observed.

"Nay, niver. 'Twould be a royalist rat, grown great on bilge shit."

"I would speak with your master." Giles felt the draft when someone lifted the rear of his nightrail with a sword.

"An' 'is scraggy arse white as a peeled parsnip." The man prodded Giles's nether cheek with the point of the sword.

"Take me to Master Ingle."

Their laughter had an unpleasant rasp to it, but they led him up the ladder, across the ship and through the splinters of the great cabin's door. Ingle sat with his boots propped on the chart table.

"Brent." Ingle didn't rise or bow. "Still with thy shoulder locks, I see. The mark of the whore of Babylon."

"That would be the only whore thou dost mislike." Giles looked coolly down his nose at him.

Ingle's smile expressed a year of simmering rancor about to be avenged. He turned to the leader of the crewmen. "Take a party ashore. Pretend they're from the Dutchman's crew. That will allay suspicion until they can lighter aboard the tobacco and beaver on the priests' landing. *Speagle* will transport the spoils to England." He grinned at Giles. "The papists' own goods will help pay for the holy fight against them."

Some of the hogshead sitting on St. Inigoes landing belonged to Giles, but he said nothing. Bringing it to Ingle's attention would only add to the man's satisfaction.

He kept silent when he was shackled and shoved into the wherry that took him to Ingle's ship, the *Reformation*. One of Ingle's men pushed him into the roundhouse and flung a pair of woollen hose and breeches and a rough shirt in after him. He slammed the heavy door and bolted it. The cabin's narrow window had been boarded shut, and Giles slammed his bare toe on a corner in the darkness.

"Death and the devil!" he muttered.

"I say, is that you, Brent?"

"Fenwick?" Giles blinked, adjusting his eyes to the gloom. Thomas Cornwaleys's steward, Cuthbert Fenwick, sat on the plank shelf that served as a bed.

"Hast thou tobacco and pipe?" Fenwick asked.

"I have little more than I was born with."

Giles swore again under his breath as he struggled to pull on the hose. He rarely had to dress himself and he wasn't skilled at it. With no points or garters to hold the stockings up, they sagged about his knees and ankles.

He sat next to Fenwick. "I wouldn't have expected to see you here, Cuthbert, what with Cornwaleys hand in glove with Ingle."

"Ingle's a treacherous dog." Fenwick brooded a bit. "He took me prisoner, then summoned me to the great cabin for a bowl of sack. We became rather merry, I laughing at his jests, to make some advantage of our mutual friendship with Cornwaleys. I asked that he allow me to go ashore." Fenwick sighed. "He said I could land if I signed a warrant authorizing him to take temporary possession of Cornwaleys's pinnace, his house, his arms and all his goods."

"And you refused, of course."

"He promised that nothing would be damaged and no one wronged. He promised to look after his friend Cornwaleys's property and swore he was as good as his word. He ordered two men to ferry me ashore, but as soon as I delivered the warrant to my wife, they seized me and brought me back." Fenwick's voice broke. "Ingle's rabble has garrisoned the manor. I fear that the villains he left there will harm my wife."

Giles put a hand on Fenwick's shoulder. "He said no one would be wronged."

"He said a great many things." Now Fenwick was weeping openly. "And all of them lies."

The two men sat elbow to elbow in the gloom and thought about the consequences of such a letter of authority in Richard Ingle's hands.

Just after breakfast Margaret sat in the kitchen watching Robert Vaughan lay waste to the venison and marrow pudding left from supper. She jumped when Anicah and Kitt came flying through the door. She was edgier than she had thought.

"Aunt," Kitt shouted, "Squire Giles's pinnace approaches."

"How many times must I tell thee not to run and shout like a common wench." But Margaret was relieved. At last something was happening. The night and day of waiting had worn on her nerves.

"Is Squire Brent aboard?" Margaret waited for Anicah to fetch her cloak from its peg.

"We could see no plumes nor colors among their duds. All dull as dust and ashes," Kitt said.

Margaret collected her pistols, picked up her pouch of lead balls and patches and her powder horns and went outside. She and Vaughan walked to the top of the path that meandered down the face of the bluff. Maybe Ingle had thought better of his rash behavior and was delivering Giles, but only he and a pack of his men rowed ashore. Ingle wore a high-crowned black felt hat, black breeches buckled at the knees, and a loose wool coat the color and texture of wet oak bark.

"I see he's forsaken his former plummage for the drab duds of a proper roundhead," Vaughan said.

"Made of wool from the black sheep of the flock," Margaret muttered.

"I have not seen such a dissolute collection of rogues since I drank too much in the stews as a lad and spent a night in the clink for brawling."

Margaret glanced at Vaughan. He smiled sheepishly, but with a trace of nostalgia for better times.

"Giles took the account books when he sailed to confer with the merchant aboard *Speagle*," Margaret said.

Vaughan grunted. The books listed Giles Brent's assets, and Margaret's too. Not the sort of thing one would want a man like Ingle to have possession of.

"Mistress Margaret." Ingle looked up at her from the narrow beach. "I pray God hath kept thee well, and all thy household likewise."

She stared down into his tobacco-stained grin, a wide curve like a brass scythe below shrewd blue eyes that weren't smiling. She leveled the pistol at him.

"Where is my brother?"

"Enjoying good health and the hospitality of my ship."

"Release him and return our vessel to us."

"I would speak with thee concerning the warrant I hold from Cuthbert Fenwick, attorney for Squire Thomas Cornwaleys." He waved a folded sheet of velum.

"Speak then."

"And what of thy hospitality, famous among ships' masters from America to Gravesend?" He started up the hill, his men fanning out behind him.

"Speak there or go thy way."

From the corner of her eye she saw Martin approaching. He carried the old Dutch matchlock he'd acquired from a Seneca he'd cudgeled during their raid on Uncle's hunting camp. It was loaded and primed. Both ends of the match sputtered in the serpentine.

Ingle continued to advance anyway. He only stopped when the mastiff raced to the edge of the bluff and snarled an assurance of painful bodily harm. The rumbling growl roused deep-planted, nameless terror even in Margaret.

"I shall state my business plainly, collect what's due, and leave thee to thy affairs." Ingle shrugged, as though surprised at such an unfriendly greeting. "According to Cornwaleys's accounts Squire Brent owes his estate six thousand weight of tobacco, neat in cask, and eight barrels of corn, or the equivalent in pounds sterling. I have here Fenwick's signature permitting me to collect Cornwaleys's debts."

He waved his men forward. The mastiff's huge front paws slid halfway over the edge of the bluff. He punctuated his growls with vast, tearing barks. The men retreated.

The snaphaunce was heavy to begin with and growing heavier by the heartbeat. Margaret thought it would pull her arms from their sockets soon. She wanted to shoot Ingle and be done with him, but she knew if she fired, Giles's life could be forfeit.

"Get thee gone, Master Ingle. Return when thou hast my brother with thee."

Ingle swept his hat in a bow and backed downhill. "Captain Brent will return to England to stand trial for piracy and assault committed a year ago against my person, a loyal defender of the king and Parliament."

The king and Parliament! Margaret was speechless with outrage. The knave was claiming, like the mutinous members of Parliament themselves, to speak in the king's name. She focused all her will on keeping the snaphaunce from wavering until the men had climbed into the lighter and pushed away from shore. Then the pistol dropped like a stone to her side.

"The rogue thinks to make war with straw men and ink." She shook her head at Ingle's chicanery. "With God's help we shall best him."

Chapter 53

M argaret eased sideways through her front gate, past a bawling heifer. Robert Vaughan and his two spaniels had to dodge and weave to keep up with her as she strode into the chaos of her own creating. The yard teemed with her men and Giles's bringing in everything useful, edible or valuable from Giles's farm and the outbuildings of Sisters' Freehold.

"Joseph," she called to a beefy redhead struggling under a hundred-pound bag of grain. "Stack all the meal sacks in the southeast corner of the great hall." She turned to Vaughan. "Thank God we dug the well deeper last spring. And I had reinforced doors and heavy locks hung on the cider and root cellars."

"Ingle's men have taken St. Inigoes Fort." Vaughan shouted to be heard over the squawking chickens, the penned pigs and cows and the mastiff who was leaping in tight circles and barking madly. "You must take your people and flee to Virginia, Maggie."

Startled by the suggestion, Margaret stared at him. "And leave my brother in Ingle's clutches, abandon my holdings to that rascal rout? I think not."

Vaughan followed her into the narrow passageway that had been the entry hall.

"Besides, we have everything in hand here," Margaret waved at the goods stacked along the entry's walls.

"You cannot stand off Ingle's army as well as every disaffected bully in the province." But looking into the parlor and great hall, Vaughan thought that perhaps she could.

Hog carcasses hung in all the chimneys. Barrels of Indian corn and beans and apples lined the walls. Strings of dried pumpkin and more corn dangled from the rafters. In the kitchen Anicah and Bess were casting bullets. The hiss of heated lead hitting water issued from the cloud of steam that rolled around them.

"I've hidden Leonard for the time being," Vaughan said. "But I must get him to safety in Virginia." He was upset about leaving Margaret and Mary. "The court records. Government papers. Baltimore's seal. Ingle must not have them."

"You'll transport Father Copley too, won't you?"

"He refuses to leave."

Both Vaughan and Margaret knew what Copley's fate might be if Ingle took him to England. Most of the priests had found sanctuary among the Catholic gentry of the west country, but half a dozen had been captured, thrown into freezing, rat-infested cells, then publicly displayed and hanged.

"I'm asking you once more to come with us, Maggie. Governor Berkeley will shelter you."

"We're in the Holy Mother's care here." Margaret made the sign of the cross, and for once Vaughan didn't grimace and wave it away. "May she and her legions watch over thee, Rob. Thou'rt the best friend—"

Her voice faltered. Her eyes stung. He had always stood unperturbed between her and whatever dangers might threaten. What if she never saw him again?

She rummaged in a chest. "I had intended these for thee as an Epiphany gift, but only just finished them." She held out a pair of knitted wool hose, thick and warm and matching.

He smiled and tucked them inside his old leather doublet.

"Captain Vaughan." Mary emerged from the parlor. "Raphael tells me thou art sailing for Virginia."

"Paddling, more like, Mistress Mary." He smiled. "I would ask you gentle ladies to care for my hounds while I'm gone."

"Of course," Margaret said.

Mary put a small lead token in Vaughan's hand. " 'Tis dedicated to Mary," she said softly. " 'Twill keep thee safe and all those in thy care."

When he left the two spaniels set up such a howl Margaret had to lock them in the stillroom.

Margaret didn't know why she came awake suddenly. She lay in darkness as absolute as the bottom of a cold, covered well. Snores scuffled in the great hall where Giles's servants slept on the rush-covered floor. A predatory wind snarled around the corners of the house and rattled the windows. In the fireplace an unburned log gave a loud crack where the sap had frozen and expanded. A branch fell onto the peak of the roof and rolled down the steep slope like an animal skittering to safety.

Wolves howled. Over the years Margaret had learned to recognize the individual voices among them. She and Mary had given them the names of the Apostles.

She heard no hissed whispers of attackers, no crunch of boots, no chime of pewter powder horns or muted clatter of muskets carelessly carried. When for an instant the wolves stilled Margaret realized that she couldn't hear Mary's slow, deep breathing either.

"Art thou awake, Mary?"

"Aye, Maggie." When Mary sat up she let in a wash of icy air. "Something is amiss."

"A great deal is amiss, sister." Exhausted by the toil and uncertainty of the past few days, Margaret leaned back onto the bolster and closed her eyes.

When Mary got up Margaret didn't go with her. Mary almost never slept through the night without the necessity of relieving herself in the bog bucket.

It was the season to set the tobacco seeds in the beds. Margaret knew she would have to rouse the household soon and chivvy them into their day's labors. But she let herself float toward the silent black ocean of sleep, felt it close in around her.

"Sister!" Mary's voice woke her with a start.

She pulled back the curtain and saw Mary standing with a pine-splinter torch in the doorway. Her pale, thin face looked spectral in the flicker of light and shadow.

"The chapel is burning."

By the time Margaret had pulled on her shoes, lit a torch, grabbed her pistols and thrown on her cloak, Mary was gone.

Margaret called for Martin to come with her. She ordered her steward to bolt the gate behind her and to let in no strangers or Protestants. She and Martin reached the path in time to see the errant light of Mary's torch wink out at the first bend. A pale gold ribbon, a false and frightening dawn, lay along the tops of the trees in the direction of St. Mary's.

Margaret waved Martin forward. "Go after her."

Martin hesitated. "Here is the link then." He gave her the pine knot and sped away.

Margaret picked up her skirts with one hand and, holding the torch aloft with the other, ran after him. The air felt like ice tearing her lungs and chest. In the wavery light the gnarled trees, the angled worm fences and the jagged stumps and corn stubble looked as though they had been writhing in place and had stopped just as she came in sight of them. Everything inanimate seemed to hold its breath. She could almost believe in Bess's pantheon of creatures of the dark—sprites and elves, witches and fauns and the nightmare that settled on sleepers and suffocated them with her weight.

Over the harsh rasp of her own panting Margaret heard the crackle of the fire even before she rounded the last turn. It lit the surrounding green and Copley's house. The roof blazed. Banners of flame streamed upward from the openings where the glass panes had been.

Two men ran past her, one clutching silver candlesticks, another the sanctus bell. Others had laid their plunder onto the priests' vestments, heavy with gold and scarlet embroidery. They gathered up the edges and carried them away on their backs like wool sellers bound for market. They were stealing the silver chalices and crucifixes, the aspergillum and patens, fine linen cloths, the ancient gospeler bound in silver and leather, sacred items that generations of the faithful had preserved at great peril.

Half a dozen men struggled to hold onto Martin. Margaret didn't stop to argue with them. The notices tacked to the door of the church were curling like spiders from the heat. Mary was heading straight for them.

"Mary!" Margaret knew her sister couldn't hear her over the roar of the fire, but she shouted anyway.

Mary wrapped the hem of her cloak around her hand as though to grab the hot handle of a kettle and she pushed the door open with it. She disappeared into a billow of smoke.

A looter staggered into Margaret's path and she shoved him so hard he tumbled end for end. The chasuble he was using as a sack flew open, scattering books from Copley's library. Men who'd come too late for plunder began heaving them into the conflagration. They capered in front of it, intoxicated by the consuming power they had unleased.

Margaret pulled her hood over her face and put her shoulder to the door. The roaring of the fire filled her skull. She could feel the heat through the heavy wool of her cloak, but when she tried to enter something caught hold of the back of it and dragged her away. She turned and struck out and hit Thomas Copley in the face.

"Mary's inside," she screamed at him.

"Dear Mother of God." He crossed himself.

Margaret turned and saw Mary emerge as the roof collapsed with a crash behind her. Her hood had fallen onto her shoulders and her hair glowed in a fiery halo around her face. Margaret threw her cloak over Mary's head and hugged her close, smothering the flames and smelling the stench of burning hair. Copley led Mary to where they could feel the fire's heat on their faces and February's chill at their backs.

Margaret touched the fragile threads that had been Mary's side locks and they crumbled in her fingers. The flames had singed off her eyebrows, giving her a startled look. Otherwise her face was remarkably untouched.

She held out the statue of the Virgin Mary. "God did not grant that I find the blessed piece of the True Cross." She winced when Margaret gently pulled the hood over her burned scalp.

"There's the priest. Seize him." The men let go of Martin and surrounded Copley.

Martin lunged at them, but one of them held a knife to Copley's throat.

"The Lord is my shield, Martin," Copley said.

They tied the priest's wrists and fastened the long end of the rope around his neck.

"Where are you taking him?" Margaret stood with her arm encircling Mary's waist.

"To the gallows, to dance for the crime o' treason."

Margaret loaded and primed her pistol. She set it at half-cock, hurried after Copley's captor and put it to his head. "Do not think to harm him in any way."

"Harm me and me men will turn ye off, mistress."

"But I will kill thee first."

"I'm only following orders," he grumbled.

"I would speak to thy master."

She followed him, her pistol ready, while Martin stalked after her, menacing anyone who came near them. They left the burning chapel and turned onto the main path through the center of St. Mary's. In spite of the uproar the houses remained shuttered and noncommittal. Richard Ingle had taken the town without a shot fired.

When the little party reached the landing the sky had paled to the color of cold ashes. In the east it glowed with the promise of a new day. A cold mist rose from the water around the lighter that carried them to Ingle's ship.

Copley was taken to the roundhouse and Margaret and Mary

were ushered into Ingle's cabin. Margaret didn't waste time on amenities.

"How darest thou pillage the house of God!"

"We are justified in taking property from popish malignants to relieve the distressed Protestants they would starve and root out." Ingle was unrepentant. "I give you Exodus, chapter twelve, verse thirty-six. 'And the Lord gave unto the children of Israel favor and they spoiled the Egyptians.' "

"Egyptians!" Margaret was stunned by his effrontery.

" 'Thou shalt not abhor an Egyptian,' " Mary recited. " 'Because thou wast a stranger in his land.' Deuteronomy twenty-three, verse seven."

Margaret chuckled, in spite of herself. Anyone who sought to use biblical quotations in a joust of wits with Mary was bound to lose. Ingle seemed to realize it too and he took another tack.

"If you would but swear the oath of allegiance to Parliament," he said, "no one will touch anything of yours, nor offer you any insult."

The women stared so long at him, Margaret with her unwavering gray eyes, Mary with her serenely fey blue ones, that he fidgeted and turned away on the pretext of lighting his pipe. Everyone knew Catholics could not and would not take such an oath.

Outside, geese honked as they left in a thunder of wings to forage on the wild celery and eel grass of the marshes. From the distance came the crowing of a tardy rooster. Everything seemed so normal, so peaceful, that Margaret dared hope the fire had been a dream. All of this, even Ingle, was wrapped in a mist of illusion. She shook her head slightly to dispel it.

"What will you do with Thomas Copley?"

"Take him to England to stand trial with the other traitors." There was no mistaking that he included Giles in the category.

"We would speak with our brother."

"Thou must leave thy doglegs here, then." He nodded at Margaret's old fish-tail pistols. "We would not have thee smuggle them to him for his escape."

Margaret pulled back Mary's hood, exposing her bare, burned scalp. "Mayhap my poor sister hath hidden a weapon in her tresses." Her icy stare never wavered.

Ingle rose abruptly. "Come with me, then." He followed her out with an odd look on his face, as though he realized that had Margaret Brent been a man, his investment of St. Mary's would not have been so easy.

Chapter 54

Some might remark on Martin's partiality to Indians, but no one was fool enough to make an issue of it. He was the largest man in the province, and the strongest. He was equally adept with cudgel, bow and firelock. The simple country yeoman was gone, replaced by someone outside the usual order and therefore undefinable. He moved with a wolf's grace and he spoke only when spoken to. Men read danger in his silences and in his eyes, the blue of midnight moonlight and shadows, and did not cross him.

Anicah ladled hominy into the wooden bowl and put it on the worktable in front of him. The raw March wind had deepened the pink of his cheeks to crimson and tousled his black hair, shot with sun-burnished copper. For these few moments she and Martin were alone in the kitchen and she could pretend it was her own hearth, intimate and sheltering. She brushed the stray locks off his forehead so she could see his dark azure eyes. The misery in them made her want to weep.

She tried again to console him. "God will care for Father White, Martin."

"The shackles had rubbed the skin from his wrists and ankles, Ani. Their weight seemed enough to snap the bones." He looked up at her, his eyes full of despair and bafflement that injustice should have such free rein in the world. "Ingle sailed all the way to Portobacco to take that frail old man prisoner and fetter him like a felon."

In Bridewell Ani had heard stories of priests accused of treason and condemned to be drawn and gutted in front of a cheering mob. She put her arms around Martin as he sat at the table. She pressed his head to her chest and ran her fingers through his curls as though comforting a hurt child.

"Martin, I know naught of religion, but I wonder of what use is faith if 'tis ne'er tested?"

He wrapped an arm around her hips. "I only wonder that I could be so fortunate to have you." When he spoke she could feel his lips moving against her breast.

"Martin!" Margaret's voice called from the great hall.

He stood up. "The mistress has finished packing Squire Giles's things for the voyage."

Anicah held onto him as though to keep him from going. "I perish with worry whene'er ye're not in me sight."

"The mastiff will go with us."

"A pack of mastiffs'll do ye no good if Ingle decides to arrest ye and carry ye to England, ye being a Catholic now too."

In the great hall Margaret closed and latched the lid of Giles's old leather chest. Bess knelt to tie the wooden pattens onto the soles of Margaret's leather shoes. Martin shouldered the chest. The maids followed him and the mistresses to the door to bid them good-bye.

Margaret reminded them one more time, "Let no one enter the gate who's not of the family."

Then she pulled the hood of her cloak over her head and led Mary and Kitt into the mud left by the spring rains. Anicah followed to bar the gate after them. As Kitt passed through it she threw Anicah a complex look—sad, defiant, hopeful. Hopeful of what? Anicah wondered. That Giles never return?

Anicah watched them disappear over the edge of the bluff, headed for the landing where the old pink threatened to founder at any moment. It hadn't been worth Ingle's while to levy it, which was what he called his plundering. Aside from the boats, he hadn't managed to acquire any of the Brents' goods, though he had cajoled and threatened.

When the sun had slid halfway to the horizon, Bess began fling-ing herself about the kitchen in the final throes of supper prepara-tions. Anicah went out into the gray chill to fetch the two buckets of lye so it wouldn't freeze overnight. She was almost to the back door when she heard the new Scottish maid, Anna, at the gate, and then a man's voice. From across the yard she could see a gray-and-brown-clad crowd through the cracks in the palings.

"Ingle intends to transport yer mistresses as popish malignants," one of them said. "Mistress Margaret bid me fetch her biggest trunk to take with her."

A roaring filled Anicah's ears. They were taking Martin from her.

"I mus'na," the maid said.

"Make haste, ye silly wench."

Harwood, Anicah thought, 'tis Robin Harwood. "No, Anna!" she shouted. She was too late.

The bar dropped with a clatter and a score of men splashed through the gate. Anicah ran into the kitchen, scattering the chick-ens pecking at the offal in the straw. She tipped back the lid of the cider barrel and poured a bucket of lye into it. It fizzed and hissed something wonderful.

"Have you gone daft?" Bess stared at her.

"Robin Harwood and his merry band." Anicah could hear the rumble of boots on the porch. She ran into the entryway. "Help me, Bess."

They put their shoulders to one of the hogsheads there and heaved. It toppled, cascading 300 pounds of dried beans the length of the floor.

As Anicah ran to the back door for the pig stave she could hear swearing and the thud of bodies hitting oak planks. When she re-turned, Bess was already using the broom to sweep a path through the beans and to thwack the men who still littered the entry hall. The last to come in carried Anna, screaming, over his shoulder. He aimed her flailing feet for the great hall and the comfort of the pallets there. Anicah walloped him behind the knees with the staff, and he sprawled facedown with Anna on top of him. Anna regained her feet first and fled upstairs, bolting the door behind her.

From the great hall came the sound of crashing and tearing, but the parlor was where Margaret and Mary kept their most cherished things. Anicah walked into a blizzard of linens there. Men rifled the chests and sideboards. They threw the crystal goblets against the chimney for the pleasure of hearing them smash. Robin Harwood was tossing petticoats, jewelry and chairs, mirrors, bolsters, Mary's silver thimble, fire irons, tablecloths and stockings onto the bed.

He had the frenzied stare of someone who'd drunk more than enough spirits already. He waved an arm to include all of Sisters' Freehold. "Soon this will be mine, wench, and you too."

"When frogs grow feathers." Anicah brandished the cudgel.

"Ye're no papist, Sparrow. Come wi' us."

"I know good folk from bad, ye mutton-headed coistrel."

When he made a clumsy grab for her she rammed two fingers as far up his nostrils as they would go. He yelped and his eyes watered with the pain. He slammed his fist into her eye and sent her flying backward over a bench.

"Now I'll have ye, me bold punk," he shouted.

Anicah scrambled to her feet and dodged his leap for her.

"Touch me, and Martin Kirk will make a garter o' yer guts."

"And if I kill him first?"

"He will rise from the grave and do ye, Robin Harwood."

Anicah's chest heaved. Her hair stood out around her face like a wreath of glossy eels. Her numious brown eyes glinted wild as a Fury's. She looked privy to dark secrets, and fully capable of summoning a dead lover to wreak her vengeance.

"To the devil with ye, ye lousy punk." But Harwood kept the bed between himself and her cudgel.

Someone was hammering in the kitchen, nailing the lid on the cider barrel so he could roll it away. Others pounded at the door of the wine cellar.

A man called from the doorway. "The papists' catch-farts are coming."

With pewter spoons jangling in their pockets, and sheets, petticoats and tablecloths draped around their necks, they hurried outside to stand off the fifteen men returning from the planting. Harwood and seven others lifted the big bedstead, but it left a spoor of plunder as they maneuvered it through the doors.

Blankets and bed curtains dragged in the mud while the four-poster careened and wobbled across the yard on its sixteen mobile if poorly coordinated legs. A man rolled the cider barrel after them while the turnspit dog clung, growling, to his stocking. Three more drove the mare and the bawling milk cows out of the pen and herded them toward the gate.

Kitt will be furious, Anicah thought. Her cows milled among them.

The Brents' servants stared at the procession and Anicah stood on the porch to bid the looters farewell.

"Yer guts will burn for this." She pointed at them, tense and ominous as a figure of doom. "Ye will feel the fires of hell inside ye." She shouted an incantation she had learned from Dina in the ordinary. *"Hocus pocus tontus talontus vade celeriter jubeo."*

She didn't know what it meant, or even if it meant anything. But Harwood's burdened army hurried off as fast as it could, anxious to get out of range of the spell. Anicah's eyes narrowed and her mouth tightened in an evil smile. She wished she could be present when they broached the barrel of lye-laced cider.

Margaret knew something was amiss when she saw the linen sheet lying in the mud of the yard. Martin had sensed trouble before that. He rushed inside, shouting Anicah's name. Margaret entered slowly, afraid of what she would find. Dusk had thickened almost into night and rushlights flickered in the dark rooms.

"We tried to stop 'em, mistress." Bess, on her hands and knees, looked up at her from the entry hall floor.

She was filling a basket with muddy beans and pouring them back into the barrel. The rest of Margaret's people picked through the wreckage. Her steward avoided her eyes. Glass crunched underfoot as Margaret walked into the parlor.

She turned to Anicah. "Did they hurt anyone?"

"Nay, mistress." Anicah's eye was red and swollen, but she almost danced in place, she was still so excited by the fight. "They are but cowardly curs."

Martin stood behind her, looking as though he wanted to feel her all over, to make sure she was unharmed.

"Where are James and Jack?"

"Joined the rabble, I expect." With her apron hem Anicah dusted the broken glass off Margaret's books and stacked them on the shelf. "Harwood promised them land and a king's riches if they absconded."

"There are such creatures in the world . . ." Margaret said, more to herself than anyone else, "who can only thrive on disorder."

"They shall find their bowels much disordered, mistress. I sophisticated the cider with lye."

"Dear God." Mary put a hand to her mouth in horror. "I must take them a palliative."

"Ye'll not find them, mistress. I expect they've gone to ground in their dens on the far creeks and swamps."

"She's right, sister. The cider will dilute the caustic soda. It should cause them no more than great discomfort."

"Whacking great discomfort." Anicah grinned.

"Leave this." Margaret waved a weary hand at the shambles. "And come with me."

With cressets of blazing fat-pine splinters for light, the household walked to the top of the bluff. Tiers of sails glowed pale in the moonlight as Richard Ingle's ship moved slowly downriver. As she stared at it Margaret chided herself for indulging in the hope that when Ingle sailed to England he would take strife with him. Instead he had left it behind to wreak havoc on decent folk.

She thought of Anicah, fierce and loyal and quivering like a hound about to be loosed on a bear. Adversity could bring out the noble as well as the base, even in a Bristol thief. Even in Giles. She remembered Giles as she had seen him little more than two hours ago. His manacles had weighed cold and hard on her neck as he clasped her in an affectionate embrace.

"Fret not on my account, dear sisters." He had been obstinately cheerful. "Master Ingle hath restored my deck of cards. Before we land I shall have won back all he stole from me."

Margaret blinked back the tears so she could see the ship sail past. She motioned for her men to hold high the torches as beacons for Giles, White, and Copley.

She prayed that Thomas Copley was right.

"God's work will continue," he had said, by way of good-bye. "Rage men and the devil never so much."

Chapter 55

The sky shimmered like a delftware bowl overhead. Sunshine gilded the river. And the liberating warmth of April enticed six more of the Brents' men to vanish. There was no court nor sheriff nor magistrate to whom Margaret could appeal for her servants' return, but at least no one had attacked Sisters' Freehold again.

Anicah and Kitt worked side by side with the maids in the field. Their wool skirts were pinned up, their arms and legs bare. Kerchiefs kept their hair out of their eyes and straw hats shaded their faces.

With her wooden hoe Anicah scraped the dirt around her leg up to her knee. She eased her foot out and flattened the top of the hill. She poked three holes in the dirt, put a kernel of corn in each and covered them up. She tried not to think of the thousands of times she must do it again.

"The curs *would* run away at hilling time." Kitt bitterly resented the servants' desertion.

"I'd rather hill corn than tobacco." Anicah arched her back to relieve the ache and squinted at the ground yet to be worked. The field seemed to stretch to the horizon.

Margaret had calculated the acreage needed to provide enough corn to feed the family. Twelve hundred hills to the acre for the large gourd-seed corn, fifteen hundred for the early ripening roasting ears, twenty-seven hundred for tobacco. Fortunately, Mistress Margaret planned to grow only enough tobacco to supply Bess and her own servants who swore it had bewitched them and they could not live without it.

Raveling chevrons of ducks—clacking blue wings and pintails with their flutelike calls—flew overhead.

Kitt looked up at them. "I would that I could fly."

"Ye'd fly to find yer love, would ye?"

They exchanged looks. Edward hadn't visited since the Nativity celebration almost four months ago. He had danced with Kitt then, but he had treated her with exaggerated courtesy, bowing and calling her by her married title of Mistress Brent. Anicah had detected anger mixed with the mockery in his eyes. Kitt must have seen it too.

To cheer Kitt, Anicah started the first verse of a popular catch, swinging her hoe in time to the beat. Kitt joined in, then Bess and Anna and Mim each in turn to give it the five-part harmony. If the maids recognized the irony in the lyrics they kept it to themselves.

> "*A smug, rich fantastic old Fumbler was known,*
> *That wedded a brisk, juicy girl of the town:*
> *Her face like an angel, fair, plump and a maid,*
> *Her lute well in tune too, could he have but played.*"

As Anicah hacked at the roots and stones that day and in the weeks that followed, she began to sense the link between the buff-colored dirt and her own stomach. No ships arrived from England with stores. None came from Virginia. The pestilence that was war had placed Maryland in quarantine, isolated from the rest of the world.

Anicah realized that if she intended to eat corn bread and hominy, she would have to plant the main ingredient. And she would have to weed it and rehill it and weed it and rehill it a third time, then weed it again and again until it was tall enough to shade out the unwanted growth.

The two months following April she named Dismay and Swoon, for the labor they required. But for the first time she understood why Martin craved his own land and the ability to feed himself no matter how fortune might plot against him. She became fiercely protective of the acres she had planted.

She took a personal dislike to the crows that stole the seeds from the hills. She watched the sky for rain clouds. She stepped carefully around the pumpkin vines that darted between the corn hills, and looked for pods on the bean plants that climbed up the stalks. She measured the height of the corn against her own body.

In June when the corn was almost waist high, the rains stopped.

Anicah crouched ankle deep in slime. She flapped her hands at the mosquitoes swarming around her and looked dubiously at the mound of sticks and leaves.

"What did ye say it was?"

"Musquash." Kitt rested her hands on her knees and looked over Anicah's shoulder. "The English call it muskrat."

"What if it's at home?"

"From what you've said of Bristol rats, this would be no bigger." Kitt poked her with her staff. "Art thou afeared?"

"Never." Anicah whacked at the mound with her own cudgel. She laid bare the vacant nest inside and the cache of roots the rodent had collected. She and Kitt loaded them into their sack and slogged away.

Their search for food had taken them to the marshy bottom of one of the deep ravines with its spring emptying into the St. George's River. Anicah and Kitt toiled through the laurels and sassafras saplings that spilled down the steep sides. Martin waited for them at the top with the sack of hickory nuts he'd gathered The three of them made their way to the St. Inigoes path, so overgrown it was almost impossible to find.

They walked through Squire Greene's weed-grown fields and collapsed fences. Vines grew up the sides of his house and over the charred timbers of the tobacco sheds. Margaret's fields had been burned by marauders. The dried black mud still gave off the odor of charcoal and tobacco smoke. Except for the birds and the autumn crickets, the country lay silent. Even with her hand enfolded in Martin's the emptiness made Anicah uneasy and forlorn.

"God keep you." Edward appeared at the top of the path to the Brents' landing and angled to meet them. He wore a breech-clout and moccasins and carried the gutted carcass of a sow across his bare shoulders.

"Anansine." Martin shook Edward's hand and thumped him on the back. "Welcome, brother."

Edward lowered the sow to the ground and nudged her shapely rump with his moccasin. "I take her from Harwoot's zhed." he said. "I'm thinking maybe zhe's his zweetheart and her brats rezemble him." He grinned. "Pork here, venizon in canoe." He grinned. "Not zo many English now. Plenty deer."

He bowed to Kitt. Over the years, his Piscataway accent had taken on traces of England's west country, but it was quite good when it came to the amenities. "Miztress Brent, I pray you are in good health."

Kitt paled, then flushed and curtsied perfunctorily. "As if my health mattered a fig to thee."

Lynx-eyed Kitt stood almost as tall as Edward now. Her bulky skirts couldn't hide the fact that the uncoordinated discord of knees and hips and elbows had rounded into lithe curves. The tightly laced bodice cinched her small waist even narrower and made admiration of her full, round breasts unavoidable. The line of her slender neck flowed up to a strong chin and out to a wide jaw capped by narrow, fluted ears.

Without shifting his gaze from hers, Edward walked close enough to reach out and pull her to him, but his hands stayed at his sides. The two of them stood silent and motionless until Anicah prodded him in the bare flank with her staff.

"Kiss her, ye rufous oaf," she said.

He leaned forward and brushed his lips tentatively against Kitt's. He had obviously never kissed before. Kitt lifted her chin and closed her eyes. He kissed her again, longer this time, as though tasting a new and exotic fruit.

Anicah and Martin went on down the path without them.

Margaret closed Leonard Calvert's front door behind her. As she and the mastiff crossed the muddy yard she shook her head sadly. This was March 1646, and the first time she had been inside Leonard's house in the year since Richard Ingle had left. Maryland's damp airs and the attentions of the riffraff had scoured the dwelling of its grace and gentility.

The water-stained plaster was falling off in chunks, exposing the laths underneath. Plunderers had stripped away the wainscoting and floorboards. The renegades had stabled cattle in the great hall and stored rusted armor, kegs of powder and piles of fist-sized cannon balls in the parlor. Armaments, she supposed, gathered by the rebel Protestants to stand off Calvert's expected invasion.

She had come here to assess the interim governor, Edward Hill. Hill was a ponderous Virginia Protestant given to nervous tics and unctuous promises to restore order. He claimed to possess a letter authorizing him to act on Calvert's behalf. When Margaret had asked to see it, he mumbled that the document was packed away at the moment. He had been equally evasive about what success Calvert was having raising an army to retake the colony.

Margaret picked her way through the brambles and broken hogsheads littering the vine-covered ruin that had been St. Mary's. Except for Hill and his cronies no one lived in town, nor had reason to visit. Fear and suspicion pervaded the outlying farms. Like an arid, choking dust it piled up in corners, slid under doors and blew through chinks in walls and shutters. It itched under people's clothes, tainted their food and crept into their dreams.

Protestants and Catholics alike had knocked at Margaret's gate in the last year. They came not knowing whom else to trust in the web of suspicion, recriminations, and petty theft. They asked her to arbitrate their quarrels or present their grievances to Edward Hill's makeshift government. Some simply begged for food or curatives. But as the honest folk gave up the struggle and left for Virginia, the requests dwindled.

At least, Margaret thought, little remains to be stolen, and few to steal it.

She wore a pair of men's boots, more practical than wooden pattens for covering distances. With her holstered pistols and leather bandolier under her frayed cloak, she and the mastiff went wherever her two and his four arthritic knees would take them. Mary said Margaret and the gaunt, gray-muzzled dog were coming to resemble each other more every year. Margaret didn't mind the comparison.

She shifted the heavy basket on her arm. It held cheeses from Mary Lawne Courtney Clocker's first batch of the year. The farmstead of Mary Lawne's second husband looked prosperous compared to those around it. They had cows at any rate, and few of the honest sort, Catholic or Protestant, had managed to keep theirs.

Margaret pondered the rude truth that it wasn't only cream that rose to the top.

She was grateful to round the last curve of the overgrown path and see the twin plaster pyramids of her chimneys and the steep, shingled roof amid the bare branches of the oak. Her world had shrunk to emcompass the palisade and dairy yard and garden, the fields and orchards and wood lot. But it was a snug world and it was hers, and she would harvest her crops this year if she had to shoot every rogue in the province first.

Chapter 56

The newer servants occupied benches farthest from the hearth fire. In the dim light they passed two clay pipes among them and squinted at the shoes they were mending or the oaken hoe blades they were whittling. Margaret's steward and Bess, Anicah and Edward had stools close to the blaze. Martin sat on the floor between Anicah's knees.

Margaret and Mary, dressed in their wool nightgowns, played piquet with Kitt inside the fireplace itself. The turnspit, mastiff, whippet and Robert Vaughan's two spaniels slept draped over their feet. Kitt had chosen a chair where she could see Edward. While her aunts studied their cards Kitt flashed him heated looks that had nothing to do with the oak logs blazing nearby.

"Join us in a hand, Anicah," Margaret said.

"Nay, mistress. Ye be too crafty for me by half."

"Dost thou imply that I cheat?"

"Aye, and skillfully too."

"Extravagant praise from one with considerable talent in the cheating rig herself." Margaret arched her heavy brows and gave Anicah a look of mock severity.

Anicah wouldn't have moved even for a seat closer to the fire. She pressed her groin against Martin's back and scissored her legs around his sides. He rested his arms along the tops of her thighs while she ran her fingers through the soft darkness of his hair, searching for lice. The expression on his face was beyond beatific.

"In games of chance 'tis Raphael one must beware of," Kitt said.

"Raphael does not divulge to me the hands of others." Mary glanced mischievously over her cards.

"I have been to heaven," Anicah said suddenly. "And seen angels."

"Ye never." Bess looked up from the stocking she was knitting from the ravelings of worn-out ones.

"How did it appear to thee, Ani?" Mary asked.

"It was lit bright as the sun, mistress. Candles everywhere. Real tapers of the whitest tallow." She rested her elbows on Martin's shoulders and crossed her forearms to encircle his neck. She laid her cheek in his hair, taking pleasure in the way it tickled her mouth and marveling that heaven could be in this very spot as surely as anywhere. "Trumpets sounded an air so beautiful that only angels could have made it. God and His host and all the littlest cherubs hovered overhead in duds of colored light."

Bess snorted, but Anicah didn't notice. She was back in Bristol's church of St. Mary Redcliffe where she had wandered to keep from freezing one February night ten years ago. The nave had shone with a thousand candles in a celebration of Candlemas that was defiant even there, even for Anglicans. Puritans condemned such displays as bribes to God and were doing their best to outlaw them.

Anicah had been staring up at the holy family and angels and apostles radiant in the pure, translucent colors of the glass windows, when the beadle chased her out into the snow and the night.

"Who does not find heaven here on earth," Mary murmured, "will seek it in vain above."

They all jumped when a voice shouted at the gate outside.

"Halloa the house. Are you dead or snoozing?"

The spaniels scrambled to their feet, raced to the door and clawed at it. The mastiff and turnspit barked wildly.

"I'll see to it." Martin took his musket and his cudgel and let himself out.

Anicah felt the lack of his warmth against her and a hint of how cold her life would be without him.

When the door swung open again Robert Vaughan stood on the threshold. "God keep you all."

The spaniels wriggled and whined and leaped around his legs. The mastiff almost knocked him over in his attempts to lick his face.

"Captain Vaughan!" Margaret hurried over to kiss him on the cheek, hook an arm through the crook of his elbow and lead him to the fire. The maids rallied to bring him cider, tobacco and the last of the thin fish chowder that had been supper.

"What news from Virginia, Rob? Hath Leonard gathered men to subdue that . . . that . . ." Margaret gestured toward the dark forest outside, unable to find words acidic enough to describe the scoundrels Richard Ingle had so easily subverted.

"Calvert can only promise payment, and the Virginians harbor little love for us, Margaret."

"We've dealt with them square and above the board."

"Our men refused to go to their aid against the Indians a few years ago. They ask why they should help us now. And they are Protestants."

"Governor Berkeley and the colony's men of influence are royalists."

"Aye. And they're fearful they'll be attacked as we have been. Besides, they're still much reduced by the Powhatans' incursions."

"And how go events in England?" Margaret asked. "We've had no word."

"Cromwell's forces are prevailing. The Puritans have outlawed the Church of England." Vaughan gave her a sad, wry look. "Now I'm as much an outcast as you."

"Rob, I'm so sorry." Tears welled up in Margaret's eyes.

Vaughan stared into the fire. "What news here, Margaret?"

"The knaves have conspired to impose upon us as governor an overinflated bladder named Captain Edward Hill."

"Ah yes, the hog in armor. I've met him."

"He has formed a band of brigands he calls the Assembly of Protestants." In spite of the bad news Margaret smiled fondly at her rumpled, wild-eyed friend. "And did a maid detain thee so long in Virginia?"

He looked wounded by the suggestion. "I had to seek employment to keep my backbone separated from my ribs. And I paddled up every pest-infested backwater recruiting men for Leonard, with little success."

"And no wench?"

" 'Twas one, a demure and virtuous maid who swore she must have marriage or no market. But her belly swoll up with a seed I ne'er planted." He grew even more glum. "And I sailed to Kent, Margaret."

"Didst thou find it deserted?"

"The rabble has despoiled your manor." Vaughan's foot tapped an angry tattoo on the hearthstone. "Harry Angell and his *mobile vulgus* attacked me at home. They burned my tobacco. They stole everything. . . ." The old grin returned. "Which may have improved the usual disorder of my house." Vaughan looked around the familiar room. "But you have weathered the storm."

"There's naught left but chaff and the scumber of rats." Margaret glanced at the empty baskets stacked along the walls and the bare iron hooks hanging from the bar in the chimney. When Bess had shaken the last cornmeal dust from the mill sacks the women had converted them to shirts and chemises.

"Thank God for Edward." Margaret pulled her shawl closer to cover her dishabille. "Without him and the baptized Indians, we should all have starved."

Mary smiled at Edward. "We thank God thrice daily for the angels He hath sent us."

Vaughan glanced at Kitt, assessing her triumphant entry into womanhood and the fact that she had become a tempter of the first order. Speaking of angels, he thought, here's one could rouse the very devil in a man.

He began to envy Giles. If the poor beggar wasn't drawn and

quartered for the edification of London's dregs, he had a pleasant surprise awaiting him here.

All morning Anicah paced from the far edge of the fields to the bluff where she stared downriver. But no sails appeared, nor oars, nor even a canoe with word of Martin. She strode past the Brents' makeshift smithy, through the apple orchard and across the fallow field, made barren by successive tobacco plantings.

She reached the collapsed worm fence dividing Sisters' Freehold from the western corner of Squire Greene's fields. Beyond it the winter forest rose forbidding as a palisade. Anicah tucked her cudgel under her arm and stuck her numb hands into her armpits. She leaned into the wind from St. Inigoes and strained to hear the muffled whump of cannons.

" 'Od's ballocks." She whirled and ran, following the fence line to where Edward was repairing it. Nearby Kitt stood watching him.

"Edward, come with me," Anicah called.

"Where would we go?"

"To St. Inigoes, of course."

"Nay." In spite of the cold he had hung his shirt over the fence. When he raised the ax the muscles of his shoulders and back rippled like waves in honey. His old woollen breeches hung low on his slender hips.

Kitt wore one of Giles's waistcoats and cast-off capes. In their English clothes they both reminded Anicah of a gentleman's panther she once had seen at the theater. The jewel-studded collar and leash the animal had worn could only have been for show. They could never have held him if he had cared to bolt.

Edward's English had improved in the last few months working on Sisters' Freehold. "We salvages kill each other for revenge. . . ." The ax bit into the wood. He braced the log with his foot and wrenched the blade free. "We kill for women, for food, even on occasion for sport, but we never kill a man for his religion."

"Shall ye not fight for the king then?" Anicah asked.

"He's not my king." Bitterness tainted his voice. She'd never heard it there before. "But for Martin and Captain Vaughan, I would not care if they all slaughtered each other." He took pity on her. "Martin will be well. He has a strong guardian spirit to watch over him."

"An angel, ye mean."

"Call it what you will."

"Now that Governor Calvert has returned," Kitt said, "and is distracting the rebels at St. Inigoes, Edward and I are going to recover my cows. He says he saw them in Robin Harwood's close."

"Ye could sue him for the return of them." As soon as Anicah said it, her eyes widened in astonishment that she would suggest going voluntarily to court.

"Rackon now his lor'ship has coom back," Edward said, "there zhall be more outcry in court than an Irish hubbub."

Anicah knew he was right. Highborn and low would be charging each other with thievery, assault, kidnapping, treason, libel, debt, stealth-of-self, impiety, impropriety, cozenage, and mopery. The legal tangles could take years to sort out.

"Good luck to ye, then."

"And to thee, Ani," Kitt said. "Thou'lt find thy Martin well at the end of the day."

Anicah trotted back the way she came but she didn't stop at Squire Greene's weed-choked field. Praying that all the wolves and panthers and bears were asleep or absent, she plunged into the forest. She had gone hardly a hundred feet when she looked around and could not see the cleared ground behind her. She pushed aside thorny vines looking for the resin-scabbed hatchet scars that marked the path. Occasionally the raked gashes of a bear's claws obliterated the blazes, establishing just who was really sovereign of this neck of the woods.

When Anicah heard men's voices she almost turned and ran, but she held her cudgel ready and waited. They approached single file, hulking and ominous in the shadows.

"What mought we 'ave 'ere?" The leader stopped and the

others gathered around him. They smelled like a shipload of rancid apples and badly tanned hides. She didn't recognize any of them and assumed they must be Calvert's Virginia mercenaries.

"I'm looking for Martin Kirk." She tried to peer past them.

"Make way, lads." The speaker was out of sight toward the rear of the column, but Anicah recognized his voice.

"Cap'n Vaughan!" She pushed through the soldiers as they continued on their way. "Where's Martin?"

"Here, Ani." Like the others, Martin's face was black with burned powder and his eyes red from the smoke.

He carried Leonard Calvert on his back, but Calvert slid down at the sight of Anicah. Martin supported him as the governor limped toward her.

Anicah curtsied. "Are ye wounded, yer lordship?"

"I sprained my ankle during the charge." Calvert seemed to feel obliged to explain why they were returning on foot. "We were to have sailed triumphantly back in the pinnace, but a stray cannonball from the fort struck her at the waterline."

"And is that yer army from Virginia?" Anicah took a firm grip on Martin's free arm and leaned around him to talk to Calvert.

"Yes."

"Shaggy as hedge pigs, aren't they?"

"Yes." Leonard laughed softly.

"Was it frightful, Martin, being in battle?"

He looked chagrined and disappointed and happy. "Aye. But the rebels went hotfoot into the forest. We found the fort empty."

"Those Virginia ninnies let them escape," Vaughan grumbled.

"Thank God no blood was spilled," Leonard said.

"And thanks to Martin Kirk," Vaughan added. "His screeching like a tribe of wild Indians scattered them."

Leonard turned to Anicah. "Are thy mistresses at home?"

"Aye."

"Good. I would sit with them on the sunny bank of their parlor fire and sip the brandy Governor Berkeley sent them."

Chapter 57

Leonard Calvert adjusted his spectacles and stared at the paper for what seemed to Anicah an eternity. She felt uneasy, in fact, that he was doing this at all. Every member of the Brents' household was wasting precious time here while chores waited at home. Besides that, a score or more people waited outside in a cold mist for an audience with Calvert. This was March of 1647. Leonard and his men had taken St. Inigoes Fort only three months ago, and he had a thousand more important matters tugging at his coattail.

For all the twenty-two years of Anicah's life, the attention of authority had boded only ill. However, Leonard Calvert esquire, lieutenant general, admiral, chief captain, and commander of land and sea of the province of Maryland, looked quite fatherly. He pushed his spectacles to the lower promontory of his patrician nose so he could gaze at her over the top of them.

"Martin Kirk and Anicah Sparrow, what is your intent touching marriage between you?"

Martin squeezed Anicah's hand harder, as if someone might try to wrench her from him even now. "She is my wife and I will ne'er forsake her." He said it in a loud, clear voice.

He looked so handsome in his freedom dues of new broadcloth breeches and waistcoat, white linen shirt and stockings and shoes, Anicah thought her heart would burst with love for him.

"Join your right hands," Leonard said, "and say the words of the marriage contract, Martin. Then loose your hands, join them again, and Anicah repeat the oath."

"I, Martin, take thee, Anicah, to my wedded wife to have and to hold for better, or worse, till death do us part; and thereto I plight thee my troth."

Anicah sucked in a deep breath and blurted the words in a rush, fearful that she would forget them. She nervously twisted the folds of her own new apron. In spite of the scarcity of every necessity Margaret had sent to Virginia for Martin's clothes and for the coarse woollen skirt and laced bodice, the apron, linen smock, stockings and two linen caps she owed Anicah at the end of her indenture. Anicah felt rich beyond any expectation.

"You are now wed." Leonard looked as happy as anyone had seen him since he returned from Virginia. "The greatest gift God doth vouchsafe us is a companion to share our joys and sorrows. May He bless your union with children to be raised in His glory." He turned to Anicah who was admiring Martin from the corner of her eye. "Goodwife Kirk . . ."

She jumped when she realized he was talking to her. Good-wife Kirk. It sounded so respectable and so odd.

"Aye, your lordship."

"Remember that thy desire shall be thy husband and he shall rule over thee."

"Aye."

Robert Vaughan laughed out loud at the thought of anyone ruling over Anicah Sparrow Kirk. He thought about the sly spark in her sleepy, dark eyes and the sensual energy packed into her sturdy, long-legged frame. Her hair today was soft and clean and fell in dark chestnut curls down her back.

Vaughan wished he'd been there to see the bath Margaret had insisted on giving Anicah for this occasion. The maids said they'd never heard such howling as when they submerged her in water and lathered her with soap. They swore they would easier have bathed a tub full of Bristol alley cats.

"Give her a buss on the neb, you thrice fortunate young hound," Vaughan shouted.

The color on Martin's cheeks spread down into the collar of his new shirt. Anicah looped her arms around his neck and pressed the length of her body against his. She kissed him until Bess observed that the two of them would run out of breath and perish, then take up everyone's time with a funeral on the heels of the wedding. When they finally separated, Margaret, Mary and Kitt kissed both the bride and groom. Even Leonard gave Anicah a peck.

"Huzzah!" Robert kissed the bride and every other woman who didn't get out of the way in time.

"Congratulations, my children." Margaret tried not to think of the tobacco waiting to be planted in the seed beds.

She was the only one in the province to have harvested a large crop the previous fall, and she had slept little until the last of the tobacco was pressed into casks and safely stowed in the first ship to arrive in two years. Now the labor must begin all over again.

People were turning to go when Anicah remembered her gifts. "I pray you, wait." She took the cloth packet out of the pouch hanging from her waist and unwrapped it. She smoothed the crumpled scraps of sacking cut into the shape of her own hand. She went around the room, giving two to each guest. "We have not marriage gloves to gift ye, but Mistress Mary helped me fashion these. When Martin and I have made our fortunes, we shall bring ye real ones, of the finest kid leather, soft as a babe's bum." Anicah kissed each person as she handed out the substitutes.

Everyone accepted them graciously. Then they put on their cloaks, retiring deep into their hoods to avoid the rain, and went outside. Leonard wistfully watched them go.

Margaret turned in the doorway. "You will dine with us tonight, won't you, Leonard? We have but rude store to garnish our table boards, but we'll shake a leg and shout out a verse or two in celebration of the wedding."

Leonard nodded, and Margaret hurried after the others. They all splashed toward home, complaining of the cold mist that formed a fuzz on their hoods and the shoulders of their brown wool cloaks. Robert sang at the top of his lungs.

"I had a love and she was chaste,
Alack the more's the pity,
But know you how my love was chaste,
She was chased right through the city."

When they turned right at the ordinary, Anicah pulled Martin left to the ancient mulberry near the blackened timbers of the chapel.

"Read it again, Martin."

The rain had dripped through the weathered board that served as a miniature roof to keep the notices dry. The ink had run on Martin and Anicah's banns, but she had made him recite them so often in the week they had been posted that he had memorized them. So had she. Her mouth moved with the words as he read them.

"This day came Martin Kirk, freeman, and made oath that he is not precontracted to any other woman than Anicah Sparrow, and that there is no impediment of consanguinity or apprenticeship on his part, nor to his knowledge on the part of the said Anicah Sparrow why he should not be married to the said Anicah."

The drizzle rinsed the tears from her face as she looked up at the blurs of brown ink on the sodden paper. She and Martin had earned their freedom and could share it together. True to her word and the articles of indenture, Margaret Brent had given Martin two hoes and an ax. Anicah had received a barrel of precious corn.

They would continue working for Mistress Margaret, but they would do it for food and wages, the promise of ten pounds of tobacco a day for him when the crop was in, seven for her.

When they saved enough they would patent the hundred acres due them for their service. Never when she wandered the streets of Bristol could Anicah have dreamed of such a life.

A yeoman's wife. A goodwife. A house and land of her own. Anicah was struck by a sudden hope that her copper-haired mother was looking down at her. She wished her father could see her too, wherever he was. Whoever he was.

Mistress Margaret had given them the use of the tiny house where she and Mary had stayed when they first arrived. It had been falling into ruin ever since, but Anicah knew she and Martin could repair it. Martin could do anything.

While Martin bolted the warped shutters for the night, Anicah pulled the old corn-husk ticking onto the hearth. She shook the dust from their blanket, a present from Robert Vaughan, and spread it over the bed. The pallet was the only furniture, and Anicah was grateful to have it.

A cold wind whistled through the cracks in the shutters and walls. The corn husks rustled when Martin lay down and pulled the blanket up. He turned on his side so he could watch Anicah rake ashes over the coals for the morning fire. With a stick she drew a cross in the ashes. She knelt on the cold hearth, bowed her head and recited Bess's prayer. It was the one she'd heard every night she'd spent under Margaret Brent's roof.

> "Matthew, Mark, Luke, and John
> Bless the bed that we lie on,
> And blessed guardian angel keep
> Us safe from danger whilst we sleep."

Martin held up her side of the blanket. She scurried across the cold of the floor, brushed the dirt from the soles of her feet and wriggled down under it. He put his arm around her and covered her with his own warmth. She felt his heart beating against her chest.

As he kissed her mouth, her eyes, the hollows of her temples, she murmured, "I wonder what we did before we met, Martin? I cannot remember a world without ye."

"Our lives begin now, Ani, in this beat of our hearts together."

Chapter 58

Margaret detoured past the weed-grown common just for the satisfaction of seeing Robin Harwood in the pillory. The July sun had burned his naked body and face until the crimson skin hung off him. His ears were nailed to either side of the hinged wooden jaws that locked his hands in place and held his neck forward at a right angle to his torso. Mosquitoes swarmed on him. A few people had gathered to pass the time of day with him and pelt him with ordure, old fish and older eggs.

As Margaret steered Mary toward Leonard's house, she used a turkey wing to fan away the flies. Flies, she thought, are the only creatures fattening in St. Mary's. Beside her, Mary murmured her devotions and fingered her heavy, clacking beads. Margaret knew her sister should be using her old rosary from England, the small finger loop that could be hidden in her palm, but she refused to insist on it. She regretted the decision when she saw Richard Bennett approaching. The sight of him sent a cold flutter of apprehension through her.

"Away to the wicked cross with thee, thou Jesuited papists," Bennett cried.

He was as solid as a side of beef, with thinning gray-brown hair that poked from under his black felt hat. His close-set blue eyes had the stare of a bird of prey. His features would have been handsome had not so much greasy flesh lumped up around them. "Thy idolatrous beads are the devil's adornment."

Margaret ignored him, though her stomach churned with anger. Mary smiled at him.

"Good morrow, goodman," she said. She sailed serenely on, picking up the paternoster where she had left it.

"Hast thou no care for thy soul's salvation, woman?" he shouted after her.

"God cares for my soul, as He cares for everyone's." Mary was always interested in a discussion of souls. She turned to gaze at him and at someone invisible just off to one side of him. "Wouldst thou not agree, Raphael?"

Bennet glanced around, perplexed, then returned to the attack. "If thou dost not forsake thy worship of the popish anti-Christ and destroy thy painted idols and apish toys, thou shalt burn in hell."

Mary cocked her head, considering that possibility. "And am I to understand thou wilt not be there?"

"Nay, sister. I shall stand among the saved elect."

"Then my care is the less." She curtsied, wafted a gossamer smile in his direction and continued intoning.

"Thou strumpet of the anti-Christ," Bennett shouted after her. "Thou art damned."

He reached up and pushed the tall crown of his flat-brimmed hat more tightly on his big head. He straightened his knee-length brown coat, stained black under the arms and in a Y-shaped line down the middle of his back. Kicking up clouds of dust, he strode away.

Margaret fanned Leonard Calvert with the turkey wing, and Mary laid cold compresses on his forehead to ease the raging fever. The doctor had ordered the shutters closed against the summer's miasmic airs. The heat in the room was more stifling than outside, and it felt hot enough to bake bread out there. Margaret instructed Leonard's man to set rosemary and bay leaves to smoldering to mask the odors of disease and death.

She hadn't the heart to ask Leonard what had possessed him to invite three hundred Puritans to settle in Maryland. They already had made such a nuisance of themselves in Virginia that Governor Berkeley demanded they leave. Richard Bennett was just the advance, come to inspect the site proposed for his followers.

Calvert had set aside land for them a three-day sail to the north. He had assured Margaret that what with clearing and building, planting and fending off Indians, they wouldn't have leisure to bother St. Mary's for several years. Margaret wasn't so sure. For Bennett's sort, bothering was not a leisurely activity, but the main order of business.

Leonard moaned. His skin had turned as yellow as onion skin, and Margaret knew that none of her infusions or powders would be of any use. She had tried them all—boneset, snakeroot, fever-few, steel dust steeped in wine. Dr. Gerard had bled him, but to no avail. Now Margaret and Mary and their neighbor, Thomas Greene, could only stand next to his bed in the parlor, pray for him and watch the life savaged from him.

All of them knew the signs. Intermittent fever was the chief scourge of that ordeal called the seasoning, and one of the ugliest ways to die. The maid who tended him spent her days washing the linens soiled by an illness that caused his stomach, bowels, kidneys and liver to malfunction. On the rare occasions that he passed water it was red as an ox's blood. When it turned black yesterday they knew he was doomed.

Leonard lay, wasted and still, under the stained cover. Looking down at him Margaret felt helpless and bereft. Ferdinand Poulton, Andrew White, Giles, now Leonard. She thought of Giles imprisoned in some filthy kennel of a dungeon, or worse, dead. One by one those she cared about were being taken from her. She wondered if eventually she would stand alone on this forsaken shore with only wolves and enemies for company.

Leonard waved them closer, then his hand dropped back onto the coverlet.

"Thinkst thou the hour has come?" Margaret asked.

"Aye." Leonard gathered himself for the effort and beckoned to Greene. "Thomas, I reckon thee to be the last gentleman Catholic in America, and I hereby name thee governor. May God guide thee in the execution of thy duties, for these are troubled times and I do not see them bettering.

"Margaret, I make thee my sole executrix." He gave her a fragile wisp of his smile. "Take all and pay all." He paused, panting. "I would speak alone with Mistress Margaret."

Before the servant followed the others out he brought a stool for Margaret.

"A pretty pass, to leave thee with such a muddle, Margaret."

"With God's help we shall prevail."

Leonard spoke slowly and with great effort. "As thou knowest, Ingle destroyed every record and account book he could find, so I can only tell thee what I remember."

Ever the careful administrator, he began listing the debits and credits and what remained of the stock and crops of his three manors on Point Lookout and of his brother's holding across the St. George's River. When he finished he lay silent for such a long time, Margaret felt with her fingertips for the pulse fluttering in his wrist.

"I always thought," he said at last, "that I would do what few English Catholics have been able to for a hundred years. When I died, a priest would be present to hear my confession, that I might do penance and receive extreme unction."

"Shall we say the thirty-first psalm, dear friend?"

Holding his fevered hand Margaret recited with him. " 'Blessed are they whose iniquities are forgiven and whose sins are covered . . .' "

" 'Into thy hands I commend my spirit,' " Leonard added when they finished. " 'Thou hast redeemed me, O Lord, the God of truth.' "

Margaret called the others in so he could make a few bequests of clothes to the two servants who had cared for him in his illness. While he did it she looked around at what she, as executor of his estate, would be listing and assigning value. Three small pieces of silver plate, a broken ax, his old flock bed with the torn ticking. An iron pot, twelve pewter spoons, worn thin and tarnished with use. He had expended his adult life here, and this was all that the plundering of the past two years had left him.

Leonard Culvert had always been separated from those around him by a barrier he couldn't define or cross, though he tried. Now he participated in the loneliest activity of all. He gave a small sigh and all movement ceased in him, though there had hardly been any to begin with. Margaret reached out and eased his eyelids closed.

Even as she and Mary and Thomas Greene recited the sorrowful mysteries, an old air echoed in the back of Margaret's mind. It was a verse Anicah Sparrow Kirk had sung when the seamen had tipped the Irish wench's corpse over the rail on the long voyage here. Margaret remembered Anicah's clear voice, angelic coming from such an urchin with tangled mane and hunger-bright eyes. Margaret sang it softly.

> *"When thou from hence dost pass away,*
> *every night and all,*
> *To heaven above thou comest at last*
> *and Christ receive thy pitiful poor soul."*

How could the colony continue without Leonard Calvert? He had been its soul, its shy center, its quiet engine. Margaret wanted to weep, but was too stunned and exhausted. Something had just ended, and something else was beginning, and she had no way of knowing how it would turn out.

She and Mary walked out into the mourning weeds of night. Millions of fireflies spangled the trees and bushes though, in a pulsing of tiny fires. They flashed in front of Margaret's face and lit in Mary's hair with a cold radiance.

Epilogue

When the knock came at dusk, Anicah put down the pumpkin slices she was stringing onto dried deer sinew and stared at the door. Leonard Calvert's mercenary army of Virginians still maintained a sullen garrison at St. Inigoes. The soldiers were demanding their back pay and they were levying chickens, hogs and corn from anyone foolish enough to leave theirs unguarded. Visitors at night gave cause for alarm.

Martin picked up his cudgel and opened the door a crack, then wider. Kitt stepped across the threshold. She had thrown back the red-velvet-lined hood of her woollen cloak, and her long, black hair fell loose across her shoulders. She carried her son, his huge dark eyes peering from the blanket that swaddled him.

Martin went out for another armload of oak from the stack that stretched the length of the house and reached the eaves. When he returned he closed the door against the October chill, but he left it unbolted. Anicah hung Kitt's fine new cloak on the peg next to her ragged one. Kitt seemed oblivious of the late hour and the fact that she had arrived unaccompanied.

"We thought to pay a call. Aunt Margaret says you'll soon be moving to your tenancy on her manor at Point Lookout, so the little one and I shan't be seeing so much of you." She never called her son by his given name, Giles. She looked around as Martin set a stool close to the fire. "Thou hast made a goodly home, Ani."

Anicah heard the wistfulness in Kitt's voice.

Giles had returned from England a year and a half ago, barely in time to take credit for the begetting of this child, though Anicah and Martin knew better. Not only had Giles escaped hanging for treason, he had brought suit against Ingle and received a judgment of a thousand pounds sterling. Now Kitt was Mistress Brent, the lady of the manor, with fine new clothes and a maid to wait on her. Even her accent was refined, though tinged slightly with the servants' burr.

" 'Tis but a humble cot," Anicah said.

A small rusty kettle dangled over the fire. A ladle and cheese toaster hung nearby, and a wooden bowl, noggin and spoon sat on a pine shelf. The old corn-husk ticking, a pair of stools and a rough board laid across two casks were the only furniture. Anicah was proud of it all.

Winter had not set in yet with its cutting winds that found entry in the smallest chinks. The fire could still warm the room as well as light it. Its glow mellowed the darkened oak of the walls. The house hadn't looked this inviting even when Margaret and Mary inhabited it briefly in 1638, more than a decade ago.

Martin had laid fresh rushes on the floor, and Anicah had scattered fragrant rosemary and thyme from her garden. Bundles of more herbs and golden sprays of shucked corn intermingled with the strings of apple and pumpkin slices hanging from the rafters. Baskets of beans and peas lined the far wall. A flitch of molasses-brown bacon revolved slowly in the wind that funneled down the chimney. Martin's old matchlock, powder horn, worm and shot pouch hung from pegs. His hoe and matlock and long-handled ax leaned against the wall by the door.

"Mistress Margaret was kind enough to send us a keg of her cider." Anicah filled the noggin for Kitt who had loosened the laces of her bodice and the drawstring of her chemise and begun nursing the baby.

"I brought you a pot of quinces in syrup," Kitt said.

"We thank ye."

"Anansine." Martin smiled as though at an expected guest.

Anicah and Kitt turned to look.

Edward hadn't so much entered the room as appeared in it. He wore his leather leggings, breechclout, and wolf pelt mantle. A sack of finely tanned doeskin hung from his belt. He had shaved the side of his head in the old way. Hawk feathers jutted from the long black hair tied in a knot over his left ear.

He left a fat goose and a mill sack of oysters on the hearth. The bag at his belt rattled as he sat back on his heels next to Kitt and stared at the baby.

"We have not seen ye in such a longsome time, Edward, we worried that some mischance had befallen ye." Anicah began laying the oysters in the hot ashes.

"I am well." The spark of sly humor in his eyes had gone out.

"Father Copley returned from Portobacco and Piscataway," Martin said. "He said he could find but few of the souls Father White baptized there."

"Nor their bodies either, I think." Edward held out a finger and the baby gripped it. He stroked the tiny brown hand with his thumb.

"Where did they go?" Anicah asked.

"The Englishmen at Piscataway Fort bought many as servants and beat them so that they ran away. Or died. The planters chase away the game and their hogs root out the corn and people starve. Or they catch the English sicknesses and they die."

"Martin, help me carry this basket of peas to the cockloft." Anicah dragged Martin toward the ladder. As they made a pretense of arranging things upstairs they heard the soft lilt of Piscataway below.

"Ani, Martin," Kitt called finally. "Edward is leaving."

Edward took Martin's hand and dropped a small pewter cross into it. Mary Brent had given it to him years ago.

"Mistress Mary will watch over you all," he said. "Her guardian spirit is very powerful."

"Have ye seen Raphael?" Anicah asked.

"Certainly."

Edward and Martin gripped forearms. They looked into each other's eyes and spoke a few words in Edward's tongue.

"God keep thee, Edward," Anicah said.

"And thee, Ani."

He opened the door and slipped out into the night. Kitt lowered her head over her baby and crooned to him. Her long hair fell forward, curtaining her face.

Anicah saw the bereft look in Martin's eyes. "He'll be back, bulkin."

"Nay, Ani. He will not."

"Why think ye so?"

"He carried the bones of his uncle and aunt. His people take such relics with them when they go to a new country."

In a light April breeze Robert stood next to Margaret on the bluff overlooking St. Mary's harbor. The first ship of 1649 had arrived. They were watching the crew prepare to lighter the 275 passengers ashore. The main deck teemed with men, women, and children in tall, flat-brimmed hats and suits of brown, black, and gray. Richard Bennett and his men stood on the landing to greet them. The rest of St. Mary's had turned out, curious to see the boatload of Nonconformists.

"They look as dreary and numerous as rats on a tanner's heap, don't they?" Vaughan stared down at the Puritans.

Margaret's laugh was bitter.

"You really must reconsider, Margaret." Vaughan returned to the discussion they'd been having for weeks.

"I've considered everything."

"You're established here. You aren't young, you know."

Margaret gave him a wry look.

"You aren't. Starting a life in the wilderness is for the young and the strong and the foolish."

"I wasn't young when I came here, though foolish enough withal."

"This is a rash and ill-considered notion."

"I know best where the shoe wrings me." Actually, Margaret

was pleased that he was trying to persuade her to stay. No one else seemed to care that she and Giles and their families were leaving.

She made one more attempt of her own at persuasion. "The land around Acquia Creek is lovely. Thou couldst come with us."

He shook his head. They were going to Virginia, and Virginia was ruled by the same sort of autocratic gentry that had held sway in Maryland. Vaughan knew he had a better chance to advance here than there. And as objectionable as the Puritans were, they were vigorous men, and hard working, and not likely to steal too many of their neighbors' pigs.

"We have lands and business here still," Margaret said. "We'll return from time to time and see thee."

"Aye." But Vaughan knew it wouldn't be the same. Not ever again.

Margaret continued to stare down at the ship. She watched its tender bounce and shy as a line of Puritans, like ants, descended the rope net and climbed into it.

"Two priests abide in Maryland now," she said. "Yet we could not celebrate mass at Easter except we secrete ourselves in some small closet and murmur like thieves. And didst thou enjoy the Nativity with Bennett and his knaves hammering on doors to ensure that no one celebrated the birth of Jesus Christ? Imagine what it will be like when they have seats in the Assembly."

"They are a hidebound and malignant race, but—"

"But me no buts, Rob. I will not spend the bran and dregs of my dotage among such as they."

More than that, Margaret's instincts for politics told her that Baltimore would never grant her or her brother any further privileges, for fear of alienating the men in power now. And he would try his best to take back what they already had. He was swinging in the wind like a man gibbeted in a cage at the crossroads; alive, but for how long?

The lighter neared shore and people began shouting back and forth. A ripple of excitement started among those at the water's edge and spread up the path to the bluff.

"Praise God. The king has lost his head," they shouted. "Long live Parliament! The king is dead."

The cheering began in the boats and followed the news up the hill. Margaret and Robert could hear the crowd shouting Oliver Cromwell's name.

"Blessed Mother." Margaret forgot where she was and crossed herself. "They've killed the king."

She looked at Robert. Tears streamed down his cheeks and into his beard. She put her arms around him and they held each other and cried together, for the loss of their king and their friendship.

At sunrise Martin and Anicah walked to the highest point of their new tenancy at St. Gabriel's Manor on Point Lookout. Mist rose from the Potomac and St. George's rivers, lying flat as quicksilver washed with pink. To the north lay St. Inigoes and St. Mary's.

"Ani, as I was leaving Sisters' Freehold yestere'en Mistress Mary gave me this." He reached into his shirt and drew out a filthy cloth bag.

"My father's testament."

"Mistress Mary said she took it from around Original Brown's neck when he died. She set it aside and quite forgot about it. She found it while packing to leave, and opening it, saw that it belonged to you."

Martin knew he should have given it to her right away, but he had been afraid of something he couldn't name. Afraid that the contents would change her or take her from him. The fact that Anicah was carrying their child made the fear even more intense.

Maybe Anicah felt the same. She stared at the bag a long time. She had received the contents from her mother's hand almost a score of years ago and a hundred lifetimes. It had assumed the quality of an amulet, a charm that held the secret to her life. Was it a secret she still wanted to know?

She opened the drawstring and with shaking hands drew out the battered snuff box. She opened it and unfolded the stiff paper inside. It was stained and crumbled at the edges, but in remarkably sound condition for what it had been through.

Her father's and her mother's hands had touched it where hers did now. It was a fragment of the past made solid. She gave it to Martin as though it were a piece of the True Cross.

He turned so the sun's rays lit the faded writing. He studied it so long Anicah had to gnaw her lip to keep from begging him to hurry.

Finally he began. "It says, 'My dearest wife and child . . .' "

Anicah's heart pounded so she feared it would snap like a drumhead.

> My dearest wyf and child,
>
> In the name of God, Amen. I Will Sparrow, being of sownd mind, tho broke body, do make my last will and testament. For transgressions wrongly emputed to me, I must suffer pain fort and dure, so that my estate may pass to thee. My keeper, in his mercy, has agreed to write this for me and see that it is deliverd.
>
> Furst, I bequeath my soul to God that gave it. Secondly, I bequeath my body to the grownd, trusting in the meritts of Jesus Christ and the life that is everlasting.
>
> To my dear wyf I bequeath the cloaths that I was wearing when brought to this cell and my death. These are all the worldly goods left me, but for a cord of fire boot, good, seasoned oak, owed me by William Dunbar of St. James parish, Bristol.
>
> This wood I bequeath to my fayre daughter Anicah as her portion. May Christ Jesus grant her his blessings and watch over her, as I cannot.

To ensure that she got the wood, Anicah's father had endured being pressed to death by weights rather than plead guilty and lose his meager estate to the king.

The sun had broken free of the net of bare tree branches when Anicah spied the pair of pinnaces approaching from the north. She and Martin watched them grow larger, sailing out into the middle of the Potomac's broad mouth to catch the tidal flow upriver.

The mastiff, grizzled and crippled in the hindquarters, barked madly from the foredeck while the turnspit leaped around his legs. Anicah recognized the two cloaked figures standing next to the dogs. She and Martin waved, and Margaret and Mary waved back.

Even though the tobacco seed was waiting to be planted in the beds, they watched the boats round the point and head upriver. They vanished around a curve and into the limitless forest.

Author's Note

The two years of relative anarchy, known later as the "plundering time," left Lord Baltimore's colony in turmoil. Governor Leonard Calvert died before the courts could begin to settle all the disputes. His entangled business and legal affairs kept his executor, Margaret Brent, busy. Besides Kent Fort Manor and Sisters' Freehold, she was in charge of the late governor's town lands and his three estates totaling six thousand acres on Point Lookout. She also acted as Lord Baltimore's attorney.

In 1649 she went before the Assembly and demanded two votes in the House of Burgesses, one for herself and one as Baltimore's representative. It was a bold act, given that women were not allowed to vote. The burgesses denied her request, and the record states that "Mrs. [Mistress] Brent protested against all proceedings in this present Assembly unless she may be present and have vote as aforesaid."

The rebellion depopulated Maryland and depleted its few resources. Contention continued even afterward. The soldiers Leonard Calvert had brought from Virginia to help him regain his brother's colony received little pay. They had almost reached the point of mutiny when Captain John Price came to Margaret for help. She gave some of the men steers from Lord Baltimore's herd and sold more of his cattle to provide their wages. She averted disaster, but her disposal of Baltimore's stock drew his wrath.

He wrote to the new Protestant governor complaining of her

actions in uncomplimentary terms. The men of the Assembly replied that "it was better for the Collony's safety at that time in her hands than in any mans else in the whole Province . . . for the Soldiers would never have treated any other with that Civility and respect." They pointed out that Mistress Brent deserved Baltimore's "favour and thanks for her so much Concurring to the publick safety, then to be justly liable to all those bitter invectives you have been pleased to Express against her."

In 1649, Baltimore sent to Maryland a document called the Act Concerning Religion. He tailored it to appease the Puritans he had invited to settle in Maryland and to provide protection for the Catholics. At the time it was without precedent. It declared that no Christian in the province could "be in any ways troubled, molested or discountenanced for his or her religion nor in the free exercise thereof." It also banned derogatory phrases such as "heretick, Schismatic, Idolator, puritan, Independent, Presbitarian [sic], popish priest, Jesuited papist, Roundhead and Separatist."

As a new member of the governor's council, Robert Vaughan signed it. One wonders what he thought of the section requiring strict punishments for profanity, another concession to the Puritans.

The Assembly of 1650 was the first in which the Puritan faction was represented. Delegates from their settlement, Providence, situated at the mouth of the Severn River, complained of great grievances and oppressions. Their main concern was the oath of fealty to Baltimore. They objected to its royalist implications and they refused to swear allegiance to officials whose spiritual head was the pope.

In 1652, Parliament appointed Lord Baltimore's nemeses, William Claiborne, and the Puritan Richard Bennett as commissioners to govern Virginia, which had also supported the king. The two men extended their authority to Maryland. To his credit, William Claiborne did not exact vengeance on the Marylanders who had taken Kent Island from him, nor did he ever recover it. He died at age ninety-five in Kent County, Virginia.

In 1654 the Puritans gained political control. After receiving sanctuary, land, religious freedom and political parity from Maryland's Proprietary government, they repudiated the Act Concerning Religion and denied the same rights to others.

The dissension between them and the other Protestants and Catholics culminated in the Battle of the Severn in 1654. The Puritans' battle cry was, "God is our strength." The royalists' was, "Hey, for St. Maries." The Puritans claimed their foes also shouted, "Hey, for two wives," meaning they intended to rape the women, although a member of the royalist force denied it in a written rebuttal. The victorious Puritans promised quarter to their enemies, then executed four of their prisoners. Captain John Price's life was saved only because the women pleaded for him.

The rule of the Maryland Puritans did not sit well with Robert Vaughan. He persevered through their administration but was deposed as Commander of Kent and fined heavily for insulting the Puritan-led court there. According to the records, he used most "opprobious" epithets, shaking his fist over the heads of the judges and swearing at the clerk.

After almost twenty years in Maryland he finally accumulated land, married sometime in 1653, and fathered three children. He died in 1668. In the inventory of his estate, his library was valued at three hundred pounds of tobacco. His old crossbow was listed among his effects.

Around 1650, Margaret Brent took up new lands in northern Virginia. She called her estate "Peace." Land grants between 1651 and 1666 indicate the Brents owned 9,610 acres on the Virginia shore of the Potomac near the present city of Alexandria. In 1663, Margaret disposed of her Maryland holdings and made her will. In 1671 she died at the age of seventy, after thirty-three turbulent years on the American frontier. Her sister Mary's death preceded hers by only a short time.

Anicah Sparrow is a fictional character, named for an indentured servant who lived on Maryland's Eastern Shore in the seventeenth century. She represents the thousands of people transported as laborers to Maryland, not always of their own free will.

At St. Gabriel manor in 1656, Margaret Brent's steward, Zachery

Wade, delivered a parcel of land to Martin Kirk by the old custom of seizen by the rod. Wade took hold of one end of a stick and Martin the other in full session of the manorial "court baron." Martin recited the oath of fealty to Margaret and was admitted as tenant. The only other mention the author found of him was a governor's proclamation accusing him and two others of gathering up and killing unmarked cattle in 1652.

Giles Brent and Mary Kittamaquund's children began a line known as the Indian Brents. In 1675, Giles Brent, Jr., fought the Indians who had begun a series of attacks, killing hundreds of Virginia's settlers. He also participated in Nathaniel Bacon's rebellion against Governor Berkeley. Berkeley, a royalist, supported restriction of trade to English imports and high duties on exported American goods. The uprising was a foreshadowing of a later rebellion much wider in scope.

Father Andrew White was released from prison, but never allowed to return to Maryland. He was buried in England in 1656. Thomas Copley did come back and died in 1658. By the 1660s the Piscataway Indians who followed White had become scattered, their numbers much diminished by disease.

Thomas Cornwaleys survived accusations of kidnapping that his enemies leveled against him in England. He returned to Maryland, transported more settlers and patented thousands of acres there. In 1659 he went back to England and stayed there.

Harry Angell and his help-meet Joan were based on a couple who lived on Kent Island. The man was granted amnesty for his transgressions during the rebellion. He was given offices and commissions, but he and his wife continued to be at the center of controversy. They were called into court for scandal and drunkenness, for severely beating servants, misappropriating muster funds, and making off with other people's goods and livestock. They buried the animal's ears and ate the rest of the evidence "all hugger mugger," as the records put it.

John Dandy's brush with the gallows reformed him only temporarily. He was executed for another murder. Mary Lawne Courtney Clocker was taken to court for theft, condemned to death, then pardoned. She and her husband Daniel prospered nonetheless.

Wonderful sources of information on these people and others equally as colorful can be found in the colony's court and council records, set into type, indexed and bound. They're housed in Maryland's Hall of Records in Annapolis.

Maryland's Puritan rule ended in 1657 after the Cromwell government in England refused to support it. With the ascension to the throne of Charles II in 1660, Lord Baltimore's position stabilized. Maryland enjoyed nearly thirty years of growth, but St. Mary's City never became the metropolis he envisioned.

In 1689 the success of the Glorious Revolution in England led to the overthrow of the Catholic Proprietor and the end of any rights the Maryland Catholics still enjoyed. In 1694 the capital was moved north to Arundel Town, just opposite the Puritans' original settlement on the Severn River. Arundel Town was renamed Annapolis, after Queen Anne.

St. Mary's City, on a bluff above the St. Mary's River, is now the site of important archeological excavations and reconstructions. Visitors will find exhibits, historical markers, a recreation of the pinnace *Dove*, and a seventeenth-century plantation house and tobacco barn. They give an idea of what life was like there when Margaret and Mary Brent walked its paths and sailed the waters around it.

ABOUT THE AUTHOR

LUCIA ST. CLAIR ROBSON was born in Baltimore, Maryland, and raised in South Florida. She has been a Peace Corps volunteer in Venezuela and a teacher in a disadvantaged neighborhood in Brooklyn, New York. She has also lived in Japan, South Carolina, and southern Arizona. After earning her master's degree in library science at Florida State University, she worked as a public librarian in Annapolis, Maryland. She now lives near Annapolis in a wooded, eccentrically surveyed community on the Severn River.